THE PEGASUS EFFECT

By Joseph E. Brown

Note for Librarians: A cataloguing record for this book is available from Library
and Archives Canada at www.collectionscanada.ca/amicus/index-e.html

Printed in Victoria, BC, Canada.

ISBN: 978-1-4251-9241-9 (sc)

*We at Trafford believe that it is the responsibility of us all, as both individuals
and corporations, to make choices that are environmentally and socially sound.
You, in turn, are supporting this responsible conduct each time you purchase
a Trafford book, or make use of our publishing services. To find out how you
are helping, please visit www.trafford.com/responsiblepublishing.html*

*Our mission is to efficiently provide the world's finest, most comprehensive book publishing
service, enabling every author to experience success. To find out how to publish your
book, your way, and have it available worldwide, visit us online at www.trafford.com*

Trafford rev. 07/3/2009

 Trafford PUBLISHING®   www.trafford.com

North America & international
toll-free: 1 888 232 4444 (USA & Canada)
phone: 250 383 6864 ♦ fax: 250 383 6804 ♦ email: info@trafford.com

The United Kingdom & Europe
phone: +44 (0)1865 487 395 ♦ local rate: 0845 230 9601
facsimile: +44 (0)1865 481 507 ♦ email: info.uk@trafford.com

This book is dedicated to the loving memory of my father.
Thomas G. Brown, 1930-2006.

My home

As I sat pondering in the university's main observatory this past nightfall, it was the end of winter, and with its last gasps, the winds howled across the flatlands here to lower the temperatures to minus thirty-two degrees. It had been the coldest day of the season thus far and the moon that evening was as white as the driven snow on a sunny day. This cold weather was typical of Park Falls for this time of year.

My name is, James Reynolds. I teach physics at the university here in, Park Falls, Saskatchewan. Our school, Sherman Patterson University, was the focal point and the mainstay of our small community.

For myself, I had been the head of the physics department at the university for the past seven years and a member of the faculty for just over twelve years. I was married to my girl Christine and we had two lovely daughters named Paula and Angela. They were teenagers, aged fourteen and eighteen years respectively, and were a handful at the best of times. Don't get me wrong though, these girls were the lights of our lives and our greatest joys. We lived on a modest little hobby farm near the waterfalls on a small offshoot of the Branson River that ran behind our home. This was a university town with a population of approximately 48,000 people. The next biggest employer in our town was that of the wheat farming industry.

I loved living here in Park Falls. This was the place where I grew up when I was a young boy. Park Falls was a simple town with small town values as well as being a beautiful place to raise children. My daughters attended, Lester B. Pearson High School in town and this year Angela would graduate with full honors and a music scholarship. Angela planned to go to a Toronto university and we were proud of her. Paula was in grade nine and she wanted to become a biologist or a geologist she said, these days, as we were proud of both of them and loved them dearly.

Christine, my wife, was the love of my life and without her, my life would be sorely lacking. Christine was my reason for getting up in the morning. She was my serenity.

Anyways, it was beginning to get a little late that evening, and as per usual, I could see that my old friend and mentor, Bernard "Bernie" Wakefield, physics professor emeritus, was coming. He was making his way down the corridor and up here to the telescope. Sky watching had become a Thursday night tradition with us. We would sit and drink some coffee or tea and do a bit of stargazing and have a few laughs. Bernie had been my friend for as long as I could remember.

"Hey, Bernie, how are you tonight? Do you want the usual?" I asked.

"Oh, not too bad, Jim, I'm a little tired though so I'll just have a cup of tea." Bernie grabbed himself a chair and sat across from me.

"So, Bernie, do tell. What are you working on these days? You were saying the other day that you got started on something new?"

"Well, Jim, I'm starting to build a full scale replica of a Native Mohawk canoe. I have to keep myself busy so I'm going to build it from scratch. Then me and you will paddle it down the Branson River!" Bernie extolled. He had a gleam in his eyes.

"Whoa, Bernie! Whoa! I hope we're going to make sure she's seaworthy first."

"We will, Jim, don't worry, we will, so how about yourself, Jim? What are you teaching the kids these days?"

"Well, Bernie, I'm afraid its engineering physics, again. So I have a class of rather grumpy students on my hands, but we'll muddle through."

Bernie and I sat in the observatory peering out at Galaxy M-88 through the university's powerful telescope. As we looked up at the stars, some soft string music washed over the room. We talked about why we chose physics and astronomy for our careers as well as our love and our dedication to the sciences. For myself, physics had become a fascinating subject of study for me ever since I was a young boy and as soon as I got into high school, I was hell bent on studying the sciences. I just turned out that way.

Bernie and I had had a long cold winter and we were looking forward to a spring that could not come soon enough.

"Hey, Bernie! Wake up! I think we'd better call it a night." I barked. Bernie had begun to drift off to sleep in his chair.

"Okay, Jim, I'm ready to hit the hay. That's it for me for tonight. I'm going home, I think." Bernie replied. He yawned.

"Go ahead home, Bernie, I'll straighten up here."

"See you in the morning, Jim."

"You too, Bernie." Bernie stood up to leave.

As I cleaned up that evening, Bernie clambered home to his wife, Stella. That night I thought of how lucky I was and how well things had turned out for me in life. I thought of how spring was on the way and how this might be one of our last summers' that we would be together, Christine, the girls, and I. I thought about how much I loved them and how beautiful they were and how truly blessed I was to be with them and have them in my life. I thanked God for my family's good health and our happy home. As I finished cleaning up I started to get tired myself so that was it for me as well. It was late in the evening and I had a good week. The following day would be a short one for me here at the university with only two classes scheduled and then the weekend was my own. I went straight home that evening and sneaked quietly into the house while everyone was sleeping. I washed up and went straight to bed trying not to wake Christine in the process. I fell asleep directly as it was almost midnight and I felt quite contented with myself.

As I awakened the following morning, the warm rays of the sun streamed into our bedroom. My morning began with the sounds of the day, squealing and squawking, "Aaie! Aaggh! Give me that dam brush back! It's mine!"

"No it isn't, it's mine!" Paula shouted. Something thrown hit the wall in the hallway.

"Girls quiet, quiet! Your mother's trying to sleep!" I scolded.

"Not anymore I'm not!" Christine yelled. The girls fell silent.

"What are you two girls fighting about now? Tell me now!" Christine shouted.

"Paula stole my hairbrush!"

"I did not! It's mine!" Paula retorted.

"Hey, hey! We don't accuse each other of stealing in this house! Are these the two hair brushes you bought that are the same?" Christine asked, tersely. They perturbed her on this morning.

"Yes, Mom" the girls answered, in unison.

"Well let me tell you what we're going to do then. I'm going to take the one of them and when you find the other, I'm going to take them both and put your names on them and then you will respect each other's property from now on, do you hear me!"

"Yes, Mom." the girls replied.

"Now pipe down and get ready for breakfast! Enough already, I'm getting a headache!" Christine bellowed. That was that. Christine had a gift with the girls when it came to obedience. She instinctively knew how to discipline them with love and understanding as well as a little yelling and hollering from time to time. This was our usual early morning wake up mayhem around our home.

"We don't need an alarm clock with these girls, Jim." Christine said, jokingly. She gave me a good morning kiss.

"Okay, let's get up and start the day." I said.

Well, our day started that way. We would all race downstairs and have breakfast together and we would talk, laugh, and listen to each other's stories. This was a precious time for Christine and me, to sit and listen to our girls, as they would talk about themselves especially this early in the day when they were peaceful and contented with one another.

Angela was our eldest daughter at eighteen years of age. Angela was tall at five feet, ten inches, and weighed one hundred and twenty pounds. She had long brown hair and big brown eyes. She was pretty. Angela was a strong willed and decisive person but she had a soft side and was compassionate towards others. I would say that she was well balanced rather than to say that she was an introvert or an extrovert.

As for our fourteen-year-old daughter Paula, well, she was still growing like a weed. Paula had short red hair and piercing green eyes and she was 5 feet, 4 inches tall, and about ninety-five pounds, if I were to guess. I think people would describe her as skinny. Paula was full of energy. She had a lot more energy than I ever had when I was her age and she was definitely an extrovert. We could really have our hands full with Paula as she could get quite wound up. Paula loved to laugh and play practical jokes, especially on her sister, much to Angela's chagrin. Hence, this is why we had our hands full. However, even with their sibling rivalries they loved one another, and protected each other voraciously. After breakfast, Christine and I would go up-stairs and get ready for work.

Christine my wife was 5 feet, 7 inches tall, and one hundred and twenty pounds. She had long light brown hair and to make a long story short she managed to look like Jeannie Nelson of the old "I dream of Jeannie" television series of the sixties, to me anyway. I was the beholder and she was the beauty in my eyes. She was an inde-pendent, honest, loving and nurturing person and my best friend. Christine owned her own small business. She operated and worked in her own hairdressing and beauty salon. She took great pride in making her salon the best. Christine was going to open her second salon in the town's west end in Park Falls' first major shopping mall. I admired her drive to be successful and to be a pillar of our community. She also wanted to do volunteer work at the town's general hospital.

Well, I was off to work and as I came down the stairs, the girls were at it again. This was Christine's department, I said to myself.

"Bye girls, love you!" I said, as I walked out the door.

"I love you too, Dad." Paula said.

"Bye, Dad." Angela said.

"See you tonight, sweetie!" Christine said, cheerily.

As I drove to work that morning, the sun was shining and it was up to minus two degrees outside. It was warmer out and a beauty of a day as I only had to wear a sweater and a light jacket. The weather had warmed up considerably overnight and the weather forecaster predicted nothing but warmer conditions for the days ahead. That day, I had a short schedule with two early morning classes and a bit of paperwork and then I would be out of there before noon, I hoped. After work, Christine and I had a big surprise for the girls. We were bringing home a three-month-old Jack Russell terrier puppy. A female, she was the cutest little dog to see. We would introduce our new family member tonight just after dinner as the girls suspected nothing. This would be a hoot for the whole family.

Paula and Angela would be home all summer and their grandparents and aunts and uncles from both sides would be along to visit them. I thought we would have a great summer and this reunion would be good for our souls and that of our extended family.

Anyway, I pulled into campus as the university was waking up. I went to my office and it was quiet, this gave me a chance to have a peaceful cup of coffee as I prepared my notes for class. As I sat and sipped my coffee, I could hear the shuffling of the student's footsteps as they filed in for the day's lessons. My first lecture that morning was my fifth year masters' class in general physics. These were my most gifted students, for the young men and women in this class were primarily twenty-four and twenty-five year olds who were working at a high intensity level. They would feed on information at a high volume. They were the senior echelon. These students would be ready to graduate at the end of the spring semester.

However, today I would give them a break and we would have a semester review. This would relieve some of the stresses they were starting to show.

As I walked down the hall and into the classroom, they looked cranky and disheveled. "Good morning class, how are y'all today?" I queried. There was a mumbling response. "Okay, listen up everyone; we have something new on the agenda for today." I said. Their eyes opened up like saucers when they heard my announcement.

"Today, we will not take up any new work, but, we will start a two week review before we have March break!" I stated. The class breathed an audible sigh of relief. I could see the stresses flowing out of them as their faces started to turn cheery again. My two top students Helen Hamilton and David Neally were delighted. They had worked hard and I was impressed with their efforts and their abilities to grasp information and to solve problems. They were sharp indeed. Well, as I had these few thoughts, the students had gotten to chattering so I decided to make this day's class a social and hand out assignments at the end.

"Alright everyone, I just want you all to plan review strategies and then you can talk amongst yourselves. I'll be back in twenty minutes." I said. I did not think anybody heard me though. I headed back to my office to make a few phone calls. The first call I made was to the humane shelter to confirm that our new dog was ready for pick up. Next, I phoned Christine at the salon. She answered. "Hi love, what are you up to?" I asked.

"Oh hell, Jim! One of my hairdryers is broken and Sheila didn't come into work today and everybody wants to look good, it's Friday! It's really hectic, hon, so did you want something, Jim?" I could hear a frantic background with people talking and lots of shuffling.

"Christine, I just wanted to let you know that I'm going to pick up the dog this afternoon. She's ready to come home."

"Oh goodness, I forgot about that since yesterday. Did you need me to do anything?"

"Well hon, did you want to pick up the chocolate cake and ice cream, for dessert tonight?"

"Wooohoo! Sure, this is going to be a party! The girls are going to flip, I can't wait!" Christine asserted, "Listen Jim, dear, I'm going to have to let you go, this place is going crazy... I have to get back to work." She said, in frustration.

"Alright then, Christine, I'll call you later on your cell."

"Sounds good, bye sweetheart."

"Bye Christine." I hung up my phone.

Well this was starting to shape up into becoming a memorable weekend. As I rested in my office for the next twenty minutes or so, I contemplated about my next class and the topics I might teach for my first year students as I tried to make things interesting for them. My first year students were just kids to me, so it was a challenge to get them interested and motivated so they could run on their own steam. As I lied back in my chair, I began to ponder about our home. I thought about what we might do with our land this summer. Being a hobby farm, it was a little dilapidated when we first took possession, so I patched the barn roof, fixed the siding as well as the loft and the fencing around the property. Over the years, as the girls grew, we spent many wonderful fun filled days fixing up the place, barbequing and going swimming and fishing. The girls would bring their friends over to play in the barn and throughout the surrounding countryside. Sometimes Christine and I would spend warm sunny days and starry nights just making love and being kids again ourselves. All I can say for this part of our lives is that life could be sweet and the experiences we had would live on forever in our hearts and memories.

Our farm had never had any animals and apart from our new dog, our daughter Paula wanted us to get a horse, two dairy cows and some chickens. I was sort of with her on this and I would not mind working a bit of a hobby farm, one day. However, I think this would be fodder for a serious family discussion in the future. A small farm would keep me humble and focused but quite busy I was afraid. I looked at the time and my first class was about to end so I rushed back to the classroom and dismissed the students with no homework, a welcomed rarity for them.

After my first class, I thought I would take a break and go visit Bernie. He was retired but he had an office in the basement. A bit of a cliché, I think, but he loved this university and was still active on the board level. After my visit with Bernie, I would teach my last class and then I was done for the day.

Sherman Paterson University had one of the most beautiful campuses in all of Canada and it was always a pleasure to walk the halls of this centre for higher learning. My daughter Paula planned to attend the university and we would probably have lunch together in the main cafeteria one day, that is, if she wouldn't mind sitting with her dear old Dad. At any rate, Bernie was in and he looked like he was in good spirits being Friday and all. "Hey Bern! How the heck are yuh?" I asked.

"Not bad, not too bad, Jim, how are you?"

"I'm okay. We're going to have a little fun today, Bernie, with the kids and the new dog and all."

"Oh yeah, that's today, make sure you've got your camera handy. You should try one of those new digital ones Jim, there the cat's pajamas." Bernie said, enthusiastically, "I haven't been able to put mine down since I got my new one. It's my favorite new toy."

"Well, I want one, Bernie and I can see by the way you play with yours your getting a lot of use out of it. I'll have to see if Christine wants a new camera though. I think our old one is going to break real soon anyway, if you know what I mean."

"I know what you mean, Jim, that's how I got mine." Bernie said. He laughed.

"Well Bernie, it's still too cold yet for a barbeque, but if you and Stella want to come over for dinner around six tonight, you're more than welcome." I offered.

"Well, we might just do that. I'll phone, Stella and see what's up and I'll bring my camera too if we come."

"Oh, I know you will, Bernie, you probably have it with you right now."

"Smile, Jim!" Bernie said. He pulled out his camera and snapped a picture. Just like a teenager.

"I knew it! Okay, Bern, you got me, you got me! I'm going to head back to class now before we start having too much fun." I said.

"See you tonight, Jim, maybe. I'll let you know either way."

"Alright Bernie, that sounds good enough for me. I'll see you later then." I headed back upstairs to my next class for my first year students. I did not really have anything prepared for them so being in a good mood this Friday I would let them go early with a small assignment for the weekend. When I got to the classroom, they were sitting attentively. I handed out the assignments and then let them go about their business.

After I tied up a few loose ends, I would head off for lunch and then to the pound to pick up our new family member. First, I phoned Christine again to see what was happening. Christine answered. I greeted her. "Hi hon! How is it there? Is it better down there now?" I asked.

"Hi Jim, yeah, it's a lot better now. Everything's in order so I'm going to head home in a couple of hours, how about you dear?"

"Well, I'm going to have lunch and then I'll be on my way to get the dog, then I'll come straight home."

"What about the cake and ice cream?"

"Well sweetie, I was hoping, you know."

"Say no more, I'll get it," she offered.

"Okay thanks, Christine. By the way, I asked Bernie and Stella over for dinner too. I hope that's okay?"

"That's fine hon. There's plenty of food at home for us, plus, with what we order and with the cake, we'll have lot's."

"Alright, hon, I'll be home by 2:30 PM, so when I get there we can hide the dog upstairs." I said.

"Wow, Jim. I can't wait to see the girl's faces. It's going to be a riot! I can't wait!" Christine said, excitedly. She had a wanton anticipation in her voice.

"Alright hon, I'll see you in a few hours."

"Okay, Jim, bye."

"Bye Christine." I hung up the phone. Well that was it for my workweek and my weekend could begin. I gathered up my things and I grabbed a bite to eat from the refrigerator in my office. I said my goodbyes to my secretary along with some of the other staff members and then I headed for my car.

I was on my way to get the dog at the Park Falls animal shelter, which was just down the road here from the university. As I pulled into the shelter to park, I saw an old friend of mine I had known since high school. His name was Paul Banks. Paul Banks was with the Saskatchewan Provincial Police Force. I had not seen him in a long while. I wondered how he was doing. I got out of my car. "Hey, Paul, hey Paul, how are you?" I called out.

"Hey, Jim, long time no see! How are you doing these days, Jim?" Paul asked. He had a broad smile. He was sparkling in his full dress uniform.

"I'm doing fine, Paul. I'm doing the family thing as usual and teaching at the university along with raising our girls, you Paul?"

"Well, Jim, I'm still keeping Park Falls safe for the good citizens and like you I'm just trying to live the good life. How's your family doing, Jim?"

"Everybody's doing just fine. We're happy, how about your family, Paul?"

"Well, Jim, Sherry and I have a new little girl, our first! Her name is, Shelly. What do think of that?" He said, beaming. I noticed his eyes start to well up.

"Congratulations, Paul! Congratulations! That's fantastic. How does it feel to be a new father?"

"Well you know she's my first, Jim and I'm really overwhelmed and excited. It feels good and Sherry feels pretty much the same. We're proud of her." Paul had an undeniable exuberance in his tone.

"That's great, Paul, that's really great!" There was a short pause. We looked at each other and smiled.

"So what brings you down to the pound, Paul?"

"Well, the detachment is looking for drug dogs so we're going to try our luck down here. Then we'll send a qualified dog and an officer off to police canine school. It's really a prestigious position. All the personnel are vying for it." Paul explained, "How about you, Jim, what brings you here?"

"Well, were adding a new family member to our clan, a little Jack Russell Terrier."

"Well that's a fine how do you do, Jim. Sounds like years of fun and joy ahead for you and your family there."

"Oh, I think it will be. Listen, Paul, when you're a little more settled with your new girl and it's a little warmer out; you and Sherry should come over for a barbeque and see the family." I offered.

"I most certainly will do that, Jim. Sherry and I would like that very much. It's been a long time since we've seen you two and your girls."

"Well, it's settled then, Paul, it's a date. I'll give you a call in the near future."

"I'll look forward to that, Jim. It's good to see you again."

"You to Paul, I'll call you soon then… bye for now."

"Alright then, Jim, bye for now, we'll see you soon." Paul said. We parted ways. It was nice to see Paul again and hear about his new baby and his wife Sherry. Christine would be happy to have them over one night for a barbeque.

I went into the shelter to get our new dog. She had just gotten her shots and the attendant attached a new collar and tags to her. I had a leash, a blanket and a toy I brought for her but it looked like I was going to have to carry her. I paid the shelter employee the fee and then I was off. As I walked out to the car, the dog got nervous and started shaking. I spoke to her softly to try to calm her and then she peed on me. I laughed. The poor little puppy did not know what was happening. I put her on a soft bed that I had made for her in the back seat and she took to it immediately. She was so cute I thought. Well, homeward bound was our destination. As I drove, the little pup slept in the back. She was relaxed and comfortable. The excitement had worn her out.

As we cruised along, I thought about how anxious I was for the spring to come. I wanted to set up my telescope in the loft of our barn again for the summer. I bought myself a telescope about six years ago and I have had great pleasure with it since. It was nothing compared to the one at the university observatory but it was mine. I saved up for it in a special fund I had to buy it with and it was my favorite pastime. We have all had fun with the telescope, my family and me and Bernie, as well as a few others. I would install it in our barn, up in the loft, on a wooden second floor area where there was a small room for general storage. I cleaned out this area and fixed it up to accommodate the telescope. I made it especially clean in the room and I furnished it with some chairs and a table. I then cut a large hole in the roof and made a makeshift waterproof observatory doors type of an opening for protection of the telescope. This made my homemade observatory in the dark country outback. The night sky out here was phenomenal for stargazing and planet watching. Only a wooden ladder that was part of the barn structure itself was access to the loft. I have had a few complaints about that though. Well maybe one day I would fix it up and put in some proper stairs. There was a small opening to the room but no door. I decided just to cover it with a blanket. There was an old rickety railing around the hayloft itself so we did not lean on the sides. I had a small pulley system to lift my telescope up to the loft and then I would pull it in onto the hay floor. It was a fantastic place to get away from it all and let the stresses of life flow away.

Being a physics professor, I taught physics in all its realms and disciplines and for the most part it was old hat for me. It was much like engineering in the sense that physics is logical and its laws are rigid. An offshoot of physics, which was part of my hobby I was most interested with, was astrophysics mixed with a little metaphysics. Much of this science was hypothesis and postulation and it was in this realm that one could use their imagination. I tried to teach my students this and remind them on a regular basis. I wanted them to think for themselves as individuals. I wanted them to be able to question, hypothesize and theorize on their own. If I quote, Albert Einstein correctly, I believe he said, "Imagination is more important than knowledge." I would try to impress this upon my students to give them a better grasp of the laws of physics and an ability to absorb information more efficiently.

Our School

Our university would be hosting a symposium of sorts in the coming weeks as the student's themselves and the student reps from each department would get together for the most part to organize this event with some of their funds and some of the university's.

The lion's share of the funding being the university's would be approved of course by the President of the university and university council who were forthcoming in instances of mutual cooperation for the common good of the school.

The students have asked, well in advance, scientists, teachers and experts from around the world who they wished to visit. They would lecture and have displays in their respective fields. This happened once every two years and was a great learning experience for everyone. This year I had no part in the planning so this year's symposium would be a surprise for me in many ways. I looked forward to seeing our guests as they arrived and the science they brought to display for all who would attend.

Well, I was almost home and as I drove up our long and bumpy driveway, a large dip startled the dog. She yelped and came to life. She pawed the sleep from her eyes, as she was nervous and excited again. As I pulled up to the house, Christine came outside and looked in the car.

"Agh, oh my God! Oh my God! Look at her, just look at her." Christine squealed. Her eyes opened wide with excitement. "Jim, she's so beautiful! My goodness, the girls are going to go bananas!" Christine exclaimed. She laughed. She opened the car door and reached in to pick up the puppy. The puppy was overwhelmed again and as Christine lifted her, she peed all over Christine's dress. We laughed, heartily.

"She's going to be a little nervous for a while, Chris, the veterinarian said."

"That's just fine, it's only natural she'd be a little nervous. Did everything go okay for you at the shelter, hon?"

"Oh yeah, there were no snags dear. Everything went smoothly."

"She's so cute. Oh yes you are, oh yes you are my little one!" Christine swooned. She held the puppy close and cuddled her trying to calm her. The puppy began to lick Christine's hands and fingers.

"I think she's hungry and thirsty dear. We'd better get her inside the house before the girls get home from school. Bring her in the house, Christine and I'll get the supplies out of the trunk. We'll get her ready and then I'll hide her in the bedroom." I said. Christine went into the house with the dog and I retrieved the food and the dog toys from the trunk. We had to feed the puppy and then hide her so we could surprise the girls after they had eaten their dinners. When I came into the house, Christine was wiping the pup with a wet cloth to clean her and feed her.

"You know, we can give her some of that hamburger from the other day and a small bit of water. The hamburger is half of her diet the vet said."

"Alright, sweetheart, we'd better hurry though the girls will be home shortly." Christine replied.

"Alright I'll go upstairs and make a little bed for her and a small blockade to keep her in the room until its surprise time." I said. I went up to our bedroom.

A few minutes later, Christine arrived upstairs with the dog.

"Okay, she ate and drank a little so she's all yours, Jim. I'm going to get supper started and make things look as normal as possible." She had a glow in her eyes and a smile on her face. After all our years together, Christine's smile still lit up a room for me.

"Alright hon, I'll try to calm her down and tuck her in and then I'll be right down."

"Alright sweetheart, hurry."

I put some blankets on the floor and made a little bowl in them for a dog bed. I thought that the next day I would have to go into town and buy something more permanent. I put the dog in her bed and she took to it right away. She seemed to want to stay there and sleep. The nervousness of not knowing what was happening and the strange environment exhausted her. She had a busy day, I must say. I closed the door slowly and I went downstairs.

"Okay all set. I think we have a few minutes or so until the girls get home." I said, as I entered the kitchen. Just then, we heard the squeal of the brakes on the school bus. I looked out the kitchen window and our girls hopped off the bus. They look tired but happy.

"Jim, we'll let them rest for awhile and then we can eat. We'll all get relaxed before the surprise." Christine said. She prepared the food and the amenities for that evening.

"Alright hon, I'll set the table and clean up a bit."

"Okay, try not to let on, Jim." Christine told.

"Don't worry hon, I won't." I replied. The girls came in from their day and they greeted us.

"Hi Dad, hi Mom!" Angela said, as she walked through the door.

"Hi Angela sweetie, how are you?"

"I'm hungry, Dad and I'm tired." Angela sighed. She looked relieved to be home.

"Hi Paula", "Hello Paula." Christine and I said, as we greeted our young girl.

"Hi Mom, hi Dad."

"How was your day, sweetie?" Christine asked.

"It was good, Mom, and I've got no homework this weekend." Paula bragged.

"Well that's good, sweetie, you can help out with more of the house work then." Christine replied, trying to tease Paula.

"Aghhh Mooom!" Paula squawked.

"Just kidding, sweetie, it looks like a nice weekend ahead. You girls can start getting outside more and enjoying the fresh air. We can all use a little of that."

"How about you, sweetheart, did you have a good day at school?" I asked, Angela.

"Yeah, I had a pretty good day, Dad." She had a dejected tone with her eyes cast down. Right away Christine interjected.

"Are you okay, sweetie, is anything wrong?"

"No Mom, I'm okay."

"Are you sure?"

"Yes, Mom." Angela responded.

Just then, the phone rang. I answered it and it was Bernie. He confirmed that he was coming over for dinner. "Stella and Bernie will be over directly sweetie!" I chimed. As I hung up the phone, I saw that Christine had sent the girls upstairs to get cleaned up and prepared for dinner. I was a little worried the way Angela looked. She did not look happy about something. I mentioned this to Christine. She said that she thought that Angela was just in a bad mood and that the dog surprise would change all that.

Bernie and Stella arrived shortly thereafter. We greeted them and ushered them into the kitchen and then we got comfortable. The girls watched television while we sat in the dining room with the stereo playing some pop music for background. Christine and Stella liked that style of music. Bernie and I were rock and rollers for the most part. We chatted for a while and then Christine and Stella went into the kitchen to prepare dinner. I ran upstairs to check on the dog. She was okay. I came back downstairs and then Bernie and I fixed ourselves a drink and sat beside our dining room window. The sun was streaming through as it was a beautiful late afternoon. We had the whole weekend ahead of us.

"So, Jim, you picked up the dog?" Bernie asked, in a low whisper.

"Yeah, she's upstairs in a cubbyhole between the dresser and the wall."

"Paula and Angela don't know?"

"No, the puppy is quiet and we're not acting suspicious to them. After dinner and just before desert we'll bring her down and present her to the girls."

"This is going to be like Christmas for them, Jim. This'll be fun. I brought my camera, Jim." Bernie mentioned.

"Oh, I know you did, Bernie."

"Listen Jim, I know you haven't been involved in the planning of this year's symposium but just to let you know it can't be missed."

"It's going to be a good one, Bernie?"

"Yeah! The students got some amazing speakers this year including, Dr. Ralph Dandridge for clinical medicine, Professor Linda Gurry from Great Britain for applied mathematics, and, Professor Barry Allen on geography along with many other great speakers. The president of Sherman P. put two staffers on it full time and after looking at the schedule, Jim, to use an old adage, they did a bang up job." Bernie explained, as he filled me in on the events to come.

"Is that right, eh? Jeez, Bernie I'll tell you, I'm right out of the loop on this one. I haven't really paid much attention to this so far. Shows you how much I'm needed."

"Huh, you may be right, Jim. However it looks like we're ready to roll next week and everything's in place."

"What about us, Bernie? Who have we gotten for physics?"

"We have three speakers but I only know one of them. Professor Hank McLaughlin. I went to school with him. I'm sure you've heard of him, Jim, he's one of our best scientists. The other two, I don't know who they are yet."

"Well, I better get an itinerary if I'm going to get into this event and if I want to earn my pay. I guess I've neglected this a bit too long and if I don't make my presence known soon, I'm going to get a kick in the ass from the university president."

"I would if I were you, Jim."

"I'll have to start first thing Monday, getting into this, with the students too."

"Sounds good, Jim, and try not to embarrass the university, eh!"

"Awe come on now, Bernie, you're just taking a jab at me."

"I know I am, Jim, I know I am." Bernie said, with a sinister grin.

"Let's have a couple more drinks and then dinner should be just about ready, Bern."

"Alright, I'll have one more."

It was half an hour when supper was ready and Christine rang the dinner bell. It was 5:30 pm and everybody was hungry and ready to eat. It did not take long for all to get to the table and then Bernie started snapping pictures with his new camera. The girls became suspicious.

"Uncle Bernie, why are you taking so many pictures? Today is only a regular dinner." Paula inquired. Bernie was not their relative but the girls had been brought up calling him 'Uncle'.

"I know it's not a special day, Paula dear but I just can't put my new camera down. It's part of me now and I can't stop taking pictures. I need help." Bernie joked.

"Oh, Uncle Bernie, you do not!" Paula retorted, as Bernie teased her. Bernie had always had a playful way of teasing the girls. I think sometimes to be fatherly with them. Bernie and Stella did not have children and I think Bernie regretted that.

"Sit down, dear and stop taking all those pictures, you're driving everybody crazy!" Stella chimed. We sat down to eat. I helped Christine serve the dinner. We were having steak that evening with some salad and sweet potatoes. We dished it out and everybody began to eat. It was then quiet, except for the munching of the food. After about ten minutes of eating the gang started talking again, laughing and telling his or her funny stories as everybody began having a real hoot. Christine talked about her wild day at the salon and all her kooky patrons. She had everyone in stitches. This went on for about a half an hour until everybody started to fill up.

"Okay everyone, save some room for dessert." I said. Each started to sigh and burp along with basking in the afterglow of another fine meal, "Don't forget to thank the chefs everyone?"

"Thanks Mom, thanks, Aunt Stella." Angela and Paula said. Bernie and I thanked our wives and then Christine signaled for me to go into the kitchen with her.

"Okay, Jim, are you ready?"

"As ready as I'll ever be." I said. We laughed.

"Alright, we'll go in and I'll make the announcement and then you go upstairs and bring down the puppy."

"Okay sweetie, that sounds good."

"Are you ready?" Christine asked, again.

"Yup."

"Okay, let's go."

We went into the dining area and stood up in front of everyone.

"Okay girls and guests, I have an announcement to make." Christine said. Our girls perked up and gave us their full attention. "This announcement is for you, Paula and you, Angela. Your father and I have seen that you girls have put in a lot of effort at school this year and we thought we would surprise you with a little gift."

"Oh my God! Oh my God! What is it, Mom! What is it?" Paula prodded, excitedly. Angela showed us her ear-to-ear smile.

"Hold on, sweetie, your father will go upstairs and get it, so you'll just have to wait for a few minutes. Jim, will you do the honors?"

"I sure will. I'll be back down in a few minutes gang!" I headed up the stairs then to get the puppy as everyone sat in anticipation. Bernie and Stella included. I went into the bedroom and the puppy was asleep. I gently aroused her and picked her up. I went back downstairs. I could hear the girls talking in the kitchen as I rounded the corner. I started to get a little excited. I rounded the final corner, walked into the dining room, and presented the dog. "Well my girls, here you are, I hope you like her!" I announced. The girls turned and at the same time, they let loose. "Aaiiee! Oh my God, Aagghh! It's a puppy! It's a puppy! It's a puppy!" The girls exclaimed, excitedly. Christine, Stella and Bernie also chimed in with a chorus of their own. After a few seconds, Bernie started to take snapshots.

"Wow! Mom, she's beautiful! She's so cute, oh look at her!" Angela beamed. I handed the puppy to Angela and she cradled her gently, like a baby. Paula moved closer and began to touch and caress her. Our girls were fawning, giggling and beaming with delight. Their eyes teared a little and so did mine. They looked so beautiful together like this, so happy. I was glad Bernie was getting some photos.

"Thanks, Mom and Dad." Paula said.

"Yes thanks so much, Mom and Dad." Angela said. They had looks of joy and love in their eyes.

"You're very welcome my girls, you deserve this gift." Christine said. She wrapped her arms around the two of them.

"You're our loves and you're welcome. Your mother and I hope you will love our new family member." I said.

"We will, we will, Dad." Angela replied.

"Yes Dad, we will." Paula responded.

Well that went well, I thought. "Would anybody care for some chocolate cake and ice cream?" I asked. I received enthusiastic and affirmative answers all round. Who says no to chocolate cake and ice cream? Well, not anyone around here anyway. "Everybody stay put and I'll get everything." I said. Christine and I went into the kitchen to get the cake and the plates.

"Jim, their so happy, I'm so happy. How are you doing hon?"

"I feel great hon, I'm elated. It's so nice to see those two so happy and us too." I said.

"Don't forget, Bernie and Stella, they look happy too."

"I know. They do don't they?"

We served the cake and ice cream and enjoyed the pleasures we were having. The evening progressed well and the girls called their friends to cancel their plans and stay home with their new puppy. It turned out to be a fine night. We impressed upon them a few rules and chores that they must do for the dog and they eagerly agreed. I saw that Paula and Angela were not going to have a problem with this, as they were mature enough to take on this responsibility. We also asked the girls to come up with a name for the puppy. The girls went upstairs and took the dog with them. They were contented for that day. Bernie and I then retired to the living room and our wives sat in the kitchen.

We had a few more drinks while we talked about the spring and the summer as well as all the things we were going to do that year. It turned out to be a beautiful day. After a while longer and a few more laughs, it was time to call it a night. It was almost 11:30 pm.

We went to the front door together to say our goodbyes and we agreed to meet in church that Sunday and then Bernie and Stella were off for the evening. As the door closed, Christine's and my eyes met and we embraced passionately. We kissed and held each other until we were tired of standing and then we laughed and knew it was time for bed. We went upstairs and looked in on the girls. They were sleeping in the same bed and they had made a little bed for the puppy. It was beautiful to see them like this, asleep and warm and happy. Christine and I went into the bedroom, tucked them in, and then turned out the lights. There was a schoolbook on the floor, where the girls had been writing down potential names for the new puppy. Some were pretty far out there but I was sure that we would have a name for the pup in a day or two. Christine and I went to our room. We hopped into bed and we talked and cuddled for a short while. We talked about how our day went and how much we enjoyed ourselves as well as the laughs we shared. We then got around to talking about Angela. "Jim did you notice, Angela today?" Christine queried.

"How do you mean?"

"Well, did you notice that she seemed to be distracted and maybe sad in some way and when I would come to talk with her it seemed she would paint a smile on her face and perk up? Did you notice that?" Christine asked. She had a mothers concern in her eyes.

"Well like you said earlier, Christine, maybe she's just in a bad mood. Why? Do you think we need to talk with her?"

"Maybe not, but let's keep our eyes on her and make sure she's alright. Maybe she's just a little stressed out."

"Alright, we can leave it at that then. I'm sure it's probably nothing, but we'll keep an eye out for her."

"Okay my dear, thanks for being the world's greatest husband. Agh, I'm tired, Jim, I'm going to sleep. Goodnight sweetheart."

"Goodnight Christine, I love you my dear."

"I love you too my dear, James." We kissed and then Christine rolled over to sleep. Within minutes, she was asleep. As I lay there, I thought about the day and the fun we had. I also began to think about how I had let things slip in regards to the symposium. I would have to get more involved or catch hell from the university president, I thought. I did not have many chores to carry out but I had to let the guests know who I was and be available to them if they needed me. In addition to that, I had to show them around and help with the tours and their personal needs to some extent. I started to get sleepy and my thoughts turned to life in general. I started to think of how ordered my life had been up until then, how I had always seemed to know what was ahead of me. I always knew what was coming next in my life. I had always known the things that were before me, more or less, and with a little perseverance, I was able to reach out and attain the things that were important to me in life. These things were my wife and kids, my job teaching and my friends and family. I knew what was ahead of me and I could attain it if I pushed hard enough and worked hard. However, I had a feeling that something was coming and I did not know what it was and that I would be somewhat powerless over the situation. I had experienced this feeling for a while. I would not say that it was a feeling of impending doom or anything like that but I felt that something out of the ordinary or something extraordinary was going to take place and it might well be all consuming. It was an uneasy feeling that gnawed at me from time to time.

I think it was on this day that it was how little I knew how much my life would change in the proceeding weeks, months and maybe years. My life and the lives of my wife and family and friends and the lives of the people of this town and the lives of all life throughout the world would change drastically. The events that would transpire from Park Falls would envelop the people of the world in an anomaly they would not understand. We would never dream in our wildest dreams that what was coming could ever happen. These events would be beyond our full comprehension and completely and entirely out of humanity's control. These events would bring global humanity to its knee's to pray for its collective mortality and the future of man on this earth. We could only watch as our futures began to unfold the way they would.

There would be one man that would be the messenger of this gargantuan change in our lives. I would meet this man in just over a week, and the start of a new destiny would begin for us. As to whether it was good or bad or if it made a difference I did not think me or anyone else would ever know for sure. To understate things, what was coming down the pike was going to throw us for a real loop. I would not be the same person I was after these events nor would anyone else be.

We woke up the next day, we felt good, and it was life going on as per usual. Christine worked until 2:00 pm on Saturdays and Paula went with her and earned some extra money sweeping up hair and cleaning up the messes as well as occasionally answering the phone. The girls phoned their friends and made their plans for the remainder of that weekend. Angela would stay with me that morning and afternoon and we would get started on how to take care of the dog after breakfast. Angela and Paula announced that they would like to name the dog "Cindy" and Christine and I agreed. Paula and Christine left for work and I instructed Angela on the care of the dog. We decided to put the dog in the back porch and put her carrier/dog house in this area. We started here and Angela volunteered to clean the area and make it home for the dog. I agreed and let her put her own personal touches into the room. The phone rang. "I'll get it, keep going sweetie." I said. I went to the kitchen and answered the phone.

"Hello."

"Hello Jim, its Marnie Greene, the university president. You remember me don't you?" the voice said. I shuddered and became nervous.

"Oh, hello, Mrs. Greene, how are you?"

"Easy Jim, call me, Marnie now." She responded.

"Yes Marnie, I will. I forgot."

"Yes Jim, I'm calling to see if you wanted to participate in this year's science symposium. You usually help us out with this. And, I think that some of your students are in need of help this year as I'm hearing through the grapevine." Marnie stated. She liked to get straight to the point.

"Yes Marnie, yes, I'm going to get into this on Monday, PDQ. I've been a little slow this year but you can count on me."

"Okay, Jim, that's all I needed to hear, nothing more to be said. In addition, Jim, I have the usual two staffers you can liaison with and I'll expect a visit from you this week in my office. So will you call for an appointment, Jim? I'll see you then, this week?" Marnie prodded. I could hear the clicking of a keyboard and the shuffling of papers in the background.

"Yes, I'll call your office first thing Monday." I replied.

"I'll be expecting your call then, Jim, thanks. So how's the family doing?"

"We're doing fine, Marnie, very well. We just got a new pet dog on Friday so our fun is just beginning."

"That sounds like a barrel of laughs, Jim. Don't worry though, you'll get used to the poop." Marnie stated, in her wry way.

"Thanks a lot, Marnie, we'll try."

"Okay, Jim, its set then, I will see you this week. Sorry to be abrupt, Jim but I am quite busy today so we'll talk later, is that alright?"

"By all means."

"Okay then, bye for now, Jim."

"Bye Marnie." I replied, and then I hung up

Whew, I did not expect that call. Anyhow, Marnie Greene was our university president and she was a good one. Marnie had been president for five years and we saw each other occasionally. I liked her and she was friendly. I figured if I did my job well, the boss would let me be, and such was the case. I went to the den and marked the dates of the symposium on my desk calendar, March 20 to April 3, 2012. I phoned my office next to see if I had any phone messages and I had two. I replayed the first one on the message recorder. "Leave a message after the tone:" "Aaghh hey he-ey, who iss thish, the world is going to hell man, the freaking world is going to hell! Anyways git lost man, get lost!" a male voice said, and then hung up. Now that was a nice phone call I thought. This person had obviously gotten the wrong phone number and sounded drunk. I fluffed it off and moved onto the next message. "Leave a message after the tone:" "Hi Professor Reynolds, it's me, Helen Hamilton, I need help or advice on the symposium, could you see me on Monday? I don't have a class with you but I can make time. My cell number is 623-8974, thank you, bye." Helen said. I wrote down her cell number and made a mental note to call her later that day. I then decided to get us a couple of pops from the kitchen. As I walked to the kitchen, I passed the porch, which was down an adjacent hallway, and I halted. I stopped in my tracks. I had just caught a glimpse of Angela as I was passing. Did I just see tears streaming down her cheeks? I leaned back and looked down the hallway and that was what I saw. She was wiping tears from her eyes. I continued to the kitchen to get the drinks and I was dumbfounded. Why was she crying? I wondered, with concern.

I got our drinks and gave it a few moments and then I headed back to the porch. I walked back into the room. She was fumbling with the blankets on the floor and I could see that only the tracks of her tears were left visible. "Are you doing alright, sweetie?" I asked. I startled her. She turned and responded.

"Oh Dad, yes Dad, I'm feeling not too bad. I'm almost finished."

"That's alright sweetie take your time, I brought you a pop. I'll put it here on the shoe rack for you."

"Thanks, Dad."

"You're welcome dear. So, is everything going well at school these days sweetheart? You know if you're having any problems with your homework I might be able to help you out. I'm pretty good in math and science." I said. I tried to engage her. She chuckled and then spoke.

"No Dad, I'm doing well in my subjects and my teachers are happy with me."

"Well that sounds good, Angela. We know you work hard at your studies. I guess you're looking forward to graduation?"

"Yeah, Dad, but I think I'm going to be nervous when you're all there watching me graduate."

"Listen dear; don't let that play on your mind, not at all. Listen it's only natural to be nervous. I remember when I graduated it was the same way and I was nervous for nothing and it turned out to be one of the happiest times of my life. So try not to fret about it sweetie. You know how we taught you to have a positive outlook and to be honest and if you do you will have no trouble getting through anything." I told her.

"I know, Dad, it's just as it gets closer I get more nervous."

"That's alright, just let it happen. God is with you, remember that."

"I will, Dad, I will."

"Do you have any other problems you might want to talk about dear?"

"No Dad, I'm okay. Look, Cindy's room is ready so we can bring her down now and put her in her house."

"Wow, that looks great, Angela, but first I'll get a newspaper and we'll put it on the floor in here. You know what that's for, eh?"

"Yes Dad, we're going to have to clean up the pee and poop."

"Yeah, that's right, we'll all take turns though. Once you get that done, you can bring her down and while you do that I'm going to go to the store and get her some more food and water dishes and a few more chew toys. So, Angela dear would you like me to bring you anything from town? Some junk food or a CD maybe, whatever you like, Angela, I can stop and pick it up for you?" I asked. I wanted to get Angela cheered up some because she still looked uneasy.

"Can you get lunch?"

"Absolutely, how does Chinese sound?"

"Yeah! Yes please, Dad!" Angela retorted. Suffice it to say, Chinese take-out was Angela's favorite food of all time.

"Alright, Chinese it is then, anything else dear?"

"Can you buy me some ginger ale, Dad?"

"Of course, anything else?"

"No that's it, thanks, Dad." Angela replied. She had a melancholic look in her eyes.

"Your quite welcome my dear. I'll be about an hour and fifteen minutes or so. So will you and Cindy be alright?"

"Oh yes, Dad."

"Okay then, I'm going to get ready and then I'll be off."

"Bye, Dad."

"Bye, Angela, I'll be back soon." I then prepared to leave.

Huneo's arrival

As I HEADED INTO Park Falls, it was another lovely day and the snow was starting to melt. First, I went to the grocers and picked up a few things for dinner. The pet store was next door so that made things convenient. I noted that it was busy this morning because people just wanted to get out of their homes again after such a cold winter and move about. It was such a relief for everyone to get out in the fresh air without the need for wearing a winter coat. I noticed that there were a lot of taxis and sedans around town. Park Falls had many guests this weekend, it seemed. I imagined that a good number of them were here for the symposium. I also read in our local newspaper that there was a car show in town. I liked to see when Park Falls entertained so many guests because then we got to show off our fabulous little town. I should have brought Angela into town with me I thought and we could have had a father and daughter afternoon together. I had to remember to get these times in whenever I could for the girls were not getting any younger and neither was I for that matter.

At any rate, I got the things that I needed and I saw a few friendly faces along the way. I saw Paul Banks again getting baby food and diapers and we had a little chat. I said hello to the mayor who seemed to be out glad-handing and there wasn't even an election. The mayor, Mayor Steven Bennett was an amiable person who seemed to be the right man for the job. I only say that because I voted for him. Lastly, I bumped into my barber, Randy Jensen, on the sidewalk. We had a brief chat as his eyes kept alluding to my ever-lengthening hair as he smiled and chuckled. "Okay Randy, I get the point." I said. I had known Randy since high school, we have always been good friends and he has always been my barber. By the way, I have brown hair and I wear glasses. I am five feet, ten inches tall and I weigh 195 pounds. I am stocky, muscular and a casual dresser. People tell me I resemble, although I do not see it in myself, former British Prime Minister Tony Blair. I told Randy that I would probably be in for a haircut in the near future and then I proceeded on my way.

I picked up the Chinese food and then headed for home. When I got in sight of the house, I saw that Christine's station wagon was in the driveway. She must have left work early and let one of the other employees close up for her. I was glad I bought a little extra food. I did not think they would be home.

I walked in the kitchen door at the side of the house and Christine's eyes lit up. "Hey there." she said.

"Hi, Christine."

"There's my favorite guy." She stood up and came towards me, "You're my favorite guy and you come with food. You're my favorite guy aren't you? My caveman brings home food to cavewoman." Christine cooed. She put her hands on my chest and bum, and gave me a big hug and a squeeze followed by a big wet kiss.

"Wow" I said, "I'm going to bring home Chinese food every day." We began hugging, kissing, and embracing.

"Mom and Dad! Me and Angela are in the next room you know!" Paula squawked. She had a cross look on her face. Christine and I laughed as our fourteen-year-old daughter scolded us.

"Alright, sweetie, time for lunch, Angela, lunchtime!" Christine called.

"So Paula, how's little, Cindy doing?" I asked.

"She's sleeping again, Dad. She always wants to sleep. She doesn't want to stay up with us!" Paula complained, in frustration.

"Well, Paula, the dog is like you when you were a baby, you slept all the time but we still decided to keep you." I said, musingly.

"Oh Dad!" she said sheepishly. The girls gathered around the table with their plates and started to dig in. They were quite hungry by the way they attacked their food. I decided to check my phone messages again but first I would bring along a few egg rolls with me just in case all of the food was eaten.

I went into the den and I dialed up my office machine and listened. "Leave a message after the tone:" "Professor Reynolds this is, Carmen from the audiovisual department. Could you please return the DVD player and the TV to our office? We're running low, thank you." I made a note of this on my cell phone and then skipped to the next message. "...Leave a message after the tone:" "Professor Reynolds, this is Helen Hamilton again. I need help, I'm in trouble. I have one of the guests here at the dormitory, I couldn't get him a room, he's drunk, and he made a pass at me. Please phone me as soon as possible! Please, my number is 623-8974." Helen stated, as she rambled frantically and then hung up. I immediately dialed her number and it rang. "Hello" she answered. "Hello Helen, its Professor Reynolds calling. Are you all right?" I asked.

"Oh thank God, Professor. I'm having a terrible day, just terrible!" she said, and then she started crying.

"What's going on, Helen? Let me know, Helen, what's going on?"

"Professor, we invited a guest for the symposium and I went to pick him up at the airport in Saskatoon and bring him to a hotel in town. The hotels were booked up and he got mad and he was drunk off the plane and started yelling at me, then he made some passes at me and then he grabbed me and I think people were following us!" she said, excitedly.

"Whoa, Whoa! Helen, slow down. Slow down dear. Tell me where you are and are you all right?" I demanded.

"I'm alright now. I'm in the dormitory and he's in the dorm guest house by himself."

"Who's in the guest house, Helen? What's this person's name?" I demanded, again. Christine popped into the room.

"Is everything alright, Jim?" she inquired.

"I think so dear." I said, "Go ahead, Helen, I'm listening."

"He's the guy we invited to the symposium,"

"What's his name? Who is he?" I asked, again. I was trying to probe further into what was happening.

"His name is, Huneo Parkas, Dr. Huneo Parkas. He's from South America."

"Who is he? What is he?"

"He's an astronomer and astrophysicist."

"You said he grabbed you. Did he hurt you?"

"What's going on, Jim?" Christine asked.

"Oh one of my students is in a bit of a jam, but I think she's going to be okay." I told her. "Go ahead, Helen." She continued.

"He was drunk when I picked him up, Professor Reynolds and he made passes at me and in the end he tried to touch my breasts and I had to scream at him to make him stop!" Helen blurted out.

"But are you alright, Helen?"

"Yes, Professor Reynolds, I'm alright."

"Where is he now?"

"He's in the guest house and he's asleep but we're not supposed to have any men in that area."

"Do you want to file charges with the police, Helen?"

"No Professor, I don't think he meant to do it. But what am I going to do now?"

"Listen, Helen, is anybody there with you?"

"Yes, the security guard and the secretary and some girls are in their rooms."

"Okay, Helen, I want you to let him sleep it off and I'll try to find a place for him to stay. I want you to try to calm down and get a little rest and when you see him again, I don't want you to be alone with him. Do you understand?" I said, sternly.

"Yes, Professor, I understand."

"Okay, Helen, I'm going to call you back within an hour and with any luck we might have a place for him to stay, alright?"

"I'll be waiting, Professor." Helen answered. She was somewhat calmer than when we started this conversation.

"Okay, hang in there then and I'll get back to you as soon as I can alright?"

"Yes, Professor…bye."

"Alright, Helen, bye for now." I hung up the phone.

Christine inquired with concern as to what was going on as she handed me what was left of the Chinese food. She sat beside me at the back of my desk and I explained the situation to her. As I was explaining, I got up and closed the door to the room and she started to give me suggestions to the problem at hand. We decided it would be a good idea for me to get in touch with one of the liaisons and see what they had to offer. I then broached to Christine a new situation. "Listen, Christine, I think we have another problem, maybe more serious in nature."

"What is it, Jim? I'm listening." Christine replied. She focused her attention.

"Well, Christine, it has to do with, Angela."

"Angela! What's wrong with, Angela?" Christine responded. She had concern in her eyes.

"Well, hon, I'm not sure. However, when we were home together around 10:00 o'clock today, we were getting the dog's room prepared when I went to answer a phone call. After that call, I went to the kitchen and on my way, I noticed that she was crying and she looked sad and I was taken aback by this. It was upsetting to see her this way and I was dumbfounded as to why if she was in such distress, why isn't she talking with us?"

"Goodness, Jim, did you try to talk with her?"

"Yes, I did. I was hesitant though and baffled, I didn't want to upset her more. This is the second time hon I've seen her sad like this. I'm not sure what to do. All I did was to be open with her and let her know that she could be open with me, but she wasn't forthcoming." I explained.

"Well, I don't know what could possibly be bothering her but we can't let this go on, that's for sure. We're going to have to sit her down and talk with her. We're going to have to do this soon. I mean tonight after dinner, we can't watch a sadness fester in her and just sit back!" Christine extolled. Her parental instincts had her alarmed with this situation.

"I agree sweetheart but I had to be with you for this. We need to be together on this. We have to deal with this together." I said. A knock at the door interrupted us.

"Mom and Dad, it's me, Paula, can I come in?"

"Yes come in, sweetie." Christine replied. Paula entered. "Did you need something, Paula?"

"No Mom. Are you and Dad coming back out?"

"We'll be out in a minute, Paula!" I said, tersely.

"Wait a minute, Jim. Where's your sister, Paula?"

"She brought, Cindy to her bed."

"Come in and close the door behind you." Christine asked of her. "Come in and sit down dear."

"What's wrong, Mom?"

"Nothing, sweetie, but listen, we've been noticing that your sister has been a little sad lately. Paula do you know of any reason why your sister might be sad?"

"No Mom, she seems fine to me."

"Are you sure you haven't noticed anything or know of any reason why she might be upset?"

"No Mom. Sometimes she's in a bad mood but I seem to do that to her sometimes."

"Well, okay then, you can go and we'll be out in a few minutes."

"Okay, Mom." Paula answered. We waited for her to leave the room.

"Okay, Jim, that settles it, we'll talk to her after dinner tonight."

"Alright, we'll have to be gentle, I think."

"Definitely we'll have to. I only wonder what could be wrong. Is it her school work, bullies, her friends, boys, what?"

"I don't know dear but we'll find out."

"Alright, I'm going out to the kitchen and be with them. I guess you have a few phone calls to make, hon."

"Yes, I'll try to get this student thing squared away and then I'll join you." I said. We both felt a little relief. Christine leaned over and kissed me. "I love you, Jim."

"I love you too, Christine." I replied.

Well, that weekend was turning out to be a little more dramatic than I had anticipated but it was nothing I couldn't handle. However, it was a respite, if it was anything, compared to the unthinkable dimensions and the sheer unexpectedness of the events that were to come.

At any rate, I got on the phone with the one of the liaisons. I got a hold of a young man by the name of Ken Davis. I explained the situation with Helen Hamilton, her guest, and the predicament she was facing. Mr. Davis explained that all the hotels in Park Falls had been booked up and the bed and breakfasts rented. He explained that there were two major events going on at the same time and the town was overwhelmed. The university staff never expected so many guests and could not keep track of them. However, he mentioned that he had contingencies ready for me and that he was instructed by the president of the university to have these plans in place for the faculty who got themselves into a bind. As I inquired as to what these plans were, he explained to me that there was an apartment out near our home, in fact, that would be available. I jumped at this offer and took down the address and phone number. He told me that it was ready for immediate occupancy. I thanked Mr. Davis for saving the day and was about to hang up when he spoke out. "Wait a minute, Professor Reynolds, I was told you have an appointment to make with the president. Would you like to make it now? Kill two birds with one stone?" he asked. They were sharp at that office, I thought. I made the appointment for, Wednesday at 2:15 pm and thanked him again and that ended the call.

I phoned the Landlord next and he was accommodating. He went through the short-term rental agreement expeditiously. I got the preliminaries completed over the phone and told him that Mr. Davis would contact him to finalize the specific details. Next, I had to get back to Helen and let her know. I phoned Helen and she was happy to hear back from me. I asked her how she was doing and she said she was okay. Helen was anxious however but when I told her about the apartment, she breathed a sigh of relief and I could hear in her voice that she was feeling much better. I told Helen that I was concerned at what she had told me and wanted her to come to my office on Monday at 11:30 am. I wanted to discuss the actions that transpired with her that day and make sure that I knew what had happened. I would confront her guest as to his terrible behavior towards Helen. Nevertheless, I told Helen to get the man out of the dorm and on his way to the apartment and then I told her to get some rest. I told her that she was not to be alone with him and to have the security guard help her out with the arrangements.

I was sitting at my desk thinking about the day and the events and I was becoming tired. I was thinking that tomorrow at church I would speak with Bernie and see if he knew anything about the fellow that the students had invited to the symposium. I got up and went to lie down on the couch for a minute and think things through. I was out like a light. When I awakened, I had a pillow under my head and a blanket on me and as I glanced up at the clock it was 3:45 pm. Wow, I was more tired than I thought. I had better get up and start moving around or I would be up all night.

I heard a chorus of laughter permeate the room so I went to investigate. I saw my gang in the living room sitting on the floor rolling a ball back and forth to one another as Cindy gave chase. They were laughing. I stepped into the room and it looked like they were having fun. Our new dog Cindy was starting to display a bit of energy. Suddenly, she saw me, stopped dead in her tracks, and let out one big bark at me. Christine and my girls laughed. "She barked at you, Dad! She barked at you!" Paula shouted, with glee. They thought this was funny and it was. I was still waking up so I sat in the chair next to Christine and joined in the festivities. We spent the next half hour tossing the ball for Cindy who looked like she was becoming a dog who was right at home with her new surroundings. We laughed and talked about her and talked to her. She was bonding with us and becoming part of our family. Then abruptly, she squatted and peed on the hardwood floor. Well that slowed things down so Paula and Angela quickly cleaned up her mess.

Christine and I decided to get supper started. I asked the girls to take the dog to her room and see if she would pee on the newspaper. I sat down at the table and began to peel the potatoes and carrots. Christine started to make the batter for the fish that we were going to have for dinner. "Well, hon it looks like you and the girls have had a good afternoon. Sorry, I fell asleep on you." I said, apologetically.

"Oh, Jim dear, don't even think of it, it's the weekend, hon, so sleep when you want to sleep. You worked hard so take the time you want, you don't have to apologize." Christine said.

Paula and Angela walked in and made a proud pronouncement.

"Cindy pooped and peed on the paper!" Each said.

"Did you give her praise for doing it on the paper?" I asked.

"Yes, Dad, I think she's going to learn really fast." Angela replied.

"Well, she's going to have her accidents and she'll take at least a few months to be paper trained properly so don't think this is going to be easy."

"We know, Dad." Angela said.

"So what are you girls doing for the rest of the day?"

"Well, were going to get together with our friends and we're going to go shopping and then we'll go to the Cineplex for a movie." Angela explained.

"What movie are you going to see?" I asked.

"We don't know yet."

"Okay, that sounds good to me. Are you guy's hungry for some fish?"

"Yeah, alright." "Yes Dad." The girls responded, unenthusiastically.

"Okay, we're going to watch TV in the living room." Paula stated.

"Alright have fun." Christine replied. Paula and Angela rushed into the living room carrying Cindy along with them.

"So I guess we're going to postpone our talk with, Angela then, hon?"

"Yeah, I think we should. It looks like they've already made their plans. She looks like she's having fun right now so I think we'll leave her be for today."

"Okay, alright, but we'll try for an opportune time tomorrow then, hon?"

"Yeah, we'll wait till the time is right I think. So did you get, Helen's problem solved?" Christine asked.

"Yeah, we did. The fellow she invited is going to get an apartment just a few miles from here at that old condominium project near the river."

"Helen is okay?"

"I think so, but maybe I'll give her a call tomorrow just to be sure."

"It sounds to me like she doesn't have much help, Jim."

"I'm going to make sure on Monday everything's copasetic and I'm going to make sure everything's coordinated!" I said, with authority. Christine looked at me and chuckled.

After our dinner, the rest of the day was the usual as the girls went out with their friends and Christine and I stayed in with Cindy and amused her while she amused us. We put on some soft music and talked until we got tired. The girls came home around 11:00 pm and told us about the incredible movie they saw and then we went to bed.

The next morning we awakened to a beautiful Sunday as the temperature looked to be warming and the snow was melting. It was March 15. It was the first day of spring-like weather and as I opened a window for a moment, I could smell the freshness in the air. I felt good this morning I thought and then I threw a pillow at Christine. "Hey, get up, lazy." I said. She moaned and reveled in the cool sheets. "Come on, get up and make breakfast sweetie!" I said. I teased her and got the pillow back in the head.

"You make it!" she squawked.

"Okay, my dear, I'll get up and make breakfast." I got up and washed. I then told the girls to get up and get dressed and that it was a beautiful day. I asked them if they wanted to go to church with us and they said yes. When the girls were younger we brought them to church with us but after the age of fourteen we let them make up their own minds on religion and spirituality and thus far they seemed to embrace both a religious and spiritual presence in their lives to varying degrees. They did not always come to church with us but we were happy when they did. So today, we would go to church together.

We arrived at church later that morning. I noticed Bernie's car had a free spot beside it so I parked beside him. As we got out of the car to go into the church, we saw that it was a full house. Everybody was happy and all smiles. We saw our friends as the girls gathered with their friends and we had a little social before the service. I saw Bernie and Stella, so I wandered over to them. I said hello to a few other people along the way.

"Hey, Bernie, how are you this morning?" I asked. I shook hands with him. "Hi Stella, how are you today?"

"Good, Jim. It gets a little harder to get, Bernie out of bed on these Sunday mornings though." Stella said. She shook her head.

"I'll bet, getting used to retirement, eh, Bernie?"

"It's the change in the weather don't you know, Jim. I need my beauty rest." Bernie said, with a devilish grin.

"It looks like your getting the rest and Stella's getting the beauty, Bernie."

"Why Professor James Reynolds, I do so declare, you are quite the gentleman!" Stella commented, as she swooned. "We had a great time Friday, Jim and thanks for the invite. How are Paula and Angela getting on with the dog?" she asked.

"You know, you and Bernie are always welcome, Stella. The girls are getting along famously with, Cindy."

"Cindy's her name. Oh, I like that name, Jim. So where's, Christine at now?"

"Umm, oh there she is, over by Paul Banks station wagon. Ah, Sherry and Paul brought their new baby girl."

"Bye guys!" Stella said. She smiled and headed over to see the new baby.

"Is everything in hand, Jim? I heard about yesterday?" Bernie mentioned.

"How did you hear about that, Bernie?"

"Oh, a little birdie told me. No actually I went by to pick up some tools from my office and I met the security guard from the girl's dorm and he clued me in."

"Really, Bern, and how do you know the security guard from the girl's dorm?" I asked, tongue in cheek.

"He's our neighbor's young lad, Jim. So is everything alright?"

"Well, I think so but I might give, Helen a call to see how she is today. So, Bernie, do you know anything about this guest she's invited to the symposium this year?"

"All I know right now, Jim is that his name is, Huneo Parkas and that he wants to be called, Dr. Huneo Parkas. He's supposedly an astronomer or astrophysicist from South America and that he may have had some training at Cambridge University in the U.K."

"I've never heard of him, Bernie, have you?"

"No I haven't, Jim, but I'm looking into it on the net and checking it out with some of my colleagues and connections. I'll keep us updated, Jim, if I can."

"Okay thanks, Bernie. This symposium seems to be off to a bit of a surprise start for me."

"There's probably nothing to it, Jim, I wouldn't worry about it if I were you."

"Well, I want to know what happened between him and, Helen to see if we need to take any action."

"Well you could ask her now, Jim. She's in the church today."

"Is she alone?"

"No, she's with her parents."

"Well, I'll make my presence known and if she wants to talk that'll be okay."

"It's your call, Jim."

"I'll just let things happen I guess. Hey we'd better get in there, Bernie; it looks like they're going to get started soon."

"Okay Jim, let's go." Bernie said. We headed into the church.

I joined Christine, Angela and Paula as we got seated for the sermon. As I was sitting down, Helen and I made eye contact. I assessed that it was not a good time to communicate with her. She was contented on being with her parents from what I could surmise.

After church, we went our separate ways. We went home to a quiet day as Christine and I were satisfied that afternoon with renting a movie and falling asleep on the couch in front of the television. Angela completed some of her homework while Paula listened to her music that afternoon in between the both of them playing with the dog and talking on the phone. It was a great afternoon to be lazy and that was exactly how we spent our time that day. It was a rare but welcome luxury around here and it felt good. After a fine dinner later that day, it got on to the time that we prepared for the week ahead and readied ourselves for bed. It was family time and we would talk about things related to one another and tell how much we loved each other. We made sure that each one of us knew that the others were there for them when they needed us, especially our daughters. After a few laughs and a few tall tales, it was about time for lights out. I think Christine had it the easiest on Sunday nights because as she used to say "Nobody gets their hair done on a Monday." Therefore, Mondays would be easy days for my love. For us in the education system however, it was a hustle and bustle environment and it was always changing. Christine was asleep when I entered our bedroom. I laid down next to her as I tried not to wake her. I reminisced about the events of that weekend and before I knew it, I was fast asleep.

Monday morning came and I awakened first. I was the lightest sleeper and I needed the least amount of sleep. Within ten minutes, Christine was up behind me and the girls were up shortly thereafter. The morning rush ensued and I was in a hurry to get out the door after the "I love you's."

I did not know why I was so impatient this morning. I said to myself that I must slow down as there was nothing to be rushing for and then to some degree I began to relax. The weather outside was foul that day. It was pouring rain and it was windy as hell. I hated the rainy weather especially here in Park Falls. We sat down for breakfast and the girls were arguing over I don't know what as Christine seemed to be in a whole other world. I finished my breakfast, said my goodbye's, and then headed off for the university. I told everybody I would be home by around four o'clock and with that, I was on my way. As I drove, I thought back to previous years that I seemed to be rushed and I surmised that it was because I was anxious for the warm weather to come. At any rate, it was raining and I could not do anything about that, so, I put on some Rolling Stones music on my CD player. I turned up the volume and that seemed to put me in a happier mood. I started grooving to the beat. Before I knew it, I was pulling into my private parking spot at the university. I truly enjoyed this benefit from my job of being a teacher. It was also a pet peeve of mine, finding the perfect parking spot. I headed to my office and as per usual, the halls were neat and quiet this morning. I filled my coffee maker, turned it on and then went to my desk to prepare for the day.

First, I set up my lessons for that day. I had only first year students and third year students so the material was easy to prepare. I then sat and enjoyed my morning respite. After a while, my secretary and other staff members began to arrive. In my office, there was a secretary and two other physics professors that were junior to me. Sandy Burns was our secretary and Larry Butler and Henry Ling were the other professors. We got along well together and we were well co-ordinated. I headed the physics department but we ran in tandem as separate entities in the sense that we did not step on each other's toes and we each had our own individual styles for teaching. We each had offices within the department and that made for a good working environment. Anyhow, the coffee was going down well so I decided to read the morning paper. These days when I read the paper, it was so depressing. It looked as if the whole world seemed to be sliding into a state of mayhem and debauchery. It seemed these days that humanity was in an unstoppable downward spiral moving toward its own self-destruction and everything everywhere was getting worse. Here in Park Falls we seemed to be so far removed from this but even from my vantage point I could see that this negativity would be knocking on our door soon enough. I was not encouraged when I read the paper these days. Being a spiritual person, I tried to live by accepting the world the way it was but it was getting harder and more difficult to accept. It seemed that turmoil and moral degradation was spreading everywhere and there was nothing that could be done about it, it was like a plague. These days quite honestly I tried to stay away from the news and its constant dismal headlines but sometimes you had to see what was going on around you so you tuned in. A soft knock came at my door as Sandy Burns stuck her head into my office. "Hi Jim, how are you?" she asked. Sandy wore a joyful smile that day.

"Not too bad, Sandy, I'm just reading the paper here. How about yourself, did you have a good weekend?"

"I had a great weekend, Jim, lots of fun and lots of parties. I partied hardy," she said, with a mischievous grin.

"Oh yeah, well I had not too bad a time myself." I replied. I thought Sandy was trying to find a new boyfriend and was at a stage in her life where she could be footloose and fancy free. I would let her call me "Jim" in the office when we were alone but in the presence of others, she had to call me "Professor" as a matter of formality.

"Jim, you have a visitor already, did you wish to see her right now?" she whispered.

"Who is it?"

"It's, Helen Hamilton."

"Yeah, that's okay, give me two minutes and then send her in."

"Yes, Professor Reynolds." Sandy replied, and then she went back to her desk.

I cleaned up my office a little and straightened up my papers and then I was ready for the day. Another soft knock came at the door and then Helen peeked her head into the room.

"Come in, Helen, come on in." I said.

"Hello, Professor Reynolds."

"Come in and have a seat, Helen. Sit in one of the bigger chairs, they're more comfortable. So how are you today, Helen?"

"I'm feeling not too bad, Professor. It's been a trying weekend for me though."

"I saw you in church yesterday with your parents." I mentioned.

"I saw you too, Professor Reynolds with your wife and daughters."

"So how are your Mom and Dad these days?"

"Oh, they're doing well, Dad is going to take early retirement and he keeps saying that he's going to relive his youth."

"Huh, good for him, it sounds like he knows what he wants. So how's your younger brother doing?"

"Well, he still loves his hockey and his basketball and he's got his first girlfriend."

"Wow, it sounds like everyone's really getting on with the things that are good, Helen." I commented.

"I thought I would come in and see you first thing today, Professor Reynolds since the weekend because we don't have a class today and I thought I'd explain what happened." Helen said, with trepidation.

"Certainly Helen, you're more than welcome. I'm here to assist you, Helen and not only in the classroom, it's part of my job especially during this symposium." I said. I tried to reassure her.

"It seems like you've had your hands full this weekend. Did no one else offer to help you with your selection for the symposium?"

"No, there were others but they were all busy with their relatives or something else this weekend."

"I see that you're alright though, aren't you?"

"Yeah, I'm alright."

"Okay, would you like to tell me what happened then, Helen?" I asked.

"Well, Professor, I went to the airport in Saskatoon to pick him up and he was drunk!" Helen blurted out. She was excited and nervous.

"Whoa Helen, slow down, listen, Helen, take your time, there's no rush. Helen you know me, I'm here for my students and I'm here for you right now. You can trust me to help you dear. What you say to me is privileged. So listen, why don't you start from the beginning, Helen and tell me who this person is and how you came about to meet him as well as how it came about that he is here for the symposium, and take your time, Helen, go slowly." I said. I tried to make her comfortable.

"Thanks, Professor Reynolds. Well his name is, Huneo Parkas. He says he wants to be called, Dr. Huneo Parkas. I met him on the internet in a science chat room and I began to find out about him and eventually thought he would be a good candidate for the symposium." Helen explained. She spoke softly.

"Go on, Helen, continue."

"Well, he works in a privately owned observatory in the Lower Antilles in Venezuela, in a place called Tierra del Fuego. The sky is most clear down there and it's a good place for astronomy."

"So he's an astronomer, Helen?"

"No he's an accredited astrophysicist, Professor Reynolds and he's a scientist. He's kind of a loner though in that observatory and he studies and maps the stars for the company he works for and takes geographical readings from satellites."

"Where did he go to school?"

"He went to Cambridge University in Great Britain in their astro-physics program but he got kicked out because he had crazy ideas they said and he did not get along with the faculty or the other students. After that, he came back to the United States and finished his graduate work at a university in California."

"Jeez, he sounds like a pretty colorful fellow."

"He was born in Mexico and grew up in Texas and he now lives in South America."

"How old is he? When did he graduate?"

"He's forty-seven and I think he said he graduated in 1990."

"Why did your group pick him for the symposium?"

"Well, it was mostly my doing, Professor. I convinced the others he would be a great speaker for us. He's known as a renegade and we thought he would be an interesting speaker."

"A renegade, how do you mean, Helen?"

"He's a person who is a bit of a loner and although other astrophysi-cists discount him he seems brilliant. I thought it would be novel to have him here to speak."

"How long have you been talking with him in the chat room?"

"We've been talking for more than a year and a half." Helen said. Her eyes started to tear up.

"That's a long time, Helen, are you two more than just acquaintances?"

"I think I love him." Helen stated, and then she began to cry. I gave her some tissues and told her it was all right.

There was a knock at the door. Sandy peeked in again with a message. "Sorry for the intrusion, Professor Reynolds."

"Yes, Sandy?"

"Yes, Professor Wakefield is here. Are you able to see him?"

"Not right now, Sandy. Could you ask him if I could call him back in an hour please?"

"Certainly I will, excuse me again." Sandy replied.

"That's alright, Sandy. Thanks."

"Sorry, Helen, are you alright?" I asked. She seemed distraught.

"Yeah, I think so. I'll be alright, Professor Reynolds."

"So you had a relationship over the internet?"

"Yes and when I met him it was not what I expected. He was drunk and mad."

"Did he hurt you?"

"No it was nothing like that, but he touched me in an inappropriate way and I did not expect that. I wanted to talk to him today, Professor Reynolds, after he has gotten up and perhaps, feels better. Maybe the plane ride did that to him." Helen explained.

"Well perhaps you're right, Helen, but if he's any trouble at all I want you to call me right away and as an organizer of the symposium I want to see him in my office today at 3:00 pm, he should have no trouble with that. I want him to explain himself to me." I told Helen, authoritatively. "I'll give this person the benefit of the doubt, Helen for his actions but he must make his explanations known and make amends to you. Do you understand? This is a matter of the university's reputation." I said, sternly.

"Yes, I understand, Professor, I'll talk to him right away. I have to pick up some packages for him at the priority post at the airport and then I'll go to see him and then I'll phone you."

"Alright, Helen, I'll write down my cell phone number for you and you call me as soon as you can, okay?"

"Yes I will, I will. Thanks for helping me, Professor Reynolds."

"Helen that's quite alright, you're always welcome. You're one of my best students, Helen, and when you need help with anything, don't hesitate to call on me, alright?" I said, in a fatherly way.

"Thanks, Professor Reynolds." she said. She had a sweet and contented smile.

"Just out of curiosity, Helen if you don't mind me asking and it's none of my business if you don't want to tell me, do your parents know about, Mr. Parkas?"

"Yes they do. They think he's my internet friend and he is."

"Alright then, Helen, enough said. I've got to get onto more important things now like, Professor Wakefield's canoe and his digital camera." I said. Helen laughed. "So you'll call me as soon as possible, okay?"

"Yes, I will." she said. She prepared to leave.

"Okay, Helen, bye for now."

"Bye Professor Reynolds, thank you."

"You're Welcome." She left looking much happier.

After Helen departed, I phoned Bernie. I told him that I would come down to his office directly and he said that he would be waiting. As I made my way down to Bernie's office, I could see that the university was gearing up for the symposium with information booths, decorations, statues and posters. They must have done this work over that weekend because no part of this display was there that Friday. I could see why Marnie was so busy. The decorations were exquisite and classy. It looked like Greek mythology and Egyptian architecture were the themes. The work looked to be expertly constructed. I made it a point to give some compliments to Marnie Greene for the work.

Well, I made my way downstairs to Bernie's office. I walked in and he was there. "Hey Bernie! How are you?" I bellowed.

"Not too bad, Jim, I feel good today, how about yourself?"

"Well I was bummed out earlier about the weather, Bernie, but I'm doing fine now, just a little bit of a slow start this morning I suppose. So how's, Stella doing?"

"Oh she's happy with the warmer weather, Jim, rain or shine. Hey, I downloaded those pictures on my computer and they came out great.

I'll get some photo paper, Jim and print you up a few pix, how about that?"

"Great Bernie, the kids and Christine would love to see them."

"So how's, Cindy doing?"

"Holy crap!" I said, "You know in my rush this morning I forgot all about her. I'm going to have to phone home and make sure not everybody did."

"Ah, she'll be okay, Jim, don't worry about it."

"So I talked to, Helen this morning, Bernie and she told me her story about, Mr. Huneo Parkas. His preceding reputation leads me to believe that he's quite a colorful fellow. Did you hear anything to that effect, Bernie?"

"Well if it's the stuff from Cal Tech and Cambridge I probably heard the same as you, Jim. However, I have a friend at Cambridge who's supposed to get back to me later today and I'll let you know what she said if there's anything to add."

"Alright that sounds good to me, Bernie, thanks."

"No problem, Jim, I'm just doing my part. So would you like to meet for lunch today, Jim?"

"Sounds like a plan, Bernie, how about 12:00 pm sharp, in the teachers' lounge?"

"Hmm, I was thinking more like 12:30 pm down at, Snicker's for some smoked meat and a beer, how about that instead?"

"Even better, Bernie."

"Okay, I'll see you there then, Jim."

"Sure Bernie, I've got a class now so I'll meet you there." I then rushed off.

As I headed to my first class, I thought I had better call Christine. I dialed up her number and she answered. "Hi Christine, it's me." I said, and then I got an earful. My love was mad at me for not kissing her goodbye and talking with her that morning, and for not helping with Cindy and for not saying goodbye to the girls. My love does not get mad at me often but today I gave her good reason. I told her that I was sorry and that I would make it up to her when I got home later that day. I have not brought Christine flowers in a long time so tonight I thought I would buy her some flowers and chocolates. I would write her a romantic note as well. I think the change in seasons has made me a little absent-minded. At any rate, I went to my first class to get that finished. The class was with my first year students and they could be a little trying at times. These students were undisciplined and essentially, for lack of a better word, they were dumbfounded but they were willing to learn. After this class, I was free until my next class with my third year students in the afternoon.

I returned to my office and decided to start a little spring-cleaning before the official start of the symposium in the event that I had visitors come to my office. I instructed Sandy that I would like her to clean the reception area and type memos for the other professors instructing them to clean up their offices as well. As I entered my office, I could see that I had to get busy on this because I had quite a little mess going. I would also rearrange some furniture to create some roominess. I called out to Sandy and asked her to phone the maintenance staff to have the carpets cleaned. Sandy then explained that she had already called them and that we were on a lengthy list and would have to wait our turn. "You snooze, you lose." She said. Anyway, I started right into cleaning my office. I was typically late starting with these symposiums but once I got underway, it was actually enjoyable. The best part was meeting all the new people and personalities. For example two years ago, I met a fellow scientist from Russia. He was an expert in electricity and electromagnetism. We had great talks about this subject and some arguments as well but the best part was his sense of humor. Boy, oh boy, could he make me laugh. I would have tears in my eyes for hours listening to his jokes. This type of sharing with new people from other countries was rewarding.

My cell phone rang. "Hello, James Reynolds" I answered.

"Hello, Professor Reynolds, it's me, Helen Hamilton calling." Helen greeted.

"Oh, hello, Helen, is everything going well?"

"Yes, Professor, everything is good and I'm doing fine. I talked to, Huneo Parkas, or Dr. Huneo Parkas as he likes to be called and he said he would be in your office for exactly three o'clock today." Helen stated.

"Okay that's good, Helen. I'll look forward to seeing what he has to say."

"You're not going to be angry with him are you, Professor Reynolds?"

"No Helen, don't worry about that. I just want to make sure for myself about him and I will be courteous. I will treat him with respect."

"Thanks Professor, he seemed a little overwhelmed after his journey." Helen said, and then she interjected herself. "Professor, I went to the parcel post today and picked up his packages with, David. He has four big boxes with some of the strangest looking instruments I've ever seen with names I've never heard of before. He has what looks like a lot of space time astrophysics documentation and other stuff that I have no idea what it is." Helen said, in perplexity. "He's got these instruments called SOLTES Calibrator 1, SOLTES Calibrator 2, and SOLTES Calibrator 3 and they have lights indicating that they are on somehow and I don't think I can turn them off. It looks like they're very sophisticated instruments. Do you know what these are for, Professor Reynolds?" Helen asked, inquisitively.

"No Helen, I've never heard of that type of instrument. However, that's his personal property."

"It's alright, Professor, he said that we could look at them and even touch them."

"Are you sure about that, Helen?"

"Yes, he said for us to bring the boxes to his apartment and we could look at them and touch them if we wanted. I think he's probably the only one who knows what this stuff is." Helen declared, "He seems to be such a brilliant and amazing scientist."

"Alright, Helen, just do as he asked. Moreover, you shouldn't fool around with those instruments not knowing what they are. Also be sure to lock the door to his apartment if he's not there when you leave."

"Okay, Professor Reynolds, I think everything is going to be alright now."

"Alright that sounds good. I'll see him this afternoon and if it warrants I'll call you later in the day. If not, I'll see you and, David in class tomorrow, alright?"

"Okay, Professor Reynolds. Thank you again, Professor."

"You're welcome, Helen."

"Bye for now then."

"Okay, I'll talk to you later then, Helen, bye for now." I said, and then I hung up. I must say that Helen has gotten my interest piqued in Mr. Huneo Parkas and his show and tell.

I could see by the clock on the wall that it was time to go and meet Bernie for lunch. I rushed out to my car to get on my way. I told Sandy to forward my calls to my cell phone. As I went out to my car, I saw that the sky had cleared and it was becoming nice outside, weather wise. As I was leaving, I saw some familiar faces and exchanged a few pleasantries. I then got into my car and was on my way. Snicker's was a medium sized restaurant and the clientele were from the university, for the most part. Snicker's restaurant had been around for more than twenty years and it had a good reputation for food and fun. When I was in my twenties, I met Christine at Snicker's, so it had a sentimentality attached to it for us. Occasionally on a lark, we would go there to reminisce and relive the early years when we first became lovers. I would recall some of the best years of my life when I sat in Snicker's and reflected upon the past. As I was driving, I noticed the large amount of visitors that our town had attracted to the two events. The car show must have been a sellout with all the people I was seeing on the streets. Our town was jammed with visitors and as I pulled up to Snicker's restaurant, it was no exception. I saw Bernie's car in the parking lot and I tried to park close to his vehicle. I went inside and there was lots of action. This was not typical of Snicker's on a Monday that is to be for sure. I would bet that owner Linda Coves was in her glory with these two events in town. At any rate, I saw Bernie and he had garnered us a small table, our usual right beside one of the coin-operated pool tables.

I went over to the table and greeted him. "Hey Bernie, wow this place is a hoppin! What do you think?" I asked.

"Yeah, I think it's great, Jim. Our town is showing a bit of life to it. What do you think?"

"Well, I think it's going to be an interesting next few weeks and we can just cruise along for the ride. Did you order anything yet, Bernie?"

"Not yet, Jim, but I'll have a cold draft to start things off with and I'll rack up the balls. Are you up for a game?" Bernie asked, knowing that I would never say no to a challenge on the pool table. We had a rivalry going and I would take any opportunity to even up the score.

"Rack em up, sucker! You'll be buying me the next beer my friend." I taunted.

"Ouch, try to keep your cool, Jim. You're going to need it." He said. We laughed.

I ordered a couple of beers from the waitress and then I sat down and soaked in the ambience. This gave us a chance to relax and relieve some stress. The beer came and I was completely at ease.

"Okay, Jim, you break, chalk a cue!" Bernie bellowed.

I broke the balls. I did not sink any.

"So, it's been a good day for you so far, Bernie?"

"Yeah, nothing out of the ordinary. Marnie Greene asked me to deliver the opening statement and introduce some of the speakers at the symposium on Thursday when it officially kicks off. I'll also help out with a few other chores as they come up on a voluntary basis of course, other than that, Jim not too much, you?"

The waitress showed up and we placed our order for smoked meat sandwiches.

"Well, I cleaned up my office somewhat, Bernie but I see I'm going to have to get down on my hands and knees to do a good job. I'm also going to meet with, Mr. Huneo Parkas in my office at three o'clock, so I have that on the agenda for today. Did you find out any more about him, Bernie?"

"Well actually, I talked to a former colleague of mine and she said that he's a kind and giving man who has a deep passion for life. That he's a man that prides himself in honesty and integrity. So what do you think of that?"

"Well if that's who he is, Bernie, you know that that's my kind of people. I'll be glad if that's the case."

"That's about all she had to say, Jim, except to say that she knew him pretty well and for quite a while I might add."

"Okay, well that sounds good then. The meeting is next. We'll see what happens then. So that's it for that then." I said. "Alright Bernie, are you ready to buy me a beer?"

"You gotta sink the eight ball son." Bernie replied. We laughed and got into a spirited game of eight ball. After a couple of games that Bernie won handily, I relented and we headed back to campus.

When I arrived back, I had to hurry to get to my next class. It looked like I was going to be late. I got that class over with and then I headed back to my office for a rest before my meeting with Mr. Parkas.

I returned to my office and prepared my desk. I reclined in my office chair and closed my eyes for a little nap. I ended up having a small sleep. When I woke up, I felt completely refreshed. Immediately there was a knock at the door. Sandy peeked her head in and announced Mr. Parkas' arrival. "Professor Reynolds, you have an unscheduled visitor. There's a Dr. Huneo Parkas here to see you. Do you have time for him? He said he was expected." Sandy stated, announcing his arrival.

"Yes, Sandy, please show him in. I forgot to mention that to you, sorry about that."

"That's alright, Professor. Dr. Parkas would you like to come in please." Sandy said. She invited Mr. Parkas into my office.

"Thank you, Ms. Burns."

"Professor Reynolds, I presume sir." Dr. Huneo Parkas said.

"Yes, Dr. Huneo Parkas is it? My name is, James Reynolds." I responded. Dr. Parkas smiled and we shook hands. I invited him to sit down. I saw that he was of average height and he was around my age. He wore glasses and his facial features were quite chiseled. He was of average build but he also looked strong. I sat down at my desk.

"Please call me, Huneo, Professor Reynolds." Dr. Parkas requested.

"And call me, Jim." I replied, as we got comfortable.

"Thank you, Jim."

"Well, I must say, Mr. Parkas, if I may be so blunt, and to get straight to the point. You've gotten our tongues wagging and our suspicions aroused with your behavior on your arrival, particularly in regards to, Helen Hamilton. I thought you could perhaps give us your side of things or elaborate on this matter to put our minds at ease?" I asked, with a directed concern in my tone. Dr. Parkas cupped his hands and dropped his face into them. He took a pause and then he looked up.

"Jim." he said. Mr. Parkas had a look of anguish in his eyes. "Jim, I'm going to ask you for your forgiveness and say that I'm so sorry for what happened with, Helen. I would never hurt, Helen, she means a lot to me. I have no excuse for my behavior from my point of view in the sense that I cannot forgive myself. Nevertheless, if there's an explanation to be had, it's my fear of flying. I have a fear of flying and this time I thought I could calm my nervousness with a few drinks. I drank more than I'd intended and as it actually turned out it made my fear of flying worse. My actions after that were inexcusable and I can assure you that this will never happen again. I hope you can find it in your hearts to forgive me or at least know that I'm very sorry for making a huge mistake." Huneo explained. I could see that he had made an honest mistake.

"I accept that explanation, Dr. Parkas and I will say that this matter is now behind us. I make mistakes too, Huneo and serious ones at that. So let's say that this is over and done with and there's nothing more to be discussed." I said.

"Thank you, Professor Reynolds. I've been troubled by this and I have apologized to, Helen profusely, yesterday and today, and I will certainly be trying to make this up to her if she will allow me." Huneo said, graciously.

"Alrighty then, so with that behind us, what do you think of our fair town and our little university?"

"Well, I think so far, that Park Falls is a beautiful place and not just in the aesthetic sense. I'm well traveled and you don't find such friendly places so often. I live in a place where there's a lot of poverty and it's not so nice,"

"Yes, I can only imagine, Huneo."

"My accommodations are large, Jim and I'm quite comfortable where I am so I must thank you for that. I'm looking forward to meeting as many of the students and faculty as I can here at the school. I haven't seen much of the university so far. However, I wouldn't mind getting a quick tour of it before I speak at my first lecture on Friday."

"Well, Huneo say no more. Let me show you around the campus. I'll personally give you the university orientation tour!"

"Hey, that sounds great!"

"Well come on, Huneo, let's go!" I said. I grabbed my cell phone and I told Sandy that Huneo and I were going on a tour of the school and I would not be back to the office until the following day.

"Alright Huneo, follow me this way." We walked out of my office and straight down the hallway to the first stop.

"Well, we can start right here, Huneo. This is the small auditorium where you'll be speaking on Friday, let's go in." I said. I held the door open and we entered the auditorium. "It holds about 400 people and it's quite cozy in here. The university will provide any audiovisual aids or equipment that you might need. Just speak with my secretary, Sandy tomorrow and she'll set it up for you."

"That sounds perfect, Jim. I'll speak with her tomorrow. It is like you said, Jim, very cozy."

"So Huneo, any hints or previews on Fridays lecture, your first lecture or subjects you might be speaking about?" I asked.

"Oh, the interested physicist asks about my lecture. He can't wait." Huneo commented. He then laughed.

"Well you know what we're like, Huneo. We always want to stick our noses into the newest science and technology and I'm afraid I'm no exception." I replied. I tried to glean some pre-lecture goodies.

"I know what you're saying, Jim. I'm the same way. I can't get enough information on science and physics. I always want more."

"So, Huneo?"

"Well, Jim, I think it'll be a good lecture related to astrophysics. I will feature some of the instruments that I've built over the years that take different measurements other than the conventional. The lecture is based on Einsteinian space-time astrophysics and there will be a new or unheard of postulation or theoretical hypotheses, mostly in regards to the sought after or more clarified grand unified theorem and its formulaic principia." Huneo explained, as those words just rolled of his tongue.

"Whoa, that sounds wild. What have you got up your sleeve, Huneo?"

"Ah Jim, I'll have to ask you to wait for my lecture this Friday. Why don't you come and listen in?"

"You bet I will, Huneo. Astrophysics is a passion of mine and I wouldn't miss it. You can count me in."

"It should be a good lecture, Jim."

"I can't wait." I replied. I could feel my cell phone receiving a call on vibrate mode. I couldn't talk right then so for that time being I ignored my phone calls. "Yes Huneo, I'll be there. I'll have to rearrange a few things but I'll be there. So let's get on with our tour, shall we. Next, we'll go to the cafeterias and the atrium garden. It's really quite beautiful, its right this way." I continued to guide our little tour.

I took Huneo throughout the general areas of the campus and we had a good time. He had a wry sense of humor and I could tell that he was a passionate person who cared about himself but cared about others first. Nearing the end of our tour he told me about his work in the South American observatory where he was employed in Argentina, in the Highlands of Tierra del Fuego. Huneo explained that a consortium owned the observatory and that he was hired in the late 1980's to oversee it and to provide and disseminate information from the telescope and the computers that were on the observatory compound. He told me that it was an easy job. He said that his employers were not demanding and the workload left him ample time to venture out on his own projects and form a relationship with the locals and others who helped with the telescope.

"I have called this place home for the last twenty years or thereabouts, Jim and I really love the people and the way they live. I like the isolation it provides from the hustle and bustle of the 21st century. It's sort of like the land that time forgot." Huneo explained, passionately. "I've been fortunate to have a job like this and with all the spare time

I have I've been able to work on my own projects and experiments. Some of these experiments I will feature at the symposium. Three or four times a year, I go to Mexico City and Texas to present my reports to the board of directors and they give me new job assignments. Other than that we keep in touch over the internet or by telephone," he told.

"Well, I must say, Huneo it sounds like a very interesting job to say the least. I can only imagine what it must be like to live in a place like that with its diverse people. It sounds like a fantasy that I might dream up for myself."

"It's also a very poor part of the world, Jim and a lot of people live in squalor and destitution. Sometimes it can be an overpowering presence that creeps up on you."

"Do you get time to help these people yourself?" I inquired. I could feel my cell phone vibrating again.

"I help out as much as I can, Jim. I balance it out with my work, my projects and my down time. I've also been able to hire a few locals and that has snowballed into a small economy of its own. This has helped tremendously in the immediate area. It's exciting to see the people build a small structured society. It's quite rewarding at times to be able to be part of this."

"I can relate to that, Huneo, helping others has had a great impact on my life as well. So we have that in common, helping others." I said. My cell phone vibrated again.

"Well, Dr. Parkas, I think for today we've gotten to the most visible parts of the university and it's been a pleasure to have been your guide." I said. I kept wondering why my cell phone was ringing so persistently.

"Well, I thank you, Professor Reynolds. I'm impressed with the school here and I'd like to see a little more of it if you get the chance."

"I'm free at lunch tomorrow if you want to drop by and we could go on another tour?" I offered.

"Maybe we can get a bite to eat in that cafeteria as well."

"Yes, by all means, Huneo, drop by and we'll do that." I said. We continued walking. "So, what is it you do down there in the observatory for your job, I mean, if you don't mind me asking?"

"Not at all, Jim. My job is not as exciting as one might think to tell you the truth. I do mostly star mapping and geological mapping by satellite. Not my field of expertise but I've developed a knack for it over the years. One of the companies I work with drills for oil and searches for rare minerals and stones. The night sky is phenomenal in Argentina though and one of the benefits of the job is being able to use the telescope for my own stargazing. So, it's mostly mapping, Jim, and reports. What I'd really like to see though is a new and nearby, but not too close supernova,"

"Oh yeah, I'd love to see that for myself too. I'd certainly like to witness an event like that in the heavens. That's a once in a lifetime event for sure. So do you have any dinner plans, Huneo?"

"I'm going to have dinner with, Helen tonight as a gesture. I think we could both use a good meal after the weekend and I'd just like to set her mind at ease and get things back on track with her."

"That sounds good, Huneo. I'll see you tomorrow then." We were about to go our separate ways.

"Okay Jim, tomorrow it is then, I'll see you at noon." Huneo said, and then he headed off toward the main entrance. As Huneo left, he looked back and smiled. I waved to him as he continued and as he walked away, I got a funny feeling about him. I was not sure how to describe it but it seemed to be a warm feeling. My first impressions of Huneo were that he was an upstanding person who had a high level of integrity. He was also an interesting person.

I went back to my office to get my briefcase and some files I had forgotten and then I headed home for the day. It was a beautiful afternoon and all I needed to wear was my spring jacket. The snow was melting rapidly and there was a lot of runoff in the streets. I noticed again as I drove down University Avenue that a lot of new traffic was on the roads. I noticed in particular, there were a number of news organizations from out of town traveling from one place to another.

Many people in general were moving about and I could see many unfamiliar faces.

It was a leisurely drive home and I traveled with the window open to get some fresh air. As I drove, I could hear birds chirping for the first time that year. I could also see a few hardy trees starting to bud. As I was a few minutes from home, my cell vibrated again. I assumed it was Christine and I could wait the few minutes until I walked in the door, I figured. I drove up our laneway and parked. I was getting hungry, I mused. I walked in the door, "Hi everyone, I'm home!" I called out. There was no response. Christine walked around the corner with a solemn look in her eyes.

"Where the hell have you been!" she exclaimed. "Why didn't you answer your phone, Jim? Where have you been?" Christine asked. She had a burning intensity and sense of immediacy about her. Christine was visibly upset.

"What's wrong, Christine, what's wrong?

"It's Angela! Something's wrong with, Angela. She's in her bedroom crying and she's been crying all day. Paula says she's been crying all day and I can't find out what's wrong. She doesn't want to talk to me or anyone, Jim!" Christine explained, excitedly.

"Is she hurt, are there any marks on her or anything?" I asked. I had become immediately concerned and worried with this situation.

"No she's fine, she's physically fine."

"Where's, Paula?"

"Paula! Paula! Come in here. Come in here we want to talk to you!" Christine sniped. Paula entered the kitchen.

"Yes, Mom."

"Paula, do you know what's wrong with your sister? Why is she so upset?" I asked.

"I don't know, Dad. I swear I don't know, Dad. She was fine this morning and around or just before lunch, she was sad and she started crying. I don't know why, I don't know, Dad." Paula said, as she tried to explain the facts. "She was sad all day and her friends tried to find out why but they couldn't." Paula added.

"Jim, one of Angela's teachers called around three o'clock and said she was upset and was excused from class to compose herself and to go to the counselor to get help if she needed. It was her math teacher, Ann Baxter and she wanted to see if she was okay." Christine interjected.

"Well, is she in her room now?" I asked.

"Yes, she's in her room, Dad." Paula replied.

"Okay, Christine, we're both going to have to talk with her together and get to the bottom of this. She's been sad for a while now and we have to find out what's going on."

"I agree, Jim but we're going to have to go slow, she's very upset." Christine said. This was upsetting for my girls and it was making me sad as well.

"Is she calm right now sweetheart?" I asked, Paula.

"Yes Dad, I was just upstairs and she's just resting."

"Okay, I think we can wait until after supper then. We can gather our wits and we all might feel a little better. What do you think about that, Christine?"

"Yes, I think so. I think we can wait a bit. I'll get supper on the table. And Paula, you can go up and ask her if she wants to eat dinner with us, and tell her it's okay if she doesn't want to eat right now and we'll save her a plate for later."

"Okay, I will, Mom."

"Tell her that we will talk with her after dinner and we're not upset with her but we want to help her, alright?"

"Yes, Mom."

"Tell her I'll come up and say "hi" to her in a few minutes okay, sweetie." I said.

"Yes, Dad." Paula replied. She then went upstairs to see her sister.

"I don't know what to think of this, Christine, she's been moody and sad for what, about a month now?"

"I know, Jim; I'm just as baffled as you. She hasn't let on about any problems she's had or has been having."

"Okay, were just going to have to wait I guess and play it by ear. Alright, I'm going to tell her I'm home and say "hi" and then I'll get changed for dinner."

"Alright sweetie, I'll wait for you down here. Be gentle with my baby."

"I will dear, I will." I said. I headed upstairs to Angela's room.

I know from time to time we have to expect girl troubles and that's part of the growing up process. I just hoped it was not too serious. I reached her room and opened the door, gently. "Hello Angela, hi sweetie, are you okay?" I asked, in my warmest tones.

"No Dad, I'm not happy today," she responded. Her face was buried in her pillow.

"That's okay dear. We're going to have supper soon. You can join us if you want."

"Maybe, Dad."

"It's okay if you want to stay up here in your room too you know."

"Thanks, Dad."

"Your mother and I want to talk with you after dinner though. Is that okay?"

"Yes, Dad."

"Okay then we'll see you in a little while." I closed the door quietly and then I went to get changed. Paula was in the hallway, she approached me to express her concern.

"Dad, I hope she's alright, she's scaring me." Paula commented.

"It's alright, sweetie. She's going to be okay. Try not to be upset. Everything will be alright." I replied. To know the truth, I was getting scared. I changed clothing and went back downstairs for dinner. We sat and ate quietly. After about a half an hour, we finished our dinner and started with the dishes. We steeled ourselves.

"Jim hon, are we just about ready to go upstairs?" Christine asked.

"Just about, Christine, I'm a little bit nervous." I said.

"We just have to be straight forward sweetie. It's in her best interest. She'll trust us, we're her parents."

"I know, so let's go."

"Alright." Christine replied. "Paula, I want you to stay down here and watch television or work on one of your projects while your father and I talk with your sister, alright?"

"Yes Mom, I will."

"Okay, Jim, let's go."

"Alright." We headed up to her room. We approached her door and knocked and Christine poked her head into the room.

"Hi sweetie, is it alright if your father and I come in?"

"Yes, Mom." Angela replied. We entered. I sat in a chair by her computer and Christine sat on the end of her bed. There was a pause as we got comfortable and then Christine began to speak.

"Listen Angela, please sit up, your father and I want to talk with you." Christine said. Angela sat up in her bed. We saw in her eyes that she had been crying incessantly and she looked sad and unhappy.

"Listen dear, your father and I and your sister, Paula, have become very concerned about your happiness. We've noticed in you that you're moody and sad, and today you have been crying at school in addition to here at home and we can't as your parents let this go on without you telling us what's happening to make you this unhappy." Christine said, gingerly.

"We are concerned for you dear, your mother and me. We know this has been going on for a while." I said, "I saw you a couple of days ago when we had first gotten Cindy and you were in the back room crying and this is upsetting us." I stated, as I added to Christine's comments.

Christine looked at her lovingly and held her hand.

"So hear me sweetie, your father and I love you so very much and only want you to be happy. We'll always be here for you so when you have a problem you can come to us. We'd like you to tell us what's bothering you and that way you won't have to face whatever it is that's bothering you alone." Christine said. She prodded her gently.

"I don't know if I can, Mom. You're going to hate me and you won't love me anymore!" Angela exclaimed, and then she burst into tears and cried profusely. Christine got upset and she started to shed tears as well. "We're always going to love you, always sweetheart! But, you're going to have to tell us! You know you can't go on like this! Your father and I must know what's bothering you!" Christine implored. We were becoming more upset. "You have to let it out now, Angela, come on and tell us!" Christine beckoned unto her.

"Alright! Alright! Mom and Dad, I'm pregnant. I'm pregnant, Mom, I'm pregnant!" Angela blurted out.

"Oh my God! Oh my God, what did you do? Who did this to you, what have you done, Angela!" Christine screeched. She banged her fist on the bed.

"Calm down, Christine, right now!" I scolded. There was a long silence. We sat and stared at our daughter in disbelief. There were no words coming out as we tried to comprehend what she had said. Angela sat with her head down as she cried and sobbed.

"I knew you would hate me!" she squealed. I could see a deep torment in my daughter's eyes and I wanted to help her and relieve the burdens that she must have felt.

"Angela, we don't hate you. We love you but you've just given us a big shock and we don't know what to do right now. Your news is upsetting in the respect that we didn't think this would happen to you." I explained, "Can you tell us more about how you came about to be pregnant?" I asked. I spoke as calmly as I could.

"I'm so sorry, Mom and Dad. I didn't think this would happen I'm sorry." Angela apologized. She cried.

"Its going to be okay, Angela, it's going to be okay." I said.

"Well, my dear, Angela, life like you knew it is now going to change, and not just for you. It's going to change for all of us." Christine said. She shook her head.

A knock at the door interrupted us. It was Paula.

"Dad, there's a phone call for you." Paula announced.

"Paula, you know we're busy. Can you tell whomever it is to call back or take a message?" I sniped.

"It sounds important, Dad." Paula said, sheepishly.

"Please take a message and leave us alone for awhile, Paula!" I said, loudly. I was touchy.

"Is everything okay, Dad?" Paula asked, with concern.

"Paula, everything's going to be okay, do you understand!" I barked, and then I regretted being so terse. I would have to apologize to her.

"Yes, Dad." Paula said, gingerly, and then she walked away.

"Angela, can you tell us how you got pregnant?" Christine asked, bluntly.

"I have a boyfriend, Mom."

"Who is he, is he from school?"

"No"

"Well, who is he then?" Christine prodded.

"His name is, Christopher Helgeson."

"That name sounds familiar. Where have I heard that name before?" Christine wondered, aloud.

"He works at, Helgeson Tires. His father is the owner." Angela replied.

"Well, why didn't you tell us this before now?"

"I was afraid."

"Oh Angela, you have nothing to be afraid of. Okay, I need a break! Let's take a break and we'll go down stairs and you can eat and tell us the rest of this okay?"

"Okay, Mom."

It was definitely time for a break and respite to comprehend this news. I had many thoughts running through my mind and a little respite was what Christine and I needed. For the time being, we each went in our separate directions and gathered our thoughts. I went downstairs and poured myself a glass of milk. Paula was watching television. I inquired as to who had called and she replied that it was Bernie and that he would call back. I dialed Bernie's home phone and there was no answer. I would call back later I decided and then the phone rang. It was Bernie. "Jim is that you? Is that you, Jim?" Bernie asked. I thought he sounded frantic.

"Yes Bernie, it's me, what's up?" I replied.

"Oh Jim, Jim, I'm at Park Falls General Hospital, Stella's had a heart attack!" Bernie blurted out.

"Oh my God, Bernie, is she all right, how is she?"

"I don't know, Jim. She's in the emergency room. I'm really scared here, Jim!" I could tell by his voice that he was in trouble.

"I'm coming down there, Bernie. I'm going to be on my way as soon as I hang up okay!" I said, with immediacy in my tone.

"Okay Jim, I'll be here."

"I'm on my way, Bernie!" I said, loudly. I hung up the phone.

"Christine! Christine!" I yelled.

"What is it, hon? What is it?"

"Come down here right away! Now please!" Christine came running down the stairs; her eyes wide open like saucers.

"What is it, Jim?"

"Stella's had a heart attack!" I exclaimed.

"Oh my God no! Oh, is she okay, Jim?" Christine asked. Her eyes filled with tears.

"I don't know, I don't know! I'm going down to the emergency right now." I told Christine. I put on my coat and shoes.

"Do you want me to go with you, Jim?"

"No, you stay here with, Angela and Paula. They need you right now. I'll call you from the hospital or soon as possible, I promise, Christine."

"Okay, Jim you go then. Tell Bernie we're praying for her, and drive carefully. Bye Jim!" Christine said, quickly, before I got out the door.

"Alright then hon, I'll call you as soon as I can, bye love!" I hustled out the door and headed for the hospital. I started driving fast so I had to slow myself down. I had to be responsible here. As I was driving, my mind was racing. This had turned out to be one of those days you only read about as if you were viewing the situation from a distance. I could not stop thinking about my daughter and her predicament, our predicament, and then I would think about Bernie and Stella. Before I knew it, I was at the hospital. I parked the car and ran into the emergency department. I saw Bernie leaning over the admitting desk. I approached him. He saw me and came towards me. He grabbed me, hugged me, and started sharing his pain. I tried the best I could to comfort him and be there for him. I asked him how Stella was doing. He explained that she was in an induced coma and effectively she would not be conscious until the following day. "Her heart is beating on its own, Jim but she has had some brain dysfunction on her tests, I'm terrified, Jim! What if I lose her?" Bernie expressed. He was alarmed.

"We're all praying for her, Bernie and we're here for you when you need us." I told him. All Bernie could do was to wait for the doctor's reports and the following day to arrive. I decided to tell him about Angela's pregnancy and this took his mind off Stella but for a moment. Bernie told me that I should take the pregnancy in stride because that was what God would want us to do. With that said, I knew this was the path I would take, that Christine and I would take. I had to face the fact that I was going to be a young grandfather and I would accept that. Moreover, with those words of wisdom I was able to help Bernie through the night. That night I would stay with Bernie in the waiting room and in the chapel. I phoned Christine and told her the situation and condition of Stella. Christine was concerned and afraid for her. I could tell my girl was getting a little overwhelmed by the events of the day. "Oh Jim, why is everything happening all at once like this!" Christine bewailed.

"It's just the way it is, Christine. We have to be strong for everyone. We're going to be alright. We're going to get through this together sweetheart." I told. And, with that, I could tell she became more at ease with our situations.

"How's, Angela doing right now, hon?"

"They're both in their rooms and they're doing their own things, Jim."

"You know, Christine we're going to have to accept Angela's pregnancy and show her love and help her get through this."

"I know, I know, it's just hard to accept from her right now. Our lives are going to change and I just can't believe it." Christine said.

"Well Granny, you're just going to have to accept it."

"God damn it to hell, James Reynolds, don't you dare call me that again!" Christine screeched. I could hear Paula in the background checking to see if her mother was all right.

"Sorry, Christine, I'm sorry, that was a bad attempt at a joke." I said, apologetically.

"It's alright, Jim, I'm sorry too. I didn't mean to snap at you."

"I know dear, it's okay, it's okay; I just wish I was with you right now. We need to be together for this, I need you."

"I need you to my love, I love you, Jim."

"I love you too, Christine." I said. I yawned. "Gosh! I'm getting tired. I want to come home but I'm going to have to stay here with, Bernie. He definitely needs to have someone around with him tonight."

"I know, I know you have to stay there, sweetie. Stay with him and I'll be here for the girls. We'll be together soon. Try to get some rest there. Are you going to go to work in the morning?"

"I don't know yet hon, I just don't know. It's still early. I think I'll wait and see what happens here and I'll call you back before midnight. Does that sound okay to you, Christine?"

"Yes, Jim, of course, you know to call me anytime you want sweetheart."

"Alright, I'll do that dear. I'm going to go back to, Bernie and see what's going on. I think he's calling his brother and he's thinking of calling, Stella's kin so I'd better get back, alright, Christine?"

"Yes, that's fine sweetheart, call anytime, I love you."

"I love you too, Christine, I'll call soon." We said our goodbyes and I hung up the phone. I found myself getting tired so I went back to see Bernie to see how things were going. After seeing, Bernie and trying to comfort him the doctor came back and gave us an update. Stella's condition remained the same. A nurse led us to a small room for visitors. There were some small beds and lounge chairs for us to sleep in. We took advantage of this and got some much-needed rest.

After what must have been a few hours, I woke up to muffled voices. I saw Bernie talking with the doctor. I wiped the sleep from my eyes and wondered what time it was. I glanced at my watch to see that it was 1:20 am. I shook my head; I have to find out what's going on. I got up and went over to Bernie and the doctor. I could see a smile on Bernie's face and a good feeling washed over me. Bernie walked over to me and whispered. "Good news, Jim, Stella's awake and she's talked to the doctor. I'm going into see her in half an hour after they've checked her over once more."

"Good, good, that's great news, Bern! That's great news." I responded.

"She's going to have to stay in the hospital for at least another seven days." Bernie said.

"That's alright, Bernie, she's awake and talking and that's the main thing. I'm going to have to tell, Christine and the girls."

"Jim thanks so much. I'm so lucky to have you here when I needed you, thanks, Jim." Bernie said, with a smile of appreciation.

"Anytime Bernie, I'll always be here when you need me."

"Jim listen, you've been here long enough. Go home, get some rest and tell, Christine the good news. I'll be in with, Stella soon so you don't have to stay here any longer, Jim, you can get going."

"Okay Bernie, if you're sure then, I'll be on my way."

"Of course, Jim, it's okay now. You go home and get some rest."

With that news, I would head off and call him the following day or as soon as I could. When I got home, I let myself in. Everyone was asleep so I slipped into bed and I woke up Christine. I told her the good news and she was happy. We hugged, kissed, and made love until we fell asleep. For me life started to move a lot faster after that evening or so it seemed.

Over the next few days we would try to come to terms with our newly thrust upon dilemmas and we would try to come to terms like others who were in the same situation. Angela had really gotten the family into a "What do we do next?" situation. We had to deal with it and get on with our lives the way they were, which they were not anymore. Everything seemed for me to be happening at the same time. It was a lot for Christine and me to deal with. Our jobs were a bit of a blur but we managed to get them done. It was hard to work when our minds were on other crucial matters. I had taught my classes and since we were in review, I could cruise on autopilot. As for the symposium, I had to give tours and help with matters that were of logistical concern for the students. It took us until Wednesday unbelievably to ask Angela when the baby was due. The baby, our first grandchild was due on, September 30, according to Angela's calculations. We also managed to get to the hospital twice to see Stella. She pulled through her heart attack but she had to stay there for at least three or four more days. Christine became emotional and broke down in tears when she first saw Stella. Stella was Christine's best friend and I think she was sad for Stella but also sad Stella was not there for her when Angela's situation was confronting her. We hugged and affirmed our love for each other. Our friendship with the Wakefield's was very important in our lives and we considered them our family. We leaned on each other in times of joy and in times of need. We also had the up and coming meeting with our new extended family the Helgesons' and their son Christopher. Diane and Bruce were the names of Christopher's parents. We had never met these people but we had seen them around. According to Angela, they were at this moment oblivious to the fact that they were going to be grandparents. We would explain to Angela that she must have Christopher Helgeson inform his parents of their upcoming grandparenthood. This was going to make life interesting for us indeed. We also had to deal with the relationship that Angela and Christopher would have and from what Angela had told us thus far, they were in love. These events were a little frazzling on my wife Christine and me but we managed to stay in tune with what was happening.

At work, university president Marnie Greene had called me in twice for updates and everything seemed to be going well on that front. I helped her office staff with our symposium guests in their scheduling of events, particularly for Mr. Huneo Parkas. Helen Hamilton had been showing him around and helping with his needs for his displays. I was looking forward to these shows and lectures. With all that was going on Bernie and I tried to anticipate the events with all that we could muster. Frankly, I thought that Huneo Parkas and Helen Hamilton had more going on than met the eye.

We headed to the hospital that Thursday to get an ultrasound for Angela. I could not believe I was doing this. Things were slow at work because of the symposium therefore I took Thursday afternoon and Friday off to attend to personal business and take in the lectures at the university. Moreover, who knows, the way things were going, I might even end up at the car show. Anyhow, we were on the way to the hospital in the station wagon for the ultrasound, Christine, Paula, Angela, Christopher and lastly and lest I forget the baby and me. We left Cindy at home to fend for herself. We would also stopover to see Stella for a cheer up visit.

"Wow, Dad!" Paula chimed, as we drove along.

"What is it, dear?"

"There are so many people in town! I haven't seen this many people in our town ever!" she exclaimed. Paula had been doing just fine throughout all of this I should mention. I think she was growing up fast with the lessons she was learning just watching us.

"It's the two conventions sweetie, the university and the car show." I responded, "But your right darling, I haven't seen this many people in town either. I can't imagine why there are so many people though. It just seems like so many. What all of these news crews are doing here I don't know, it's got to be for the car show."

"Are you all right back there, you two?" Christine asked, of Angela and Christopher.

"Yes, Mom" Angela replied. She sat in the back seat nestled in with her beau. Angela had become comfortable with her situation and she and her new boyfriend were not shy to be affectionate.

"Are you nervous about the test, dear?" Christine asked.

"No Mom, I'm excited to find out the sex of the baby."

"You're going to find that out today?"

"Yes, Dad."

"Getting nervous, Jim?" Christine asked. She giggled, and then laughed.

"No" I answered, in a coy, deer caught in the headlights manner.

We arrived at the hospital and decided to go our separate ways. I went to see Stella and Bernie. Christine, Angela and Christopher went to the ultrasound department and Paula went to the cafeteria and gift shops. It was a fair day outdoors that Thursday and warmer. I went up to Stella's room and entered. Bernie was at her bedside and they were watching the hospital television. "Hi guys, how are you, Stella?" I greeted.

"Hi Jim, oh, Jim it's so good to see you! Bernard here is starting to get on my nerves, but I'm doing okay." Stella replied. She had a big smile. She looked much better than a few days previous.

"Are you guys making out all right? Can I get you something or do you need anything done?" I asked.

"Oh no, Jim, you have your own hands full already, and it's a pleasure just to have you visit."

"Well, were here for, Angela, too. She's going in for an ultrasound."

"That's a good idea, Jim. She should have one at her young age."

"We agree with you, Stella, she certainly should." I concurred, "So Bernie, are you ready for the first presentation tomorrow by, Huneo Parkas, our opening speaker?"

"You bet, Jim, I wouldn't miss it. Are you going to the opening ceremony tonight?"

"No Bernie, I'm planning to get some sleep tonight. I've had very little over the past couple of days."

"Well, make sure you get what you need. What time is the first presentation by, Huneo Parkas?"

"His first presentation is at 10:00 am, Bernie and it should start right on schedule. Marnie Greene wants all shows and presentations to start exactly on schedule this time round on account of all the complaints she received the last time."

"Okay, Jim, I'll meet you in the auditorium around 9:45 am, alright?"

"Sounds okay to me, Bernie, just call me on my cell if you have a problem." I answered. After a short while socializing and having a few laughs the rest of my gang showed up and offered Stella their get-well wishes and sentiments. After another half hour or so, a nurse came in to shoo us away. With that, we took our cue and headed back home for the evening. After getting home, I decided to take a nap. I went to our room and quickly fell asleep. While I slept, the rest of the gang did their thing. Angela and Christopher watched television in the living room and Christine cooked dinner with Paula. At about 7:00 pm Christine came up to our room and woke me. She said she let me sleep because I needed it and I did. I felt much better after that nap.

"I let you sleep through dinner, Jim, are you felling rested?" she asked.

"Yes, Christine I do. Is there any dinner left, I'm hungry, really hungry."

"Of course, dear, I wouldn't let the kids eat your dinner. I might, but not the kids." She said. We laughed.

"Well, let's go down and eat." I said. We went down stairs and had a peaceful dinner together. Christopher went home to tell his parents his news and Paula and Angela sat in the living room and watched a movie. Christopher would phone either later or the next day and give us the reaction of his parents. After dinner, we retired to our bedroom and talked about Angela, Paula and the new baby and how we would take care of him or her and then it dawned upon me that I had yet to ask the sex of the baby. "Oh my goodness, I forgot, am I going to be a grandfather to a little boy or a little girl?" I asked.

"We're going to be grandparents to a little boy, Jim. What do you think of that?" Christine asked. That was when a new realization hit me. My little girl was going to have her own little boy and at that point, some tears welled up in my eyes as this fact overwhelmed me. Christine rubbed my shoulders to comfort me and after a while, I was fine. Christine and I knew our first-born girl Angela was going to need all our support in this situation. Angela's life was leaving its current path and taking a new one. She was going to have to grow up sooner rather than later.

After about an hour of talking and having a few laughs, we decided to have a cup of tea and some cold pizza as a late night snack. The girls decided to order some Chinese food as one of Paula's friends came over and they played video games. Everything was starting to feel like things were getting back to normal again. My feet felt like they were back on the ground once more. A little bit of cuddling and sweet talk ended the evening as we fell asleep in each other's arms and a warm glow enveloped us as we drifted off to sleep.

Part of a divine principium

THAT NIGHT WOULD BE the last night that I saw things the way that I did. The next day would exist for a few hours the way it had been and was and then a gargantuan revelation would be let loose for the people of the world and probably the entire universe. Nothing would ever be the same again and Huneo Parkas would be the man who would enlighten us. He would be the messenger. Professor Huneo L. Parkas would announce the origins of an unbeknownst event that was taking place. This event of Mother Nature's would blindside the world and bring humankind to the brink. It would be on that Friday that the announcement Huneo Parkas was about make would awaken the world to an event that would begin to consume all living and non-living entities as we understood them.

I woke up the next morning feeling refreshed and happy. I was actually quite happy. I thought that after looking at the big picture, I had handled things well and was ready for anything or so I thought. Life was good again and I was ready to take on the day. That Friday, all classes were suspended and I could spend time with Bernie at the symposium before he went to see Stella at the hospital. We could watch and hear some of the best scientific minds of our time show us what made them who they were. I got up with Christine that morning and we went down for a slow unrushed breakfast. The girls were at the table and we sat together and ate. "How are you girls doing this morning?" I asked.

"Fine Dad, I have a science presentation today!" Paula chirped.

"You do, do you?" I wondered, aloud.

"Yes, Dad. I'm doing a presentation on whales!" she said, with all the enthusiasm young girls have.

"You are? How come you never told me about this before?"

"Oh, it's not that important, Dad."

"Sure it is. You're darn right it is! I want to know more about it."

"Well, after my presentation, I'll bring it home for you, Dad." Paula said, with pride and glee.

"That I can't wait for, I sure want to see your project sweetie."

"Okay, Dad."

"How about you, Angela, how are you doing today?" I asked her, again.

"I feel a little queasy, Dad." she answered, with a wincing stare.

"That's alright dear just do what you need to do today."

"Listen girls, I need to know if you're going to be home for dinner and what your Friday night plans are." Christine asked.

"I'm going to be home for dinner, Mom." Paula responded.

"I'm going to stay in with one of my friends and maybe, Christopher will come over for a while." Angela replied.

"Did he phone you yet and let you know how his parents took the news." Christine asked.

"Not yet, Mom, he said he would call me at 10:30 am or a little later."

"Would you call me at work and let me know what he said when he calls you? You can call me at work at any time."

"I will, Mom, I promise."

"Are you going to school today, Angela?"

"I don't think so, Mom."

"It's alright if you want to take a rest, Angela."

"Maybe I'll stay home too." Paula asserted.

"You're going to school little lady, don't ever kid yourself!" Christine barked.

"I'm just kidding, Mom."

"Well I'm not!" Christine snapped, as Paula got her riled.

"Okay Christine, I'm going to take off. Thanks for a great breakfast. Angela, since you're going to be home, do you want to do the dishes?"

"Sure, Dad."

"Okay, I'm going to get ready."

I went upstairs to finish getting dressed. I cleaned up and grabbed my briefcase and then I was off for the day. I said goodbye to Christine and the girls and on my way as I left, I noticed that my little girl, my young woman, Angela, had a beautiful glow in her face and eyes. I looked at Christine and she looked back at me. We smiled together at her. "Wow" I thought to myself. It was images like this in life, that would be burned into our memories. I then headed out to the car and off down our old dirt road as a glorious day began that morning. The sun was blazing and the snow was almost gone. The clouds in the sky were wispy and they looked like angels had painted them. It was an awe-inspiring sight. As I drove, I listened to the local radio station. They advertised both the symposium and the auto show. Both events sounded good and started that day so it was going to be a full weekend for many Park Fallsers. As I got closer to the university, the atmosphere was almost carnival like, even at this early hour. It was March 20, 2012 and this year had gone pretty well so far, overall. I drove up to the faculty parking lot and I could see that a few news crews had already made their way into the building. I guessed our little symposium was becoming famous. I parked in my assigned spot and made my way into the building. When I got onto the campus, it was bristling with early morning activities. I did not remember it ever being so busy here at the university except for perhaps some of the larger sporting events. I rushed to my office for a cup of coffee and then I would go straight to the auditorium. Sandy had a pot of coffee on as Larry Butler was sitting with her shuffling papers and talking quietly. I inquired as to whether they would take in any of the lectures or displays that day and they were both non-committal. I grabbed my coffee and headed towards my office. I looked at the time and in all my daydreaming the time had flown by and it was now 9:35am. I gulped down my coffee, threw my briefcase down under my desk, and went straight to the auditorium. I made my way down the corridor and around the corner and I was there. The place was packed. I looked around and I spotted Bernie. We got together, went in, and sat down. The auditorium was noisy and filled with people I had never seen before. There were news crews set up, down in front, on the floor, and students from our university had webcams set up to feed live video and sound from our lecture to other schools. There was a buzz in the room and it was exciting but I think it was a little overboard. I saw Helen Hamilton and asked her what was going on and she said there were a great many invited guests from out of town. She also informed me that she would be Huneo's partner in the display aspect of the lecture. Bernie and I were very interested in seeing this lecture. Bernie then spoke to Helen. "Is the lecture going to start on time, Ms. Hamilton?"

"Yes, Professor Wakefield, it will. Oh my God, I have to go! I'll see you after, Professors!" Helen exclaimed. She rushed off for the audio-visual room.

"So Bernie, do you have any idea of what the subject matter might be for this lecture?"

"No Jim, I'm in the dark just like you."

"What do you make of some of these people here, they look like undercover cops?" I commented.

"I have no idea, Jim, invited guests I suppose."

"Alright, Bernie, it looks like they're going to start."

"Yeah, their starting."

The auditorium became quiet and then one of the liaisons from Marne's office appeared and introduced herself. "Hello everyone my name is Naomi Hester and I am one of Sherman Patterson University's masters of ceremonies. And today, I would like to say hello to all of you wonderful people and welcome you to our 19th Bi-annual Symposium for the Sciences!" She said, cheerfully, "It looks like a packed house today and that's just great, and over the next two weeks we will feature some of the best scholars in the sciences of our times." Naomi Hester announced, "And today is no exception, so for our first presentation this morning we have for you fine people a display and talk format lecture with a short question and answer session at the end of the presentation. So feel free to take notes or record with whatever media you wish. Therefore, without further adieu, I will introduce to you today's speaker. He is I'm sure you already know by now an astronomer and astrophysicist and he currently works in the private sector and has been invited by students of our own physics department. So would you please help me in welcoming, Dr. Huneo Parkas and his assistant from our own physics department, Ms. Helen Hamilton." Ms. Hester announced. Huneo and Helen walked on to the stage and received a warm greeting and applause. The audience was enthusiastic and in a good mood. Professor Huneo Parkas walked up to the microphone with Helen and stood at the ready. He adjusted his clothing and he began to speak. "Good morning everyone, how are y'all this fine morning?" He said. He smiled. He then continued.

"My name is, Huneo Parkas. Some call me, Professor or Doctor Parkas and this is my close friend and assistant, Helen Hamilton. I know a lot of you don't know what my program is about today, however, with that being said, some of the audience has been invited and so has some of the media." Huneo stated, with an air of confidence. There was a short pause and he continued again.

"I'm very happy to be here today and I have been invited here to the university by, Helen Hamilton. I have gotten to meet a lot of the students and faculty, they have treated me like an honored guest, and I am grateful for that. This town has taken me by surprise. I find this town to be one of the most beautiful places I have ever had the pleasure of visiting and that is all due to the people. I feel truly welcome at this university and to find a finer school of higher learning would be an elusive undertaking indeed." Huneo said. I could feel the sincerity in his words and I felt comfortable listening to him. Everyone focused on Huneo and Helen. They looked confident in the beginning of their lecture and it was a perfect introduction to the symposium. As Huneo went on with other pleasantries towards the university and

President Marnie Greene, the sun was moving ever so slowly across the room giving it a summer like atmosphere. I looked at Bernie and he looked so comfortable, I thought that he was ready to drift off to sleep. Huneo continued.

"With my introduction now being completed I would like to introduce to all of you my friend and associate, Helen Hamilton. Helen would you like to tell the audience a little about yourself?" Helen stood up and looked a little nervous. She began to speak.

"Hi everyone my name is, Helen Hamilton and I'm a student here at the university. I'm a physics under-graduate in my final year in, Professor James Reynolds curriculum and I am dedicated to my studies." Helen stated. Our eyes met and we smiled. "I have been following, Dr. Parkas' astrophysics website for two years and I had decided along with some of the other students in my class to invite him to our symposium. I'm an avid amateur astronomer and this is my favorite topic in physics, back to you, Dr. Parkas." Helen said, confidently.

"Thank you, Helen. The timing of this symposium and the invitation is both practical and advantageous for my presentation for the fact that a new theoretical hypotheses and postulation will be unveiled for you to judge." Huneo stated. He then paused for a sip of water.

"I will be presenting two lectures. One of which will be today of course and the other is yet to be scheduled. The lecture consists of an oral and a hard display of my developed apparatus. This lecture is the culmination of twenty-three years of study and development. What you see on the tables here are devices that I have constructed myself and developed over the years. I have kept a lot of my work secret until this day in fact. My lecture will be short and in nonprofessional's English for the sake of brevity and understanding. What I would like to talk about today is in the realm of astrophysics and more specifically in the realm of Einsteinian space-time astrophysics. My experiments and developments have been in some ways or in most ways prompted by the human condition and natural science coming directly from our planet." Huneo explained. It sounded like he was about to get to the core of his presentation. He had everybody's attention including Bernie's and mine. He continued.

"I will get right to the point for that is my way. Helen if you would, could you please undrape the calibrators for everyone to see." Huneo requested. Helen grabbed one end of the covering and pulled it back across the table to unveil three unfamiliar electronic looking devices approximately the dimensions of a medium sized television set with a small array of displays on them. I had never seen this type of equipment before.

"Thank you, Helen. These pieces of equipment are sixteen years old and have been running for fifteen years, more or less. I've developed and built this equipment and take great pride in these devices. Well, I know, now, you're all asking yourselves, what is this equipment? What does it do? Well these devices measure time. However, these devices do not measure time in the way that we are mostly familiar with. When I was in university, I postulated that time on earth was changing speed. What I meant by that was, is that time always passes wherever you are, or in whichever part of the universe you choose. However, this time passage can happen at different rates of time speed in relationship or relative to another part of the galaxy or the universe. An entities velocity through space governs this variance or inconsistency, whichever it is you choose.

Time speed is relative to an entities velocity in relationship to the gargantuan speed of light. Time speed to a lesser degree, a vastly lesser degree can also be influenced by gravity or proportional gravity fields." Huneo explained. He said this to the audience with authority and confidence. Bernie and I agreed with his talk thus far. He continued.

"This leads me to my equipment here on the table. These devices I have named SOLTES calibrators. There are three of them and they each do exactly the same thing. SOLTES is an acronym for Speed of Light, Time Existence Speed calibrator. And, what these devices do, is this, they measure and record time speed. The calibrators electronically create an artificial light speed medium and then they integrate the time that is passing into this medium. The devices then store the time speed electronically. The results can be reproduced to compare with future readings of time speed or the present time passing. Therefore, when the artificially recorded time clock runs, it is not running as a clock, but as a representation of the speed that time was passing as it was captured at that particular moment in human history, and is not affected by any changes. I mean specifically changes in time speed that may have occurred that are affecting our solar system. The calibrator displays its artificial time speed clocks with the present passage of time clocks and then a comparison can be made between the two. As an entity speeds up and advances towards the speed of light or suspended animation, time passage slows down and conversely as an entity slows down and moves toward velocity loss or NE/TL or Non-existence / Time Loss, time passage speeds up. I will now speak of my findings and try briefly to explain them in this lecture. I will also turn on the calibrators to give you a demonstration. This is not overly sophisticated equipment. I find that keeping things simple is the easiest way to get my points across and achieve my goals. I think that the universe is also simple and man has tried to make it more complicated than what it actually is. This is just a personal observation from my own insights as to the way scientists see the world and galaxies and the universe around them." Huneo explained. We sat in anticipation. Huneo then asked Helen to turn on the calibrators. There was a short pause in the presentation. Helen stood up and then started the devices and they came to life. There was very little sound coming from them. There were a few beeps and whirs, as they seemed to become operational. From my vantage point, I could see small clocks and digital readouts as Huneo and Helen moved about talking quietly to one another while they smiled at the audience. "So, Bernie, what do you think so far?" I asked.

"It's an interesting start, I'm anxious to see what he's got here. He's holding us in suspense. What do you think, Jim?"

"I don't know, Bern, I'm in suspense too, or maybe we're in suspended animation." I said. We laughed as I cracked wise.

"Okay, Bernie, it looks like their ready to begin again." They continued with their presentation.

"Alright folks, they're on and running. After the lecture I have CD ROM's that show how the SOLTES calibrator is constructed so that it may be copied. Okay, ladies and gentleman, what I'm about to show you, you are probably not going to believe but over the next while, weeks or months, you will see that this hypothesis will be proven to be true. This hypothesis or hypotheses are as far as I know are not in consideration for any scientific revue or study because they were not in a realm where anything could be proven until now, this realm being the vastness of the universe and man's inability to go beyond theoretical hypothesis and present hard facts. As I speak, the SOLTES calibrator is showing today's time and date, of course, and it is now 10:26 am, March 20, 2012. Two of the SOLTES calibrators were turned on in the year 1995 on November 12th to be exact. At that point in time, the calibrators measured and recorded their first time speed calculations. The time was recorded on two of the calibrators that day using one for a backup. A third calibrator came on line eight months later and started recording as well. It did not take long for the calibrators to start recording differences. To put it simply with the comparison of the first recordings and the readings up to this present day's time speed, the time speed has increased close to three percent. In other words it is March 20, 2012 and we all agree to that if I maybe so bold, as the time has passed since 1995. Had the time passed at the same rate of speed it was passing on November 12, 1995, the first day these SOLTES calibrators recorded the time speed, the calendar date would now be October 19th, 2011. This is a difference of approximately 5 months." Huneo announced, to the audience. I could not believe what he had just said. Some people started laughing and some were in disbelief as some yet still were talking amongst themselves. Huneo had stopped talking and was looking at the audience. A few people heckled him at this point. He remained calm. Some people began to leave but most stayed. Helen had a glazed look in her eyes and people then began to settle down a bit as they tried to continue.

"Holy Christ!" Bernie exclaimed, "Is he crazy or something?"

"Easy, Bernie, let's hear him out." I replied. What Huneo had told us was the most unbelievable and outlandish thing I had ever heard and I quite honestly did not know what to make of this pronouncement. The room quieted down and Huneo started to speak again. "I know you're all taken aback by this and I don't blame you, it's a gigantic step to take in and understand and come to believe in a concept that is so far removed from you." Huneo explained. People began to ask if he was sure of his devices and if he had his information correct. He explained that all the information he had and how he had accumulated it, would be given to everyone and they could judge it for themselves.

"I know that all of you are familiar with natural science and this is exactly what this is. It's Mother Nature's events on a grand scale. The decision for me to make this public was a big one. The event that is taking place has colossal implications and there is no way to know where this is going. It's part pure scientific principle and the greater part is of a divine principium. I know that you are all skeptical and I don't blame you, however even to this day I still sometimes wonder if what is going on is actually happening." Huneo said. Abruptly, some news reporters jumped in with their questions.

"Dr. Parkas, Jeff McGillis KTTV News in Toronto, if you will, Dr. Parkas, if this is really happening what is causing this?" The reporter asked.

"Well, Jeff, you ask a loaded question. This event could be taking place for a number of different reasons but one thing that I believe for sure is, is that our solar system is losing velocity in the galaxy or the galaxy is losing velocity in the universe or the universe is slowing it's expansion."

"Dr. Parkas, Dr. Parkas, Mike Walters of the New Science Observer Magazine. Are you seriously putting this forward as a postulation of an astronomical event that is new?" Walters asked.

"Well, I better lay it on the line. Yes, I'm informing the world of a natural event that they will have no control over. This event may be increasing or manifesting itself exponentially. Also some of the other indicators that I have of this event occurring other than the SOLTES calibrator is that of a circumstantial nature."

"Mike Walters again, Dr. Parkas, What are these indicators, c'mon, Doctor what are they?" the reporter pressed, "I mean this is crazy, I've never heard of anything like this!" he exclaimed, Huneo continued.

"Well, I believe the effects of Non-existence /Time Loss on the human population are some beneficial and some negative. However, if the phenomenon increases it will mean global extinction. If it stabilizes, I don't really know. However, some of the effects are what would be deemed evolutionary in the fact that they would change all life on earth. Time speed variations change the evolutionary process. Some of the effects are higher intelligence in man and beast, neurological disorders associated with memory, unexplained species extinctions over the past decade or so, global stress and rage, tighter rings in certain species of trees, corruption of the evolutionary process and perhaps a, Sodom and Gomorrah effect in all aspects of humanity." Huneo said. These statements dumbfound the audience. At this point in the presentation, Huneo decided to invite everybody down to view the calibrators for themselves. Bernie and I got up and made our way to the stage. People suddenly wanted to know more about what Huneo had accomplished, if he had accomplished anything.

"What do you think, Jim?" Bernie asked.

"I don't know, Bernie, I really don't. I want to find out more about that Non-existence/Time Loss theory he's talking about."

"Yeah, me too, I want to see those calibrators though, let's go have a look, Jim."

"Yeah, go ahead, Bernie, lead the way." We went down to get a place in line. I could see that some of my advanced students had made their way to the front of the line and were queuing up for a look at the SOLTES calibrator. People started to crowd around and get in on the now frenzy.

"Jeff McGillis again, Dr. Parkas, if this is true, Doctor, why don't we feel the effects of this?" the reporter asked.

"Well, Mr. McGillis, you do feel the effects of this phenomenon. The fact that they are so subtle is what fools you. In addition, there is the fact that time is not relative to man's perception. Man knows time is passing, man can feel time passing, however man cannot accurately tell how much time is passing. That is why we have clocks to tell us what time it is, and without them, we do not know. If time were relative to man, he would not be impatient, he would not be human.

Time would always pass at the same speed seemingly and time would go on virtually unnoticed." Huneo explained. Bernie then jumped in with his own question.

"Professor Parkas, Professor Parkas what is this Non-Existence/Time Loss factor you keep mentioning? I've never heard of this before, what is this?" Bernie asked, pointedly, as others chimed in for the answer to that question. Huneo looked up at everyone and then spoke.

"Non-Existence /Time loss is a theoretical hypothesis that is converse to the special theory of relativity in regards to the speed of light and a postulate substratum that governs my claims. The logic of this hypothesis is based in Einsteinian astrophysics and is just simply looking at special relativity theories in opposite directions. In other words or quite simply put, there is light and its speed that comes first in three dimensional space and/or our universe. Light and its speed are everywhere in the universe and by itself, light and light speed garner no mass. Light and its speed are constant throughout the universe and it is in this light medium that all else exists that is not constant. Mass, velocity, gravity, temperature, time and distance are not constant. There are varying velocities of mass that govern the speed of time, time not being constant in the universe. Heavenly bodies vary in speed, for example our solar system is traveling in relative terms to the best of our human guesses at 3 million miles per hour plus, plus maybe add millions to that even and that governs our speed of time. As an entity advances towards the speed of light, time slows continually until the speed of light is attained. Once the speed of light is attained, we have no time or suspended animation. In addition, as I have said, conversely, as velocities decrease, time speeds up. At the ends of the two opposites, there would be at one end the speed of light at which point you would have suspended animation or time being frozen, if you will. And, at the opposite end of that spectrum, if all entities were to slow to if it were possible and I believe it is, slow to a true stop in three dimensional space, time would gain enormous speeds until all entities would age away and flow out of existence. It would be a fray where mass would flow out of existence, gravity would flow out of existence and in the end or NE/TL, temperature would disappear, then distance and three dimensional space would disappear and then time and of course light itself would flow into the fray of non-existence." Huneo explained. He became a little nervous looking and breathless. "It is with these logical theories that I have based my work on the SOLTES calibrator. My findings are quite final and meticulous. I believe there is no error in my calculations and I put these forward for the world to prove or disprove. My final conclusions are that time as we know it is speeding up and we are mostly unaware of it until now." Huneo stated.

"Dr. Parkas, Mike Walters again, how long have you known about this and why have you waited till now to share this discovery?"

"Well, Mike, I've known about this from the beginning when the SOLTES calibrators were put into operation and even before that. I have always had this hypothesis in my head when I was in university and when I tried to put it forward as a theory, I was dismissed as a kook."

"But why now, Dr. Parkas?" Mike Walters asked, again.

"I bring it forward for many reasons but most of all I bring it forward because the NE/TL phenomenon is increasing and its effects are becoming more pronounced and self-evident."

"That's a long time to keep this type of thing a secret Dr. Parkas."

"Well, that's just the way things went. There's nothing I can add to that. Anyways, what I have given you is the crux of my presentation, short and sweet. I will in my next lecture speak of the full effects of this phenomenon on mankind and what its ramifications might be." Huneo stated.

"Professor Parkas, Professor Parkas, how come we don't see these changes on our clocks and watches?" Kelly Brown, one of my students, piped up.

"Well, Miss, like I've said, our clocks and watches, even our best atomic clocks and timepieces measure the time that passes and the amount of time that passes. The SOLTES calibrator measures the speed in which the clock time passes. All clocks and watches register the time that is passing in the velocity they are traveling at, if that velocity changes they change with it and run the way they always do.

For time to be compared to itself on earth from one day to the next we must have a constant medium for time to be recorded in and a constant medium for it to be played back in, a recording and playback if you will. The only way to record time speed this way and lock it into a recording, is to record it using in effect the speed of light as the recording medium. The speed of light is unwavering and constant throughout the universe and it is the only way an accurate time speed recording, translation and playback can be made." Huneo answered, with authority, as Kelly, asked a good question.

"As for now, I will not take any further questions." Huneo said. He looked a little dejected or let down. "I hope you have understood my lecture and it has been my pleasure to speak here at Sherman Patterson University. I will make one more presentation near the end of the symposium and you're all invited again. As I have said, there are CD-ROMs here for everyone and there is literature if you're interested. So with that, I thank you very much and I would also like to ask you to show your appreciation for my assistant and partner, Helen Hamilton, so again thank you ladies and gentleman." Huneo said, hastily. He finished his presentation. The audience then gave Huneo and Helen a round of applause, albeit it was subdued, it was appreciated nonetheless. I found the conclusion to Huneo's lecture a little abrupt but this seemed like no ordinary lecture. I decided I would ask Huneo and Helen to lunch.

"Bernie, I'm going to see if those two want to go to lunch, are you interested?"

"Ah, not right now, Jim. I'm going to go back to the hospital to see, Stella. That was a helluva lecture though, eh?"

"You got that right, Bernie. Listen, say hello to, Stella for me and will you give me a call later, Bernie?"

"I'll try and give you a call after dinner, Jim."

"Okay thanks, Bernie. I'll see you later then."

"Alright, Jim, bye for now." he said. He left hurriedly.

I made my way over to Huneo. He was packing up his materials and talking with a few of the stragglers left over from the audience.

"Professor Reynolds there you are. Did you enjoy the lecture?" Huneo asked, with trepidation. His eyes were evasive.

"Hi again, Helen, how do you feel?" I asked.

"Hi Professor Reynolds, I'm drained I think." She replied. I laughed.

"Is that what this was, Dr. Parkas, a lecture, or an announcement?"

"Call me, Huneo, Jim. A little bit of both, I suppose."

"You've really got my mind going here, Huneo. We have to talk more about this. These postulations of yours are well… unbelievable. I don't know what else to say, Huneo. As a man of science, I don't know what else to say."

"That's alright, Jim; I would be just like you I think. I would not know what to say to something that was this unbelievable and if were true was going to change my life so. It's hard for me to know what to say, Jim. This is my first time doing this, believe me."

"Listen Huneo, do you and Helen have time to go for lunch today?"

"Well, today I'll have to decline, Jim. I'm a little tired and I've made some other plans. If you want though, Jim, how about we go tomorrow afternoon?"

"Yes of course, Huneo, definitely, you have my number?"

"Yes, I do. I'll call you promptly in the morning, Jim."

"Okay good, good, I'll look forward to it. Okay I guess I'll let you guys finish up here, I know you're busy."

"Ah Jim, I've got a favor to ask of you."

"Sure, Huneo, what is it?"

"Well, Jim, I need a safe and secure place to put my equipment and the calibrators. Can you help me out with that?"

"Absolutely, Huneo, you've asked the right person. I'll call the university president, Marnie Greene and we can arrange to have your materials put in one of the university's archive vaults and you can have complete security and access to them."

"That sounds perfect, it's not too much trouble is it?"

"No not at all. Don't worry about it. Have you met the university president?"

"No, not yet, Jim, but I'm looking forward to it." Huneo said.

"Listen, Helen, I'm sorry here for hogging all the conversation, please forgive me. I'm not giving you a chance to speak."

"That's alright, Professor. I'm happy just to listen." Helen said, graciously.

"Thanks, Helen. Alright, I'll call Marnie's office right now and I'll have things arranged for you."

"Thanks again, Jim."

"You're welcome, Huneo."

I immediately phoned Marnie's office and arranged to have Huneo's equipment put into the archive vaults for safekeeping. Her office sent two maintenance staffers to help Huneo and Helen right away.

It was close to noon and I was hungry and tired. I phoned home and Angela answered. I asked her if she wanted lunch. She was as "hungry as a horse" was how she put it so I decided to her delight that I would bring home her favorite, Chinese food. We would have a nice lunch together and enjoy the afternoon. My work was finished for the day and again it was the weekend so I would start relaxing early. I went back to my office and gathered up my things. I said goodbye to my staff and some of my students and then I took off for the day. As I drove to the restaurant, my mind was preoccupied with Huneo's presentation. I really did not know what to think of his assumptions and assertions. They were just so extraordinary and difficult to fathom. I mean if there was anything to this, why had it not been discovered before then, I pondered. If his calibrators were authentic, I thought it was possible this would make sense or be logical. Moreover, if his calibrators were real and I followed his logic, it would mean that I had witnessed a major scientific discovery that would change all science on earth or have some sort of ramifications on its principles. I arrived at Ming-Lee's Chinese restaurant as they were receiving the lunch crowd. They were busy but I would order takeout and be on my way. I sat in the reception area and waited for my order as people passed along. As I sat there, I began to ponder Einstein's special theory of relativity and how it was set apart from the general theories of relativity. How the theory pertained to the speed of light and time and distance. The theory that light in and of itself and in its broader spectrums with its relative band of waves and frequencies was consistent or constant with respect to its speed in relation to all mass regardless of its speed or direction throughout the three dimensional universe. I knew that light traveled at the same speed everywhere, always. After a while, they called out my name and I grabbed my takeout and exited. As I drove home, I kept wondering about this and realized that the theory was taking over my thoughts. I began to think that there was something here, that Huneo's postulations were not flights of fancy. As I was driving, I decided that I would call Huneo later and invite him for lunch the following day. I finally arrived home and Angela was in the front yard beside the porch with Cindy. I wished I'd had my camera with me to have taken a few pictures. She was training the dog and giving her some fresh air. I exited my car and walked towards her. "Hi sweetie! How are you doing?" I said, cheerily.

"Good, Dad, I feel better. How are you doing?"

"I'm happy it's the weekend, sweetie and I'm doing well. I got your favorite, Chinese food!"

"Oh wow! Thanks so much, Dad!" Angela said. She glowed with happiness. She looked beautiful in the shimmering sun.

"My pleasure, Angela, how's our little, Cindy doing?"

"Well, I think she's getting used to our house and the yard, Dad. She's not shy anymore, she even barked at me today!"

"She's staking out her territory dear." I said. I grabbed the food and headed into the house. "Did your mother call dear?"

"No Dad, did you want me to call her for you?"

"No that's alright, Angela, I'll call her later, are you coming in, I thought you said you were hungry?"

"Oh yeah, Dad, I'll be right in, I could eat a horse!" my daughter said, as I chuckled heartily. I felt the stresses of the week wearing off and I could feel myself becoming more relaxed. I spread the food on the table and we sat down to eat.

"Angela, your big beautiful smile is back, it's so nice to see that dear." I commented.

"Thanks Dad, I feel good about myself today and I feel happy."

"That's great dear, your mother and I want you to be happy. Now go ahead dear and dig in!" I had a big smile myself. "So my, dear, did you find out how, Christopher's parents reacted to your news today?"

"Not yet, Dad, but he promised to call me later. They're very nice people, Dad."

"Oh, I'm sure they are, Angela, but sometimes people can surprise you in the way they react to unexpected events in their lives." I said, as I dug into the food.

I heard a rumble in the driveway. Christine and Paula arrived home. Moments later, they burst through the front door with shopping bags and a pizza. "Hi Dad! Mom picked me up at school and we went shopping! Hi Angela, I have a new CD for you, I bought the one you wanted!" Paula squawked. She greeted us with her wild exuberance.

"Hi Paula, Hi Hon."

"Hi Angela, are you feeling better?" Christine asked.

"I'm feeling great now, Mom."

"That's good hon."

"How about you love?" Christine asked. She put her bags down and we kissed.

"I feel great hon. I had an interesting day that's for sure."

"Well, you're just going to have to tell me all about it then, hon." Christine cooed.

"Mom, do you want to hear my new CD?" Paula asked.

"Paula, I want to hear your new CD but first you have to eat! Now sit down and eat please!" Christine chirped. "God, Jim, I wish I had just half the energy she has, it's just go, go, go with her all day long." Christine whispered.

"Yeah, she seems to be full of piss and vinegar today." I said. Everybody sat down to eat. Paula and Angela started talking together as Paula showed her sister her new treasures. Christine and I sat and ate quietly with a little background music on. We stared longingly into each other's eyes and just slowed down and enjoyed the moments. I looked outside and I could see that clouds were starting to roll in as it looked like the weather might turn chilly.

"Let's everybody listen for a weather report!" I called out.

"It's going to snow, Dad!" Paula bellowed.

"It's not going to snow is it, you're kidding right?"

"That's what they said, Dad, on the radio."

"Oh well, that'll be one of the last ones. I hope."

"Everybody leave your plates on the table. I'm going to see if, Cindy wants any of our human food for a little treat." Christine requested. I noticed our small pet on the sidelines watching us eat. She looked famished.

"Hi Cindy, Cindy looks hungry, Dad."

"Yes she does, Paula. We'll feed her unless you want to feed her?"

"I'll feed her lunch, Jim." Christine stated.

"Alright hon."

Our lunch went leisurely as my gang and I drifted about the house doing our chores for the afternoon. We relaxed and got into our weekend modes. I went into our bedroom, laid down, and had a nap. I had a twenty-minute rest and then Christine came in and woke me up before I ended up sleeping my nighttime sleep in the afternoon. I got up and decided to call Huneo and ask him out for lunch on Saturday with Christine and me. He accepted. We set a date for 1:30 pm at Maurizio's, an Italian-Canadian restaurant in Park Falls, our finest, I do believe. I asked Christine if that was okay with her and she was fine with that. Maurizio's was close to the mall so she could check on the hair salon at the same time.

"Jim hon, are you fully awake?" Christine asked.

"I'm up dear, I'm up, why?"

"Well, Angela, just got off the phone with, Christopher Helgeson."

"And?"

"Well, it looks like Christopher's parents are upset with the pregnancy and feel that this is all, Angela's fault. They started calling her terrible names and they don't want, Christopher to see, Angela again." Christine told.

"Well sweetie, it takes two to tango and their just going to have to get used to the idea and they will. We'll see what they say after a few days."

"I think you're right," she said.

"What does, Angela think of this?"

"She says it doesn't bother her and she'll just stay away from their home for a while until they come around."

"It's a big shock for them just like it was for us."

"I know." Christine said. We went downstairs to sit in the family room. I turned on the television low and tuned it into one of our local channels for the news. The girls were in the kitchen and they were listening to music.

"So what are they going to do tonight?" I asked.

"Angela says, Christopher is going to come over and they're going to watch a movie and, Paula is going to the mall with her friends and then she's going to her friend, Linda's house to watch videos. So how did your lecture go today, hon?"

"That my dear was a one of a kind lecture. I don't know what to else to say about that."

"What do you mean by that, Jim?"

"Well hon, Huneo Parkas was the speaker and he made some of the wildest claims I've ever heard in my life. They were just astounding." I said.

"Like what, Jim?" she asked. Just then, on the television news, a report aired from a Toronto station.

"This is, Jeff McGillis reporting from, Sherman Patterson University here in Park Falls, Saskatchewan for KTTV news," It was the journalist I had seen reporting that day. "Where today at a lecture at the university during their bi-annual symposium, it was unveiled by one of their guest speakers what seemed to be a huge if not the biggest scientific discovery of our time, if it is proven to be true." The reporter stated.

"Hey, that's you guys!" Christine said.

"Shhh" I said. "I'll turn up the TV."

"Today at the university here in Park Falls, a Professor Huneo Parkas unveiled what may be a giant discovery in astrophysics that could change life and science on earth as we understand it," the reporter explained. I could not believe my ears as he went on with his story.

"The Professor, at the university, with the aid of scientific instruments that are apparently foolproof has proven that we are living in a world where time is changing. That here in Park Falls it was revealed by the professor that time is indeed speeding up in our lives. That the actual time we experience is the same but moving faster as we travel through space," The newscast cut to a clip of Huneo in what looked like the main atrium of the university. The phone rang and one of the girls answered.

"Dad! Uncle Bernie wants you to turn on the news!" Paula bellowed.

"I have it on sweetie, tell, Bernie, I'll call him back!"

"Okay, Dad."

The newscast continued with Huneo explaining the SOLTES calibrator and the NE/TL or Non-existence/Time Loss theorem to the reporter. There were shots of the auditorium and shots of the university as well as comments from the university President, Marnie Greene. The newscast then cut back to the reporter and he wound up his segment.

"Wow hon, you guys made the news in Toronto!" Christine exclaimed. She laughed. "So what's all this stuff they're talking about dear? What does all this SOLTEK stuff mean?" Christine asked, quizzically.

"It's SOLTES Christine, its pronounced SOLTES. It's an acronym for Speed of Light, Time Existence Speed calibrator. It's an instrument that measures time taken from a different prospective than what we're used to." I explained.

"What's that, Dad?" Angela inquired, as she peeked her head around the corner. Paula sneaked her head under Angela's and displayed her mischievous smile.

"Okay, girls, if you want to hear about this, come in and I'll explain it to you." I said. They rushed into the family room and took a seat. "Well, girls, you know I've been to these symposiums before and for all intents and purposes they're run of the mill. They discuss existing science." I said, "Today however, an astrophysicist from South America has decided to make our little symposium the showcase for his discoveries." I saw that I had a captive audience. "Today at the university, a Dr. Huneo Parkas, has made a claim to what amounts to, I guess if it were to be proven true, the biggest scientific discovery in the history of mankind." I stated.

"What is it, Dad?" Paula asked.

"Shhh, Paula! Quiet while your father speaks." Christine scolded.

"Well, what he postulated, or what his theory is quite simply, is that as we travel through space, time passes for us the way it does. We see it pass on our watches, we see it on our clocks, and we take it for granted that it never changes. However, Dr. Parkas has invented a device that apparently shows, that in certain respects, time is changing."

"How do you mean, hon?" Christine asked.

"Shhh, Mom, Dad is talking." Paula said, irking her mother.

"Paula! Mind your manners!" Christine snapped.

"Well, Huneo Parkas speculated that the same amount of time always passes. For example, twenty-four hours is always twenty-four hours. However, at different velocities, twenty-four hours passes at different speeds. As for an example, we feel the twenty-four hours pass on our earth the way it does but if another earth was traveling through space at one hundred times faster than ours is right now. The comparison might be that the earth that traveled at one hundred times faster when it experienced the passage of twenty-four hours relative to our earth at the speed that it is traveling now, that our earth would have experienced hundreds or maybe even thousands of years passing. This is part of, Albert Einstein's special theory of relativity. What Huneo is saying is that our earth is slowing down in space and time is passing faster."

"So we have less time to live, Dad?" Paula asked.

"No Paula, you have the same amount of time to live it's just going to happen faster."

"So we're going to die sooner, Dad?"

"Well, sooner than we would if we were going at a faster speed in space."

"Jim enough!" Christine exclaimed, "Enough with the death talk!"

"Sorry hon, listen girls, what Dr. Parkas is saying is far from proven fact. I'm surprised that it even made the news. So let's try not to read too much into this." I said. I tried to reassure my girls.

"Jim, is this the person we're having lunch with tomorrow?" Christine asked. She had a look of trepidation in her eyes.

"Yes, dear. I think you'll like him though. He is an honest and an upfront person."

"If you like him, Jim, I'm sure he'll be fine with me."

The phone rang while we were talking.

"Paula, would you answer the phone please?"

"Yes, Mom."

"Dad it's, Uncle Bernie."

"Alright, I'll get it…thank you."

I went to the phone and picked up.

"Hello, Bernie."

"Hey Jim, I guess you've seen the news?" Bernie asked.

"Yeah I did, Bern. It's got tongues wagging over here that's for sure."

"Yeah, over here too, I'm at the hospital, Jim."

"How's, Stella, Bernie?"

"She's doing fine, Jim. It's a much brighter day for the both of us today."

"That's great, Bernie, we're glad to hear that."

"I just called to see if you'd seen the news broadcast, Jim. I tell you, Jim, one minute I come to think this postulation could be happening and in the next minute I think it's just stuffing nonsense." Bernie stated.

"I know, Bernie; I'm going through the same thing in my mind. I'm going to have lunch tomorrow with, Huneo and I'll definitely talk about this some more with him. I'm going to pick his brain, Bernie."

"That's good, Jim. Other than that everything else is okay?"

"Everything's fine."

"Angela's doing well?"

"Yeah, Bernie, she's doing great."

"Okay, Jim, I'll touch base with you later on then."

"Alright, Bernie thanks for calling, and say 'hello' to, Stella from the gang here."

"I will for sure, Jim, you take care now, bye."

"See you later, Bernie." I said. I hung up the phone and returned to the living room where my girls seemed to have gone back to each one's business.

"How's, Stella doing?" Christine inquired.

"She's doing well. Bernie said she's feeling a lot better. I'll tell you, I'm sure happy for that."

"That's great, I think I'll go visit her tomorrow morning. Just her and me, she's probably in the mood for some girl talk."

"That's a good idea, Christine. She's probably looking for a good friend to be with now that she's in recovery." I said. After that, everybody got back to normal and we had a quiet Friday.

The girls went about their business and Christine and I went out for a quick dinner and some shopping. Later in the evening, we watched a movie in our bedroom. We fell asleep in each other's arms.

The next morning, I awakened refreshed and feeling well. I had a euphoric feeling and a warm feeling inside as if I was in tune with the rest of the world. There was a note on my nightstand from Christine. The note explained that she had gotten up extra early and did not want to disturb me so she could get dressed and leave for the hospital to visit Stella. The note went on further to explain, that she would be home as soon as she could after completing a few other errands. The sun was shining in our room and I could hear the girls getting up and arguing in the bathroom, the usual. Well, I decided that dear old Dad would get up and cook breakfast for his good daughters and of course my grandson and Cindy. I did so post haste and then I went into the family room with Paula and Angela. I spent a lot of fun time with my daughters that Saturday morning watching television movies, and talking and laughing with them. I did not get to do that as much as I liked but when I got the chance, I tried to savor each moment with them. Before I knew it, it was 12:00 pm. Christine was plowing through the front door with the groceries, and then I realized, I had to get up and get ready to go to lunch with Huneo. "Jim! You're still in your pajamas! What've you been doing all morning?" Christine asked, loudly. She gestured to the girls to help her using her eyes.

"Mom did you buy us anything?" Paula asked, excitedly.

"I bought everybody some food my dear, is that what you were expecting?"

"Yes, I guess, Mom" Paula moaned.

"Okay, your father and I have a lunch date so you two are going to have to fend for yourselves. And, and... I also want you to do some cleaning around this house this afternoon or you'll be helping me clean it tonight! Do you hear me?"

"Yes Mom" the girls answered.

Christine and I ran upstairs, got ready, and immediately left for town. As we drove into town, we listened to the news on the radio. The news had the regular town stories and then a story about the discovery announcement by Dr. Huneo Parkas. I was brought back to reality all of a sudden. This was not just an ordinary lunch I was going to and Christine would meet Huneo for the first time. We drove to the hair salon and Christine ran in as I sat in the car listening to music. After about twenty minutes, she came back out and we left for the restaurant. I commented to Christine about how beautiful the day was turning out weather wise and she agreed. Christine added how God painted such a beautiful picture for us on days like this and then started in with a little self deprecating humor that got me laughing pretty good. After a short drive, we arrived at Maurizio's. As we pulled in, I saw Huneo walk into the restaurant with someone. I did not make out whom it was. We walked into the restaurant and we were greeted by the hostess. She guided us to our table. Huneo was with Helen Hamilton. I did not expect this and I saw that Christine was also a little surprised. "Hello Huneo, hello Helen. Huneo, I would like to introduce you to my darling wife, Christine. Christine, may I introduce to you, Professor Huneo Parkas." I said.

"Hello, Professor Parkas."

"Please, Christine, if I may, please call me, Huneo, that would be great." Huneo said, graciously.

"Thank you, Huneo. It's my pleasure to meet you."

"And, Christine, of course you know, Helen. We all know, Helen, how are you, Helen?" I asked.

"I'm good, Professor Reynolds, how are you?"

"I'm good, Helen, very good today, thank you."

"Hi, Mrs. Reynolds, how are you?"

"I feel great, Helen, but call me, Christine please."

"I will." Helen replied.

"Well, I hope everybody's hungry, let's sit down and order some drinks." Huneo said. We took our perspective seats. It took a few minutes to get comfortable and then we ordered our drinks. Christine and Helen started to talk together as Huneo and I exchanged some pleasantries. The waitress came back with our drinks and then we were given our menus. We started to browse through our menus and after about ten minutes the waitress came back to see if we were ready to order. We asked her to give us another five minutes while we made our selections.

"Are you very hungry, Huneo? They have a fantastic lasagna here with three cheeses. It's definitely one of my favorites." I suggested.

"You've made up my mind for me, Jim. I'm going to have that. How does that sound to you, Helen? Would you like lasagna too, or something else, sweetie?" Huneo asked. Christine and I looked at each other. Helen told Huneo that she would order spaghetti and meatballs.

"Oh, oh, I think its out. I can see that by the way you looked at each other, Jim. We've been trying to hide this but it's futile. Jim, Helen and I are a couple now. We've been lovers for some time. I think we're going to have to let everybody know considering the circumstances." Huneo said. I saw Helen wincing and squirming. Helen was a novice in the world of adult relationships.

"I don't know what to say, Huneo. You caught us off guard here." I said.

"Speak for yourself, hon. People have relationships you know." Christine chirped. Suddenly, I felt like I was the babe in the woods. She could do that to me. Christine said that I was old fashioned but she loved old fashioned.

"So how long have you been together like this? If you don't mind me asking."

"Not at all, Jim. Including the time we met on the internet, about two years now."

"You're in love?" Christine probed.

"Yes, yes we are, Mrs. Reynolds."

"Well that's good enough for me. And call me, Christine please." Christine said. She displayed a warm approving smile. The waitress arrived and she took our dinner orders. Everybody was hungry judging by the long list of appetizers and entrees that we ordered.

The house music began to play and we started talking about our day and our daughters. Huneo talked about his job in South America and the people who lived in and around the area where he worked and resided. Helen more or less sat quietly but talked some as lunch progressed. Christine then started talking exclusively with Helen so I took advantage of this time and tried to get a few more of Huneo's insights.

"Huneo, did you see yourself on the news out of, Toronto yesterday?" I asked him.

"No, Jim. However, I stayed up late and saw myself on the late news out of, New York."

"You were on television down there?"

"Believe me; I'm as surprised as you are, Jim."

"Huneo, I've got to tell you, I still find your assertions extraordinary and hard to fathom."

"I know they are, Jim. In the beginning I found them hard to believe myself but after a while you begin to accept them."

"But why now, Huneo, why are you presenting this here and now?"

"Because the effect is increasing, Jim, and because of, Helen, I'm here because of, Helen, Jim."

"The effect is increasing?" I prodded.

"Yes, Jim, I believe our solar system's velocity is decreasing and time is speeding up even faster, not exponentially but on a graduated increasing curve most likely. Nevertheless, as I said before, Jim, I don't know if it's the solar system or the galaxy or the universe or even if we're on the outer axis of some sort of ellipse as we travel through space. This I don't know, Jim. When it comes to the astronomy game, I'm just average in that category. I do believe there's a possibility that this effect is leading astronomers to conclude that the expansion of the universe theory in which it is postulated that the universe is expanding even faster are fooled by the fact that time is passing faster for us. Light from the stars seems to be moving out further in the cosmos when in fact what we are seeing is ourselves moving ahead further and faster in time giving us the false impression that the stars and galaxies are moving away faster." Huneo explained.

"That's incredible, Huneo, but I mean the ways things are going you're going to have lots of detractors."

"Well, that's the way things are probably going to go. I think things are really going to take off now. I'm ready for it though, I think, I'm ready for it." He said.

"So what's next, Huneo, what are you going to do next?"

"I'm going to stick to my plan, Jim. I will promote the SOLTES calibrator and get ready for my next lecture at the end of next week. That's about all I have in the cards for now."

"That's right, you have another lecture. What's the next one about?"

"I think you're my friend now and I consider myself your friend, Jim, but all I will tell you, Jim, is that my next lecture deals with the speculated effects of the Non-existence/Time loss theorem on our physical and biological world. My lecture will deal with the effects that this astronomical event is having and will have on the human mind, the individual and the entire human race. This lecture will include the animal world and the entire planet that it affects." Huneo explained.

"I don't know what to say, Huneo. I just don't know what to say! I'm starting to feel like I'm dreaming all of this. That this is not real and I'm going to wake up." I said. Huneo started to laugh.

"Oh sorry, Jim, I'm sorry but I don't know what else to tell you."

"Hey, are you guys going to talk with us too?" Christine asked, as the girls tried to join in our conversation.

"Go ahead ladies don't let us slow you down." Huneo replied.

Our second round of drinks arrived and then our appetizers arrived shortly there afterwards. Everyone jumped right in snacking on his or her food. The mood in the restaurant was festive and warm sunlight streamed into the dining room. The music was soothing and we were relaxed. We talked again about our lives. Christine talked with Huneo about our daughters and I talked with Helen about her brother and her parents. I asked Helen if she had told her parents about Huneo and she answered she had not but would talk with them on the coming Sunday. She seemed to think that they would be approving of their relationship and I did not see any reason why they would not. After a while, we took bathroom breaks and then the main entrée came and we started to enjoy our meals. After eating quietly for a while, Christine started a conversation off by telling some of her best jokes and making some of her witty remarks. Christine was the comedian in our family and she could always pick up our spirits with her great sense of humor. I tried to keep her in check while we were eating though because Christine had a devious way of telling jokes as people were eating or having a drink, causing them to laugh their food or drinks out of their mouths, sometimes in a projectile way. I think she did this on purpose but she would not admit to the fact. I know she did this with Angela and Paula. We were having a good time and then the women decided to go to the bathroom again. I could talk to Huneo one on one again. "Huneo, how long are you planning to stay? Have you got plans to leave right after the symposium?" I asked.

"I don't think I'm going back to, South America, Jim."

"What do you mean?"

"Well, quite frankly, I don't know where or what direction I'm going to be headed but I have a feeling my journey begins here."

"You mean because of your pronouncements?"

"Yes exactly, especially now because of, Helen." He said.

"Well, I hope while you're in, Park Falls, Huneo, if you ever need anything you can call on me at anytime. I think of you as my friend too."

"Thanks, Jim, I'll remember that." Huneo said.

The girls came back from the bathroom and sat down again.

"So guys, are we about ready to leave?" Christine asked.

"Yeah, I think we're just about ready." I said. After a few more laughs and some conversation, we headed off together. As we walked out to the parking lot, I mentioned to Huneo that I wanted to talk with him more about his theories. Huneo offered to explain them to me in depth. He said that he would be around the university throughout the week and that he would try to visit me in my office during the day. I went on to give him a list of times that might be opportune for him when I did not have any classes. We then said our goodbyes. As they walked away, Huneo and Helen kissed and held hands. Christine and I then got into our car and drove off. "So what did you think hon?" I asked, Christine.

"They seem to love each other and I must say for a man who is a little older than you he keeps himself in pretty good shape. He's a handsome looking fella." Christine said, as she slurred her words. Alcohol affected Christine particularly as she was not a drinker.

"You think so, hon?" I asked.

"Yeah, I think they make a nice couple." Christine's eyes looked like they were getting a little heavy. I decided to let her rest in the car as we drove home. She slowly drifted over onto my shoulder. It was a nice afternoon and I did not think we would be having a big dinner that evening. I found being around Huneo that afternoon to be a little unsettling. I thought that inevitably, we were headed on a journey that would bind us together and I was a little frightened of that scenario. I thought of Huneo's theories and the effect that they were unleashing and it seemed more like the beginning of an unstoppable juggernaut that was going to ensnare me and my family and everyone else in the world into who knows what. We got home and Christine woke up. We spent the rest of that evening quietly. Christine developed a headache from too much alcohol at lunch. The girls went to their friends homes for the night but they left us a clean house. I was impressed. The rest of the weekend passed uneventfully for us.

Monday morning arrived and I was just about at my office. We had a quiet weekend I thought to myself as I entered the building. I walked through the door of the office and my secretary, Sandy, announced that I was wanted in Marnie Greene's office immediately. She told me to turn around and go to Marnie's office and she would inform them that I was on my way. She said that something was up and I would have to go there directly. I turned around and headed towards her office. As I walked to Marnie's office, I began to get nervous.

When I arrived, her secretary ushered me in, hastily. I walked through the door and to my surprise and shock; Huneo and Helen were there along with Paul Banks and another police officer. Marnie Greene sat behind her desk. "Good Morning, Professor Reynolds, how are you this morning?" Marnie asked, with somewhat of a smile on her face.

"Not too bad, Marnie. This looks rather ominous if you don't mind me saying."

"Well calm yourself, Professor, it's really just routine. Have a seat please, Jim. Listen Professor Reynolds, late Saturday, during the night sometime, there was a break in the university's archives and one of, Professor Parkas' calibrators was stolen. There was some damage done to the archives so the police were called immediately. Mr. Parkas has asked if you would be present at this meeting this morning. Are you okay with that?" Marnie asked.

"Yes of course, Marnie, no problem, anything I can do to help."

"Well, I would like you to help, Mr. Parkas, and the police in any way that you can assist them. It looks likes the thieves were specifically interested in the calibrators and they took one of them, like I said." Marnie explained.

Huneo interjected. "Jim, I have decided that the two remaining calibrators I'm going to give away. The CD-ROM I gave away at the first lecture shows how to build them and they're easy enough instruments to build for the most part. I'm sure the CD-ROM will end up on the internet soon. This is no longer a secret. Of the two remaining calibrators I'm going to donate one to the university here under your supervision and the other I have not decided where it will go yet."

"Well, I thank you very much, Huneo, from myself and on behalf of the school." I said.

"Hello there, Jim, I wish we could have met again under better circumstances." Paul Banks interjected. He greeted me and joined in the conversation. "We were called in late Saturday night by the janitorial staff and started our investigation. Jim it's not kids who did this and we will pursue this matter. However, Jim, it is not a high priority. Mr. Parkas does not want to sign a complaint so we're going to be listing this theft under a vandalism folder. Personally, I don't think we're going to be very successful with this one, I say that off the record of course." Paul explained, as he took notes. "We think it could be one of the visitors that have come to town and once they leave... well."

"So listen, Professor Reynolds, we'll keep, Mr. Parkas' equipment in another part of the archive that's more secure and access will be limited as well as tighter security being put in place." Marnie stated.

"That sounds alright to me."

Marnie then asked Paul and the other officer if they had what they needed and then gave them a personal escort out of the building.

"Are you and, Helen, okay, Huneo?" I asked.

"Yes, we're fine, Jim, we're fine."

"Everything's okay, Professor Reynolds." Helen said.

"Jim, I've decided to stay in town for an extended period of time for various reasons. Actually it may be a much extended period, I have not fully decided yet." Huneo said. He held Helen in his arms. I was still not used to the idea of these two being a couple.

"So I guess that just about finishes this matter then." I said.

"Jim would you like to have lunch today?" Huneo asked. I told him that I would be free at 1:00 pm and that I could meet him in the university's cafeteria in the section reserved for teachers if he wished. He agreed to this suggestion enthusiastically as we wrapped things up. I then reminded Helen that she had a class with me in just over thirty minutes. She replied that she would be on her way. I said goodbye to everyone as I left for my office to get ready for my first class. Well that woke me up, I thought. As I left Marnies' office, her secretary asked me to come in for an appointment, Tuesday at 8:00 am. I agreed. I rushed back to my office and grabbed my books, I made a few phone calls and then I went to my first class. I rushed down the hallway and walked in the door and I was out of breath. I made a mental note to myself that I needed more exercise. In any event, it looked like everybody was here including Helen Hamilton. "Hi everybody how are y'all today?" I inquired. I saw an attentive class as they were all staring at me. I became a little self-conscious.

"I trust everybody is in full review mode today, without exception, I hope." I said, to a few affirmative responses. "We're going to have a few quizzes next week so it's important that you study. It'll probably go better if you have partners so try to pair up. Any questions?"

"Professor Reynolds', are these quizzes going to be typical in format and content as the final exams?" Robbie Platt asked.

"Robbie, the quizzes will be similar but expect some surprises and some difficult work in the finals. Any other questions before we get started?"

"Is the Non-existence/Time loss theorem a true theorem Professor Reynolds?" Janice Davis asked, to my somewhat being taken aback. It was at that exact moment that Huneo's theories clicked in and made sense to me. And. It was for the first time, I felt that this was indeed a plausible postulation. It was at that moment that I also felt or started to feel different. I was starting to feel that something was changing inside me.

"I saw you at the lecture on Friday, Janice. There was certainly a lot that could be said about that show and tell that we witnessed." I said.

"C'mon Professor what do you think?" Robbie Platt pressed.

"Is the universe coming to the end?" Janice asked.

"What do these theories mean to our lives if they're true?" another student quipped.

"Yeah, what does this mean, Professor?" Janice asked again, as a chorus of questions and a feeling of excitability permeated throughout the classroom.

"Easy everyone, easy, I can see that, Dr. Parkas' lecture had a great impact on you. All right then, if you want to discuss this, we'll calm down and discuss this in a civil manner. So how many of you, by a show of hands, went to the lecture?" I inquired. I scanned the class-room. "Ah let's see, three, five, six, alright eight of you, out of twenty. Okay how about the rest of you? How many of you know what the lecture was about? Raise your hands if you know what's going on here." I said, "Alright five more of you, okay most of you know what's going on. The rest can just listen in for now and you'll be filled in later. Okay we can probably discuss this over the next few days in class and we'll make it a project. Is there anyone willing to volunteer a name for this project?" I asked.

"How about we call it, Pegasus Project?" Janice Davis offered.

"That sounds alright; does everybody agree to, 'Pegasus Project'?"

"Yes, yes!" The students replied.

"Alright! Pegasus Project, it is then. Okay, we'll start off with a discussion of the theory and its plausibility. We'll discuss Dr. Parkas' hypothetical theories and postulations and their ramifications, if any. This project will be an exercise in the hypothetical." I explained. My students were more interested in this subject than I had seen them about any other so far that year and I had their complete attention.

"Would anybody like to start us off? And remember, one at a time please."

"Professor, Professor what is the Non-existence/Time loss theorem that I keep hearing about?" Student Ben Ross asked.

"We're you at the lecture on Friday, Ben?"

"No, Professor, but I keep hearing people talking about it, what is it?"

"Well, Ben, it's a postulation that is based partly on Einsteinian astrophysics and a hypothesis put forward by Dr. Huneo Parkas. I wonder if, Helen Hamilton... would you like to explain the hypothesis to us if you wouldn't mind, Helen it would be our pleasure being that you're his assistant?" I asked Helen, putting her on the spot.

"I will gladly explain the theory, Professor Reynolds." Helen replied. The students applauded her. Helen clasped her hands together, took a deep breath, and then began to explain the postulation that was put forth.

"Well, it is a theory based a lot on velocity, gravity and mass but most of all it speaks to the way that these elements of the universe affect the way time flows in the universe in relationship to our earth. These scientific theorems are part of a hypothesis that, Dr. Parkas has put forward with his work on the SOLTES calibrator." Helen explained, "In its simplest forms the hypothesis' are in the realm of the special relativity theories put forward by, Albert Einstein in his revolutionary theorems. In the Special Relativity theorem, in regards to the propagation of light, specifically the speed of light, the gargantuan speed of light. Einstein stipulated, that as an entity, when a mass advances towards the speed of light, the speed of time passing for that entity begins to slow down, as it would appear to us. The speed that time is passing slows down, not the amount of time passing but the speed at which it passes slows down. What I'm saying is that the time passing for an entity, let's say for example, that is traveling at five hundred million miles per hour and we take that in comparison to the time passing for us on earth that are traveling colossally slower. The amount of time passing is the same. However, it is happening at a slower rate of speed, the amount of time passing is the same but at the colossal speed the entity is traveling at, the time is passing much slower in relationship or relative to our own time speed passing. The theorem stipulates that if the entity were to travel at the speed of light, time would be suspended or time would in effect be halted. What Dr. Parkas postulates is, is that in the opposite direction in which the Special Theory is commonly looked at, in his opinion, that if an entity were to slow down towards no speed, time would speed up and eventually at no speed or velocity, the elements of the universe would disappear and all time and entities would be consumed. Light, gravity, mass, temperature, time and distance would become non-existent. There would no longer be any existence. The elements of the universe would be crunched into non-existence." Helen explained, impressively. She continued. "Professor Parkas' theory sets out to prove that our solar system or galaxy is slowing down in the universe or we are in some sort of elliptical orbit in some way or possibly we are on the outer axis of an ellipse in the universe and time is beginning to speed up. What he is saying is that the same amount of time is passing for us except that it is happening faster and faster. Thank you." Helen stated. She then sat down as it looked like she had finished her explanation.

"Thank you very much, Helen. That was a very accurate explanation for the students. Does anybody have any more questions, comments or observations?" I asked to my mostly silent and now reflective class. Then, a voice from the back of the room piped up. She was one of my top students. She was a petite, frail and a shy student. Her name was Connie Beaton.

"Professor Reynolds, if this is true, what is going to happen to us on earth?" she asked. A stunned silence fell over the classroom. I think for the first time that question finally struck me. What was going to happen to humankind on earth if this were true?

"Well for arguments sake, Ms. Beaton, let's say hypothetically this is happening. I want to ask you the students to come up with the answers to that question and also what can be done to deal with the problems that may arise from this phenomenon." I asked, of the class. I was as much in the dark as they were. I was an unwitting participant in this project myself, the so-called "Pegasus Project". My immediate concerns were for my family. I wondered how this anomaly might affect us in the future if indeed this theorem were true.

"Are we going to write all this down or take notes or what professor?" Ben Ross asked.

"Well, Mr. Ross, I think for the time being I want everybody to document in their own words what they would like to contribute to the discussions. You can work independently or break off into groups, it's up to yourselves. So, in a separate notebook that you can provide for yourself, if you want, this will all be optional of course. In that notebook, you can divide it up however you like, into sections if you want or it could be general notes and separate categories or a list format, it's up to each person. This is general interest assignment remember, and it is not part of the curriculum so it is all informal. You can use whatever media you want but remember most of all, this can't interfere with the rest of your regular curriculum!" I explained. I emphasized these points to my students. "So for today just use your notebooks to start with and we'll continue this discussion in the next class for a small portion of it and perhaps after class as well."

"Professor Reynolds, will we have access to the SOLTES calibrators?" Janice Davis asked.

"Actually, I think we might have access to the calibrators, Janice, but I'll have to double check on that and get back to you."

"Professor, do you think we have anything to worry about with this theory of, Dr. Parkas'?" Student Robbie Platt asked.

"I don't think there's anything to worry about, however, we will continue this discussion as if there are no boundaries and that this is a hypothetical event phenomenon."

"So this theory is a conceivable one professor?" Janice asked.

"Yes, this is definitely a conceivable theory, Janice. Like the old saying goes, anything is possible under the right circumstances. Okay everyone, for tomorrow we'll each give our own thoughts and ideas on how this phenomenon would affect the earth and all life on it and remember to use different scenarios, different rates of the speed of time passing, will it continue, will it stop, what is driving this phenomenon and how will it affect us as a biological entity. What happens to human beings as this process continues, one way or the other?" I asked, of the class. "But you must also keep up the work on your review. That is your prime objective!" I stated. I then handed out some small assignments and we continued with the regularly scheduled class. The rest of the class was routine except for the fact that in the back of my mind, I continued to think of this theory. I could see as well in the eyes of my students that they too were distracted by the NE/TL theories of Huneo Parkas'.

Dawn of a new day

AFTER ANOTHER HALF HOUR, the class was finished and I dismissed the students. I decided to go for a walk around the campus for a breather and for an opportunity to be alone with my thoughts. As I walked around the university, it was a pleasant day. The sun was shining and it was warm enough to wear a sweater. As I began thinking about things, I noticed that the sky did not seem right to me. I did not know what it was but it just seemed different and I had a feeling that somehow things had changed. It felt as if I was living in a new world and nothing was the same as it used to be any longer. It was a feeling that I never experienced before and it made me feel sick. I thought of Huneo's theory and the more I thought of it the more it made sense. The theory was just so conducive to making sense in the respect that it logically linked up with the science of our day and the fact that it could easily be explained to anyone. I started to think that maybe his calibrators were accurate and this was actually happening. Was it possible in a universe as large and boundless as our own that a new and completely unexpected event that could be explained naturally and consume a large part of the galaxy or the universe itself was taking place? At that point, I decided to call Huneo on my cell phone and ask him to lunch. I phoned him, he accepted my invitation, and he would meet me in a half an hour at Snicker's restaurant. I went back to my office, grabbed my keys, and took off for Snicker's. As I pulled into the restaurant, I saw that Bernie's car was there as well. I went in and saw Bernie sitting at a table with a smile on his face so I went over and sat with him.

"Hey, Bernie, how are you? More importantly how's, Stella doing? I asked.

"Hey Jim, I'm doing fine and Stella's feeling a whole lot better. She's coming home later today and I'm going to pick her up in a couple of hours from now!" Bernie said. He had a new vigor in his tone.

"That's great news, Bernie. The best I've heard in a while. I bet you can't wait?"

"It's going to be nice to have my sweetie back home where she belongs. I'll tell you, Jim, the house just isn't the same without her."

"I can only imagine that feeling, Bern. I'm happy, Stella's getting out. She must be so happy."

"So are you here alone, Jim?"

"No actually I'm going to meet, Huneo here. He should be along any minute."

"Is it a business lunch or just pleasure, Jim?"

"A bit of both, Bernie, a little bit of both. I'm going to ask, Huneo if the students can have free access to one of his calibrators."

"I heard there was a break-in over the weekend, is that right?"

"Yeah! I almost forgot about that. Yes, Bernie there was a break-in on Saturday night and one of the calibrators was stolen. It's a crazy thing, I'll tell you, Bern."

"Any suspects?"

"No, but it looks like it was a professional job though, that's what the police think. It's not any of the kids at the university, thank goodness." I said. Huneo walked in the main entrance. I gestured for him to join us. "Over here, Huneo." I beckoned. He saw us and rushed over.

"Good day, Huneo, have a seat with us. How are you doing today?"

"Good, Jim, I feel good today. Hello, Professor Wakefield, how are you this fine day?"

"I'm well, Huneo and you can just call me, Bernie. Professor Wakefield is too formal for me."

"I will, Sir. How is your wife doing these days?"

"She's doing fine, Huneo. Thanks for asking. We've gotten an extra menu, Huneo, would you like to see the lunch specials? The food is good here. Have you eaten here before?" Bernie inquired.

"I believe this is my first time, in fact I'm sure of it. I would have remembered this place."

"Well don't be shy, Huneo, the food is great here and the price is right. I'll be picking up the tab guys. I'm celebrating." Bernie offered, in a gesture of happiness.

"Okay, I guess we're all settled in then." I said. "Huneo, I have a favor to ask of you. My class of advanced students has seen your lecture and they're concerned with the postulations that you've presented us with. I am as well and we were wondering if we could use one of your calibrators for a project that we've started, to study your postulations and theories?" I asked.

"Well, I must say, Jim I'm honored that you've decided to study my hypotheses and equipment. It's like I said, Jim, the SOLTES calibrators are a donation to the school and they're in your care now. You may use them however you wish. You can get the keys and the combination from your university president."

"Well, thanks very much, Huneo. I also have one more little favor to ask of you, and that is, that I might need a tutor to show me the operations and functions of the calibrator?" I asked, sheepishly.

"I'd be glad to show you how it works, Jim. If you want, we could set something up for tomorrow at your convenience. I could come and show you and your students anytime you'd like."

"That would be great!" I said, "Perfect, Huneo, I can assemble my students in no time."

"Listen guys, I hate to break in here but can an old professor get in on this too? I can do my share to help out you know?" Bernie asked. He inquired with a zip in his tone.

"Certainly you're invited, Bernie. You know what, we could all get together after school around 4:00 pm and we could take one of the calibrators into one of the labs and do our thing in there. Would you guys be able to make it for that time of day, in the labs?" I asked. Our lunches arrived at the table.

"I'm available at four o'clock. Stella will probably want her first break from me since getting home." Bernie chimed.

"Okay, Huneo, all we need is you. Are you in?"

"Oh, I think I can make it. Yeah, I'll be there." Huneo replied.

"Great then, so what I'll do is tell the students in the morning at class and whoever can attend will, and then I'll go to the archives and get one of the calibrators and have it brought up to the lab for that evening."

"I can give you a hand, Jim. I can get there a little early." Bernie offered.

"Alright, that would be great then, Bernie, and I could get a few of the students to help out with the set up. I can get some of the maintenance staff to help out a bit too, I think."

"Okay listen, Jim, I'll be either right on time or a few minutes late, I have some personal business to attend to at that time but I'll get there as soon as possible." Huneo mentioned.

"Yeah, there's no problem there, Huneo. We won't start the class without you. We'll just have discussion period until you arrive."

"Okay, I should be there right on time, though."

"Good, that's just fine then." We started enjoying our meals. Having lunch at Snicker's restaurant seemed to get us in an upbeat mood. We were enjoying ourselves. As our lunchtime wore on, we got to know Huneo a little better and became friendlier with him. Huneo seemed to be a down to earth person and we seemed to bond well. I decided not to push him anymore about the class on Tuesday or the lecture he would give later in the week. I ate my lunch and then I had to get back to class. I excused myself, said "good afternoon" to Bernie and Huneo, and then went on my way. They ordered a few more drinks as I left. I wished I could have stayed but I had class. At any rate, I headed back and arrived at my office about a half an hour later. I grabbed my briefcase and went off to teach my last two classes. After this, I was pooped out and could not wait to get home and relax. My workday had ended and I finally got to head home.

After getting home and having a good shower and dinner, I was able to sit down, relax with my daughters, and enjoy the cool evening. I sat in the living room with Angela and Christine while Paula was upstairs listening to her music and dancing in her bedroom. Angela was half reclined on the couch with Cindy in her arms, petting her gently as she watched television and relaxed. Christine was reading one of her magazines and occasionally talked with me. "Angela, dear." I said. I began speaking.

"Yes, Dad."

"How are things going with the, Helgesons, is everything going well?"

"Not too bad, Dad. I think they're starting to accept me a little more now. Mrs. Helgeson asked me over for lunch on Wednesday with Mom, if she can take some time off from work. She phoned me today and asked me."

"Why aren't you in school today?"

"C'mon, Dad, it's spring break for our high school, don't you remember?" Angela replied.

"Oh yeah, that's right. How are you feeling these days, are you feeling okay?"

"I feel great, Dad. I was sick this morning but that's normal for a pregnant woman."

"Really?"

"Daaad!"

"Don't tease your pregnant daughter, dear." Christine chimed in.

"I'm not teasing her hon, I'm just chatting with her."

It was about then on the television that it was announced that ahead on the American National News that a report out of a New York university about a major scientific discovery related to a scientist in Saskatchewan, Canada would be forthcoming and that it could change the face of science and life on earth. Right away, I knew this report was about Huneo.

"Jim, it sounds like that could be about the symposium and, Huneo Parkas." Christine expressed.

"I think you're right dear, I'm going to turn it up a bit." I sat waiting for the news to begin. I sat in anticipation as Christine and Angela talked quietly in the room. Cindy woke up and then she started to yawn. She shuffled around a bit and then abruptly she let out a little bark. We laughed at the sound of the little puppy bark and as fast as she woke up she fell back to sleep. The evening news began. It started with political stories about upcoming elections in the United States so I turned the volume down and waited patiently while watching the television. We talked quietly as I kept one eye on the news. A few more stories came and went and then a news bit called "The Science File" appeared. "Okay here it is, here it is, listen." I said. A reporter from the news program began to speak. "Good evening everyone." He said, "Tonight out of New York University, comes a story of national importance dealing with new science. Hello, I'm Richard Jenkins reporting and we're here at the labs of New York University where scientists are hastily assembling a device called the SOLTES calibrator. They're trying to complete their work as soon as possible to determine if a scientist who made a surprise announcement in Park Falls, Saskatchewan in Canada was in fact making accurate statements in what is believed to be an absolutely stunning claim. A scientist at a symposium in Saskatchewan, Canada claimed that the expansion of the universe is slowing in velocity causing a natural event to occur that is related to the passage of time. He claimed in his announcement that this event or another event of unknown origin is causing our time that passes to pass faster." The reporter stated. They cut away to scenes of what looked like technicians working on a project as his voiceover continued. "I know you're all asking yourselves, what exactly is this guy saying? Well, the professor of astrophysics in question, a Dr. Huneo L. Parkas of South America, a displaced American citizen, has at a symposium in, Park Falls, Saskatchewan unveiled a device that measures the rate of speed at which time passes using a medium that mimics the speed of light electronically. He has made a claim at a lecture at the Sherman Patterson University for the Sciences, in Park Falls, that his

SOLTES calibrator, an acronym for the Speed of Light/Time Existence Speed calibrator has measured the time it takes for time to pass." the reporter said. He continued. "This is completely new science and in a move to prove this, the scientist, Dr. Huneo Parkas, has released the blueprints for the construction of the SOLTES Calibrator via the internet for the whole world to build and see for itself. Scientists here at the university tell us it will only be a matter hours before their first calibrator is functional and we will see for ourselves." The reporter commented. The station cut away to a New York scientist who further explained the calibrator and how it worked as well as other points of view from various experts who were either enthusiastic or skeptical about the announcement. The reporter then came back and ended his segment. "Well there we have some early opinions as the juries are still out on the legitimacy of this science. However, in the days ahead this news agency will stay close to this story indeed, I'm Richard Jenkins for the American National News reporting." He said, as he finished his story and signed off.

"Well holy cow, Jim, this Huneo Parkas thing is really starting to taking off, I mean what gives?" Christine inquired.

"I don't know, Christine. I really don't."

"Dad, what's going on with this? It seems to be getting bigger and bigger." Angela inquired, with concern in her eyes.

"I don't know sweetheart, I really don't, but I can only say that we might be living in a time when the foundations of science and God only knows what else are going to be shaken to their cores. I don't know but I think this effect might put this world into a tailspin and I don't even think, Huneo has told us the half of what's going on yet." I said, to my loves. Their eyes grew dark.

"Dad, you're scaring me with this!" Angela said.

"Honey, honey, its okay, don't get bent out of shape because of this. Remember nothing has happened yet, nothing, so don't worry." I said. I tried to calm her fears.

"Angela it's alright, you're worried about nothing. I brought you up to weigh things for what they are and not what you think they might be. Just worry about your healthy choices for your baby and your school and friends." Christine echoed.

"Okay, alright, listen you two, there's nothing to worry about so calm down and relax. I'm sorry I scared you so I'll change the subject and the channel." I told. That seemed to end the excitement. We forgot about the news report and went about our normal family evening. Paula came downstairs and started telling us about the adventures of her day and we started to get a little laugh festival going. We were together as a family that Monday evening, laughing and enjoying ourselves. Cindy got up and became a little rambunctious herself. We had an enjoyable night that just happened spontaneously and we would remember it for a while to come. The evening ended with a lot of "I love you's" and hugs and kisses before we tired out in front of the television and started to get ready for bed. We put Cindy in the back hallway and then Christine, the girls and I retired to our bedrooms. As Christine and I lay in our bed, we cuddled together and talked quietly about our new grandson on the way and our girls. Then Christine changed the subject. "Jim, are we in any kind of trouble, if this theory of, Huneo Parkas' is true?" she lamented. She had a quaver in her voice.

"Hon, I don't think so but right now no one knows for sure. We're just going to have to give this thing time to run its course and see what happens. But remember my love you always know who's with us, don't you."

"Yes Jim, I know God is with us and may God bless us and our home and the whole world." Christine said. She sighed.

"Amen." I said. We fell asleep in each other's arms.

After a good night's rest, I woke up the following day contented. I awakened Christine and then we got our daughters up and did our daily thing. It was another fair weather day as I headed off to the university on that dreary Tuesday. I went straight to my office and then right into my first class of the day with my fifth year students. As I walked in, there was clamoring and shuffling going on. The students were disorganized. I sat down and tried to capture their attention. "Okay can everybody hear me, please can everybody hear me?" I called out. The class started to settle and become quiet. Everybody took to his or her seats and I was able to begin the class.

"Are we going to start off with our Pegasus project Professor?" a student asked.

"Yes, are we going to start with the Pegasus project this morning?" another student asked. The class began to speak out.

"Okay, okay it looks like you've all got bees in your bonnets this morning so we'll start with, Pegasus Project. Y'all look eager to go. So who's first?"

"Professor, did you see the news last night?" Janice Davis asked.

"Yes, I did."

"What did you think of what they said?"

"What part of the story do you mean, Janice?"

"The part that the Chinese have made a calibrator and they said it is true that the calibrator is a functional device that does what it is intended to do."

"Whoa! I didn't hear that report. When was that on?"

"11:00 o'clock." Janice replied.

"How many news reports were on last night?" I inquired.

"There were a few, Professor."

"Well, I think we'll have to wait for more corroboration than that one report."

"But Professor everything points to, Dr. Huneo Parkas' theories being true!" Robbie Platt exclaimed.

"First of all, this is not a proven theory yet, it is a hypothetical postulation that has yet to be proven. However, I would agree that proof one way or another is just around the corner."

"Professor, I've been on the internet and other universities are now trying to see if this is true too and they're doing what we're doing." David Neally stated.

"Well, all I can say is that it looks like this thing is starting to run on its own steam. I have no idea where we're going with this. However, sometimes in science, this type of discovery or non-discovery happens and as far as I can tell this is an aberration in our scientific community and it's anybody's guess as to where we're going with this. I think that's all I can really say on this right now. Are there any other questions?"

"Professor Reynolds, are we going to get to use one of the calibrators?" Ben Ross asked.

"Oh yes, before I forget, late this afternoon we're going to get together in one of the labs and bring a calibrator in and everybody will get a chance to see and use it. Is anybody interested?" I asked. Without exception, everybody raised his or her hand.

"Also, listen up everyone, Professor Bernard Wakefield and Dr. Huneo Parkas will be there as well. So were going to be at the center of the universe tonight."

"Where, where do we meet Professor?" a student asked.

"Okay, we'll all meet in lab 2 at 4:15 pm today. Is that okay with everyone?" The students enthusiastically agreed to meet in Lab 2 at 4:15 pm.

"Okay, it's settled then. All right, in order for me to earn my money, we're going to have to return to our regular curriculum. So listen everyone, later today we will go into a full depth discussion on this subject, so try to be patient." I explained. We then settled into our review of the semester.

I could see as I presided over my class that my students had their minds set on the Pegasus Project. I could see that my student's were becoming aware, as I was as well, that this scientific postulation was starting to consume us and everything was starting to point to the fact that this event was actually taking place and had been for some time. I decided that I would finish off that class with a small assignment and then I asked my students again to meet me in lab 2 at 4:15 pm, for those that were interested. After my next class of first year students, I thought I would go for a walk again and take some time to think. Lately, I have had many thoughts running through my mind and a good brisk walk might be just the thing I needed to gain some prospective on the events that have transpired. Things have been starting to get a little stressful lately and they have begun to creep up on me. The unexpected pregnancy of Angela and the future arrival of my first grandchild by my first born daughter, Stella's heart attack, the

pressures of the university and now the revelations of this new postulation by Dr. Huneo L. Parkas. My next class went well and the students
were actually a welcome change. Being first year students their lack of
knowledge about physics that day was quite amusing. Their misbehav-
ior in class was laughable, so I enjoyed myself and went along with the
flow, chuckling and shaking my head at their antics and silliness.

I felt better after that class. I wrapped up some business in my office and I went for my walk. I went out the door by my office, a rarely
used door that leads to a brushy and rough landscape at the side of
the university that faced the north. There were natural pathways that
wound around the trees and lead off campus, creating a shortcut for
students in a hurry to go for lunch at the mall and for those students
who caught the bus. The weather was fair as well as being a little cold
maybe and the only real color was in the sky and the fir trees. As I
walked, I felt good. I felt better than I had earlier. Sometimes, I got a
feeling that things were closing in around me and I needed some time
for myself. The fresh air felt good on my face. I noticed that somebody
else was coming down the path. It was Bernie Wakefield. "Hey Bernie,
over here!" I called out.

"Hey, Jim! Hi Jim, wait there! I'll come over there." he called back.
He ambled over to my location.

"Hi Bernie, I see that great minds think alike."

"Jeez Jim, it's still a little cool, eh?"

"Yeah it is, Bernie. It certainly is. How's Stella, Bern?"

"She's a little under the weather today actually. She thinks she's
coming down with cold. I think I'm getting a touch of it myself."

"I think I know what you mean, Bernie. I've been feeling a little run
down myself. I need to find some way to recharge myself and get my
energy level back up." I said.

"Well sometimes a little exercise and a good meal can go a long way
with some quality rest of course." Bernie recommended.

"You're right, Bernie, that's probably what I need. Are you still going to come tonight after school to the extra class for, Pegasus project?"
I asked. I wanted to confirm this with him.

"Yes, I'll be there, Jim. Stella wants a little extra time for herself. I'll get dinner out after the class."

"Everything's alright isn't it, Bernie?"

"Oh yeah, yeah, Jim, everything's just fine."

"Alright, let's go down this path then, Bernie."

"Lead the way, Jim." We walked down a path that wound behind the university and then around behind the shopping plaza and onto a public nature trail.

"It's refreshing to get out here, eh, Bern?"

"It's nice, Jim. We should do this a little more often now that the weather is getting better."

"We can do that, Bernie."

"How's Angela doing? Is she doing well these days?"

"She's doing just fine, Bern. I think she's going to grow up fast though. I think her pregnancy is making her stronger as a person and more responsible, so far anyway. How about you, Bernie, are you doing okay these days?"

"I'm making out okay, Jim. It gets a little hectic sometimes but I can usually muddle through pretty good."

"Well, if you ever need help, Bernie, you know you can always come to me and I'll be here for you. So you keep that in mind, alright?"

"I will, Jim, and the same goes for you." Bernie replied. We stumbled through the brush, mud and leftover snow of the trail.

We went on walking and talking for another half hour and then we made our way back to the university. It felt good to get out and have a frank talk with my mentor and best friend. After we got back to my office, I arranged for the maintenance staff to go and retrieve one of the calibrators from the archive and bring it to lab 2. I asked them to set it on a table for us so we could have good access to it and a good view of the calibrator. I then had a bit of a bite to eat with Bernie and then he headed down to his office for a nap. After that, I would go to my last class of the day and then straight to my office and then to the laboratory. My last class was actually a math class for English students who had a compulsory sciences class as part of their curriculum. I found these classes to be a great waste of time for these students and me; however, it was part of the program. The students in these classes had no interest in what you were trying to teach them and it was usually a class of people staring off into space, falling asleep or just staring at me with blank expressions on their faces. I went to this class and it was the same as usual, and after about an hour it was over. "Thank God." I sighed. I left for my office. I got to my office and Sandy was there typing something or other. She mentioned that I had a phone call from Christine and that I should call her back. Sandy also informed me that a SOLTES calibrator was delivered to laboratory 2 by the maintenance staff and that she had the key to the lab for me. I took the key, thanked her, and told her to go home. I went into my office and called Christine. "Hi hon, how are you doing?" I asked her, "Was there something special you called for, Christine?" She explained that she had tried to call me on my cell phone and could not get a hold of me and that she just wanted to say hello and that she loved me. "I love you too, sweetheart." I replied. I explained that I had gone out for a walk and turned off my phone and forgot to turn it back on. I asked her how the girls were and mentioned to her that I would be late for dinner, perhaps as late as 7:00-7:30 pm. My love was understanding and said that she would have something special ready for me when I got home. I told her that I loved her again and then I hung up, as it was time to go to the lab. I grabbed my briefcase and locked up my office for the day. I had not seen hide nor hair of my counterparts over the past few days and their offices were locked up as well. I wanted to find out what they were up to and what their takes were on this NE/TL theory of Huneo Parkas'. I must say they have been quiet these days. Well, I was off to the labs and as I walked down the hallways, I could see some of the other guests in the auditoriums speaking. I had almost completely forgotten about our other guests and I was probably going to catch hell for this neglect. I thought also that I had missed a meeting with Marnie Greene earlier in that day. She would have my rump for this. Marnie does not take kindly to being stood up that was to be for sure. I was going to have to make amends if I could. I turned the corner to the labs and the students were waiting. A few of them playfully looked at their watches and there were also a few tongue in cheek remarks as I looked at my watch to see that it was 4:40 pm. "Oh my goodness everyone, I'm sorry I'm late. I have the key here. I'll let you all in right away." I said, being a little surprised at myself for being tardy. I was not usually late for classes but I was human and I got caught up in things too. "Hi Huneo how are you?" I asked. Everybody started to shuffle into the lab.

"Not too bad, Jim, how about yourself?"

"I'm good, Huneo. Thanks for coming, I appreciate this."

"Jim, it's my pleasure. I've been talking to some of your students and I'm very impressed with their knowledge of physics. They must certainly garner the high marks I'll bet."

"Yeah, they're a pretty good bunch, Huneo." I replied. Bernie rounded the corner.

"Am I late guys?" Bernie asked.

"It's impromptu, Bernie, so you're right on time."

"Hello again, Professor Wakefield."

"Dr. Parkas I see, just call me, Bernie." Bernie responded. We filed into the lab. Everybody took a chance to socialize before we got started. I saw that the SOLTES calibrator was in the center of the room and it was covered. I started to arrange the chairs and tables in a semicircle. Bernie and Huneo helped as the session was about to begin. After approximately five or ten minutes, I decided to call the class to order. I went to the table in the center of the room with the calibrator on it and I pulled out my notes, pens and chalk. "Okay everyone, could I have your attention please." I said, "Everyone please take a seat and we'll get started." The students began to take seats and settle.

"Hello everyone, it's nice to see that so many of you could make it out to our special class tonight. I hope you're all in good spirits. So, like I said before, this is a special class and we have a few guests with us to help in the discussions. So let's say hello again to, Professor Huneo Parkas, and Professor Bernard Wakefield." I stated. The students greeted our guests. "I don't have to explain to you why we're here tonight. Over the past number of days, we've been put on the plank so to speak as we are on the cusp of a new theory in science that has presented itself to us and now seems to maybe have some legitimacy or does have legitimacy in theoretical astrophysics. We are perplexed, and in a conundrum of sorts. This information is spreading throughout the world and people want to have answers to this hypothesis and most certainly with a sense of immediacy. Today, I hope we can make things a little clearer for everyone and maybe gain a better understanding of what's really going on in the universe. I suppose that's the best way I can put it to you. The first thing I would like to do is ask Dr. Parkas to speak to us and tell us a little more if he might." Huneo gave me a nod and a smile in the affirmative. "After this I would like to have a question and answer period for everyone to maybe shed even more light on this topic. So with no further delay, please welcome, Dr. Huneo Parkas." The students applauded as Huneo made his way up to the podium. He wore a big smile on his face. I took notice that Huneo was looking like a contented man these days and he was quite a striking figure. I also noticed Helen Hamilton applauding with a sparkle in her eye for Huneo. Their feelings for each other were obvious and they looked good together. I hoped it was a match made in heaven as they both deserved to be happy. Huneo stood at the podium, a small portable one. He shuffled a few papers as he collected his thoughts. I sat at the back of the class with Bernie and we got comfortable.

"I bid you good evening, Sherman Patterson students. How are you this evening?" Huneo greeted. The students welcomed him in response. "You certainly look like a nice group and you look like a happy bunch of students tonight." He said, as he began his talk. He took a sip of water and continued. "I can recall back to when I was your age, or a little younger perhaps, and I was learning physics. I had the same look in my eyes that I see in your eyes these days as I tour your campus. I'm happy to be here today, as well I am happy to be part of this symposium. When I was in my early teens, I gained an interest, a natural interest, in the sciences, and then after a while I became obsessed with science. I became determined to make science a part of my life. One day I would be studying volcanoes and the next day I would be studying rockets. I loved it all and I couldn't get enough of it. I would forgo the usual teen social events and spent my time in the libraries reading book after book, magazine after magazine and going to science shows.

I was like a wild mustang though because I only learned what I wanted to learn. This got me into trouble sometimes because I could not follow the curriculums properly, and I almost did not get my degrees. My marks were not high. However, in the end, I prevailed and as I persisted, I completed my education. I believe it's the way that I learned the sciences that has led me to the discovery of the, Non-Existence/ Time Loss theorem and the changes that are now affecting our solar system. The ideas just came to me. They just hit me right in the face and they stunned me. In reality, I have not discovered anything. The theory and its physical and relative functioning in the universe has always been there, is there now, and will always be there in three dimensional space physically or in relative theory or principal forever. It's a constant. I believe that this hypothesis and now proven theory is partially above us in the sense that it is part of the divine realm and or of a divine providence. It is principals such as these that have shown me where my heart and soul lie and have shown me who I am and what my place in the universe is and why I'm in existence. Today, I'm a contented man. My questions about life and my questions about everything in general have been answered for the most part. I know that that's an egotistical sounding statement, but it's not. It's a place of great inner peace for me, and now with this experience I can give of myself and share my experience with others to make a contribution for a better world. Today, I try to keep myself humble and I try to live my life in a positive direction striving to push myself to the limits of my capabilities, always! Meaning, I try to always to be honest, respectful of others, self respecting and outwardly loving and giving." Huneo stated. The students were entranced by his words up to that point. "Nonetheless," he continued, "This theory in its most simplistic form is just that, it is not complex! I believe that God made the universe a simple place. I believe that others try to make the universe out to be an overly complex entity that only they can understand when in reality young people can understand the universe because it is simple, the way God had intended. However, I believe there are mysteries out in space that we cannot see and it is because of the vastness of the universe that we are blinded. Think of how much man complicates things and makes things different on our little blue ball we call earth. We build airplanes and hydroelectric dams and make electronics and tennis balls and so on. There are literally hundreds of millions of different things that man has made and perhaps, literally, billions of different things of material. But when we look up into the heavens, God has created trillions upon trillions of stars in the universe, and basically they're all the same, it's simple." Huneo stated. He expressed his thoughts and paused for a moment. "The theory is simple. It involves three dimensional space, mass and velocity, more specifically the lower end of the velocity spectrum in regards to the speed of light associated with the special theory of relativity. Not light itself, but the speed of light. As these theories evolved in my mind, when I was younger, I decided that I would try to discover ways of understanding them as they related to man and the human condition. One of the ways that I saw this was through the way man was evolving. How was he changing? And why was he changing, the way he was?" Huneo told. He had me enthralled with his words. I looked over and saw Bernie on the edge of his seat. "The changes that proved the theory to me on a less scientific basis were intangible. They were intangible because they could have more than one root cause but together a common thread closely linked them. The most common changes were the tighter rings in trees and the unexplained species extinctions, which I believed to be the direct result of the NE/TL effect. They are attributable to the speed of time passing increases. I believe that the central nervous systems of the smaller species in nature that are becoming extinct with no explanation are being overloaded with electrical activity that is too fast for them due to the time speed increases. Therefore, the species dies off as a whole. This is where man gets fooled. These effects and manifestations don't look abnormal because to us twenty four hours is still twenty four hours. We cannot gauge the difference in the speeds of the electrical impulses in the brain of a small species because to us their brain looks and functions the same at different time speeds when in fact their brains and our brains are functioning faster. Man comes with speed limits. If man travels too fast through space his mind fires too slow and he dies, and conversely if man travels too slowly through space his mind fires too fast and he will die. Biological entities do not function relative to non-biological entities or principals. In the case of the tree rings, I believe they tighten again by the speed of time passing increases. I think tonight in honor of the students in this class I am going to call this event the Pegasus Effect, I think, after you so aptly named your project. Therefore, as I was saying, the Pegasus Effect, I believe, has also been responsible for the higher intelligence in man. I believe it is responsible for the technological revolution that man has recently gone through and is going through not unlike the past industrial revolution. Humankind has gone onto technology never before seen or thought of in the past and it all seems to be driven by one common denominator, and that is speed. It is humanity's need for speed and our constant wantonness to do things faster that our minds are in essence working faster due to the time speed increases. Our brains and time are not relative to one another. What I mean by that is, is that as time speeds up our brains do not adjust to stay the same, they change. If our brains and time were relative, our brains would not change. However, our brains do, and as we think faster, we want things done faster and combined with the fact that the mind is running faster and it is learning faster and learning more as its electrical impulses fire quicker. We become more intelligent but not wiser. As we become more intelligent like a computer, we want more storage space in our brain and we try to overload it. The Pegasus Effect is also I believe a cause of neurological disorders in the human population. Medical statistics show that the problem of neurological disorders is seemingly on an exponential rise. The Pegasus Effect has a for sure true effect on all biological central nervous systems. The Pegasus Effect could be our greatest natural disaster and a global calamity that could render us extinct. It is a natural disaster unlike any other in its nature. For example, in a hurricane, we can build fortifications and walls to shield us, or in a tornado, we can seek shelter underground or in reinforced structures. In a natural disaster like an earthquake, we can build stronger structures and for tidal waves, we can set up warning systems that direct people away from the danger and can help minimize the losses. With the Pegasus Effect, there is no solution to protecting ourselves.

We can harness the power of the waves and the wind but we cannot harness the power of the universe. It is for this fact alone that we are now at the mercy of the Pegasus Effect and divine providence. Huneo explained. He paused, took a sip of his water, and then continued. "I don't know where the NE/TL effect is going to end up taking mankind, but what I do know about this event is, is that the same amount of time is always passing, however the speed in which that time is passing is happening faster and faster." Huneo stated. The class sat in stunned silence. Not a sound was to hear in his pause of speaking, not the students breathing or swallowing even. Huneo continued. "In regards to global stress and rage and the corruption of evolutionary processes, the NE/TL theorem supports both circumstances. In the past fifteen years or so, we have seen the world's level of personal and collective rages and stresses increase dramatically, all due to the need for speed causing increased impatience. The people of the world have become driven and obsessed with doing things faster and going faster and to what end? To no end, except that we are changing subtly and unknowingly to effects that are beyond our control and up until now the human population has been totally oblivious to these facts. Lastly, we have come to the corruption of the evolutionary process. This is now self-evident as we witness the unusual and unexplainable mutations in different animal species and non-compliance of the long held beliefs of a natural order." Huneo said. He paused. It surprised me, the things he was explaining. Moreover, it all seemed to make sense. I looked over at Bernie and he was shaking his head in amazement. I believed Huneo had now laid bare a conundrum of gargantuan proportions. An untenable situation foisted itself upon the world and it left humankind with no tools to deal with its outcome. "What are we going to do?" Huneo asked, as he had begun to speak again. "I'm not trying to be an alarmist, but I think society as a whole must immediately start taking this seriously and try to do something about it if there is anything that can be done. This is important to the human race as a whole as well as to all other biological life forms on earth, in the highest order. So, for now I would like to thank you all for listening and being patient and with that, I will hand the podium back to,

Professor Reynolds and we can look at the SOLTES calibrator up close and personal. I will also have more to say in my lecture this Friday at 12:35 pm in the main auditorium and I invite you all to be there of course. Thank you for listening." Huneo said. He concluded his talk and then went to take his seat. The students sat in silence for a few moments and then gave him an enthusiastic round of applause. I thought the students did not know what to think and frankly neither did I. Nevertheless, I got up made my way to the podium. I gave my thanks on everyone's behalf to Huneo for taking the time out to be with the students for this special request. I tapped my pen on the podium a few times and then I spoke. "Okay, alright everyone, we'll have a short question and answer period. So if you've got a question please raise your hands." At that point, all of my students raised their hands. "Whoa, whoa!" I said, "Okay, we'll go one at a time, first we'll go to, Connie Beaton, go ahead, Connie." Petite and shy Connie stood up and began to speak.

"My question is for, Professor Parkas. Are we going to be okay? Is this, Pegasus Effect going to go away?" She asked. Huneo then stood up and turned to respond.

"Well, Ms. Beaton, all I can say is that in the case of this phenomenon I do not know what will happen or how we will fair in the outcome of this event. There is no known documentation of this event ever happening before but it most certainly could have happened without man ever realizing or even knowing it was taking place. Its effects in the beginning are subtle and it could have happened before in history and was not an inconvenience. Its effect would not have been attributable to the then effects on biological entities and might have been an unbeknownst factor. It conceivably could have taken place numerous times without man knowing and either got to a point where it went into remission or it reversed itself. I think what might help us, Ms. Beaton, is knowing what event in the universe is taking place that is causing this to happen. Is it localized? Is it some sort of orbital feature of the galaxy? Is it on as grand a scale as to involve the whole of the universe? I don't know. We'll have to look to astronomers I think to find our answers if we can even hope to have a chance at finding the answer. This could also remain a mystery forever." Huneo said. He answered eloquently and sat back down in his chair. I continued. "Alright good question, Connie, is there any others? One at a time, please." The hands shot up again. One of my best students David Neally had his hand up and I chose him. "Yes David, you're next, ask away."

"Thanks, Professor Reynolds. My question is for Professor Wakefield." I chuckled. It had been a long time since Bernie had been in the limelight. I said, 'Show em, Bernie, show my students you still got it what it takes.' I thought, as David Neally began to ask his question.

"Professor Wakefield, do you think this event is taking place? And if you think it is, why do you think it is?" David asked.

"Well, Mr. Neally, that's a good question. I guess to answer you I'd truly have to say that I'm on the horns of a dilemma. First, the science is theoretically sound. Next, the SOLTES calibrator looks like a bona fide scientific instrument and its functionality is legitimate. Everything points to the NE/TL theory as being a true and proven theory. Yet, I cannot bring myself to accept it. It is so extraordinary a theory that I cannot fathom it. To me it is so outlandish I just can't come to grips with it. I think a little more convincing might help me out. To answer the second part of your question, why is it taking place? If it is. Well, I'll just have to go along with the common sense answer of, Dr. Parkas' and that is to say that a celestial event of unknown proportions, with unknown parameters is taking place, and the only way we will unravel this mystery is to put our best astronomers to work and see what they can come up with. I hope that helps you out, Mr. Neally."

"Thanks, Professor Wakefield, it does." David replied.

"Okay, we'll take a few more questions and then we'll move on. Okay, who's next? Someone new this time, ah okay, let's see, ah, Diane McLeod, you have a question?"

"Yes, my question is for, Dr. Parkas. Dr. Parkas, if your discovery is true; would we not be moving faster?"

"Yes, Ms. McLeod, we are moving faster. The relative speed of everything we do and everything that happens is in fact happening slightly faster than it used to happen, it is imperceptible to us. The same amount of happenings happens in the same amount of time in respect to let's say a person walking a mile in ten minutes ten years ago and a person walking a mile in ten minutes ten minutes ago. Except the latter is happening slightly faster because the ten minutes ten years ago was happening at slower rate of speed than the ten minutes, ten minutes ago. So time not being relative to us we adjust by moving slightly faster. This is due to our immediate velocity slow down in the galaxy or the universe. The same amount of time is passing but it is passing faster. You will understand this easier if you think of the two times relative to one another and their time passing at different rates of speed because of their differing velocities in relationship to the speed of light and how masses with different velocities can have different rates of the speed in which time passes. Try to remember that in all instances that the same amount of time is passing, it's just happening at different speeds. I hope that answers it for you, thanks for your question, Diane."

"Thank you, Dr. Parkas." Diane replied.

"Alright thanks, Diane. That was another good question. I think what we'll do is take one more and then we'll move on to looking at the SOLTES calibrator, so anyone else with a question? Okay let's see, okay, Ryan Bell, you've got a question?"

"Yes Professor, my question is for you," he said.

"I was wondering when I would get my turn. Okay, Ryan, let me have it."

"Thanks, Professor Reynolds. I would like to ask you if the Pegasus Effect gets worse and worse, let's say, and the speed of time passing goes faster and faster as the earth slows down, could it wipe out all life on earth?" Ryan asked, in a facetious tone. I thought this question would bother me, but it did not. At that moment, I accepted the facts of the NE/TL theories and it would be different for me as I answered.

"Yes Ryan, if time speed increased to go fast enough it could conceivably wipe out all life on earth." I responded. There were a few gasps. "But don't go out and start looking for burial plots just yet! We don't know what's really going on here but I'm sure you have lots of time. I'm sure one day you will bounce your grandkids on your knee and enjoy your retirement." I said, not really having much confidence in what I was saying. It seemed to appease everyone and that was good enough for me.

"Okay, Ryan thanks for your question. All right, listen up everyone, we're going to take a ten minute or so break and then we'll come back here and look at the SOLTES calibrator and then after that we'll wrap it up. So go and get a soft drink or a snack or whatever and we'll meet back here in ten minutes." I told. The class dispersed for a break. I went over to Huneo and Bernie. They were talking quietly.

"Hey can anyone get in on this conversation?" I asked, in jest.

"Yeah c'mon over, Jim, what do you think? Do you think the class is going the way you wanted it?" Huneo asked.

"Oh yeah, it's going all right. Why, what do you guys think?"

"It's alright." Bernie replied.

"So how do you feel, Jim on being on the cusp of the beginning of the biggest event in the history of mankind?" Huneo asked.

"I don't know, Bernie; I don't know, Huneo, God Damn it! I don't know, I think I'm going to be sick to tell you the truth, I think I'm going to be sick!" I growled.

"It's okay, Jim, I was sick for three weeks when I first took acceptance of the NE/TL effect. Don't worry. The best is yet to come." Huneo said.

"Goodness, Huneo, what the hell do you mean by that?" I asked. I had a moment of frightened anxiety.

"In due time, Jim, in due time." Huneo replied. The students started filing back into the classroom.

"I don't know if I can take anymore."

"Easy Jim, you have nothing to fear." Bernie reassured, "Just take it easy, Jim and we'll muddle through like we always do."

This reassurance from Bernie was always comforting to me and I started to relax again. We talked more as the students strolled in and started to take their seats. I reminded them that they could not leave a mess in the classroom and they must clean up after themselves. I took a few deep breaths and then I headed to the front of the class. I looked at my students and I was in wonderment of how beautiful they were, as the young people they were and the adults they were becoming. I breathed easy and felt a little euphoric. "I'm okay." I said to myself. I got up and started the class again as a few stragglers came through the door.

"Alright everyone, take your seats and we'll get started again. We're going to look at the SOLTES calibrator now so what I want is for everyone to pull their chairs in a little closer and we can begin." Everyone moved closer. I went up to the calibrator and undraped it. There was a small light on that indicated it was off. I asked Huneo if he would come up and give us a demonstration. He agreed. Huneo walked up and began to speak. "Hello again, that was a short break." he said. A few students laughed. "Well everyone, I know some of you have seen this calibrator and some of you have not so I'll explain it again before I turn it on. First off, this device is now available free to the world on the internet and it is quite an easy device to build and operate. I made it available on CD-ROM at my first lecture when I presented it and it's available for anyone to access now. It works simply by incorporating three measurements. The first measurement is the present time, the time that has been passing on all the clocks that we use in our daily lives throughout the world. The next measurement is the time that would have passed if the speed of time passing for the last fifteen years had remained constant from the time this calibrator was turned on, on November 12, 1995. It is now March 27, 2012 and when I turn on the calibrator, it will show the time of the latter aforementioned. The latter time will be the time that has been passing in perfect constancy in a spectrum that holds it in its speed in relationship to the speed of light. The last gauge that is of significance is the gauge that shows its current potential or shows any great changes in its current speed or increase in the speed of time passing." Huneo explained. My class seemed to grasp this easily.

"Alright, I'll turn the calibrator on and it will take a few minutes to get its information gathered and measured," he said. The students watched intently. The calibrator came to life and made a few beeps and whirs as it lit up and started to function. Suddenly, there was a reading.

"There we go." Huneo said, "Our first reading is the current time and date March 30th and it is showing 6:55 PM," he said. I realized how late our class was running. I did not expect to have that session run so long. At any rate, Huneo continued.

"Okay, the next time you see will be the time that would have passed if the time had remained constant. Hmm, okay there it is. There's the time of the second indicator and it's showing that the time would have been, October 10th, 2011 at 1:11 pm." Huneo explained. He looked at his calibrator in delight. Some of the students were in awe of the device. I mean you have to be in awe of a device that is showing you such incredible and astounding information. Then, the silence was broken.

"My God, is that thing for real!" Janice Davis exclaimed. She had a look of dread in her eyes.

"Yes, Ms. Davis it is." Huneo replied. The other students stared in amazement and could not believe their eyes. They were talking and asking questions of each other excitedly as Huneo continued.

"Alright, the comparison clocks are on and what they will do is if you watch them for about ten minutes, you will start to see the time separate from one clock compared to the other. In other words, you will see their differing time speeds. So we'll keep it on until we see a change in the speeds of the two clocks." Huneo explained, once again. The class was transfixed on the calibrator.

"Okay, the last display is the rate of the increase in percentage and that will show up when it is tallied. It reads around the very low end of the percentages, about 3.39% rate of increase as compared to the time speed recorded on November 12, 1995 when it comes up. The other gauges are functional gauges that show the power levels and a few other minor functions that the device registers to operate." Huneo explained.

For a while, everybody talked quietly and watched the calibrator for changes. After some time, things died down, and then. "Ah, oh my God, Professor, the calibrator is showing a change!" Diane McLeod called out. She observed a change on the time indicators as suddenly all the eyes were on the calibrator. Huneo smiled and moved closer to explain what was happening. "As I said, the calibrator is registering a change. It is only fractions of a second right now but the gap will grow as the calibrator is left on calculating the difference."

"Well, Dr. Parkas, how do you know the gap after all these years is about six months?" Janice asked.

"Well, Ms. Davis, I built this device with micro circuitry that is always running and has been since 1995. The time difference can also be calculated mathematically to a fair degree of accuracy from the information it yields. However, I have let the device do the work and it's extremely accurate."

"Thanks, Dr. Parkas." Janice replied. The class clamored and was transfixed by the happenings. I let the class do as they wished and essentially the class had ended for the evening. I went over to Huneo and realized that Helen was not with him. "Huneo, I just realized this is one of the few times I've seen you without, Helen. I haven't seen her for a while, has she gone home, if you don't mind me asking?"

"Not at all, Jim, she's taking time to be with her parents. She's been with me so much lately that she feels that she's neglecting them. So, she'll spend some time with them and she'll also talk about us and explain her feelings."

"You and Helen are doing okay aren't you?"

"Yes Jim, everything's fine. It's just a small lull in the relationship that's going to keep us apart for a few days." Huneo replied. He yawned and then his eyes grew wide and he began to shake.

"Huneo are you okay? What's the matter? You look like you've just seen a ghost!"

"Nothing, Jim, I'm alright." he said. He went over to the calibrator and then turned it off, abruptly.

"Okay, I think we'll turn the device off for now and let it cool down." I knew something was wrong. He was acting completely out of character. I had to find out why and I was not going to let him off the hook this time.

"I will now turn the class back over to, Professor Reynolds… Professor." he said. Right away, I got up, thanked the students for coming and then dismissed the class. I told them they could stay for ten more minutes and then they must be out of the lab. Immediately,

I went to speak with Huneo. "Huneo, what exactly happened there while I was talking to you?" I asked.

"Listen, Jim, it's nothing, I just got a little excited." He said. He was being evasive.

"I don't think so; I want to know why you turned off the calibrator so abruptly. I think you owe me that after your arrival fiasco. I want to know and if we're going to be friends you're going to have to be honest with me."

"Okay, alright Jim, I'll tell you but you have to clear the room."

"Alright, the students will be out of here shortly."

"Professor Wakefield too."

"Alright, Huneo everyone goes, whatever you want." I replied. He sat back down and we waited. We milled around some and then I started to egg the students to be on their way. I told Bernie that I needed to talk to Huneo privately and he agreed to see me the following day. The students filed out slowly and after about ten minutes, the classroom was empty. There was just Huneo and I in the classroom then and I could feel the tension between us rising. Huneo started to make small talk about how the class went and I let him go on for a few minutes as I talked about the students with him. Finally, I asked him directly.

"Huneo, what went on in the class that upset you so?" I prodded.

"Alright Jim, turn on the calibrator and I'll show you." he said. This made me feel unsettled. I asked myself what might be up with the calibrator that he did not want to talk about. Anyway, I walked over and pushed the on/off button and looked at him as he had this dead look in his eyes, it was as if he was not there or he was looking right through me. I beckoned unto him. "Huneo, are you alright?"

"Yes Jim, I'm okay. I'm just thinking. Jim it'll take at least thirteen to sixteen minutes for the calibrator to get to where I want it so we're going to have to wait for a bit."

"That's alright, Huneo, we've got nothing but time."

"I'm not so sure about that, Jim. I mean about the time, in general." Huneo responded. I did not know what he meant by that.

"So you and, Helen are alright?"

"Actually, Jim, we're going to move in together and I'm going to ask her to marry me."

"Goodness, Huneo, are you that serious?"

"Yes, we are, Jim."

"Well congratulations to the both of you, Huneo. I wish you all the happiness that life can offer."

"Thanks, Jim. We'd like to have children soon and well, we're trying."

"That's great, Huneo. All I can tell you is that from my own experience, my daughters have been the greatest joys of my life alongside with my wife. For me, I could see no other way to live than to be married and share our lives with our children." I told, Huneo. He seemed a little bashful about this. "I'm going to get a soda, Huneo, would you like one?"

"Yeah, I'll have a pop, any kind, Jim, please, if you don't mind."

"I'll be right back." I said, and then I raced off to get the drinks. As I walked, I phoned Christine to let her know that I was going to be late. It was almost 8:00 pm and I had been here longer than I had anticipated. However, Christine did not mind. I told her that I would be home as soon as I could. I had gotten the drinks and as I headed back and walked in the door, I saw Huneo standing in front of the calibrator with a sick look in his eyes. I walked up to him and handed him his drink. He looked at me.

"I didn't see this coming, Jim." He said.

"You didn't see what coming, Huneo?"

"Come over here, Jim, please, look." I walked over and looked at the calibrator. It looked to be functioning normally.

"What am I looking for here, Huneo?" I asked.

"Look at the rate of increase indicator."

"Yes, and what about it?"

"Jim, it was reading a 3.39% rate of increase and that was a cumulative rate leading up to that reading over a decade. Jim, now it's reading a 4.79 % rate of increase compared to the November 12th, 1995 readings, that's an increase of almost twenty five percent in the last ten days. I don't think this is good news. Jim, this is a bad thing." Huneo stated. His eyes now dark, like black pools.

"What do you mean? What does this mean?" I asked.

"Jim, it means the speed in which time is passing has taken a huge leap and that we're slowing down rapidly in the universe, if that's what's happening."

"How do you know that, Huneo?" I asked, intently.

"The indicator is showing the time as it is passing right now, Jim compared to what it was in 1995 and it's not wrong."

"How do you know that, Huneo?"

"I just do, Jim! Time is passing at a much faster rate than it was ten days ago. I know we can't feel it, Jim but if this keeps up like this, it will kill us!" Huneo exclaimed. He had an unshakeable air of certainty about him.

"I don't believe this. This is crazy! Do you know what you're saying for God sake? Huneo, do you know what you're saying?"

"I'm afraid I do, Jim, I don't know what else to tell you except that time is passing faster and by the looks of this pattern, it's going to pass even faster." He stated, dejectedly.

"This is insane, Huneo!"

"I know, Jim." he replied. Moreover, with that, we fell silent. We looked at the indicator on the calibrator with the time separation growing further apart on the comparison clocks. After a while, I asked him again if he was sure about the calibrator readings and he said there was no doubt. He then told me that he was going to leave to be with Helen. This disclosure stunned me as we decided to end our evening. It had not sunk in for me yet because aside from the readings there was nothing tangible really on which to base his assertions. I told him that I wanted to see him the next day. He agreed to see me around noon the following day and then we said goodbye to one another and went our separate ways for the evening. I phoned the night staff to come, get the calibrator, and bring it to the archive vault for safekeeping. This news was upsetting and I must tell Christine about it I thought. I gathered up my things and I headed for home. I was in a hurry. It was going on 9:00 pm. I was late. I felt unsure of myself and vulnerable.

As I drove home, I looked at the night sky and the stars and I could not imagine for the life of me that this was happening. I could not believe that the discoverer of the greatest natural phenomenon and aberration in science has come to Park Falls to drop this bombshell on us and that this was actually taking place in the heavens. It all seemed so unreal as I drove. I wondered how this was going to play out and if we were in mortal danger from this astrophysics event. As I pulled into my driveway, the lights were out except for the porch light and the kitchen light. I stopped the car and I tried to sneak into the house. Nevertheless, as I walked in the door Cindy let out a staccato of sharp puppy barks which I was sure awakened everyone. I calmed her and then I went to our bedroom. I saw that Angela was asleep and Paula was still watching television. I said hello to her quickly and went to our bedroom where Christine was reading a letter in bed. I crawled up next to her and gave her a kiss. I told her that I loved her and she said she loved me too. I went to the bathroom to brush my teeth and get undressed for the night and then I returned to our bed and slipped under the sheets. "How did your class go hon?" Christine asked.

"It went well. The students had a good night. We got a lot accomplished in understanding Huneo's theories and the effects they're having on the planet and I guess the rest of the galaxy or the universe. I mean who knows right now what's happening!" I said, in frustration.

"Are you alright, Jim?"

"I am, Christine, don't worry about me, I'll be alright."

"It's my job to worry about you, dear, and it's also my passion."

"I know, Christine but this thing has just gotten me out of sorts lately."

"You know hon, while you were in school, this Huneo theory stuff was all over the news. I mean it's been on every station and it seems to have spread all over the world." Christine told. Her eyes widened with concern. I could that tell she wanted to talk about this.

"What were they saying on the news, Christine?"

"They were saying that the calibrators are being built by everyone and that they're working like, Dr. Parkas said they would and then they were saying that this was potentially the culminating event of mankind sort of thing and that there was no way to know what was going to happen next. They also said that countries and scientists wanted to talk to, Dr. Parkas to see if they could get more information." Christine explained.

"Well, there is more and I just found that out tonight."

"What is it, Jim?"

"I hate to say this but this is all starting to seem so real after what you just said about the news reports. Huneo discovered tonight that the speed of time passing over the last ten days has increased by almost twenty five percent of what the last recordings were that were steady he said for almost a decade or longer. This frightened him enormously and now I'm starting to wonder myself, how bad of a situation are we in?"

"Jim, they said on the news that the President of the United States might make an address or statement or say something on this tomorrow night."

"Christine, this is very serious now I think."

"Jim, don't say that, you're scaring the shit out of me!" Christine said. She grabbed my arm and dug her nails into my skin. She had a look of fear in her eyes.

"I'm sorry sweetie, don't be scared, I'm here with you and I will stay with you." I held my love as close to me as I could and held her as tightly as I could. I could feel her clenching me to make sure I was there for her.

"We're going to have to be strong for this, Christine, you know that, eh?"

"Yes I know, I know, Jim." She whispered.

"We have to pray, Christine and we have to take care of our girls. That's our job."

"I know, I know." She said, softly. I held her tightly.

"This is going to be the biggest test of our lives I think, Christine. It's going to be the biggest test of everybody's life. We have to be strong and not jump to conclusions, or let rumors or hearsay lead us in the wrong directions. We have to try to take advantage of the knowledge of the science that is propagating this phenomenon for the sake of our kids, our family, our friends and this town and lastly ourselves."

"I know, Jim, I know. I'll be strong, but it scares me what's happening. It's like God is mad at us and he's going to end the world." Christine said, in angst.

"I know, Christine, I know, but we're living the way we were meant to live. We have nothing to fear, Christine. We have nothing to fear. God loves us and God will always be with us, remember that, and we will remind ourselves of that all the time."

"I will sweetheart, I will." Christine replied. We embraced until she became sleepy. Christine started yawning and then she slowly fell asleep in a few short breaths. I gently laid her on her pillow and kissed her goodnight. I then got up to check on the girls to see if they were where they should be. I went to their rooms and Paula was listening to her rock and roll CD's. Angela was in her room and she was fast asleep. She had a smile on her face. I turned her light off and then I went downstairs to fix myself a snack. I saw Cindy staring at me so I decided to sit with her and share my food. Cindy was hungry and gobbled her eats in a few seconds as I ate slowly and savored my food. After my snack, I finally got tired and went to sleep thinking that in the morning this would all be gone and life would be back to normal as it had been in the past. Alas though, I knew deep down, this was not going to happen.

INTO THE FRAY

I BREATHED IN DEEPLY and then out. I was awake and it was, Thursday, March 26, 2012. I felt warm inside and good this morning. I turned over and I saw Christine curled up in the fetal position. She looked contented but cold. I had pulled the blankets from her in the night, so I covered her and then hugged her as she came around and then dozed off again. I let her get all the rest she needed. I got up quietly, tiptoed into the bathroom, and then went downstairs for breakfast. I was the first one up or so I thought. "Oh, good morning, Angela, sweetie, I didn't know you were up. What are you doing up so early my dear?" I asked her.

"I couldn't sleep, Dad, my mind's been racing and keeping me up." my young girl said. She yawned. I looked at her in her pajamas and t-shirt and I noticed that she was starting to show. There was a noticeable tummy starting to appear and she looked beautiful my first-born girl.

"Is there anything I could help you with, Angela?" I asked.

"Well, Dad, I just hear people talking about, Professor Parkas and his theories, and my friends and I are wondering what's happening and if everything is going to be alright. And I'm pregnant, and it worries me that a lot of people are talking about this and not a lot of us understand these concepts," she stated. She had a concerned tone.

"Do you understand what, Dr. Parkas' theories are about?"

"I think so, Dad. I know he's talking about our time is passing the same amount, that the same amount of time is passing and as time goes on, the same amount of time is passing faster."

"Yes, I think you have it sweetie, you seem to understand the main gist of the theory."

"Yes, I think I do, I know I do."

"Dad?"

"Yes, dear?"

"Dad, when I understood the theory, I understood it right away, it came to me instantly." Angela stated.

"Well that's good, Angela."

"Dad, after I understood it, things seemed to change for me, everything changed."

"How do you mean changed?"

"Well, I don't know how to describe it, Dad. It was as if the whole world changed when I understood it. Everything changed, I mean even the sky wasn't the same anymore and I wasn't living in the same world any longer and I felt sick but I knew nothing was wrong or I thought nothing was wrong." she explained. I listened to her intently.

"Are you sure this just isn't your pregnancy and morning sickness and the change in your moods?"

"No Dad, I know all that stuff and it's not the same, it's something different. I'm not sure really how to describe it."

"Is it bothering you a lot?"

"It's not bothering me as much as it's just on my mind most of the time," she said.

"How about your sister, Paula?"

"Paula?"

"How does she feel about this?"

"Hah, Dad, Paula's in another world! She pays no attention to this. She's just on a quest to have fun and see what she can get away with." Angela said. She laughed while thinking of her.

"Yeah, I guess she's not one to be too concerned about the immediate world around her these days." I said. I chuckled.

"I wish I was more like her, Dad."

"Footloose and fancy free, I wish I had a bit more of that in me too." I said. I stared into Angela's eyes.

"Dad, what is it?"

"Oh nothing, sweetie, you know your mother and I love you very much don't you?"

"Yes Dad, I love you too."

"Well, well, well! What about me? Doesn't anybody love me?" Christine exclaimed, as she popped around the corner.

"Mom, yes of course! I love you too."

"I wish I could put into words how much I love you my dear daughter but I think in a matter of a little while you'll know what a mother's love is." Christine said. She gave Angela a big hug and a kiss. We sat down and talked for a while as we woke up and said what our daily itineraries were.

"What's going on?" Paula said. She stuck her head around the corner with her eyes half open and her pajamas disheveled. She was still half-asleep.

"We're telling each other how much we love each other, are you going to join us?" Christine asked.

"Yes, Mom."

"Come here, Paula." Christine commanded. Paula went over and Christine grabbed her and gave her a wild hug and kiss. Angela and I laughed as Paula struggled in her mother's grips.

"Moooom!" Paula whined. Christine let her go and said that she loved her as we each told Paula that we loved her. All were awake and in good spirits so the hustle and bustle of another day began. I turned on the radio and then I went to get ready for work. As I dressed, the 7:30 am news came on and the headlines were announced. "SOLTES calibrators from four different countries confirm the NE/TL theories.

The successful operation of the devices confirms the acceleration of time speed," a reporter rattled off. The reporter went on to announce the discoverer and inventor of the calibrator. He reported how this news was traveling rapidly around the world. Things could not be more obvious as I thought that the planet was in serious trouble and time was something we did not have to fool around with any longer. I could hear the girls downstairs talking about these reports. I could hear their concerns, especially Angela's, and her concern for her unborn child.

I knew that the vast majority of the human population on earth did not understand this theorem and that education was going to be crucial for them in comprehending this astrophysics event. The people of the world would have to learn quickly because of the extraordinary nature of the problem. I dressed swiftly and decided to leave for work right away. I said goodbye to Christine and my girls. I gave them a big kiss along with a hug each and told them I would be home early to help make dinner. As I drove into Park Falls, I thought to myself how unreal this all seemed but I knew it was happening. Much of what Huneo had said in his first lecture made sense to me about how the world had changed psychologically as well as how the need for going faster along with the loss of patience around the world was one of the factors that were part of the effect. I could feel it myself, that there was not enough time in the day any longer. It was only a few short years ago that I seemed to have all the time in the world. I never rushed for anything. I thought of how the Pegasus Effect would cause the electrical impulses of the neurons in the brain to fire faster in our compressed time passing. This would account for the higher intelligence in humans and the remarkable gains in technology based science we have had in the past twenty years. I could see the need it caused in people and that the higher level of wanting and greed had caused a Sodom and Gomorrah effect. People throughout the world seemed to have become immoral and less caring of their fellow man, like life had become not worth caring about any longer. As I got closer to town, I noticed that there were many news crews from outside the area driving around. No doubt, these news people would find their way to the university and well I guess they would be looking for Dr. Huneo Parkas. I could see the town was bustling that morning with more traffic than usual. The symposium was in its final days and the final lecture would be Huneo's the following day at 12:30 pm. There would be a few important lectures on this day, but none I could imagine would come close to the importance of Huneo's lecture. I remembered that the first thing I had to do that morning was to go to Marnie's office and apologize for my brushing her off on Tuesday. I knew that she did not take kindly to her subordinates being lacking in integrity. Moreover, tardiness and missing appointments fit right into that category. I pulled into my parking spot. I noticed that for the time of day the university parking lot was almost full, which was unusual. I went to my office and Sandy was already working. I said good morning and engaged her in some small talk. I then asked her if she would try to get me a morning appointment with Marnie, but to make sure it did not conflict with my schedule. She said I had an appointment in twenty minutes. Well, here goes, I thought. I proceeded into my office to get settled. I heard one of my subordinates enter and I called him into my office. It was Larry Butler. "Larry, come in." I beckoned.

"Hi Jim, how's it going?" he asked, sheepishly. He sauntered into my office.

"Hey, I haven't seen you or Henry Ling in weeks it seems. What are you guys doing? Are you avoiding me?" I asked. I was quite serious about this. "So what's going on?" I asked, again.

"Well Jim, like you, we've been very busy. I've been working till 8:00 pm most nights and so has Henry. We've been taking on a lot of work with this symposium. I thought you knew that?" He explained.

"Well if that's the case, Larry, I'm sorry. I've been busy myself and I haven't had time to keep in touch with you guys. So we're going to have to at least try to communicate a little better." I told him.

"Okay Jim, we'll make the effort in future." Larry replied.

"Thanks, Larry. Say listen, Larry, I'm going to see, Marnie to catch a bit of hell, so if there's anything we need in the meantime, in the department, I can ask her for it while I'm there?"

"All I can think of is office supplies, Jim. Everybody's running low on office supplies."

"Alright Larry, I'll bring it up. I better get going, if I'm late again, well you know."

"Okay Jim, I'll catch up with you later then."

"Alright Larry, I'll see you later." I walked out the door and rushed down the corridor and up to Marnie's office. I came into the reception area and her secretary ushered me directly into her office.

"Have a seat, Professor Reynolds, Mrs. Greene will be with you momentarily." her secretary offered. I took a seat in Marnie's office. I became nervous. The walls hung diplomas and photos in large wooden frames. Marnie Greene had graduated university with a Masters degree in business and she was a shrewd investor from what I had heard told. Marnie entered. "Well, well, well, if it isn't the late, Professor James Reynolds." Marnie commented, with a sneer.

"I'm sorry Marnie; I apologize for missing my appointment with you the other day. I have no excuse. I just forgot about it, Marnie, I'm sorry." I blurted out. I tried to apologize.

"Jim, Jim it's alright! Listen Jim, I got busy myself and I wouldn't have had that much time for us, so don't worry about it. So how are, Christine and your lovely daughters doing these days?" she asked, with a smile.

"Oh, they're doing just fine, Marnie. The girls are doing well in school and, Christine; well she's planning to open up another hair dressing salon in the new mall, so we're excited about that."

"So what about you, Jim?"

"Well to tell you the truth, Marnie, I've been going through the ringer with the big announcement made at our school as of late."

"You mean the, Dr. Parkas affair?"

"Yes, yes it's quite a revelation for us, quite a revelation for the whole world."

"Yes, I know, Jim. It's kept me up a few nights over the last little while and I agree with you. We're facing a real global dilemma here. So what do you think will come of all this theory stuff?"

"Well, Marnie, we've got to remember that it's not just theory anymore, it's the real deal now that it's been proven."

"Alas that is true, Jim, but I think we should take things slow for the sake of the school. We're going to be in the spotlight over the next few days and I've given permission to several news organizations to attend the last lecture of, Dr. Huneo Parkas. I've also given permission to dignitaries and special envoys as well as representatives of about twenty different governments and who knows who else might show up." Marnie stated. She paused for a sip of tea. "Listen, Jim, the lecture is in the main auditorium and we're going to beef up security just to give you a heads up. I think we're going to have a lot of people show up and we'll probably have some pushing and shoving. So just be aware, Jim and spread the word, easy does it." Marnie requested.

"You think it's going to be like that?"

"Jim, you know as well as I do that when we fill the auditorium it's always mayhem. Our students are okay until their in a large group and then we have to babysit. And that, Jim, brings me to my next item of business, babysitting."

"How's that, Marnie?" I was perplexed.

"Well correct me if I'm wrong, Jim, but through the grapevine or the ivy, whichever the case may be, I've heard that you're going to be a future babysitter yourself, is that right?" Marnie asked. She had a devious smile and a wink in her eye. I laughed and then Marnie laughed as she was trying to tease me.

"Yes Marnie, I am. It was a big surprise for us I can tell you that. Christine and I were in shock for a few days over that." I told her.

"Well that's what we humans do, eh, Jim, we have babies."

"Yeah, but I thought that it would be..."

"I know what you thought, Jim but you'll get over it. Congratulations by the way."

"Thanks, Marnie, I appreciate that."

"Huh, Grandpa." she said. She shook her head and we laughed again.

"Well, Jim, that just about wraps things up. Is everything else all right? How about your students, Jim, how are they doing?"

"Everything's good and on schedule or was on schedule. This NE/ TL stuff has the students by the tail. It's got all of us by the tail."

"Well let's try to stick to the curriculum, Jim and not miss anymore appointments, alright?"

"Sounds good, Marnie, I'll certainly do my best." I replied.

Marnie and I talked for a while longer as I got a few more heads ups and then our meeting was over in the blink of an eye. I guess being university president you get accustomed to getting out of meetings as fast as she does. I left her office and decided to go downstairs to see if Bernie was around. As I headed down to the basement, I passed by the main auditorium as news people were already setting up their equipment. There had to be a hundred and fifty people there already. I saw that it was going to be an intense lecture. I finally made it down to Bernie's office and he was not there. However, a note on the door informed me that he would be back in one hour. I went back to my office and started my prep work and then I tended to teaching my classes. My morning went well. I had my first year students again. They were an outlet for me with their naiveté and carefree ways. It is funny how as we grow older we become wiser and more serious about our lives and we lose a sense of naiveté that kept us wide-eyed and fancy-free. We seemed to lose a God given innocence that shielded us from the rest of the world. After my classes, we had a staff meeting and we discussed the events of the past few weeks. I got the staff's input and expressed my views on the matters of the day, which seemed to be about the same. Our world was in a dire predicament of an unstoppable nature and we may be doomed by this astronomical event. We agreed that as physicists, this was the nature of our situation and realization was the hardest part. Sandy, Larry, Henry and I agreed to be supportive of each other and to try to overcome any obstacles that may arise because of this event. We had a few coffees and a few laughs as we tried to make the best of the situation, which up to that point, was not too unsettling. After an hour, we decided to end our powwow and each go about our own business. Larry and Henry have been teaching their classes regularly and on top of this, they have been putting in many extra hours with our invited guests at the symposium. This was something I had neglected to do due to my closeness with Huneo Parkas and recent events. Sandy, my secretary had been doing a bang up job in coordinating our schedules and keeping the office running smoothly, all the while the university was in a state of turmoil with the current events that surrounded us. I was impressed with the jobs my subordinates had been doing and perhaps a little disappointed in my own performance or lack thereof. In any case, I was resolved to try my best in the future. Everybody in the faculty by the appearance of things would be attending tomorrow's lecture of Dr. Huneo Parkas' in the main auditorium. This was a much-anticipated event I must say, to say the least. I would spend the rest of the day having lunch alone and teaching my third year students who had just as many questions as my fifth year students. It seemed to be a grueling afternoon and when my classes were done, I was ready to go home and get some rest and relaxation away from the school and everything else that was on my mind. I finally got to leave as it seemed like I was one of the last teachers left on campus. I hopped in my car and drove home. Along the way, I saw a little flower stand and I decided to buy some flowers for Christine. We could put them on the dinner table and admire them while we ate our supper tonight. The air was fresh and I was getting tired as I drove home. After twenty minutes, I was home, it looked like a full house and that was a welcome sight. I pulled in and turned off my car. Christine came out to greet me. I received a big hug and kiss. "I haven't seen you in a while stranger, do you want lie down by my side stranger and rest your weary bones with me?" she said, with a come-hither look. She smiled. The fresh wind blew through her hair as it audibly wafted through the trees. It was at that point I felt contentment come over me that I do not believe I had felt before. I could have passed out in her arms I was so entranced. I was home, I was with the ones I loved most in the whole universe and I was happy. After a few minutes of embracing, she gazed into my eyes and spoke softly. "Jim, are you okay?" she asked. Christine had concern in her eyes.

"Yes Christine, I am, I am, I'm with you and I'm okay, don't worry." I responded. I guess I got a little dreamy and sleepy. I shook my head and yawned. I took the flowers out of the car and presented them to her.

"Oh, Jim, thanks so much, these are beautiful. Let's go in the house and I'll put them on the table for supper." We walked into the house and sat down for dinner. We had chicken legs for our meal, one of my favorites, along with potatoes and salad. The dinner was mouthwatering and succulent and we enjoyed the meal. Angela was especially hungry now that she was eating for two. Paula was a fussy eater but she liked the chicken especially the way her mother cooked it. After dinner, I was exhausted. Christine and I decided that we would go to bed early and get a good night sleep. Christine by chance was also exhausted, so we were in a perfect synchronization with each other that evening. The girls did whatever they wanted and we tried to stay up as late as we could but around 8:30 PM, we decided to go to bed. We staggered up to our room. We were so tired. We laughed and tried to hold one another up. It was quite comical. Our girls thought it was embarrassing but I guess that was a parent's job sometimes to embarrass their children to teach them humility. We went into our bedroom and undressed and when we got into bed we said our "I love you's" and as our heads hit the pillows we were asleep. That was it for our evening.

Friday March 27th, 2012 arrived. I awakened. It was a big morning for me, for my family and the world. Christine was already up and downstairs cooking breakfast by the sounds of the pots and pans. I could hear the murmur of my daughters bickering quietly. I supposed they were trying not to wake me. I arose slowly and had the remnants of the previous day's exhaustion in my muscles and bones. I washed and got dressed and went downstairs to start the day. "Good Morning my love!" I sang, to Christine.

"Hi hon, did you sleep well? Do you want some bacon and eggs?" Christine asked, in her soft feminine tones. This was welcome to my ears early on that morning.

"Yes my dear, I'm famished. Could I have a coffee too please?"

"Sure, you know where your cups are, dear." I retrieved a cup. I sat down, put sugar in my coffee, and begin to stir.

"Christine, today is, Huneo's big lecture. Would you be interested in going with me to the auditorium today, hon?"

"You know, Jim I think I might just do that. I haven't been to Sherman P. in a long time. I think it would be interesting. Can you get me in if I go?" she asked.

"I sure can babe. It's going to be a helluva show, I think, the way it's getting hyped."

"I'll be there for sure then. What time do you want me to be there?"

"It starts at 12:35 pm sharp so come at around 11:00 am and we can have a nice lunch together in my office."

"Okay, I'll come to your office at 11:00 am." Christine said. Paula walked into the kitchen.

"Hi Mom, hi Dad."

"How are you this morning, Paula?"

"Fine, Dad. We're going to the river today on a field trip for science." Paula announced. She wiped the sleep from her eyes.

"What are you going to do at the river?"

"We're going to collect samples of rocks and trees to bring back to the classroom to study."

"That sounds like an interesting and fun trip, Paula. Do you need anything from us?"

"I need money for lunch and shopping."

"Shopping? I thought you were going to the river?"

"Daaad! We're going to the mall too!"

"Jim, can you give her thirty dollars please, I promised her." Christine requested.

"Thirty dollars! What are you buying, a new car?"

"Daaaad!" she whined.

"Alright, alright!" I exclaimed. I gave her the money and told her that she had to eat a good breakfast before going to the river. "Paula, could you go upstairs and call your sister for breakfast please?" Paula left to fetch Angela. "My God, those girls are growing up fast, eh, Christine?"

"They sure are, aren't they?" Christine replied. The smell of bacon and eggs permeated our home. I sat and watched Christine cook. I looked out the window at the spring season rolling in. Angela and Paula came down and we sat together and watched their mom cook breakfast.

"Do you want some bacon and eggs, Angela? Are you feeling well this morning?"

"Yeah Mom, please! I'm hungry like a lion this morning!"

"Well you do feel good don't you. Don't eat too much though dear, you'll get bloated." Christine suggested. She began to serve the girls their breakfasts and they started to eat. They seemed hungry this morning that was for sure. Anyhow, we got to talking about the weekend as Paula and Angela shared their plans. It was certainly nice to have a big breakfast together on a workday. Angela planned to be with her friends and her boyfriend and Paula planned to go to the mall and the movies again. They were carefree that day and I was happy for that fact. My girls were at the age where they should be having all the fun they could. After breakfast, they helped their mother clean up. I went upstairs and got ready for work. I dressed in a hurry and I had to get moving for class. I said goodbye to everyone and confirmed with Christine our lunch date and going to the symposium together. Next, I thought, Christine had not been to the university in a long while. Perhaps six or seven years, I surmised. I would have to show her around again. I walked downstairs and pet Cindy. I snuck her some leftover bacon and then I was on my way. It was sunny and warm outside and as I walked to my car, it seemed to me that everything had changed. I got in my car and drove off and I had this strange feeling come over me. Again, everything seemed different. The sky seemed different, like it was not the same sky, and the air seemed different, like it was not the same air. I don't know what it was, but I recalled what my daughter Angela said to me the previous day about the way she felt. I thought she had described the way I was feeling. I could not figure out what it was but something was definitely different. I kept on driving. I wondered exactly what was going on with the feeling I was experiencing. After a while, the feeling abated. I headed straight for the university because I was running late. The traffic in town was the worst I had ever seen it and it looked like I would not make my first class if I could not get around the cars ahead of me. I took a side street and found a hole that I could drive through to get to the university. I made it there in time. I arrived at my office and greeted my staff. I then grabbed my books and ran to my first class. My early class again was my first year students and they were sitting waiting for me. I greeted them and they responded in kind. I told them that we would get started immediately. Right off, one of my students, Shauna Binns, raised her hand. "What is it Shauna?" I asked.

"Yes, Professor Reynolds. We were talking before you got here and we were talking about something we had heard of, Pegasus project, could you tell us what that is Professor?" she asked. 'Oh well,' I thought. I was going to have to sit down and explain Huneo's theory to the students. I began to explain Pegasus Project to the class. I realized that it was important that as many people as possible understand the phenomenon as soon as they could. People had to spread the word from person to person so as many people as possible would come to know and understand that a great event was occurring in our current times. I made sure I told the class every detail so they understood it well and I encouraged them to go to the auditorium for 12:30 pm for Dr. Huneo Parkas' lecture. The class was awestruck as they were in a bit of shock. They did not seem to know any of this before that class, not even from news reports. I told them that their homework assignment was to write a two thousand-word essay on their understanding of the NE/TL effect and have it ready for their next class on the Tuesday of the following week. We would then discuss the topic in finer detail. I surmised, this would be one of the best introductions to physics the students could receive. After a short while conversing with them and addressing some of their concerns, I dismissed the class and the rest of my day was free. This was the last day of the symposium. I had cleared my schedule and cancelled the remainder of my classes. I decided to go down to Bernie's office and see if he was in. I arrived at his office and I knocked, the door was open and he invited me in. "Hey Jim, come in, how are you?" Bernie asked.

"Not too bad, Bernie, I haven't seen you in a few days."

"You missed me, Jim?"

"Yeah, Bern, I did. So how about you, how are you?"

"I'm good, Jim, I'm good."

"Are you going to the big lecture today, Bernie?"

"You bet, I think that this'll be the most important lecture that we'll have ever attended." He stated.

"That important you think?"

"I think it will be, Jim, I can't think of anything more important in our lives right now besides this, can you?"

"Not really I guess, Bernie." I replied, shaking my head. "Christine is coming today, Bernie, and I think we'll try to get there a half hour early and sit near the top middle of the auditorium. So if you want to find us or come and sit with us, Bernie, I'll save you a seat at the top."

"Alright Jim, I'll try to sit with you. I'll try to get there for noon too,"

"Good Bernie, we'll be waiting for you. So Bern how's that canoe you were building coming along?"

"I had to stop building it, Jim. I just don't have the time these days being with, Stella and the circumstances going on at the moment."

"I don't blame you. I've been swamped myself. You know it's funny, Bernie. This theory dictates that our time is speeding up just as we're complaining that we don't have enough time in our lives. Do you think there's a connection?"

"I think there's a connection indeed, Jim, I most certainly do." he answered. I did not expect that answer. We talked for a while longer and our talk was somber. After that, we lightened up. I then left as we agreed to meet in the auditorium later that day. It was 10:00 am and the time was coming for Huneo's lecture and the closing events for the last day of the symposium. I went to the cafeteria on the way to get lunch for Christine and me. I found a complete chicken dish, the last one, so I picked that up, brought it back to my office, put it in our mini fridge, and waited for Christine to arrive. I was getting anxious and impatient with anticipation. The office was empty so I turned on my radio and listened to some soft music from a classical radio station. This seemed to calm me. I began to feel better. I peered out the window and looked toward the side of the campus at a large field that was unused when the feeling I had earlier came back and I felt strange again. I felt like I was in a different world and that nothing was the same any longer. I found this feeling hard to describe because there was also a serene feeling that went along with this sensation of being in a new and different place. I felt like I was in a different world. After some time, the feeling abated again. I made a mental note to talk with Angela about this over the weekend.

A knock came at the door and it was Christine. "Come in sweet-heart, come in and sit down, sweetie." I greeted her.

"Hi hon, I brought you some desert. I hope you have a sweet tooth today. So, how are things lover?" she asked. Christine was in a cheery and upbeat mood.

"Oh, not too bad." I replied. Christine put her bags down and sat on the couch in my office. She stretched out and made herself comfortable.

"I just had strangest feeling today, Christine. I had a feeling like everything was different in the universe." I told her, "I mean that's the only way I can describe it. I've had this feeling a few times today and it sure is a strange one. I've never felt this way before and Angela seems to have had the same feelings too." I explained.

"Jeez Jim, what do you think it is?"

"I don't know, but I don't think it's anything to worry about."

"Maybe you're having sympathy pains for, Angela's pregnancy?" Christine proselytized.

"I don't know, you may be right, Christine. Anyway let's eat." I replied. Christine's answer to my quandary made me laugh at its suggestion.

"Okay." she said. I went to the fridge and got the chicken entrée.

"So?"

"Yes, Jim?"

"What do you think of the university, you haven't been here in years?"

"Oh, it's so much different than I remember. I had to ask someone how to get to your office. I don't really remember any of this area."

"Well, there's been a lot of work done and a lot of the inside has been reorganized or renovated."

"I'll say!" Christine replied. She wasted no time digging into her chicken.

"Hungry, hon?"

"I'll say. If you hadn't noticed, Jim, I didn't have too much to eat this morning."

"I did notice that my dear."

"So do you like it?" I asked.

"Like what?"

"The university and the new additions?"

"Oh yeah, yeah they look great hon." she replied, in a devil may care way. We ate voraciously until the chicken was gone and then we started in on the dessert. It was chocolate cake with chocolate sauce. This was my favorite.

"Oh boy, Christine, this is good, this is delicious, thanks hon."

"You're welcome, Jim." We smiled at one another as we ate. I savored the chocolate. We talked for a while longer and then I realized it was 12:05 pm.

"Oh my goodness, Christine! Finish up. We have to go to the auditorium." I said, frantically.

"Alright, alright, don't panic." Christine said. She became annoyed at my impatience.

"C'mon, Christine, finish eating please."

"I am I am!" She exclaimed. She then gave me an evil eye. I quickly threw everything in the garbage while she finished her meal.

"Okay let's go, Christine, grab your purse." I told her. I tried to rush her.

"What's the panic, it's only down the hallway isn't it?" she squawked.

"Yes, but it'll be busy, C'mon Christine, let's go!" I begged.

"Alright alright!" she growled.

As we went into the outer office, we could hear a clamoring. As we got out into the hallway, it was a sight. The halls were crowded to the hilt. Most people I had not seen before and the noise level was increasing. I could see that the auditorium doors were opening and people were starting to be let in. Flash bulbs were going off and the crowd was strained.

"Holy shit, this is wild!" Christine exclaimed.

"I know it is, eh?" I replied.

The amount of people as well as the people who did not look like they were from around our town was amazing. I could not believe the anticipatory mood that was in everybody's eyes. It was something I had never seen before in a crowd here. We started to file into a line going in and Christine and I shuffled along, going with the flow. As we got past the entry doors, the auditorium was filling quickly and there was electricity in the air. I started to see people I recognized. I saw many of my students. I saw the university president, Marnie Greene, sitting in the V.I.P. seats, reserved for her of course. I saw the presence of the local police including Paul Banks. He saw me and waved, I waved back.

"C'mon Christine, I see some good seats at the end of this row." I said. I tugged her by the hand and she gave me a cross look. We sat down.

"Sorry I'm so pushy, Christine, but I'm excited."

"Don't give it a second thought hon, I know this is important." She said. Sitting down we scanned the auditorium and it was almost full. I think just under four thousand people were here. This was your typical auditorium with the main stage being front and center and the school emblems and banners on top of the stage. In the front sections of the auditorium, news camera operators, reporters, and official looking people filled the area. There had to be five hundred of them. It was a good thing the auditorium was well sloped or we would have not been able to see the stage. There was an incessant clamoring and the noise level was high. I looked around for Bernie. However, I could not find him. Suddenly, Huneo Parkas and Helen Hamilton walked onto the stage and the clamor built to a fevered pitch. They sat down near the podium and waited as the time approached 12:35 pm and passed. Security guards and police stood posted in many places, especially around the stage. I was sure to deal with the invading media. I looked down at the stage. I could see both the remaining SOLTES calibrators, with various books and papers placed about. The audience seemed to settle and the situation became quieter. I saw Huneo on the stage. He looked composed as Helen did as well. The time ran past 12:45 pm and the lecture was not any closer to beginning. I looked over at Marnie Greene. She was conferring with one of her aids when abruptly, the aid walked briskly down to the stage and then up to the podium. She turned the microphone on and began to speak. "Good afternoon everyone, my name is, Sharon Roberts and I'm today's spokesperson for the university on this Friday the 3rd day of April, 2012, and I hope you are all feeling well today!" Sharon announced, as she opened the lecture, "Today is the last day of our, Symposium of the Sciences for Sherman Patterson University, 2012. Congratulations to everyone! We've had a very successful symposium this year. Our speakers were some of the world's leading minds in their fields and we thank them for their patience and hard work dedicated to making this a successful event. Today on the last day, on behalf of, University President Marnie Greene, we extend our sincerest thanks for again making this a successful event. In addition, of course without you this event would not be possible. With that said, we are coming to a close of this year's symposium with our last lecture. We know at the university the significance of this last speaker and the events that have unfolded over the past few days and weeks and for whatever the outcome, we will present our last guest. Ladies and gentleman, please welcome, Dr. Huneo L. Parkas, Astrophysicist." Sharon Roberts said. She then walked from the podium and returned to her seat. There was a subdued but respectful applause for Huneo as he stood up and walked to the microphone. You could hear a pin drop. The room became dead silent and all attention focused on Huneo Parkas and what he was about to say. Huneo began to speak.

"Good Afternoon and welcome to the last day of, Sherman Patterson University's bi-annual symposium. I want to thank the University for the Invitation and the opportunity to speak here and I also want to thank the faculty and students for the support and help they have provided me with over the past few weeks." Huneo said, as he expressed his gratitude. He paused. A few moments passed and then Huneo continued.

"You all have an idea of what I will speak about today. You all know about the SOLTES calibrators here on my right. The governments it seems and the scientific communities from around the world have built and tested the SOLTES calibrators and have found that in some countries so far, the calibrators are a functional and legitimate device. I know that the information that the calibrator yields is hard to embrace because of its very nature and that it's not a perceptible or tangible entity, as of yet. We know what the readings mean and that they put us in awe of what may be happening. The speeding up of time passing and the NE/TL theorem are the result of an event that is happening on a galactic or universal magnitude and it is happening on a scale of size and scope that humans cannot comprehend, by any means! I might add. What is happening is anybody's guess at this juncture." Huneo explained. He paused again and sipped on a glass of water. He adjusted his tie. After a few moments passed, he continued again.

"The calibrators are proving that a monumental shift is taking place in the velocity of our solar system while it is traveling throughout the galaxy or the universe. We are slowing down in velocity and time passing is speeding up. I believe that this occurrence is a happening from the realm of a divine providence. I didn't want speculate in this realm, however, if I were to quote scriptures, one that comes to mind is in, Matthew, in the new testament in The Horrible Thing and A Lesson from a Fig Tree. In Matthew chapter 24 verses 21 and 22, it reads in 21, this will be the worst time of suffering since the beginning of the world, and nothing terrible will ever happen again. And, in 22, if God doesn't make the time shorter, no one will be left alive. But because of God's chosen ones, he will make the time shorter." Huneo stated. The audience drew its breath and then one person called out to Huneo. "What do you mean by that?" The audience clamored.

"These are my own thoughts and I'm not stating these scriptures as facts or anything else." Huneo explained. The audience started talking amongst themselves. This statement also took Christine and me aback…what was he saying? I thought. Huneo continued. "I want to talk about the effects of this, in my opinion, that I believe are occurring or have occurred. I believe the first thing I noticed was the extinction of a number of small animal species for no apparent reason. I believe that in the smaller animal species, their central nervous systems cannot handle the increase in the speed of the electrical charges that occur in them as time speeds become faster, compared relatively to the speed of time passing twenty years ago. Therefore, the smaller species are dying off. Man is a biological organism and as time speed increases, our brains function in relationship to our brains function twenty years ago has sped up along with the aging process in comparison. In addition, with these processes and changes taking place in the human being, we in fact change in the evolutionary sense, in that we will evolve differently at different rates of speeds of time passing. I believe that the evolutionary process is affected by time speed changes, and by no doubt, this is a major affectation. In the past twenty years or thereabouts, our technological progress has exploded and we do not attribute this to anything in particular.

We called it the 'Technological Revolution' and we did not question why it was happening or whether or not something we may not have looked at was responsible. It was a giant leap in a short time frame… why?

The next anomaly I would like to talk about is the corruption of our behaviors, that being as serious an aberration as there is. Our first corrupted actions were the need for us to get things done faster and to go faster and the rage it produced over the passing years. It began seemingly with road rage then moved along to air rage and then to a global rage. Wherever we go, for the most part, our rage has become problematic. The effect on the human mind is almost a tangible change for us. We are changing and we are changing fast, too fast!" Huneo explained. The audience was silent and looked dumbfounded. Huneo continued. "I believe we are encountering neurological disorders because of this. As an example, an anomalous and increased amount of unnatural stuttering is occurring in everyday speech. This is beginning to be perceived by all people.

We are encountering an age where everything is becoming acceptable and we are going through a Sodom and Gomorrah effect, if you will. People are literally abandoning their moral bedrock with one taboo after another being brought down. There has been more moral degradation in the past twenty years than the first two thousand. The internet is a prime example of moral degradation gone rampant." Huneo stated. The audience gasped and started muttering. I looked at Christine and spoke. "This is incredible isn't it?"

"I don't know what to think, Jim. This is so wild." Christine replied. She had a stunned look in her eyes.

Huneo took a sip of water and continued again. "Physically, I can only speculate about the things that I think are attributable to this effect. One is the tighter configuration of rings in certain tree species showing some sort of evolution of the tree or its natural recording of time speed passing. The next is the amount of solar UV light we seem to be detecting as the Sun is burning faster as well. I know this is hard to digest but you will and you will know when you have because you will experience an effect that goes along with the realization of this event. People will manifest a feeling that everything has changed and a feeling that everything is different. People will feel that the sky is different and people will feel that the air is different and people will feel that the whole of the planet has changed. This effect comes along with the realization process of the NE/TL theorem. This is an aspect with relative connections to a 'Grand Unified Theorem', which governs our universe and is part of a divine realm. This is the way an astrophysicist or scientist may see how universal principals apply to our lives in a metaphysical sense. This effect will come over everyone who comes to the realization of these theories as they manifest, as they are happening to us, as I speak, and is only one of the many effects that will take place.

We are preoccupied as human beings with the need for greater speeds so much so that we fail to look in other directions as to what might be happening. For example, we do not look at the special theories governing the speed and propagation of light and how they relate to us in conceptual ways that we don't already understand. We know light's speed. We know how wondrous it is and that at the speed of light we have the effect of suspended animation. But, what if we were to have absolutely no velocity, no velocity for earth, or the solar system, around the galaxy, or throughout the universe, absolutely no velocity? It would make sense that we would have no time or all time would be consumed and everything would happen at the same time as it is crunched. I believe that this is a theory that Albert Einstein tried to perpetuate to the world community. This is what I believe. We look at stars more than 5 billion years old and more than 10 billion light years away and go 'Wow, look at those stars.' However, those stars are probably no longer there, they have lived their lives and died. Those stars no longer exist, so what does that say about the perimeters and parameters of our universe. Is it collapsing in on itself? Moreover, if it were, would we ever even know it? Hence, in the book of Matthew A lesson from a Fig Tree. Matthew 24 verse 34 and 35, in 34; I can promise you that some of the people of this generation will still be alive when all this happens. 35, the sky and the earth won't last forever, but my words will." Huneo stated, as he quoted The Holy Bible. The audience gasped and started muttering. Again, people called out to Huneo. "What do you mean by that? What are you talking about here?" I found the lecture restrained to that point. The reporters were active with their cameras flashing and their video cameras recording.

Huneo again sipped his water and continued. "I've gotten a little off topic but I will answer your questions at the end of the lecture, thank you. We are in flux on this planet and an anomaly engulfing probably vast regions of, or even all of interstellar space of some sort or another is affecting our time speed passing and it's that simple, simply put. Over the past few days, I've been reading the SOLTES calibrators. The calibrators tell me that our time speed is increasing, and if, and I'm sure they will, the scientific community will confirm these results. The only real important conclusion that can be drawn from this is that planet earth is in a heap of trouble and global extinction is now at hand!" Huneo exclaimed. The reporters jumped to their feet and started hollering questions at him. The auditorium broke into pandemonium. Police and security guards blocked the stairs to get onto the stage as the place went crazy. I saw Marnie Greene's aid run down to the stage and try to get through the reporters. I was shocked. I know I heard it before but now it was real and this was not a dream any longer. I looked at Christine "Can you believe this?" I said. She looked back at me.

"Is this true, Jim? Is what, Huneo is saying true, Jim? Is it true, Jim, tell me!" she begged. I saw her eyes dark with a frightened look. I could not lie to her or try to protect her.

"Yes Christine, it's true."

"Oh my God, Jim, Oh my God, Jim! What are we going to do?" Christine cried out. I grabbed her by the shoulders, hugged her, and told her that I did not know and that no one knew what to do. At that point, I looked back and saw that Marnie's assistant had made it onto the stage and was about to speak as the auditorium was in total chaos. "Quiet, quiet please! Everybody please! Everybody please be quiet!" The noise did not die down as the reporters where jostling each other and then abruptly a fight broke out between them. The security guards raced over and jumped on them to break them up as the assistant started yelling over the public address system. "Everybody calm down right now or this event is over! Everybody calm down! Please!" At that point, the audience became quiet as police arrested the three men that were fighting and whisked them away. The police took over at the P.A. system. It was Paul Banks and in a booming voice, he commanded to the audience, "Everybody calm down or this event is over right now and I am specifically talking to the media. Cease and desist or else!" He bellowed. He then stood silently. The audience became quiet. There was a pause as Paul stood there and watched over the room. After a few moments had passed, Paul handed the microphone back to Marnie's assistant. She came back to the podium and prepared to speak again. I noticed Huneo was no longer present and neither was Helen. The assistant Sharon Roberts then addressed the audience.

"Please everyone, I have a message." She said. Sharon paused for a few moments and the audience became quiet. "Dr. Huneo Parkas has decided to cut his lecture short because of this disruption. Dr. Parkas has determined that because he was close to the end of his presentation he would stop for the sake of having a peaceful end to the symposium. He has cancelled the question and answer session and said he would conduct one and only one press conference in the near future in our small auditorium open only to a select number of invitees. Dr. Parkas has asked me to extend his thanks for your coming to the lecture today and I would like to ask all of you for a nice round of applause for him and all our other speakers on this the final day of the Symposium at Sherman Patterson University for the Sciences. Thank you very much." Ms. Roberts stated. She finished her statement and walked away from the microphone. The audience offered a spontaneous applause. A number of reporters started to call out some questions that went unanswered and then the crowd dispersed and headed towards the exits. I looked at Christine and spoke. "Well we better leave hon, let's go to my office until things die down."

"Okay let's go." she replied. As we walked through the throngs of people, we heard them expressing their disbelief or we heard them wondering aloud. Wondering how they were going to deal with this revelation as well as wondering how the rest of the world would deal with the time speed changes. The people had a genuine sense of urgency and worry in their voices and looked upset. Christine and I reached my office. I unlocked it and we walked into the reception area and locked the door behind us. We then went into my office. "Whoa! What the hell? Huneo, how did you get in here?" I said, in shock. Christine flinched and gasped.

"Sorry to scare you, Jim. We had your secretary let us in. Helen and I needed a place to go where the reporters would not hound us. We were chased around by them most of the morning and we just wanted some peace." Huneo said.

"That's alright, Huneo. You just scared the hell out of us. We didn't expect anyone to be in my office, it's okay. How are you there, Helen?"

"I'm holding up, Professor Reynolds, but those reporters are pretty tenacious, I must say."

"From now on, Helen, call me, Jim, alright, at least when we're not in class." I requested.

"Thanks Professor, ah, I mean, Jim. Thanks."

"Mrs. Reynolds are you okay?" Huneo asked. I looked and saw that my love was looking pale. I rushed to her side. "Hon are you alright? Hon answer me, are you okay?" I beckoned unto her.

"Yes, yes Jim, I'm okay, I'm just overwhelmed by all this excitement. This is a lot of excitement for me in one day, more than I've had for a long time. I'll be okay, Jim." She answered. She began to regain some color.

"Are you sure, hon?"

"Yeah, I'm okay, Jim, I'm okay."

"Alright then hon, we'll sit down and take it easy for awhile." I said, "Huneo, what do you need to do?"

"Jim, I need a place to stay for tonight, Helen and me. We need a place that no one knows where we are, can you help us?"

"You can stay with us, Huneo. We have a spare room, is that okay for you?" I replied. I offered him the guest room at our house.

"That would be perfect. Jim and Christine, thanks very much."

"Is there anything else, Huneo?"

"For right now, Jim, no. Jim, I just want to lie down on your couch here for a while if you don't mind. Helen and I want to rest here for a bit." Huneo said. He and Helen looked rather haggard.

"Take your time, Huneo. We'll leave you here and you can come over to our house after you've rested. Please just lock the door behind you when you leave, alright?"

"Alright, Jim thanks. I'll do that for sure."

"We'll have dinner around 6:30 pm if you're interested? We'd love to have you." I offered.

"Thanks again, Jim, I think we will." Huneo replied. He laid down with Helen sitting beside him.

"Christine hon, I'll get my things and we'll head out and give them some privacy. Christine, are you doing alright hon?"

"I'm fine, Jim. I'm back to normal,"

"Alright, is there anything I can do for you?"

"No thanks, not right now, hon."

"Helen, is there anything you need?" Christine asked.

"No thanks, Mrs. Reynolds."

"Helen!"

"Sorry, I mean, Christine." Helen said. They laughed.

I gathered up my things and with stealth, we slipped out the side door, made our way to the parking lot and took off for home. It was starting to cloud over and cool off. I didn't know why but it seemed like a fitting end to that day.

As we drove, Christine was silent. I asked her if she wanted to talk. She was hesitant and quiet and she had a look like she had been betrayed on her face and then she spoke. "Jim?"

"Yes sweetheart?"

"Jim, what are we going to do about this? Are we all doomed?" she asked. She had a solemn demeanor.

"I don't know, Christine. I don't know how this will unfold or why it's happening but I think we're going to have to stick together as a family and deal with this thing together and not hide anything from each other. I think our next best course of action is that we're going to have to talk to the girls about this. It's important they know. And then next, we'll start to pray." I said. She did not respond.

"Alright." She said, eventually, and then as I was looking at her and looking at the road, she began to cry.

"Christine hon, don't cry. It's going to be okay hon, try not to cry sweetie." I said. I put my arm around her to comfort her.

"I'll cry if I want too," she retorted. She buried her head in her hands and wept. At this point, tears began to run down my cheeks as I saw that my love was so distressed. I tried to keep my eyes on the road. We drove along silently for the remainder of the ride home. I took a few deep breaths. I thought of how this was so unreal but it was happening, and I could not do anything about it. I could not do anything about it! As we arrived at our house that day, we gathered our wits about us in case the girls were home. We went into the house. Cindy jumped on Christine to greet her as I saw the smile return to her face. The girls were not yet home so we were able to talk before they arrived. We sat in the living room on our love seat with Cindy huddled beside us. We talked about what was happening and how we would explain this situation to Angela and Paula, our two beloved daughters. We would look for an opportune time that we could sit our girls down and have a talk with them about something that we did not know the outcome of ourselves. We talked about our lives together and life itself. We talked about how, that as people on this big blue planet, we were truly blessed. Our lives were, by all principles that were important to a human being, rich indeed. We agreed that the love in our family was the greatest of God's gifts and the only one that really mattered in our lives and situations. We talked for about an hour and a half and before we knew it, it was 4:00 pm and there was a knock at the door. It was Helen and Huneo and they looked tired. I let them in and I saw that they had brought a suitcase and a knapsack. I guessed they were going to stay for a few days. That was okay with us. I thought it would be fun to entertain for a time seeing it had been a while since we last had houseguests. I beckoned them to follow me into the guestroom. When just as I got the words out, Paula and Angela burst through the door. They had big smiles and shopping bags containing the trinkets and baubles from their excursion. Each stopped dead in their tracks when they saw Huneo and Helen, and their luggage on the floor. I wished I had Bernie's camera at that moment to capture the looks on their faces. It was priceless and funny. After they picked up their jaws from the floor and the looks of surprise departed from their faces, I introduced them to one another and then we continued with the house tour and bedroom assignment. It had been a long week and I could see that everybody wanted to rest and have some dinner. Huneo and Helen stayed in their room while Christine and I prepared the meal. Paula and Angela were in their rooms as we unwound. The weather was getting gloomy and I knew that it would be raining soon. It was the perfect weather for staying indoors, turning up the furnace and hunkering down for the evening. We decided to cook homemade spaghetti and salad for supper. I continued with the cooking while Christine went for a nap and a shower. Next, it would be my turn to shower when she took over from me. I felt despondent at this point in the day. I was a person who was in a good mood most of the time, although sometimes, I could get a little depressed. However, it always passed. After my shower, I felt better. I got dressed, headed downstairs and things were happening. Christine and Huneo were cooking and Helen was playing some music on the stereo. Angela and Paula watched television quietly in the living room. I came into the kitchen and offered up my culinary expertise, which they promptly rejected, so, I decided that if they did not want me to help, then I could just loaf around, which is exactly what I did. After another half hour, it was time to eat. We sat down in a festive mood and dug into some fantastic spaghetti and salad for dinner. We opened a nice bottle of red wine. It was delicious as everybody had two glasses except for Angela and Paula of course. When dinner was finished, I offered to do the dishes and got no resistance. I threw everything into the dishwasher and turned it on. It was time to relax again so we retired to the living room. Angela and Paula had plans to be with their friends and took to their separate endeavors in haste. They took the station wagon for their excursion that evening. Angela would drive Paula to the mall and then she would go to Christopher Helgeson's home and talk with their parent's about herself, Christopher and the soon to come baby. Therefore, it was just the adults. We decided to have a few drinks and maybe watch a movie on the DVD player. We had some movies we had not yet seen so I would read off the titles and a selection would be chosen by popular demand. As I fumbled through the DVD's, Christine made everybody a drink. We talked about the events of that day and Huneo explained how nervous he had become in the middle of his presentation.

"You know, Jim, I left the lecture because I thought I was going to be sick. I mean I was doing fine until everybody started yelling and then it dawned on me the impact of what I was saying to them and that got to me." Huneo explained.

"I was very scared! I thought I was going to cry." Helen added.

"Well, you're safe here so you can relax and just put your feet up." I said, to comfort them. They relived the day, which I believed was quite stressful for them. Christine came in with the drinks and we sat back. I continued on flipping through the DVD's and came across a comedy that was recent and looked entertaining. I suggested it to all as everybody agreed with the choice. Christine then turned on the television and set up the video machine. Huneo and Helen again thanked us for our hospitality. We were more than happy to have them as our esteemed houseguests and they could always help with the chores around the house I suggested, in jest. They laughed and looked like they were becoming more relaxed.

Christine turned on the television as an announcement concerning the upcoming 8:00 pm news was playing. I left this channel on for a few moments to catch the highlights of world events. As we sat enjoying ourselves, an anchor for the Canadian news appeared on the screen and began the broadcast. "Good evening ladies and gentlemen. Today, in stunning revelations of a scientific nature from Park Falls, Saskatchewan, there have been claims that humanity may be facing the worst natural disaster in its history. There is word of a natural disaster that potentially may spell the end to humanity and indeed all life on earth. This natural disaster now confirmed by most industrialized nations as an occurring astrophysics event of mammoth proportions. The natural phenomenon has to do with the speeding up of the passage of time and the catastrophic effects that it may have on our planet and the universe itself. Scientists from all nations are struggling to figure out what is happening and to see if there is a course of action that can be taken. At this time, we are about one hour and fifteen minutes away from an unscheduled press conference by the President of the United States and we will interrupt regularly scheduled programming to bring you this live event," the anchor stated. He pounded out these words as we sat taken aback by this report. I was not surprised however. "Well, Jim, I guess the proverbial you know what is hitting the fan now. This day was a long time in coming, but its here now." Huneo said.

"It's alright, Huneo, you can swear out them words."

"It's not my way, Jim," he said. Christine came into the room and sat down.

"Did he just say on the news what I think he said?" Christine asked.

"I'm afraid so my dear. He said what we didn't want to hear." I replied. The newsman continued.

"It has been confirmed in Saskatchewan, Canada today that the discoverer of the astronomical event, a Dr. Huneo L. Parkas, who gave a lecture at the Saskatchewan University in Park Falls also added suggestions of new parameters surrounding the event. Researchers, scientists, and governments from all over the globe are racing to find out exactly what is happening. So far, the public and civilian understanding of this event has not kept pace with the breaking speed at which this natural disaster is unfolding. There's speculation from all quarters that this is not just a natural event but something that is in a religious realm as well," the newscaster reported. I decided to check and see if this was the only channel playing this news at that time. As I switched the channels there were quick protests but they were silenced by the news that was coming through the television. Station after station was reporting the events that were transpiring leading up to the American President's press conference about an hour away.

"Are we going to watch the movie?" I asked, facetiously. Looks of seriousness permeated. "I'm only kidding. We'll have to watch this and the Presidents press conference. We'll save the movie for another time." I said, not realizing that it was going to be a long time indeed before I ever watched another movie, if ever again. We sat and watched as the newscasts showed their varied points of view and differing scenarios. We watched as they showed how this news was spreading to all corners of the globe and filtering into the masses. The problem with this natural disaster in the aspect of people understanding it was the complexity of the physics, although the physics was not that difficult. It was a matter of focusing, learning and understanding. It was also a matter of communicating it and getting it out there to the people. Next was the hard part. It was for me anyway, and that was the believing that this was actually happening part, which was no longer an issue for me.

"Jim."

"Yes, Huneo?"

"Jim, I have a little surprise for you," he said. Huneo displayed a devilish grin.

"Oh yeah, what's that, Huneo?"

"Jim, I have one of the SOLTES calibrators out in, Helen's car."

"What!"

"Yes, Jim, that's right. The school has had its use of it. I talked with Marnie Greene today, and she said that since this was probably the only remaining one left that I built that I could have it back. She said the school would not need it and I was welcome to it, seeing they already had the other one. The knowledge is out and they can easily be copied so it's a not so coveted a device any longer." Huneo explained.

"What are you going to do with it?" Christine asked.

"Well, I thought I would have a calibrator for myself and I could see with my own eyes how my invention works and what it will show me, good or bad."

"So where are you going to keep it, Huneo?" I inquired.

"Well, I thought I would keep it here for now if that's alright with you, Jim?"

"Sure, as long you show me how to operate the calibrator."

"Sure Jim. I'll give you a crash course."

"You know what; I have the perfect place for it."

"Where's that, Jim?"

"Out in my observatory, in the barn."

"Your observatory, Jim?" Huneo inquired. He looked amused.

"Yes Huneo, I have an observatory in my barn. I own a high-powered telescope that my family, friends, and I use. We could keep it out there if it can stand a few cold nights until the warmer weather comes."

"Will it be safe out there?"

"As safe as in the house, and I suppose we could chain it to a post, and the barn door has a heavy padlock on it."

"It'll stay dry?"

"It will, the barn is dry and there's a wood stove inside. We can heat the place up when we go out there."

"Sounds good to me, Jim, I think we've found a home for the calibrator." We sat back to relax again. Christine and Helen had left the room and sounded as if they were rummaging in the kitchen and having a few laughs. There was an announcement on the television. "Ladies and Gentleman stand by for the President of the United States," a news voice said. A shot of the pressroom in the White House, by the looks of things, was displayed on the screen. In the center was a podium with the Presidential seal and in the foreground, reporters were at the ready.

"Hon, the President is coming on now, come on in!" I called out.

"Alright dear we're coming!" Christine answered. Some dishes crashed and then there was the shuffling of feet as Helen and Christine appeared with a tray of snacks.

"Wow hon, this is great!"

"Yes, this is great, Christine, I'm still so hungry after the day we had, this looks so good!" Huneo said.

"Well, you're welcome guys, dig in!" Christine said.

"Eat well sweetie you deserve it." Helen cooed, to Huneo. She sat down, put her arms around him and then kissed him passionately. I still found this awkward, one of my students with a much older man. However, with things being the way they were this was not much to fret about, I mean really. A White House representative came up to the podium and began to speak. "Good evening ladies and gentleman and welcome to the White House. The President will be out in a moment and there will be a brief statement as well as a short question and answer period." The spokesperson stated. He then paused, held his hand to an earpiece, and listened for his next instructions. There was a stirring and then the pronouncement. "Ladies and Gentleman, the President of the United States." He announced. The President walked through a parted curtain and up to the podium and stood looking at the reporters. He took a pitcher from the podium and poured a glass of water. He took a few sips.

"He looks debonair." Christine commented.

"Yes he's handsome, isn't he?" Helen added. The President began to speak. "Good Evening my fellow Americans. I offer you my humblest greetings and my best wishes on this evening," he said, a long pause followed. After thirty seconds, he began to speak again. "It is with great trepidation that I have come to you this evening to make an announcement that nobody had ever conceived of, even in our wildest dreams. I'll get right to the point. It has come to the attention of this Government that a natural phenomenon, and that's the best way we can describe this to you, is occurring, and that this natural phenomenon is moving in the direction of becoming a global natural disaster. Much of the civilian masses around the world have heard of this but have not grasped the true nature of the science that pertains to it, leaving them not able to understand fully what is going on and what it means to them. We urge our population to become informed as soon as possible and others around the world to do so as well." The President stated, as he took a sip of water, "For those of you listening now who do not fully know what I am talking about. I am talking about the discovery of the fact that our planet is slowing down in the galaxy or our galaxy is slowing down in the universe for whatever reason and the effect this is having on the speed in which time passes. You must become informed! This is known as the Non-Existence/Time Loss effect or for short the NE/TL effect. An American astrophysicist named, Huneo L. Parkas and the device that he has invented that measures time in comparison to, has discovered this event. Our best scientists have confirmed that the event that is happening right now as I speak has been happening for at least fifteen years or longer! This is going to continue to happen as far as we can predict at an increasing rate into the unforeseeable future. As I have said, we have our best minds at work on this trying to figure out what exactly is going on and what we can do about it. We are also asking for input from anyone who may be able to help the world and its people with information that might shed light on what is happening. My fellow Americans, this is a very serious event indeed and I ask you not to panic and to live your normal lives the best you can. My fellow Americans, I did not think that I would ever have to make an announcement like this to you and would have done anything to make this not so. However, it is. I urge all of us in our future hours and days to see what we have and reach out to help anyone who is in need. I will inform you on a regular basis as your, President. I wish you a good evening and good days ahead and may God Bless you. I will take a few questions." The President said. He had concluded his statement and the press started hollering for their questions. "Mr. President, Mr. President, Mr. President!" they called out. "Yes, you in the second row, right there." The President retorted, as he pointed out a reporter. "Yes, Mr. President, Jake Durbin, Cable News Television. Mr. President, what steps are being taken to overcome the time loss effect?"

"Well, Jake we don't have any concrete steps or plans or contingencies to put into effect due to the very nature of this problem. This is completely new to us as it is to the whole of the world's population. We will try to inform the public at large the best we can and from here on in, we will be working around the clock to find the answers we need to know. Next."

"Mr. President, Mr. President!"

"Okay, you in the first row here, the young lady on the end."

"Yes, Mr. President. Julie Delorme, United News Service. Mr. President, could this happening be considered a potential extinction event?"

"For obvious reasons, Julie, that question cannot be answered fully or properly at this time. We have not had the time to decipher what is going on and what the ramifications might be, however, I will tell you this and that is we will hold nothing back from the population of this great nation or the rest of the world. What we find out and then come to conclusions thereof, we will report to the American public and the world post haste. This is not an American only problem. The world as a whole has an interest in what is at stake here. We will go at this problem all together and all for the common good. Thank you, Julie. I have time for one more," the President said.

"Mr. President, Mr. President!"

"Yes, one more, in the second last row, with the blue sweater."

"Yes Mr. President, Margaret Chin-Lau, Japanese Cable News, Tokyo. Mr. President, how much time do you estimate we have before the effect takes on a physical nature? Meaning, how much time do we have before we start becoming sick?"

"Margaret is it? I believe that is a loaded question and a bit unfair. We have no conclusive evidence real or otherwise that points directly at that scenario thus far and we will keep you informed as to what this government thinks. In the meantime, I expect that the fear mongering will be kept to a minimum in any case, for the good of the people of the world so as not to spread unsubstantiated rumors. We must remain responsible and this government will be watching that situation as well. Thank you for your questions, God Bless you and good night." the President said, and then he walked away from the podium. "Mr. President, Mr. President, Mr. President!" the press hounded. With the last question answered, the press conference was over and the camera panned away. The broadcast then returned to the news commentator.

"So what does everybody think?" I asked.

"It doesn't sound like they're any further ahead in their search for answers, Jim than anyone else. I guess they're just as baffled as I am as to what's going on." Huneo stated.

"I think they're just getting started in the search for the answers and I think that the astronomers are going to figure this thing out." Helen commented.

"I just want this to be over with, like it never happened." Christine said.

"I know you do sweetheart, we all wish that."

"We're all going to hang tough for each other and have patience." Huneo stated.

"Let's turn off the news, Jim and not talk about this for awhile, that's how we're going to have to live with this from now on." Christine said, "We have to put this out of our minds and not think about it." She added.

"Well, I don't know about that, Christine. I think we have to think of it a certain amount each day." I replied.

"It's a matter of balance and attitude." Huneo said.

"Can we not talk about this for the rest of the night?" Christine said. She had a sad look in her eyes."

"Sure sweetheart, okay we'll change the subject." With that said, we began talking about other things as the evening was almost over. Christine and Helen decided to go to bed and Huneo and I decided to stay up for a while and talk. We had a few more drinks and had a few laughs and we were not very serious, but we decided that the next morning we would take the SOLTES calibrator into the barn and set it up. We would chain it to one of the posts. Whether Huneo was here or not the calibrator would stay here at least for the immediate future. After this, we got a little drunk and ended up waking everybody in the house. After that, it was just a blur. However, I did remember going to bed.

As I awakened the next morning, I did not feel well and my head was pounding. I could hear that everybody was up and starting their day. Christine walked out of the bathroom and stared at me with cold eyes. "I hope you're not going to have a repeat performance of last night anytime soon! You behaved very badly last night, James Reynolds and that is not any way to show an example to our daughters!" Christine scolded. She had a tremble in her voice and angst in her eyes.

"What do you mean, Christine?"

"I mean you were drunk last night and you woke up the girls and went in their rooms and talked gibberish to them and then you came in here and you were very drunk and I didn't like it!" she said, angrily.

"I'm sorry, Christine, I won't do that again. Christine, I had too much to drink and I should have been more responsible. I'm very sorry hon, please forgive me." I begged.

"Yes, Jim, of course I forgive you."

"I won't do it again, Christine, I'm sorry."

"I know, Jim. It's okay. You know how much I don't like being around drunken people though."

"I know, Christine, I'm sorry."

"You tell, Angela and Paula you're sorry too." She demanded.

"Yes, I'll definitely tell them I'm sorry and ask for their forgiveness too."

"Okay then, what do you want for breakfast? I'm going to bang some pots and pans," Christine said. The smile came back to her face.

"Christine, could I have some bacon and eggs please, and some coffee and a few aspirin?"

"Headache eh! You're not going to throw up are you?" she asked, smiling at me.

"No, dear."

"I'll fix you up sweetie, don't worry." she said. She came over and gave me a kiss on the forehead.

"By the time you get washed and dressed your breakfast will be waiting for you, so get to it."

"Alright hon, I'll be down in a bit." I then proceeded to wash up.

When I came downstairs, I noticed the newspaper headlines. "President warns of impending disaster." I made a mental note to read this report as soon as I could. I walked into the kitchen, which sounded more like a party with Angela, Paula, Christine, Huneo, Helen and Cindy all in good moods, laughing and talking. I saw that Christine had held nothing back on breakfast. She had two large frying pans with steaks cooking, two toasters, and two dozen eggs at the ready. The girls were getting the plates and condiments prepared as it looked like Saturday was going to be a nice day if we could just enjoy ourselves. I sat down to have my morning coffee and greet everyone. "Listen, Angela and Paula, I want to talk to you later, okay?" I asked them.

"It's okay, Dad, you don't have to say anything." Angela said.

"Yeah, it's okay, Dad, we love you." Paula said. My girls forgave me.

"Thank you girls, I love you too." I said.

Well that was that then. We then proceeded to have one of the best breakfasts I had ever eaten. Huneo and Helen concurred and were thankful. The phone rang. Angela went to answer it as Huneo and I discussed putting the calibrator in the barn and me showing him around the homestead later on in that day. We started giving a shopping list of things Huneo and I might need to Christine and Helen who decided all the girls would go shopping and have lunch together along with partying the day away. I suggested we have our first barbeque of the year and everyone was hip to that idea. Right then, Angela walked back into the room with a stunned look in her then glossy eyes. She was not speaking. "What is it, Angela, is anything wrong?" I inquired. She looked at me and said nothing, "Who was that on the phone?" I asked, to no reply. Again, she stared at me.

"Angela, for God's sake answer your father, what is it? Angela!" Christine beckoned. In a small trembling voice Angela spoke.

"The nurse called from the hospital," she said.

"What is it, Angela?" her mother beckoned unto her.

"They said, Aunt Stella had another heart attack and she died!" Angela cried out.

"Oh no, oh my God, no no no!" Christine cried out.

"Oh no, no, are you sure that's right, Angela?" I asked.

"Yes, Dad." She then burst into tears.

Christine started crying and then Paula and then me. We went from being happy to being devastated in the blink of an eye that morning. I tried to comfort my girls in our grief. The girls and I wailed as we tried to comfort one another. We cried for what seemed like an eternity. Huneo and Helen could only watch in despair and sympathy with weepy eyes. We moved into the living room and sat down to try to gain some composure. We sat in the living room crying. Huneo and Helen asked if there was something they could do for us. I told them they could not do anything, except let us grieve. They expressed how much they were sorry. Huneo articulated how much he knew that I loved Bernie and Stella and how the whole family must have loved them. Huneo said that in the short time that he knew Bernie that he grew to become fond of him and respected him. Helen however, knew Stella more intimately and cried as Huneo tried to comfort her. They decided to go to their room and let us have some privacy together as a family. We sat in the living room and began to talk about Stella. After a while, we gained composure and stopped crying. We sat and talked about the last times we saw Stella. We talked about who she was and how well she got along with everyone. I told the girls not to bottle in any of their emotions. I told them that God wanted us to grieve. God wanted us to grieve openly and let out our feelings. We were taught that grief was love and this was how love was expressed in one's passing.

I let the girls know that grieving was not only for sadness but also for love to be shown for a person who has passed from their earthly bonds. I told them that we would see Stella again when we go to meet her. My thoughts then turned to Bernie. We had to put on our best faces and go down to the hospital and be with him in his time of grief and sorrow. I excused the girls from the first meeting with Bernie. I told them that their mother and I would go directly to the hospital. Christine and I went upstairs and got dressed to leave. We sobbed, as the house was quiet and solemn. As we dressed, I thought to myself about Stella and the years we had together and how she became part of our family along with Bernie. We were their extended family and the ones that provided them with a sense of young people to love and to be around. Stella was a joker and would often tease Paula and Angela. She was also a stern woman who put up with no impudence from others but most of all she was Christine's best friend. As I looked over at Christine, I saw that my wife was heartbroken and injured by this. I knew that I must be the pillar that she was going to have to lean on. After an hour or so, we were ready to leave for the hospital. The ride to the hospital was quiet. As I drove, Christine sobbed and cupped her face in her hands. "I know it hurts, Christine, I'm here for you." I said, softly.

"I know." she whispered. The day was beautiful and sunny. Not a day that you would expect the worst to happen but I guess weather really has nothing to do with death and passing. We arrived at the hospital and went to the front desk. We were directed to the morgue waiting room. Christine and I walked silently towards the morgue and that was when we saw Bernie sitting with his face buried in his hands. I walked up to him and put my hand on his shoulder, he turned, and his grief weathered face bursts into tears. He stood up and grabbed hold of me moaning and crying. Christine started crying. She came and put her arms around him. We just held him for the next twenty minutes as we grieved. We stayed at the hospital with Bernie for the next two hours while arrangements for Stella's transportation to the funeral home were put into place. We drove Bernie home after this and I stayed with him that evening as Christine took the car and went home to be with our girls. Over the next few days, I stayed close to Bernie and helped him with whatever his needs were as one of his brothers arrived in town to help and attend the funeral. Bernie had a number of family members who had come to town to pay their respects whom I had never met before. It was because of the sheer distance and availability that they did not come to Park Falls before then to visit. The next few days were surreal and passed in a dark haze. We attended the funeral and laid Stella Wakefield to rest. I decided to take a few days off from work and let my counterparts take my classes being that the symposium was over and we were getting back to normal at the university. Bernie seemed to be coping well with his loss but that was only on the outside. I knew how hard these things could be.

Bernie had his brother Michael staying with him and that seemed to suffice for the time being. Bernie and I had talked about how his grief would get better over time. He faced the deaths of loved ones before and knew he must let grief take its course. I was verifying this with him so it would give me some peace of mind as well. I went home to Christine and the kids and even though we were a family and lived together, it was as if I had gone away and was returning after a long absence. It was time to concentrate on their feelings of loss, especially my wife, Christine's. I was home again, where I should be. Huneo and Helen were still in our home of course but they were low key. The town of Park Falls became quiet after the symposium. It seemed like for the next few weeks life was rebuilding itself. We seemed to catch our breath and little by little, we started to get back to normal. The crying for Stella had calmed and we went on with our lives. It was mid April and Christine and I were sitting having morning coffee when Huneo and Helen walked in and sat down with us. They had big smiles on their faces. "Whoa! You guys look happy this morning, what's up?" Christine asked. They poured some coffee and sat down with us.

"Oh, not too much, how are you guys doing? Are you feeling better these days now that a few weeks have passed?" Helen asked, with a smile.

"We're doing okay. The big shock of, Stella's passing is easing up quite a bit, I must say. How about for you, hon?" I asked, Christine.

"I'm over the big shock of it, Helen, but it'll be a lifetime of remembrance for me." Christine replied, with a tear in her eye.

"So again what's up with you guys, you look so happy?"

"Well we found a house to move into and we're going to live together so we're going to move out on you guys!" Helen stated, with glee.

"Oh yeah, where?" I asked.

"It's about six miles from here near the big hills. We bought the house and we're going to move in right away." Helen said, with a smile. She hugged Huneo and kissed him as they embraced.

"Are your parent's okay with all this, Helen?" Christine asked.

"They gave us their blessing." Helen said.

"Their blessing?"

"Yes, they gave us their blessing because, Huneo asked for my hand and I said yes!"

"Said yes?" Christine retorted, perplexedly.

"Huneo and I are getting married!" Helen squealed.

"What? Oh my God! Congratulations! Are you really?" Christine asked. She looked shocked and surprised.

"Yup, we're getting married!" Helen exclaimed. Huneo and Helen laughed and kissed and then laughed some more.

"Congratulations, Huneo, congratulations, Helen or should I say, Mrs. Parkas!" I said.

"Thank you, Jim, thank you, Christine. Thanks very much, it's much appreciated." Huneo replied.

"Yes, thank you so much, Mr. And Mrs. Reynolds, you've done so much for us!" Helen expressed. She had a sheepish look in her eyes.

"Hey hey there, my girlfriend, what did I tell you, from now on it's, Jim and Christine." Christine said.

"Thanks, Christine." Helen responded.

"Congratulations again you guys." I said.

"Christine, I have something to ask you."

"Yes, Helen?"

"Well, in school I don't have many friends, and I don't relate well with a lot of the others in my class. I was pretty much a loner till now and I was wondering…"

"Yes, Helen what is it? Spit it out." Christine prodded, in anticipation.

"Would you be my, Maid of Honor at my wedding?"

"Oh my goodness, Helen, I never expected that. I never thought you would have ever asked me that." Christine said. She paused with a solemn look on her face. I looked at Helen. She had the look like someone who had just done something wrong. She sank into her chair.

Christine then turned to her and looked her straight in the eye. Helen cowered.

"Listen, Helen." Christine said, "I have considered your request and I have to say it would be my greatest honor and privilege to be your, Maid of Honor. Yes, Helen, I would be delighted!" Christine blurted. Helen jumped for joy and wrapped her arms around Christine. The tears began to roll down both their cheeks. Huneo and I laughed. I congratulated them again.

"I guess we're going to a wedding!" I exclaimed, with joy.

Paula and Angela rushed in and took us by surprise.

"What's going on down here?" Angela squawked. A look of concern was on both the girls' faces.

"Helen and Huneo have announced that they're getting married!" I told.

"Oh my God! Congratulations, congratulations!" Our girls cheered.

"Thank you, Paula and Angela."

"Yes, thank you, Paula and Angela, thank you very much." The Parkas' said. Everybody then sat down to a wedding announcement breakfast that just happened out of the blue. We sat, ate, and laughed as we told the girls about their mother being the Maid of Honor and they were ecstatic. Then Helen spoke up, again. "Paula and Angela would you like to be my brides maids?" Helen asked. Their eyes opened wide. "Yes, yes I will." they said, together. They squealed and laughed in delight, as everybody was happy and elated in the moment. It astonished me that we could wake up in the morning in a rather glum and depressed mood in dealing with our loss and in the span of minutes, unbridled happiness abounded, as there was joy and cheerfulness in our home once again. Angela got up and went to the refrigerator. She opened the door for something. All eyes were upon her. It was then I noticed why they were looking at her so intently. They were looking at my beautiful pregnant daughter. She had made a fuss that morning to look nice and she looked especially beautiful. That morning, Angela had a glowing aura and an angelic loveliness about her as everybody watched the beauty of a maturing young girl becoming a beautiful young woman right before his or her eyes. "Angela dear you look beautiful this morning, very beautiful." her mother complimented.

"You do, Angela, you look beautiful." Helen said.

"You're very pretty, Angela." Paula said, with a big smile for her sister.

"Thanks so much everyone, thank you." she said, with watering eyes. She then came over and hugged me, to my surprise.

"What are you hugging me for, Angela? I didn't say anything?"

"I could see the compliment you gave me in your eyes and your face, Dad. Thank you." Angela said.

"My goodness, your Dad's that obvious, am I?"

"Your heart is on your sleeve this morning, Dad."

"Well, you're welcome sweetie; I meant every part of that look." Everybody laughed. And, that's the way our morning went, happy and joyful and I thanked God for the blessing. The rest of our day went that way as well. That day being a Sunday, we went to church together and prayed for our blessings as we prayed for others that were less fortunate. That day was a turnaround for us in our grief that led to hope. However, not thinking because of our happiness and our human frailties of not having a long forethought, it was also the beginning of the world's nightmarish plunge into a global hell that was taking humanity to the brink. It did not hit me again until I picked up a paper the next day before class and read. "World's calibrators synchronized as time speeds increase!" This headline blazed across the front pages of Toronto's main newspaper. It was Monday, April 20, 2012. The natural disaster, the paper said, was taking on the mainstream name the "Pegasus Effect." Each day the newspapers were reporting the results from the calibrators and informing the citizens how the "Pegasus Effect" manifested itself. They would explain the mathematics involved as well as the astrophysics to the best of their abilities to try to get people to understand what was happening. The newspapers reported the suspected effects of the phenomenon and speculated on the future effects. I decided that I had to learn how to read the calibrator. I had to see for myself the increase in the time speed readings, but most of all I wanted to see the incremental rises and perhaps calculate how much time we had left. For this, I would need Huneo's help and I had one of his calibrators right here. I decided to wait until Huneo got up that morning and then I would find out what was going on with his calibrator. I was the first one up and I did not want to wake anyone else so I went, sat on the couch for a while, and ate a piece of cheese and toast. I laid back to rest and within minutes, I was fast asleep again.

I woke up about hour and a half later and everybody was being quiet as the gang was trying not to wake me up. I woke up to whispers and muffled laughter. I watched and listened to everyone for a few moments and then I got up and joined the gang for the morning ritual. The girls were about to leave for school and Christine was about to head off to work. Helen was also on her way to classes. This would be great. Huneo and I would have the house and the calibrator to ourselves. Huneo and I were eating as everyone left and then we were alone. "Huneo?" I inquired.

"Yes, Jim."

"Is your offer still open for the calibrator?"

"Oh yeah, I think I'm going to leave it here, Jim." He replied.

"Is it still in, Helen's car?"

"No Jim, actually it's in your barn in your observatory. I chained it to a post and locked your barn door. Until now, I was the only one who knew where it was except for, Helen of course plus your wife, Christine. She gave me the key to the barn so I could set it up. I put it up there myself when you were with, Bernie Wakefield. Is that alright?" Huneo asked.

"Yeah, Huneo, that's fine, that's okay. Huneo, I wanted to learn more about the calibrator and its readings and I was wondering if…"

"You want me to explain it to you and show you how it works" Huneo said, with a grin.

"Yes, yes exactly if you wouldn't mind doing that for me?"

"It's the least I can do, Jim. You know aside from, Helen, you and Christine are the closest friends I have now."

"Thanks, Huneo."

"It's my privilege, so when would you like to start, Jim? I guess I'm the teacher now, eh?"

"Hah, hah, yeah you're the teacher. Now I can sit and relax and learn from you."

"Well, would you like to start now?"

"I was hoping you were going to say that. That sounds pretty good to me."

"Well, let's finish up in here and then get our coats on and go out to the classroom."

"Alright Huneo, I'm ready to go." We finished our breakfasts and then proceeded out to the barn. Today was a sunny day and a little brisk, but it was not too cold. I thought I would bring Cindy out to the barn and give her a good dose of fresh air today. As we went into the barn, I mentioned to Huneo how much I wanted to get my telescope out and set up for the summer. We began to load up the wood stove. We loaded it up good because it would probably be the last burn of the year so it may as well be a good one. I lit it up and we could feel the heat from the stove almost immediately. Cindy started barking at the furnace in a puppy bark that was quite amusing. "Come on, Huneo, we'll go up and leave her down here, she'll be okay by herself." I said. Huneo concurred.

"How did you get the calibrator up here by yourself, Huneo?" The calibrator was a large enough device that he could not have climbed up the ladder with it alone.

"I had a rope in the trunk and, Helen found another rope over by your furnace. I lifted it while she held it steady with the other rope. It wasn't that hard to lift really."

"Yeah, that's the way I lift my telescope up here."

"You don't bring it out in the cold weather, Jim?"

"No, in the deep cold it can damage the small gears that rotate the barrel, but I think it's almost warm enough now to think about bringing it out."

"So how are you making out these days with the loss of, Stella, and your situation with, Bernie?" Huneo asked. He had a concerned tone.

"I think it'll take time, Huneo, but I know relief will come. We'll always have the memories and the love from now on and that's what's important."

"That's good, Jim. How's, Bernie making out?"

"Well, he's taking it pretty hard but that's to be expected. I'm going to check in on him and try to visit him every other day and I'll talk to his brother every now and then as well. He's here for another week, I think."

"Well, here we go, Jim, grab that end and we'll uncover it."

"Okay. Lift." I said. We uncovered the calibrator and then Huneo grabbed a rag and dusted it off.

I opened the observation hatches for my telescope to let some sunshine in and a little fresh air. I looked over the railing to check on Cindy. She was snooping around the barn.

"Good girl, Cindy, good girl!" I cooed. She looked at me as if I was crazy. I then threw her down a dog treat and went back to the calibrator with Huneo.

"I can feel the heat from that stove now, Jim."

"It takes a little while but you can get it nice and toasty in here. I put some bales of hay in some strategic locations around the barn for some insulation here and there. I also have a few double walls with dead air spaces so I can get it pretty warm in here when I want to."

"Alright Jim, you can turn it on now, you've seen me do it a dozen times."

"Okay." I flipped the main switch and the SOLTES calibrator came to life. Why is it you call it the SOLTES calibrator again, Huneo?"

"S-O-L, Jim, meaning Speed of Light, the speed of light is the medium the original time speed was captured in on November 12th, 1995. In addition, all other time speeds are recorded in the speed of light medium. As I explained before, Jim, it's the best and only medium to record time in because the speed of light is constant throughout the universe. Next is T-E-S, Time Existence Speed, and that is just what it does. It measures time speed right down to non-existence. That is theoretically, Jim. The calibrator would, when velocity got slow enough, oxidize away and turn to dust itself as time would be passing at such a high rate of speed. For example, take the speed time speed is passing now for us in the twenty-four hour period that we're in, then compare that to a velocity that got slow enough for another example hypothetically to almost absolute zero movement. Thousands of years or even millions of years would be passing perhaps in the same amount of time a few hours passed for us. I mean isn't that amazing, Jim?" Huneo explained, and asked.

"Yeah it is, it is. It's funny we never think of some of the aspects of the special theory of relativity in the opposite extremes when we think of them. We think of the great extremes of high speed yet not realizing we are traveling millions of miles per hour or tens of millions and we don't ask ourselves what happens when we slow down and move closer to non-movement or I guess non-existence."

"Exactly Jim, now you've got it." Huneo replied, "Okay Jim, it's all set to give us readings. The calibrator is very simple to operate. The way I see it, Jim, at the speed of light or for example, let us say, Gamma rays, which travel at the speed of light but have no mass and we know as physicists, Jim that mediums that travel at the speed of light have no mass. If however, the rays were to drop below the speed of light, they would explode and create mass. At the other end of the spectrum, let us say, at absolute non-movement or no velocity you would also have no mass or non-existence. In the case of no existence if you wanted to start a clock running you would probably have to have a big bang. Perhaps with an entity decelerating from the speed of light or who knows? Anyway, to start a clock running you would have to have a big bang to initiate time via the introduction of mass with velocities and gravity fields on a colossal scale. The clock in the beginning would run unimaginably fast or it could run unimaginably slow and then it would slow down or speed up as higher or lower velocities are attained. Therefore, at one end of the spectrum, at the speed of light, time goes so slow that it comes to a halt or stops or does not exist hence you have suspended animation. At the other end of the spectrum towards no velocity, time is going so fast that eventually at a pure stop in velocity all time and entity would be consumed. Hence, there is no time, therefore no existence. What do you think of that, Jim?" Huneo asked, flippantly. I chuckled at his demeanor.

"I don't know but it certainly sounds logical to me." I replied.

"Okay look here, Jim. Now that we have all the functions up and running on the device, the first one I want to show you is the current date and time function, which is just an expensive digital clock I installed." Huneo said, as he went on with his 'class'.

"Okay, yeah, I see."

"The second readout I want to show you is the start up time and date clock marked, 'Master Time Originator.' This is the read-out for the time and day this clock was started and is a clock with the original time speed from November 12, 1995. The time you see running here is the speed the clock was running on that day in, 1995, locked into the speed of light medium. The clock just runs in a loop, Jim and repeats itself continuously for that twenty-four hour period. Are you with me so far on this, Jim?" Huneo asked.

"Yeah, go ahead, Huneo, it's clear to me, I know what you're saying."

"Okay, the next two gauges here represent the time as it is now and the one beside that time date current, is the time and date running at the time speed it was on November 12th, 1995 again. These two clocks are reset-able so that we can compare the speed of the two clocks together."

"I got it."

"And lastly one of the most important displays is the 'Time Speed Difference' in percentage indicator which up to this point is the most important because of its alarming rise." Huneo explained. Right then, Cindy barked and I went to see what all the fuss was about. I looked over the railing to where she was down on the barn floor and it looked like she had killed a mouse.

"Huneo, Huneo! Come over and take a look!"

"What is it, Jim, what is it?"

"Look at, Cindy, Huneo, she has her first kill. She's showing it to us." I said. He looked over the edge and started laughing.

"That's funny," he said. We returned to the calibrator.

"Alright Jim, I'll show you the last readout and that should be it, it's quite simple, as you can see."

"Okay, let's have a look."

"Okay, once again the last one shows the percentage of rise in the speed of time passing. All right, Jim the readout measures 6.334%. That means that compared to November 12th, 1995 the time speed is going that much faster and if I use my calculator here that would mean that that day in November in 1995 when I first started recording a time speed. Let us say that the master day had 1440 minutes in it and with that 6.334% rise in time speed, which is what the time is running at right now this minute, if we were to fit this day into that day on November 12, 1995. This day would register 1349 minutes. It would be registering 91 less minutes in it than the November 12th, 1995 day." Huneo said. His words rolled of his tongue like nothing.

"Are you sure about that, Huneo?" I asked. I was in disbelief.

"Jim, that's why mankind is becoming so rushed, we're experiencing an astrophysics phenomenon that if it doesn't stop it's going to kill us."

"But 91 minutes, Huneo, how can that be?"

"We see this day with 1440 minutes in it right now. However, if we stick this day on the November 12 clock, it would register 1349 minutes. As compared with that day, Jim, we are moving into the future faster, it's that simple."

"It's that simple, Huneo! It's not that simple!" I snapped, in a tone of frustration. I looked at Huneo and shook my head. "I guess every time this percentage goes up we're one step closer to dying?" I stated.

"Exactly."

"We get older faster, everything degrades faster and it's no wonder we want to do everything faster."

"That's right, Jim, that's exactly right."

"Huneo, there's only one thing that can stop this."

"Oh, and what's that?" Huneo asked, with one eyebrow raised.

"Divine intervention."

"I agree, Jim. That's our only hope for the future."

"So we can only ask for, God's mercy and pray for his mercy and hope that, God will save us." I said.

"I agree again, Jim. There's nothing else we can do except to live whatever life is left in his image and pray."

"So that's it then."

"What's it?"

"The Grand Theorem, velocity of mass and gravity is time and space and everything in it and what we don't know is in the realm of a divine principle or of a divine providence."

"That could very well be. I don't think we'll ever really know for sure." Huneo replied. We stood there staring at each other trying to understand our predicaments.

"I can see by the look in your eyes, Jim, I can tell what you're thinking. Ours is not to question why, Jim but only to imagine."

"Imagine?"

"Imagine and have faith." Huneo said. At that moment, I did not think anything could be truer.

"Okay, that's enough for me, Jim, I'm getting depressed."

"Alright, alright, turn the calibrator off and let's get out of here." That was definitely enough of the calibrator for one day. We left the barn. Huneo decided to go to the university to visit Helen and I decided to see if I could do anything for Bernie that day. I gave Bernie a call but he was not home. I knew his brother Michael was taking good care of him so I was not too concerned. I decided then to go into town and spend the afternoon in the shops. I thought that I might also visit Christine and perhaps see if she was not too busy. I could take her out for lunch. I got ready to leave and as Huneo was walking out the door, I said goodbye to him. I gave Cindy a dog treat and then locked up the house along with the barn and left for town. As I got into town, I felt better. It was a sunny day and it seemed to be getting comfortably warm for this time of the year. I went down to the main street in Park Falls, which was Union Street, and I parked at one of the parking meters. I got out and went for a stroll through the town and the shops. As I started walking down the street, I noticed that for a Monday the town was quite busy with people. As I wandered about, I saw that things were different. People were quieter and there were not the smiles on the people's faces like there once was. It was an unsettling feeling to see the entire town seemingly in a collective depression. There was the odd smiling face but overall it was a palpable depressive mood, which was abounding on the street. As I continued, I could see that many people were reading the newspaper and I could overhear the odd conversation and then the fact hit me that the whole town was becoming aware of the Pegasus Effect. It was starting to be a concern for everyone in the town. As I was walking, a person that looked familiar, but whom I did not recognize, walked up and greeted me. "Hi Professor Reynolds, it's me, Dave Baker, how are you?" He asked. He had a cheery smile.

"Not bad," I replied, "You look familiar but I can't place you, I know we've met before." I said. I tried to figure out where I had seen this person in the past.

"You don't remember me, Professor? I fix your family's shoes here in Park Falls. I'm Dave Baker of Baker's Shoes and Shoe Repair," he explained.

"Okay, that's right, now I recall you. How have you been, Dave?"

"Good Professor, very good actually, I'm happy here in Park Falls and I think me and the Missis will certainly retire here to watch our family grow," he said, with a smile.

"I know you don't remember me that well, Professor, that's because I've mostly dealt with your wife. She always brings the shoes into the shop."

"Yes, that's right; she takes care of that for us."

"Professor, you would know about this, Pegasus Effect thing. Am I going to be able to see my grandchildren grow up?" he asked. This question surprised me.

"Well, Dave, you've caught me off guard here. I can honestly tell you, Dave that I don't know where this phenomenon is going any more than you do. It's an act of God. It's natural event of some sort in our universe that is really without explanation as far as I'm concerned." I blurted. I was not really thinking about what I was saying.

"I'm very concerned about this, Professor, the wife and me. We want to know what kind of trouble we're in."

"I know you do, I know. I want the answers to this myself."

"Well, if you find any answers, Professor, you'll let us know here in, Park Falls, won't you, Professor Reynolds?"

"I certainly will, Dave. I can assure you that I would not hold back any information from the people of this town. I love this town, Dave and the people in it and I have a feeling that we'll stick together like a family during this crisis."

"That's good to know, Professor. It's reassuring to know that."

"Listen Dave, from now on call me, Jim. I prefer to be called, Jim."

"Okay, Jim, I'll call you that." He said. We chitchatted a while longer and then we parted ways. As it turned out that day, I made a few new acquaintances. People in town, some that I knew and some that I did not, stopped me and asked me about the Pegasus Effect and what was going to happen to themselves and all of us. I was seeing the news of this saturating into our community. The townsfolk were concerned as they were talking about this everywhere I went. As the day wore on, I was getting tired. I made my way over to the mall and stood outside of Christine's salon, which was the actual name of her business. I peered through the window and watched her as she worked inside. My Christine was a beauty to watch working as well as being so professional and attentive with her customers. I was going to watch her until she noticed I was staring at her, to see her reaction. I watched her as she did her thing. Some of her antics made me laugh and then finally I caught her eye. It reminded me of when we first met in school. We both started laughing as her customers were in perplexity of her merriment. I could see why I loved her so every time I looked at her. Nevertheless, when she had a free moment we got together and talked. She told me that she had the whole day to work with appointments and would even be home late that evening, which was unusual for her. I told her that I would meet her at home. It was also decided by Christine that I would make dinner that day. Therefore, I went over to the grocery store to see what I could find. Christine wanted a surprise for dinner and it would be my big project for the day. This was something that I thought would be fun especially the way things were working out. I went into the grocery store and started looking around for what we might have for dinner. I found fish and seafood to be my choice. We had not had seafood for dinner in a long while. I knew that one of Christine's favorites was sea scallops and smoked oysters so this would truly be a surprise for her. She would be expecting some meat or some takeout but this time I would surprise her good. I rushed through the market and I got plenty for all and then bought a few extras. On the way out, I also bought some flowers for Christine to compliment the dinner. I would put them in our room with a romantic note for when she came home. I started driving home and as I did, I put some music on the CD player and started thinking. I was thinking again, about what was happening and that I should try to keep my mind off the current events as much as possible. I would try to divert my attention to other things that were going on in my life and the lives around me. I would try to see what I could do to help my family and friends in these times of uncertainty of the unknown. I thought that I would steel myself as the man and patriarch of my family. I would be there for everyone when needed and my family would be able to count on me for whatever the future had in store for us. I wanted to protect my family from anything that might be negative for us and I wanted to make sure we headed in a positive direction in our lives. As I pulled in the driveway, I saw that a taxi was dropping off

Angela. She got out of the taxi and waved to me as I pulled in. I was happy to see her home. I got out of the car and she called out to me.

"Hi, Dad! How are you?" She was near the front porch.

"Good, sweetie, are you going to help me with these bags here?"

"Sure, Dad, I'll help you." My daughter replied, with her beautiful smile. We grabbed the bags and flowers and went in the house where Cindy was there to greet us. Cindy was growing fast and she was spunkier and more rambunctious, which was nice to see in her. That meant she would be a good protector and a friendly dog. She was becoming Angela's protector, which was because of her instinctive knowing that Angela was going to become a mother and needed protection. We went into the kitchen and put our goodies on the table.

"Dad, what did you buy for dinner? Are these flowers for me, Dad?" Angela prodded.

"No sweetheart, those are for your mother."

"That's nice, Dad. Mom's going to love these."

"I hope so."

"Are they for something I'm missing, an anniversary of some kind, or something?"

"No, Angela, they're just for a surprise."

"That's nice, Dad."

"I'm going to go upstairs and get changed, Dad and then I'll be right down to help you. Dad, I want to talk to you, alright?"

"Okay sweetie, I'll be waiting for you." I said. I ran upstairs and changed into a more comfortable pair of pants. I brought the flowers up and I put them in the empty vase in our room. I wrote the note to Christine. "Christine, you are late from working today my love but you are never late in my heart, you will always be there. To my loving wife, from your loving husband, Jim" I wrote and then I put the note by the lamp on her night table. My cell phone rang and it was Huneo calling to say that he would be late tonight with Helen and they would be missing dinner. I tried to entice him with the seafood but he did not bite. So, as the crow flies, it was just as well. It would give us some time together as a family. I went back downstairs and Angela was in the kitchen getting some condiments and dishes prepared.

"Huh, you beat me to it, eh sweetie. You're faster than your dear old, Dad."

"Oh, Dad, you're not old." Angela responded.

"Thanks darling, that's kind of you to say."

"So what are we cooking, Dad?"

"Well we're going to have seafood baked and fried, with different sauces, and potatoes and green beans. So, I was wondering, Angela… would you like to make us one of your famous garden salads?"

"Sure, Dad, I'll do that." she replied. Her youthful exuberance shined through."

"So, is everything going okay for you these days?" I asked.

"Well, I'm going to start working for, Christopher's father at the tire shop next week on Wednesday and Thursday nights, Dad; part time."

"That's great, sweetie. What are you going to be doing?"

"I'm going to do clerical work like answering the phones and working the cash register."

"Do you think you'll like that?"

"Yeah Dad, I think I'll like that type of work and it's only four hours a night so I can save a little money for my baby."

"You know sweetie, I never thought I would hear those words come out of you. I just never thought of you having a baby until well, here we are!" Angela giggled and then she started to prepare our salad, "So you said you had something you wanted to talk to me about dear?" I queried. We continued to prepare dinner in the kitchen.

"Yes, Dad." she said. She then paused. After a while, I saw that she was trying to get something out so I prompted her.

"Angela, you can talk to either your mother or me about anything. Don't be shy."

"I know, Dad. Well, Dad, I want to tell you that this, Pegasus thing, has got me thinking and I've been dwelling on it really. I watch it on the news and any chance I get, and Dad I'm scared, and not just for me but mostly for my baby and then for the family. I'm young, Dad and I want to live and have my baby and I want my baby to live and grow up and I want to grow up too." She stated. She stopped talking. I waited to see if she had anything more to say and then she spoke again. "I went to a Catholic Priest today after my classes, Dad and I had a long talk with the Father. Dad, I think I'm religious and I want to live a religious way of life. I want to be as pure and clean a person, as I can be, Dad. Today, when I went to him, he seemed to know what was happening and he was there for me with what I needed to hear and how I wanted to practice my faith." Angela explained. She spoke in a concerned and anxious tone.

"I'm glad to hear you say that, dear."

"You are, Dad?"

"Of course I am, Angela. I think that living a pious way of life is a very rewarding way of life. Your mother and I try to live that way and we try to instill that in you girls. We took you to church when you were younger and we don't swear in front of you and we do unto others as we would like done unto ourselves. We would be happy to see you live that way too, Angela." I told her, in my fatherly way. I tried to calm her fears.

"Dad, I'm scared about the future with the way things are going with this, Pegasus thing. I think we're in real trouble, Dad,"

"Listen Angela, I want to tell you something you already know and that is that God loves you and the future is not for you to see. You can control some of your future, Angela, to a certain extent, with the way you live, and you can determine some of your fate, dear, but your mortality will always be in, God's hands. Do you understand that fact? That, it is your mortality that will always be in, God's hands?" I asked her.

"Yes, Dad, I understand that."

"The best way you can live Angela is one day at a time. To live in this day only and not worry about tomorrow or yesterday, those days are either gone or not here yet." I explained, "Angela, if you live in this day only you will live a much happier life. What do you think of that?"

"I'll try to do that, Dad. I think your right,"

"Does any of this make you feel any better?"

"Yes, I feel better when I talk about these things with somebody."

"Well don't be shy, Angie, your mother and I are always here for you, anytime you need us, always." I said.

"Daaad!"

"What is it, sweetie?"

"You haven't called me that in ten years."

"What's that, Angie?"

"Daaad!" she squealed.

"Alright, Angela, I'm only teasing you." I said. Angela laughed shamefacedly.

"I love you, Dad," she said, sheepishly.

"I know you do, Angela. Your mother and I love you more than you can imagine, so never be afraid to talk with us, ever, okay?" I told her. She smiled and lowered her head and sat down. Angela began to cut the vegetables and I started to marinate the seafood and cut some potatoes. We were sitting in the kitchen and it was afternoon. The sun was streaming in the kitchen windows and the house was warm and bright. It was a beautiful day to be doing this with my daughter. As I watched her cutting the vegetables, my mind went through all the years we have had with her. Everything was right there in my mind when I thought about her, Paula, and Christine. For the time being, she was placated. I knew that we would be talking about this again but for the time being I just wanted to relax and enjoy this day with her. Cindy wandered about the kitchen and every once in a while we would give her a snack. She was becoming quite a voracious little eater at her tender young age. It was then Christine called and informed us she would be picking up Paula at one of her friends homes. Christine said that she would be home in exactly one hour and fifteen minutes. She tried to find out what was for dinner over the phone but I would not tell her and she became excited. "Tell me what's for dinner, hon!"

"No, you're going to have to wait just like, Paula." I retorted.

"Oh, I hope it's good, I'm so hungry, so hungry, I could eat a horse, I could eat two horses!" she exclaimed. I told her that the sooner she came home the sooner she would be out of her misery. She laughed and screamed at the same time. I laughed too. We said our goodbyes and I hung up the phone.

"Well, that was your mother, Angela. She and Paula will be home in an hour," I mentioned, "So, what was this priest's name, Angela, the one you saw today?"

"His name is, Father Alan Mulvey, Dad."

"I'm not familiar with him. I only know the priest your mother and I go to, Father Matthew McPhee."

"Father Mulvey works at our church, Dad."

"I don't think I ever met him." I said, as I tried to place him. "What does he look like?"

"He has reddish hair like, Paula," she said. I then interjected. "Say no more, sweetie. I think I know the one you mean. He's about thirty years old and drives an old Camaro with mag wheels, right?"

"Yeah that's him, Dad."

"He seems like a nice enough fella. He sure is a car enthusiast though I must say. Every time I see him, he's polishing his car. He must really like that car."

"Oh, Dad… okay the salad's ready. I'll put it in the fridge for now, alright, Dad?"

"Sounds good, my dear, what're you going to do till your mother gets home?"

"I'm going to lie on the couch and watch television. Dad, I'm tired." Angela yawned and looked groggy.

"Yeah, Angela, go lie down on the couch and rest. You're moving around for two people now so you've got to get your rest when you can. I remember when your mother was pregnant with you. She was tired all the time. She used to say that she thought she was carrying around an elephant with you and that she was going to lose some of her height with all your weight, she would say." I told, Angela. She burst out laughing.

"Did she really, Dad?"

"Oh yeah, she would say that all the time." I said. Angela thought this was so funny.

"When she gets home, Dad, I'm going to ask her if I'm her little elephant!" Angela said. She laughed again.

"Go ahead, Angela dear, I'm sure she'll remember."

"I've got to lay down for awhile, Dad or I'm going to fall asleep standing up."

"Go ahead and lay down, Angela and get some rest. I'll finish the rest of this." Angela headed for the couch and I continued with the food preparations. As I did, there was a knock at the door. I went to see who it was. There were two men outside, whom I had not seen before. They did not look as if they were a threat, however, I chained the door, opened it a crack, and asked if I could help them. "Are you, Mr. Reynolds or Professor Reynolds?" one of them asked.

"Yes, I am. Who wants to know?"

"Well we do, Mr. Reynolds. We would like to talk to you about, Dr. Huneo Parkas, if we may?"

"Like I said fellas, who wants to know?" I prodded. I became agitated at their lack of respect in regards to identifying themselves.

"Well, we're friends of his and we wanted to talk to him about old times." the other said. I knew right then they were lying.

"He's not here anymore. He flew to, South America and then he went onto, Australia. He's gone for good." I replied. They seemed puzzled and angered by my response.

"Listen fellas, I'm busy. So, I'm going to have to ask you to leave, so if you don't mind."

"Listen, Professor Reynolds, we'd like to come in and maybe ask you a few questions if you don't mind?" The first man asked, in an intimidating tone.

"Listen fellas, you'd better leave or you're going to be in a heap of trouble." I said, tersely, and they backed off. They went back to their vehicle and they drove off. I wrote down their license plate number so I could call Paul Banks at the Park Falls police detachment and maybe find out whom these people were and if they did in fact know who Dr. Huneo Parkas was. Anyways, I paid no more attention to them and went about my business. As I prepared dinner, I decided to call Bernie to see if I could reach him, given that a few days had passed. Bernie answered the phone but he sounded a little depressed. "Hello, Bernie, how are you?" I asked. He responded by saying that he was not doing too badly. He mentioned that he went to the university to visit me and it was okay that I was not there. Bernie explained how he was spending most of his time with his brother catching up on all the time they have been apart and that they were even managing to get in a few laughs here and there. I mentioned how I was doing and then he asked me if I wanted to go out for dinner that coming Wednesday and I gladly accepted. Bernie said he was happy that I called. It was a phone call I was thankful I made.

After my call, I went into the living room to see how Angela was making out. She was sound asleep and snoring quietly. I sat in a chair and watched her for a while. I could not believe how far we had come with her. It seemed like only yesterday I was changing her diapers and walking her to the school bus and now she was a beautiful young woman who bore my first grandchild. There was the sound of muffled voices and then Christine and Paula burst through the door. I rushed to the front door and tried to quiet them. "Shh, ladies, quiet!" I whispered. I tried to hush them.

"What's going on, Jim?" Christine asked.

"It's okay, Christine. It's Angela. She's asleep on the couch. I want to let her rest for a bit, she's tired."

"Okay, we'll be quiet, Dad." Paula answered.

"What're you cooking hon? Oh my God, are you cooking seafood?"

"Surprise!" I said. Christine dropped her bags and threw her arms around me.

"Oh, Jim thanks so much. Now that's a real surprise, thanks sweetheart, I love you," she said.

Christine and Paula came in and settled. Christine then went upstairs and Paula promptly went into the living room and awakened her sister. They squabbled. I told them to stop and get along with one another and they became quiet and watched television.

Christine beckoned for me to come upstairs to our bedroom. I went upstairs and entered. She was in the bathroom. She started to thank me for the flowers and then she jumped from behind the door wearing a tiny almost non-existent red and black baby doll nightgown with a pearl necklace and her hair tossed in a mess. "This is for you later Tarzan!" she growled with a wicked stare in her eyes. I was breathless. I could not think of a thing to say as she ambled over to me in a slinky, sultry manner. "Christine you take my breath away," I muttered. She got closer and we embraced and kissed. Then abruptly, "Mooom!" Paula shrieked. She and her sister walked by. Angela started laughing and then Christine blushed.

"Close your door! Why do you do this, Mom?" Paula squawked. Angela laughed at her sister and our little predicament. I closed the door and Christine dropped her nightgown to the floor again, I was speechless. After that, we went downstairs for dinner.

"Where are, Helen and Huneo?" Christine asked.

"They went out for the evening or late at least."

"So were alone then?"

"Yeah hon, it's just the six of us."

"The six of us?" Christine mused.

"Yeah, there's you and me, Paula and Angela, our new grandchild, and Cindy."

"Right, how could I forget?" The girls came downstairs. We got set to have dinner.

We had our dinner as I saw that I had made the right decision with the menu. There was almost no talking and lots of gobbling up of all the food in sight. It was a welcome dinner as the girls thanked the chef and helped me clean up afterwards. After supper, we went our separate ways. Paula and Angela went outside with the dog and Christine and I sat in the living room and decided to watch television and cuddle. We talked about how Angela and Paula were doing. I told Christine about my talk with Angela that afternoon. Christine thought that it was great for Angela to want to be so pious but she also thought that Angela should not restrict herself too harshly in her lifestyle choices. I agreed. We then talked about Paula and some of the friends she was starting to keep or some of the ones we heard about from our friends and Angela. Paula was starting to hang around with a group of teens that were a little unkempt and suspected of delinquent behavior and the missing of their school classes.

We agreed that we had to sit her down, have a talk with her, and try to see what was going on in her life. Paula had become more secretive over the past few months and had started dressing differently. This was typical of setting off alarm bells for parents, we thought. We agreed to concentrate our attentions on our girls more because of our circumstances. Christine and my parents would be visiting that summer but in the meantime, the girls would get calls from their grandparents and the occasional letter. I thought it would be soon that the girls were going to want to cut the apron strings themselves but I also thought in the back of my mind that they would need us more than ever in the near future.

As we cuddled, Christine turned on the eight o'clock news. We listened in to the broadcast. The headlines started with a news newscaster's pronouncements "Startling scenarios ahead for the world and other news about the, Pegasus Effect ahead next on the nightly news!" This statement transfixed Christine and me. "Oh God, Jim, I hope it isn't too bad this time."

"I hope not either, sweetie." I replied. We watched the television quietly. The commercials at the beginning of the newscast rolled by and we held each other's hands. Then, the broadcast began. "Good evening folks this is, Bill Adams with the evening news for, Monday, April 20th, 2012. This evening in regards to our top story, we have reports from differing sources tonight about what to expect in the future as well as the latest calibrator updates. Our first report comes from, the Surgeon General of the United States." The anchor said. They faded to a scene of an old but official looking building and then to an office.

"Thanks, Bill. This is, Jake Turnbull for the National News, reporting. I'm here with, Dr. Evan Berkeley of the Surgeon General's office who is also an affiliate with the, Centers for Disease Control," the reporter stated. They sat together in what looked like a media room. Both looked to be in a somber mood. "Hello, Dr. Berkeley."

"Hello again, Jake."

"Now Doctor, you and your associates have been studying this phenomenon and the effect it might have on the population since the outset and you say you have come up with or have a preliminary report that can be shared this evening?" the reporter asked.

"Yes, thank you, Jake. Well first, we at the Surgeon General's office have come up with a list of adverse human physical and mental effects that may and will come out of this phenomenon known as, the Pegasus Effect." Dr. Berkeley stated.

"Well, Dr. Berkeley, would you be so kind as to share with our viewing audience what we might expect in the immediate future and then down the road some?" the reporter asked.

"Yes, Jake. Well, the effect is already taking its toll and has been for some time with the effects of global stress and raging. Humans are for the most part going to be intolerant to the effects of this anomaly and will probably suffer the most. The Pegasus Effect seems to be picking up speed and we'll find the effects becoming more pronounced and serious as time goes by. We can expect in the immediate future that we as the human race will become more easily agitated on all levels as our time speed passing accelerates. Some of the first of the more pronounced adverse mental effects will be a greater sense of frustration, depression, anger, delusional thinking, suicidal thoughts, immoral behavior, and a general loss of caring. Despondency may set in, that's very taxing on one's energy level, and a person's will to push forward. These symptoms will differ from person to person and will be more visible in some as compared to others and these symptoms will worsen as the effect intensifies." Dr. Berkeley stated.

"That's quite a chilling prognosis, Doctor?"

"This is the most serious health threat the world has ever faced, I believe, and we have to take this seriously and fast. It is by the very nature of this effect, the speeding up of time passing that's really giving humans an ultimatum."

"What do you mean by that, Dr. Berkeley?"

"Time is not on our side and we have no benchmarks for this nor do we have a real starting point as to where to begin looking."

"We have nothing, Doctor?"

"Well, we've been looking at drugs to help alleviate some of the mental effects but we don't have a supply that is sufficient and we don't want to get people addicted to drugs."

"What kind of drugs, Doctor?"

"We have drugs that slow down the mind in a manner of speaking and take away the stress. These are common drugs known as benzodiazepines, like valium or diazepam. They will keep people from getting too excited, manic or out of control from the Pegasus Effect," the Doctor explained.

"Will there be any physical effects, Dr. Berkeley?"

"Yes, Jake, there will be if the effect continues to intensify. And there's every indication that that is exactly what's going to happen."

"Could you share them with us, Doctor, if you will?"

"Yes I will. In the beginning, the effects can easily be masked but they will intensify. The immediate effects will be nervousness and twitching as well as tremors and muscle fatigue. We suggest people try to get as much sleep as possible. We will and are going to age faster than normal for the time that passes and we will grow weaker. The effect will take our natural energy and strength away and make us sluggish. We might experience headaches and gastrointestinal upsets. These symptoms will be chronic and will affect people differently."

"How so, Doctor?"

"Well, the most affected we believe will be persons who are already in bad health, physically and mentally. They will fall to the effects easier than the rest of us, and then the next group will be the aged and the very young populations. The young and old are always affected the most, obviously because of their more fragile natures. After this it'll probably be woman before men as the best we can figure out but the opposite could hold true as well."

"A real battle of the sexes eh, Doctor?"

"By no means is this a joking matter, Sir!"

"You're right, Doctor, I'm sorry about that, I truly am. Forgive me."

"It's alright." Dr. Berkeley replied.

"We'll move on then, Doctor, if you don't mind."

"Go ahead, Sir."

"What will be the more advanced symptoms of this effect?"

"Well, the more advanced symptoms will be very serious indeed, and if we're right they'll include headaches and stomach upsets and then that will proceed to a great nervousness and then painful debilitating tremors. It will affect the central nervous system the most, where the brains electrical signals take place and that will filter throughout the body. Eventually, the circulatory system will be affected and blood pressure will rise. There will probably be a lot of vomiting and bleeding in the stomach. You may have bleeding of the eyes and ears and bladder and anal bleeding. This will be followed by convulsions, kidney failure, heart attacks, brain hemorrhages, strokes and death," the Doctor stated.

"And for whom will this apply to, Doctor?"

"This applies to everyone! If this effect does not slow down, stop or reverse itself, the people of this earth will die off in the order I've specified. First, we will die off in small pockets and then we expect all of humanity will die off in large swathes!"

"Jeez, Doc you say that so matter of factly." The reporter responded, alarmingly.

"I know, I know. We're on orders from, the President of the United States not to under any circumstances be holding anything back from the people of this nation." The doctor said, with a solemn manner. Then,

"Oh! My baby's going to die! My baby is going to die!" We heard. Christine and I bolted around and see Angela and Paula at the back of the room listening. "Mom and Dad, my baby is going to die! We're all going to die!" Angela squealed. She burst out crying.

"Christine, turn off the TV, turn off the TV!" I exclaimed.

"Are we all going to die, Mom?" Paula asked. Tears welled up in her eyes as we rushed to our daughters. They were crying. We looked at one another and we began to cry. We really knew this was happening and our time was finite. I embraced Angela and her mother embraced Paula. They cried and we cried for the fact that our daughters were in agony. There were no words to be said. It seemed like everything that could have been said, was said. We held them and then brought them to the couch. We sat down and held them in their angst and fear. We held them for what seemed like hours. We tried to comfort our daughters with positive thoughts and our physical contact until they became calmed, until we became calmed. We were experiencing the Pegasus

Effect, it was just beginning but I did not say this to the girls. However, I thought they knew this as well. After a while, the sobbing stopped. The girls expressed how they wanted to know if there was anything we could do for ourselves. I told them that for the time being, for that evening, we would go to bed and we would pray for each other and all our loved ones and ask for God's help. If we asked God to help us with something in our hearts, sometimes God would help us and protect us I told them. I instructed our daughters to pray for each other and ask God to bless them. Our girls were once again serene but they looked fragile and unhappy and it made us sad to see them that way. We held them for a while longer and then we got them to bed. They were quiet and then Christine and I went to bed. As we lie there, we looked at each other and then Christine spoke.

"What are we going to do, Jim? What are we going to do for our girls, our treasures, what?" Christine begged, "This is it, isn't it, Jim. This is the end for us isn't it? I mean really, there's nothing we can do, nothing, is there?" she expressed. Christine was anguish ridden. I grabbed her and held her tight.

"I don't know sweetheart, I truly don't know." I replied. I held her until she eventually fell asleep. I rolled over on my side and as I tried to fall asleep, I heard some rustling downstairs. I went to the stairs to see what the commotion was thinking it was Cindy flopping around in the night. However, it was Huneo and Helen. They were quietly sneaking into their room trying not to wake us. I had forgotten about them. They saw me at the top of the stairs and we waved to one another. "I locked the door, Jim. We'll see you tomorrow." Huneo whispered.

"Okay, goodnight." I replied. I went back to our bedroom. As I walked by Angela's room, I heard her crying. I knocked softly and entered her room. She was sitting and weeping. I went to Angela and told her to lie down. I then pulled the covers over her and stayed with her as she gripped my hand. So tightly, in fact, it was uncomfortable. I stayed with her until her grip loosened, she finally let go and fell asleep. I went to bed next for I was exhausted and I really needed my sleep. It took me a while to fall asleep. I realized I was filling with anger and many other negative emotions. I knew I had to try to change my way of thinking if I was going to be of help to my family and whomever else. I decided to try to concentrate on being as spiritual as I could and as positive as I could at all times. I would try to look at all situations from then on in the most favorable light and try to instill hope in others. After a short while, I fell asleep.

The next day arrived and I had slept in late. The gang was headed out the door when I got up and Christine rushed in, gave me a peck on the cheek, and said she was off for the day and she would call me later. Christine explained she let me sleep in because it was my second day off and I looked like I was in a deep sleep with a smile on my face. I got up and went downstairs. Huneo was at the kitchen table. He was having a coffee and he offered me some. I heartily accepted a cup. I was in the mood for a good cup of coffee or two.

"How are you this morning, Dr. Parkas?" I asked.

"Not so bad, Professor Reynolds, why so formal this morning?"

"No reason, just fooling around, I suppose." I said, with a melancholic resound.

"Is everything okay, Jim?"

"I guess, I suppose. Where's, Helen?"

"She went to classes today."

"Is everything alright with you guys, Huneo?" I asked, as I poured my coffee.

"Actually it is, Jim. We've set a date for the wedding," he said. I chuckled.

"When's the lucky day?"

"It'll be on Saturday, August 8th, 2012 at 12:00 PM."

"Congratulations again, Huneo."

"I have another announcement for you, Jim."

"Oh yeah, and what's that, Huneo?"

"Helen and I have decided we're going to move out this weekend and move into our new house. We feel we're no longer going to wait. We're going to set up our household right away and enjoy our new love nest." Huneo said. I laughed at the latter part of his statement.

"Jim, are you sure there's nothing wrong? You look like you've got something you want to get off your chest. You can talk to me about it if you'd like. I'm your friend you know, Jim and I'm discreet." Huneo offered.

"Since you make that offer, Huneo I'd like to bounce a few things off you, if you don't mind?"

"Jim, I've got all the time in the world for you today. I've got nothing else to do for the next little while so fire away."

"Well, I think my family and myself of course and not to mention the rest of the world are on a collision course with our future and our mortality, in the most odious way. My girls are getting quite worried about the family and others of course but we're a family and they're getting more upset I think as the days pass and the news becomes more grim and hopeless." I expressed. I spoke in a dejected tone.

"Well, Jim, you've got me over a barrel here because we're in the same boat, Helen and I. We have the same feelings that you're having and we're saying the same things that you're saying. Jim, when I first made this announcement I did not realize how much things would change. In hindsight, I know that making this announcement was the right thing to do. However, I should've made it a lot sooner than I did and I regret that now and I think I'll regret that more as each day passes." Huneo said. He bowed his head.

"Huneo, I don't think it would have made a whole lot of difference."

"I don't know about that, Jim?"

"Nobody does and nobody ever will." I told him. We sat in the kitchen sipping our coffee in the morning sun. It was such a beautiful day and it just seemed so ludicrous that in contrast to this inviting beauty that the destiny of humanity was seemingly racing to an end as this barely registered in our cognizant thoughts.

"Huneo, I just feel that there's nothing we can do to stop this and we just have to let the end happen without a fight. There's no enemy. There's no enemy except time itself, and the universe."

"I know, Jim. We feel the same way, Helen and me. There's nothing we can do to help ourselves. This is too big, Jim. It's in the realm of the divine. All I know to do is to pray for our lives and ask for forgiveness and that may sound corny to you but that's all I know what to do for,

Helen and me, and live like there's no tomorrow, and live for today the best we can." Huneo replied.

"It's not corny, Huneo, we feel the same here and we're going to be doing a lot more praying in the future, what there is of it, and hope and try not to lose hope." We both sat there for the next four or five minutes in silence.

"Are you all right, Jim?"

"I will be. I have to be, for my family and myself, don't I?"

"Me too, Jim, for Helen and me I think the best thing we can do is to try to live our lives in the most normal way we can and to try to have fun and do the things and say the things that we must say to each other in the days ahead. We have to be strong for our families and have hope for the future, at the very least, I think."

"Before I forget, Huneo, yesterday, two men came to the house here looking for you and they were quite rude." I stated. I wanted to mention this to Huneo before it slipped my mind.

"Was one of them middle aged with reddish hair and the other about twenty eight and had brown hair in a brush cut?"

"Yes, those were the two, do you know them?"

"I don't know them, Jim but I know who they are. They're from the U.S. State department and they've been hounding me for information." Huneo said. He had a perturbed demeanor. He started scratching his head.

"What information?"

"Jim, they wanted to know if I've disclosed everything that I had to disclose at the symposium. They wanted to know if there was something I might have held back from my lecture or if there was something I had forgotten to mention," he said, still scratching his head.

"Is there?"

"Is there what?"

"Anything you're holding back?"

"Well, there's another tidbit that I have kept to myself and I intend to keep it that way." Huneo said, with conviction.

"You mean there is more about the Non-Existence/ Time Loss Theorem that you haven't told us? Told the world?" I asked, with disdain.

"Jim Listen! Listen carefully! This other tidbit has nothing to do with the Non-Existence/ Time Loss theorem or the Pegasus Effect or anything else that is involved with this effect. Not directly, however, it has something to do with unrelated topics that have no bearing on this. Do you understand, Jim? This is my own private scientific endeavor and I'll keep this to myself period," he said. Huneo was getting upset with me for prying.

"Alright Huneo, I'll mind my own business." I wondered deep inside as to what it was he was keeping concealed and how important it might have been. "So Huneo, you're moving out on the weekend? What are you going to do with the calibrator in the barn?" I asked.

"Well, I'd like to keep it there, Jim, if that's alright with you? I've decided to keep it here, Jim, as long as I can come and use it whenever I'd like to. To read the measurements for my own information, if that's alright?"

"Of course you can, Huneo. I'll give you a spare key and you can have twenty four hour access."

"That's great, Jim. That's all I needed. In any case I'm going to be taking off for now to do my chores along with a few other things, so, I'll see you later today, alright?"

"Okay Huneo, we'll see you later then." He rushed off. Huneo was probably going to buy flowers for Helen, I thought. I decided to clean up the house and spend the rest of the day doing housework and other chores around the yard. It was not often that I had to clean the house since we have gotten the girls trained to do this task over the past few years. It gave me a chance to think and unwind by myself. I had a lot of time to think that afternoon, just Cindy and I, and I concluded that our family would try the best that we could in the near future. We would also try to help whomever we could along the way and pray for our futures here on this earth. I would talk with my family later that evening and we all agreed that this is what we would do for each other and our community here in Park Falls. In addition, later that afternoon, I phoned Bernie to confirm our dinner for the following evening and where we would go to eat. We decided on Maurizio's and we would meet at 6:30 pm. The girls came home at their regular times and we had a good evening compared to the night before. We had that talk and then we moved on.

Humbled to our knees

THE NEXT DAY WENT by pretty much the same. The evening came along and I found myself driving towards Maurizio's restaurant to have dinner with Bernie Wakefield. I went into the restaurant and saw Bernie at a side booth. It was a booth with lots of privacy. "Hey Bernie, how are you doing buddy?" I asked. I whisked in and sat directly across from him.

"Oh, good and bad, Jim, I have my good moments and I have my bad ones." Bernie replied. He had a sad look in his eyes. His feelings of loss for Stella were still palpable.

"I know, Bernie. I know it's hard to deal with but I'm here for you and I'll always be here for you so don't ever think you'll be abandoned. The whole family is here for you as well as all your friends." I wanted to reassure him of our commitment in these difficult times. "We'll have to be there for each other, Bernie and that means you'll have to be there for us too." I stated. He nodded in agreement. The waitress arrived and we ordered our drinks and food at the same time.

"So Jim, I've been following the Pegasus Effect on the TV and radio and the newspapers and I must say it doesn't look good." Bernie said.

He grabbed a bread stick and started to munch away. "Jim, I don't think it's going to be very long before we're in real trouble right here in, Park Falls along with the rest of the world. And I agree with you, Jim that we have to stick together on this." Bernie stated.

"It's good to hear you say that, Bernie. It gives me lots of confidence. I've been lacking some fortitude lately and I think I need to be propped up every once in a while."

"I'll be here for you too, Jim, remember that as well."

"I will, Bernie. Thanks." I said. We shook hands and I patted him on the shoulder. After that, we enjoyed a good spaghetti dinner that Maurizio's restaurant was famous for around Park Falls. We talked about everything with the fact being that we had not seen each other in almost a week. Bernie also filled me in on the happenings and events concerning his brother and the rest of his family. We even managed to get a few good laughs in after dinner as we indulged in a hearty dessert. At the end of the evening, we agreed to try to keep in contact every day in one way or another and we decided that we would not falter on this resolve. After dinner, we both headed to our homes and to our loved ones. When I got home, everybody was up waiting for me to see me and to know that I was home. They corralled me at the front door for hugs and kisses as we spent the rest of the evening together. Huneo, Helen, and Cindy included. We took it easy watching television along with just sitting and talking with one another. We talked until midnight and then we went to bed for a good night's sleep for the days ahead.

As the next few days and weeks passed, our town of Park Falls became a different place. Our once vibrant town was no more and transformed like the rest of the world. Park Falls became a place of desperate uncertainty and fear. The mayor of Park Falls, Mayor Steven Bennett, issued a bulletin that in fact stated that the mayor and city council would set up a help and support office that would deal strictly with the problems that might arise from the NE/TL effect. The office would deal with medical problems in conjunction with the hospital and anything else that might be related to the Pegasus Effect. The mayor also called upon the people to turn out for the information sessions. He wanted their input at the town Hall meetings over the next few weeks. On that Thursday, I went back to work at the university and let my counterparts have a few well-deserved days off. The university was the place I think I needed to be for the next little while. Our university president, Marnie Greene, wanted me to be on campus as an advisor to her in these uncertain times, primarily because I was an expert in the field of physics and to some degree astrophysics. Marnie wanted to keep the school open until the summer break without too much upheaval, and to keep the morale of the students up as well as to explain the situation to them truthfully and in a timely manner. The students, the faculty and the residents of Park Falls would start to become despondent over the next few weeks and months with the continuing news from leading scientists and governments from around the world that the NE/TL effect was intensifying. It also became obvious that the world's problems were increasing and the average death rate of the world began to climb. It was not a large increase but it was reported that there was a noticeable increase. Crime rates and incidents of rage had jumped tremendously as the statistics and reporting could not keep up with the escalation. People were becoming sick from the effects both mentally and physically. Our town of Park Falls was no exception. Usually a quiet town, Park Falls was more noticeably interrupted by the blare of police, ambulance or fire sirens. People were being brought to the hospital, in many cases, with symptoms that were indicative of exhaustion, mental fatigue and high stress levels. The increase in time speed was cramming our brains and overloading them with faster electrical impulses. The brain of a man and the central nervous system being biological entities would not function relative to time speed changes and would not adapt to rapid changes in time speed well, if at all.

Around the house and in our daily lives Christine, Paula, Angela and I would grow to become tired easier and earlier in the day. We would also be snappy with one another sometimes but we always said we were sorry and knew what the real cause was. Angela had complained to me that her sister was becoming more aggressive with her and began to hang around with others whom we would not approve of and persons that were out of her age range by many years. This became a source of family upheaval and eventually caused arguments between us on how to handle this situation with Paula. We were growing concerned as time passed on and the Pegasus Effect was taking its toll. I also had to be close to Bernie over this time, as he was growing more despondent as the effect wore on and was taking its toll on him as well. In addition, the added pressure of his grief and the lost love in his life was placing a heavy burden on him indeed. I tried to see him at least every second day and tried to encourage him to keep active and have a stiff upper lip along with trying to think positively. I acquired some books for him on the subjects of dealing with grief and a book that inspired positive thinking.

As for Huneo and Helen, they had long since moved out. They were living like it was their honeymoon but they too were having their problems, albeit small ones, that were related to the Pegasus Effect. They would visit and talk with us every two or three days or they would visit me at the university and we would talk there as well. The national and international news had become grimmer with each day that passed as the leaders of the leading industrialized nations started emergency meetings trying to come up with answers as to what to do about the Pegasus Effect. One of their solutions called for the general populations of each country that were unnecessary in keeping the infrastructure, utility and food supply operations of the countries running, for these people to stop working and save themselves from the effects, and possibly help other workers when it became necessary. In addition, as per usual, like in other national or international emergencies, the militaries of all nations went on standby for whatever possible scenarios that a military might be utilized for, whether it was positive or negative in nature. For that time being, calmer heads prevailed, which was one encouraging sign for us. It seemed as a collective, people were making the correct decisions as to what to do, so far. Astrophysicists and astronomers were also trying to figure out what was going on in the universe that might be causing this phenomenon. They seemed to keep pointing to the slowing down of the expansion of the universe. They speculated that maybe some pockets of the universe might be speeding up and some may be slowing down. Some speculated that this was a midway point in the universe's life, while others believed it was the universe in a sense showing its old age and that it was nearing its death. This would be billions of years off however but just the same the universe was making radical changes that were really only starting to be discovered by the human race. Some astrophysicists and astronomers speculated that in deep far off parts of the universe as well as parts of the universe not so far off, in large expanses of interstellar space that were free from gravity fields, mass and velocity there might be pockets of non-existence present. Scientists thought that throughout our universe there might be areas where time did not exist. The scientists began to speculate on alternative theories of black holes in space and some postulated these black holes were able to consume parts of the universe as well as expand limitlessly and effect time. Some astronomers wondered, still yet, if empty space itself could have velocity. The speculations came fast and furious and I believed they only served to confuse people.

These were the best educated guesses for humankind as man could only speculate about what was going on in the universe. Moreover, that left for us the realm of divine providence and divine principia, which to us was only in our hearts and souls and the scriptures of the world's great religious books. Around the world, it seemed that two sides or two camps manifested. The first was the ever-growing populace that was turning to prayer for hope and change as more of the masses were returning to their respective religions and praying for their lives and the lives of their children as well as the rest of the world's population. There were also speculations that had religious implications and some sounded valid while others were wild. In the town of Park Falls, churches were overflowing and not only on Sundays. The churches were holding masses everyday and our family was in regular attendance as well as many people we knew.

The next camp was that of persons, to put it bluntly, who where immoral and lawbreakers. It seemed they would take advantage to the end and take whatever they could and could get away with, in their desperation. The crimes they were committing were becoming more frequent and heinous. In Park Falls, the police were arresting unprecedented numbers of people for sex crimes against the young and the weak. The number of break-ins in town was epidemic and the number of assaults was rising. The mayor had also announced town council would hire more police to combat this problem but in the interim, he was asking the townsfolk to be vigilant and watch out for one another. It was obvious that if things did not change in the not too distant future that global chaos was going to envelop the world. The bleakness of the future wiped the smiles from people's faces. The world was becoming a place engulfed in despondency, distress and a general sense of impending doom. Huneo's SOLTES calibrator was in my barn and I would read it daily in the hopes that the readings would stabilize or slow down or reverse but that would be to no avail. The SOLTES calibrator was registering steady increases and showed no sign of abating. It was June 17, 2012 and the summer was about to dawn. The digital incremental/ exponential time speed indicator on the SOLTES calibrator was reading 6.983% or 100 minutes and 32 seconds differential from the time recorded November 12, 1995, as compared with a recording on April 23 of 6.334% or 91 minutes and 15 seconds in differential to the November 12, 1995 reading. This difference was huge and disheartening.

That Saturday, warm sunshine greeted us as we arose. We could finally wear our summer clothing comfortably outdoors again. Christine and I awakened slowly as we got up, washed and got dressed. We could hear Angela in her room moaning softly as she struggled to get up. Angela was six months pregnant and affected the least by the time speed changes. Christine went to check on her to make sure that she was all right. I went downstairs and started breakfast and at the same time, I called Bernie. Bernie was downcast this morning but I managed to perk him up. I told him that Christine and I would be going to his first barbeque of the season. I told him that we were going to see Huneo and Helen for a light lunch and then we would be by to his house for supper. Christine and Angela came downstairs and they were a little ruffled. "Good morning, Angela." I said, with a smile.

"What's good about it?" she said, with a frown. I looked at Christine and she shrugged her shoulders. "I'm sorry, Dad! I'm sorry!" she blurted out, and then she started crying.

"It's okay sweetie, its okay darling." I said. I went over, gave her a hug, and started to rub her shoulders to try to comfort her. "I'm going to cook you a nice breakfast this morning dear and that'll give you some energy and make you feel better." I said. She began to calm down. Christine took out the sausages for sausages and eggs that morning. We knew Angela was bothered and deeply troubled by the situation we were in, especially because she was bringing her baby into a dying world and she would die herself. We no longer kept the radio on to listen to the news because of its depressing nature. When we received our newspaper, we turned it face down so whomever that was not in the mood to read the latest revelations of the Pegasus Effect did not have to be continually bombarded with the news. The television was kept on quietly those days so as not to bother anyone, and it was only turned on in the evenings.

"I'm feeling a little better now, Dad." Angela said.

"That's good dear. You'll be feeling fine after you eat. Angela, do you want to come with your father and me today to, Huneo and Helens, and then we'll go to, Uncle Bernie's for a barbeque after?" Christine asked.

"Thanks, Mom, but I have plans to go to, Christopher's house. I want to spend some time with him and his parents. Christopher has set up a room for me for when I stay there with the baby and he wants me to see it, to see if it's okay for the baby and me. His parents are going to have a barbeque and I'm going to eat there, if that's okay?"

"Of course it's okay, sweetie. You're a grown woman. You can do whatever you please."

"Thanks Mom, I love you."

"I love you too dear." Christine replied. She gave her a big hug as they smiled at each other and that made me feel better as well.

"What's your sister doing, Angela? Is she coming down for breakfast?" I asked.

"I don't know if she's awake yet, Dad."

"That's okay, its Saturday, we'll let her sleep in." I said. I poured some coffee and put some bread in the toaster.

"Dad, Mom?"

"Yes, Angela." Christine and I responded.

"I don't like to say this, but I think, Paula is starting to have sex and she's starting to drink booze and take drugs."

"My goodness, Angela, are you sure about that?" Christine inquired.

"Yes, Mom."

"How do you know this, Angela?" I asked.

"I saw her at the mall doing this in the parking lot with some older men." Angela said, to our shock.

"Oh my God, are you sure it was her you saw?" Christine asked. Her voice was hushed as not to be overheard.

"Yes Mom, and she has condoms and spermicidal gel in her purse and I seen her drinking out of a liquor bottle with her friends. My friend, Jenny saw her at, The Blue Bird Club. She was with her friends. They got in with phony I.D. I guess and then she saw, Paula go outside with two men and get into a van. Jenny followed her and as she walked by the van they were taking her clothes off and theirs," Angela told.

"My God, Jim! What are we going to do about this?" Christine asked, with a disparaging howl.

"I don't know but she's too young and she can't be doing this. There's no way we're going to let her do this. She's a minor and if we have to confine her, we will! Oh, God. Why is this happening to her?" I said, letting down my defenses. "We're going to talk to her as soon as she gets up." I said and then Paula walked around the corner. "What's going on?" she asked.

"Why don't you tell us what's going on young lady?" Christine questioned. She jumped right on her.

"What do you mean, Mom?" Paula responded. She had a surprised look in her eyes.

"What do you mean what do I mean? I hear you're turning into a dirty little drug addicted slut! What do you have to say to that?" Christine retorted. She then started to approach Paula.

"Christine calm down, right now!" I exclaimed.

"Is that true, is it!" she exclaimed. Paula's eyes opened like saucers. "Is it? Is it!" Christine yelled.

"Easy Mom, please!" Angela begged. Just as Paula was about to answer, Christine smashed her across the face with her closed hand.

"You dirty slut!" Christine yelled. Paula cried out and crashed to the floor. I jumped in front of Christine and threw my arms around her.

"Christine stop! For God's sake, what the hell are you doing?" I yelled. Paula lay crumpled in a ball, screaming and crying on the floor. Angela looked on in horror with her hands cupped to her face.

"You get to your room right now you little cunt!" Christine yelled.

"Christine shut up! Shut up Christine! Right now, Christine, shut up!" I yelled. I tried my best to restrain her.

"Angela, take your sister to her room right now!" I shouted. Angela got up and tried to help her sister.

"Get out of my sight you dirty slut! I'm not having a whore in this house!" Christine yelled, again.

"Shut up, Christine, please shut up!" I implored.

"Get your hands off of me you rat!" Paula yelled, at her sister.

"I'm sorry, Paula, I'm sorry, Paula, forgive me!" Angela begged.

"Go to hell you bitch!" Paula screeched.

"Paula go up to your room right now!" I yelled. Paula picked herself up off the floor and went screaming and crying to her room. Angela sat back in her chair with her hands pressed to her cheeks. She was in complete shock and disbelief.

"Christine! What are you doing! What are you thinking?" I exclaimed.

"Oh my God, ah, ah, what have I done!" she cried out, "Jim, what have I done? What have I done!" she called out, again. I held her and Angela cried. I spotted Cindy under the pantry cringing and shaking with terror in her eyes. I did not know what to do or say but I knew I had to take over the situation.

"Angela, can you turn off the stove and go to your room?" I asked. She promptly complied.

"C'mon, Christine." I led her into the living room and on to the couch. I sat her down and held her. She sobbed. I tried to comfort her. After about ten minutes, she was calm again.

"Jim, what have I done to my youngest daughter?" she asked, despairingly, "What have I done, Jim?" she begged.

"You lost control, Christine, you simply lost control."

"Jesus Christ! What have I done to my daughters?"

"Easy now, Christine, let's calm down."

"What's happening to me, Jim? What's happening to me?"

"Easy Christine, you have to calm down and get some prospective."

"Okay, alright, I'll try!" she squawked. She rocked back and forth. Our house was quiet for the next hour as I prepared the rest of the breakfast and served it in their respective bedrooms. In Paula's room, she was under her sheets crying with her head buried. I put her breakfast on her dresser and closed the door. I figured the best thing was to have separation and quiet. After some time passed, I reminded Christine that we had to leave for Huneo and Helens. She said she could not go but I told her that she must stay by my side and keep away from Paula for the remainder of that day. I told Christine that Angela would take care of her while we were away.

"Jim, I'm ashamed of myself. Jim, I've done a terrible thing," she said.

"Okay, Christine, but you must have a cooling off period and you must reflect on this before you move on with it, do you understand?" I said. I tried to explain to her what she must do next.

"Yes, Jim, I understand." she answered. I went up and asked Angela if she could delay her visit with the Helgeson's until at least the early afternoon until we got back. She agreed to do this and phoned them to change her plans. I asked Angela to watch her sister and try to calm her. I asked her to get anything for her sister that she might need. I could see in Angela's eyes that she was willing to do anything for us, to save us. "I will Dad, I'll take care of her and try to calm her, I will, Dad, I promise." she replied.

"Alright good, call me on my cell for anything you might need okay, or for any other reason."

"I will, Dad, I will." Angela had a look of sadness in her eyes. I went to retrieve Christine's sweater and we left immediately for Huneo and Helens. As we drove, there was silence in the car. I could see that Christine was hurt by what she had done and it was coming home to roost. She stared out the window of our car and winced in the emotions that were churning inside her. I kept quiet and drove.

Our trip to Huneo's was a planned event and we could not cancel it at this juncture. We were going to discuss the more intricate details of the wedding plans with Helen. As we got closer, Christine worried about how she looked since she had been crying. I told her she looked fine. We drove up to their house and they were waiting for us. They had big smiles for us as they welcomed us. We said our 'hello's' and then went into their family room and discussed the girl's roles in the wedding. We shared a couple of drinks and appetizers. Things seemed to be a little more relaxed and Christine was smiling although I knew that deep inside, her thoughts were on what she had done to Paula. Huneo and I broke off and went out to his new garage and workshop to see his latest acquisitions. As we went into the garage, he turned and asked if everything was all right. "No, not really, Huneo. This morning we had a blow up with one of the girls and things got out of hand." I told him.

"Is there anything that, I or Helen, perhaps, might be able to help with, Jim?"

"No Huneo, for now I would just as well like to keep it a family matter, for now anyway, but thanks."

"Say no more, Jim. I just thought you were a little out of sorts today, especially Christine. She looks upset." Huneo said. We paced around his garage.

"We are Huneo, but for now we're going to have to struggle through this episode ourselves and do our best to resolve it." I said. He fully understood. We talked a little more and then we returned to our significant others. Huneo pushed things right along with Helen to get us out of our predicament and back on the road again. I could see in Christine's eyes that she was just roiling inside and wanted to leave as soon as possible as that moment finally came and none too soon.

We slipped on our sweaters and said our goodbyes. I could see that Helen was upset and sensed that something was wrong. I leaned over to Huneo and asked him to tell Helen that none of this was her fault and she could count on us in every way for the wedding. I told him I would call him later about this and we could talk more. Christine and I waved goodbye, walked to our car, and got in. I started it and we got under way again. As we drove down the road, Christine gritted her teeth, pounded her fists on the dashboard and screamed.

"What is it hon? What's the matter?" I asked.

"Oh God, Jim, I'm screwing up everything! Helen must think she did something wrong or something. I couldn't concentrate on what she was saying and I kept avoiding eye contact with her," she said. Christine buried her head in her hands. "What's happening to me, Jim? What's happening?" she bewailed. I said nothing and then I saw a diversion ahead in the road. I turned off towards an old lookout we used to go to when we were younger. This gave us the opportunity to be alone for a while without interruptions. I headed up the road to the top of the hill, which looked out over Park Falls. Christine protested. "Where are you going, Jim? I don't want to go up here!" she squealed.

"We're going!" I continued driving. When we got to the top of the hill, I pulled over and parked. We looked out over Park Falls. We had not been up here in a long time, it was beautiful, even more so than I had remembered. We sat, looking out over our little town, viewing the beauty that was before us. The wind was wafting through the surrounding trees and the sun shone brightly. It was warm. Christine looked lovely up here on the hill but I could see a deep pain in her face that tore me up. The fact that everything was going so wrong in our lives was starting to eat at me. Christine started to sob. "Christine hon, I think we need to sit here and talk things out. What do you say to that?" I suggested. She closed her eyes and lowered her head again.

"I think something has to happen or I'm going to go crazy, Jim."

"Is there anything you want to talk about in particular, Christine?"

"I want to know what future we have, Jim? Do we have a future or is the whole world going to die from this thing?" she asked, disparagingly. "I want to know why I laid into, Paula so badly and I want to know why I hit my young daughter whom I love so much, in the face… I want to know what's happening to me?" she begged.

"Christine the first thing you've gotta do is calm down and try not to be so hard on yourself. You made a mistake and the first thing you have to do is recognize that. Then, once you've admitted that to yourself, you can take corrective action."

"That sounds so easy, Jim but it goes deeper than that. I went way too far and it is not going to be fixed with a simple 'I'm sorry.'" Christine said. She began to open up.

"Listen, I think for now this is the place we have to start, Christine. This is not the only predicament you or we are in and we have to get this behind us fast. We're in a fight for our lives too and this really doesn't measure up." I stated.

"What do you mean, Jim?"

"I mean our mortality is at stake with this Pegasus Effect and it's probably one of the reasons you blew up the way you did and it's probably one of the reasons Paula might be behaving the way she's behaving!"

"Oh, it can't be that, can it?" Christine asked. She looked at me perplexedly.

"Christine, I think things are going to get a whole lot worse in the days and weeks to come and we have to be strong for the girls. Don't you agree with that?"

"I just can't seem to come to grips with this. It is so horrible and insidious."

"I know, I know sweetheart, I know. We have to come to grips with this and we have to forge ahead to try to save ourselves. Christine, we have to come to grips with this! Look, we're going to make mistakes but we need to keep focused on our family and friends because this is going to get worse, Christine. It's going to get worse and I'm not trying to scare you. There's no fix in sight for this!" I said.

"Jim, you're scaring me. Jim, you're taking away my hope! That's all I have left!" she said. Christine started to cry again.

"I know it's scary but the whole world is scared and you're not alone, we have each other and we have God with us."

"God, what do you mean, God? If God were with us, he wouldn't let this happen to us! God is not helping us at all!" she exclaimed.

"Christine, Christine you know that's not how it works. You know that, now c'mon."

"I don't know what I know anymore!"

"Christine we're going to go to, Bernie's and then we're going to call, Angela to make sure everything's alright. Then we're going to have dinner and then we'll go home and try to fix things with, Paula, alright?"

"Okay, I'll do that. I mean what other choice is there?" she said.

"We're going to get by hon, don't worry. I'll always be here for you." I said. I started the car and we drove to Bernie's house for dinner. It was around four o'clock. The afternoon was beautiful, and we started to feel better as we travelled. I cracked a few jokes that I had heard recently and I finally got a smile onto Christine's face. I even got a few hearty laughs from her. After approximately 20 minutes, we arrived at Bernie's home. He was in the front yard working on his flowers or should I say he was taking care of Stella's flowers. We pulled in and he had a big smile for us.

"Hello Bernie, how are you?" Christine greeted him.

"I hope you guys are hungry. I took out some big steaks. I'm not doing too badly today, Christine, how about you?"

"I've had better days, Bernie."

"Oh, oh, that doesn't sound so good. Anything I can help you with?"

"Not right away, Bernie, I just want to relax a bit and have some light conversation."

"Alright then, get out of the car and let's go into the back yard. I'll show you what I'm up to around the house this summer."

"Sounds good, let's go." Christine replied. We got out of the car and walked around to the back of his house. Bernie lived on a large piece of property with lots of natural foliage. Stella and Christine had built some impressive flowerbeds and gardens on the property over the years. Bernie and Stella's home was on a large hill and had a beautiful view of the university. He had one of the nicest homes in Park Falls. Stella Wakefield was responsible for the beauty both inside and outside their residence. She had the magic touch when it came to the home and garden. As we walked to the back yard, Bernie offered us a drink and we graciously accepted. "I'm famished and I'm thirsty." Christine said.

"Alright I'll fix you up. White wine, Christine?" Bernie offered.

"Yes, a big glass please."

"A beer for you, Jim?"

"Sounds good to me, Bernie?" I replied. Bernie went into the house to get the drinks as Christine and I looked around the backyard. I could see Christine looking at the flowers, while in her face, memories of Stella and the afternoons they would spend together in the summer growing these gardens and having their friendship bloom over the years was evident. I took this opportunity to call Angela to see how things were going at home. It took a while for Angela to answer but she eventually picked up. She was anxious to get going to Christopher's home to have her visit. She told me that Paula was still angry and would not come out of her room and she would not talk with her. She said Paula was in a bad mood as she was throwing things, slamming doors and crying. I asked Angela to stay with her as long as she could and to leave quietly when she had to so her sister would not think she was alone. I told her that we would be home as soon as we could and to take care of one another and then I hung up. I told Christine about the call and she took it in stride. Bernie came back out with our drinks and we started to unwind. We were like at our parent's house or at a second home when we came to Bernie and Stella's and it was easy for us to relax and be ourselves here. Bernie brought us around the property and gave us the latest updates on the landscape and I could see in his face that Stella was right there with him as he pointed out the features of his property. I was sure she was always on his mind. After awhile we sat down and got to talking. "So Christine, you looked like you had something on your mind earlier. Did you want to talk about it?" Bernie inquired.

"Well, today, I got into a big fight with, Paula. Actually, I attacked, Paula and said some pretty terrible things to her and then I hit her in the face and knocked her to the floor screaming and crying." Christine said, without trepidation.

"My goodness, Christine, that's pretty rough. She must have done something quite serious for you to react like that?"

"We found out, Paula has been up to no good. She's been smoking drugs and who knows what else and she's been having sex with much older men and if I find out whom they are!"

"Easy Christine, remain calm now." I said.

"Well I'm sorry, Jim, I can't. Our young daughter is becoming a whore right in front of our eyes and I'm not going to let that happen. She's not going to throw her life away and destroy our family in the process. I'm not going to let that happen!" Christine retorted.

"Okay dear, okay, but we have to be calm about this."

"What do you think, Bernie? What should we do about this?" she asked. Christine had hope in her eyes and wanted an answer that would appease her.

"I think if it were my daughter, I would do everything in my power and use every resource I could find to help me. I would look for people that had been through the same thing. I would see what they had to say and see if this might help me. You'd really be surprised what a few people who have been through the same thing might be able to offer you." Bernie explained this in his learned and professor like manner. This answer helped Christine right away. They began talking about Stella and Paula and getting out what needed to be said to help them ease their pains. I did not interject even though I knew that the main problem we faced was our own survival from the Pegasus Effect. They had their minds focused on other things that seemed more normal to a normal world so I let them be. I only butted in to find out where the food was to get things started for dinner. After awhile, they joined in the preparation and before we knew it, we were eating some big, world famous, Alberta steaks. A meal that was welcome to us. Both Christine and I were getting tired with all the days' events. We ate voraciously and not much was left to waste.

"Alright, Bernie, it's our turn." I said, "I want you to know that, Christine and I will be at your disposal twenty four hours a day if you need to talk with us or you don't feel well, okay?"

"Thanks, Jim. I knew you would be here for me. I know I still have a lot of rough days ahead before things get better."

"Well that's the operative phrase here, Bernie. You know that as time passes, things will start to ease up in your mind and you'll have only the good memories of, Stella and the love."

"I know, Jim. I know it's going to be a long road to recovery."

"We'll always be here for you, Bernie, always." Christine said. She emphasized our commitment.

"I know it's going to take about a year and it's been almost three months now so I'm slowly going to be getting there."

"That's the spirit, Bernie. And remember, Stella will always be with you."

"I will, Jim, I will." he said. We finished our dinner and after some coffee, we told Bernie that we had to leave because of Paula. He encouraged us to be on our way. I told him I would call him first thing in the morning and we would talk or maybe go out for breakfast or lunch. Bernie agreed this would be nice but he reminded me that the next week was the last week of school and he was going down to work in his office. He planned to do some cleaning out of his old files and get ready for the summer holidays. I remembered that I had to do the same. At any rate, we would see each other at the university that following day. Christine and I said our goodbyes and then we left for home. It was almost 7:30 pm and Christine was not looking forward to seeing Paula to apologize but she knew that this was the most important thing to do right then. When we got in the door of our home, the house was quiet. Angela had left a note on the bureau by the front door telling us she had gone to Christopher's house.

The radio was on quietly and the curtains were drawn. Christine decided to go upstairs and see Paula in her bedroom. Christine walked into her room, saw that Paula was fast asleep, and decided not to wake her. She came back downstairs and I turned on the television. We decided to watch the news to see the latest stories. As we sat down, we held hands and got comfortable. The news was about to come on as a tag for the upcoming broadcast played. "Ahead on the news at the top of the hour, calibrator numbers rise as the world prays for a miracle." A spokesperson announced as we braced ourselves for what would be next. Some commercials played, then ended, and then the national news began. "Good evening everyone. This is, Bill Adams, reporting for Thursday, June 18, 2012. Tonight in our top story, SOLTES calibrators the world over are recording higher than usual jumps in their readings as this has raised alarm bells for governments around the globe," the commentator reported. He looked sternly into the camera and continued. "Sources in the government have concurred and the speculation is more grim than expected. Researchers within the scientific community say that at this pace the general populations of the world will be wiped out in 6 months to a year. These catastrophic predictions are on the heels of the government of the United States announcing that there is no defense against the effects of the universe slowing down and that the people of the world must brace themselves for their final days," the news anchor announced. He looked downward and said nothing for the next dozen seconds. He finally raised his head and with a look of sadness, he spoke. "In a related story, the peoples and populations of the world have begun praying en masse. In churches and synagogues around the world, the populations have begun to pray for salvation. People feel that this is their only hope for themselves and their children." Christine and I sat there dumbfounded as we could not believe what we were hearing and seeing. We sat and stared at the television for the remainder of the broadcast. There were reports of people from all over the world succumbing in large numbers to the first symptoms of high levels of stress. The news broadcast reported that people throughout the world were developing tremors and shakiness. It was at that moment, I noticed a tremor in my hand and it was not coincidental. Christine looked down in shock at the tremor I had developed. She gasped. As I looked at Christine, I could see that she was getting more gray hair and she was developing age lines. It was not much but it was enough to be perceptible. "God help us, Jim. God please help us, God help my babies, please!" she cried out. We hugged tightly. It seemed like all our hope had been taken away and there was nothing left to do except to wait for death to come. We were sad. At that moment, the phone rang and it was Christine's parents. As Christine spoke on the phone with them, she began having an emotional conversation. I noticed at this point, through an open blind, that a light was on in the barn and I could see Huneo's car in the driveway. He was out looking at the calibrator I was sure. I got dressed and excused myself to Christine. She waved for me to go ahead. I proceeded out to the barn. When I got to the barn, Huneo was sure enough up in my observatory starting the calibrator. "Hello, Huneo!" I called out. He turned and saw me. "Hello Jim, I'm just satisfying my curiosity. I didn't disturb anyone, did I?"

"No that's fine, Huneo, you're welcome here anytime. Is everything okay?"

"As well as can be expected, Jim for our situation at hand. Are you coming up?"

"Yeah, I'm coming." I started climbing the ladder up to the loft.

"Is there a reading yet, Huneo?"

"No Jim, I just turned the calibrator on now so it'll be a few minutes," he said. I got up to the top, grabbed a seat, and tried to get comfortable.

"So is this a normal visit, Huneo or are you doing something special?"

"No, I'm just concerned."

"How's, Helen doing?"

"She's irritable lately, Jim. She's visiting her parents tonight."

"How are her parents?"

"They're in a depression and are not coping very well. This is starting to upset her to no end. Her younger brother is not helping much. He has no experience in life situations or wisdom as to know what to do." Huneo explained.

"So what'll you do about that situation?"

"Well, the way things are going it doesn't look too good. Perhaps they'll have to move in with us till the end."

"You think that's where we're headed?" I asked.

"What do you mean, Jim?"

"The end?"

"Yes, I think that's exactly where we're headed, Jim." Huneo stated, with conviction.

"Okay here we go. I'm getting the reading. It's a 7.019% increase, Jim over the November 12th, 1995 time speed recording,"

"What's that in minutes?"

"Well let's see here, Jim. I'll punch it in on my calculator," He fumbled with his calculator. I looked at the calibrators' readings, as the device seemed to be functioning normally. "That's 101 minutes and 4 seconds, there or about." Huneo replied. He shook his head.

"That's about a half a minute more than on Tuesday." I said.

"You measured the time speed on Tuesday?"

"Yeah, it was 100 minutes 30 seconds."

"Well Jim, at this rate I'm afraid we don't have much time left at all, four or five months if we're lucky."

"Yeah, I think that's about right." I said, dejectedly. We sat there for the next little while and stared at the calibrator as it kept running. It would run without feelings or emotions as it would give us a rough countdown to our impending doom. After awhile, I said goodbye to Huneo for that evening and then I would head back to the house. I gave Huneo a hug and he hugged me back. We agreed that we would try to work together for our families when the need arose. I left him to lock up and then I started walking toward the house. As I got closer, I could hear voices and then closer still, I could hear yelling. It was Christine and Paula and they were fighting. I ran quickly into the house. Christine and Paula were fighting in the living room. I ran into the living room as Paula took a swing at her mother. I pushed the both of them to the couch. They were screaming but I did not know what they were saying. I yelled at them to stop and then I led Paula up to her room. She was crying and saying we had no right to do this to her. I told her to keep quiet and I would be back later to talk with her. I told her that she was grounded for two months and slammed the door on her. She screamed at me and pounded her fists. I went back downstairs to see what had happened and Christine was pacing in the kitchen. "What's happening now, Christine!" I demanded.

"She just came downstairs and wanted to fight with me, Jim. She just wanted to fight with me!"

"Well, what the hell was she saying to you?"

"She said I had no right to run her life. She said that we treat, Angela better than we treat her and she has the right to do whatever it is that she wants." Christine explained.

"I know she's out of control now. We have to take control of her, Christine. She sounds a little like I was when I was her age. She doesn't know what she's doing."

"Do you think that's all it is, Jim? Do you think that's all it is?"

"No I don't think that's all it is! It's the Pegasus Effect as well. Christine you seem a lot less upset than you were about all this a little while ago?"

"I know, I know, Jim, I think I must be over the first scrap I had with her. I have to have a long sincere talk with her, Jim. I've got to try to help her and calm her down." Christine said.

"Listen hon we're going to have to talk with her but we're going to have to put more emphasis on this Pegasus Effect starting now!" I stated, "Huneo and I have been talking and there isn't much time left for us. We have to come to terms with the realization of this, it's more important than anything else." I said. Christine fell into the chair and dropped her head in her hands.

"Christine are you…"

"Jim! Jim! Could you just leave me alone for awhile, please," she said. She spoke in a tone of frustration.

"Are you..."

"Jim! Please! For awhile, just let me be," she said, again. I walked away. I figured it was best. I walked up to our room, as I did I saw Huneo getting into his car and I wondered if he had witnessed what had happened. Not that it would have mattered. I went to our room and got ready for bed. I had a bit of time to think and I wanted to make things better but I was getting frustrated. I really did not know what to do about this and I could feel that I was becoming more tired.

I could feel with each passing day that I was becoming less energetic and as I looked in the mirror that night, I could see new lines on my face and more grey hair. I was taken by surprise with these changes. They were happening so fast. I examined myself and I could see that my muscle tone was softening and my skin was becoming dryer.

I heard the dog yelp and the door opened and closed. I went to the stairs to see that Angela had come home. I watched her take her shoes off at the door and her mother come and greet her. Christine put her arms around her and they embraced. This made me feel better. I went back to our room and got into bed. After awhile, Christine came upstairs. She quietly slipped in beside me and we went to sleep. It was not the best of days but at least we were together.

Over the next few days, things were not much better as I noticed that everyone in town with the exception of the very young was getting grey hair. Angela, Paula and Christine also started turning grey and this bothered them immensely. They were young women and they were aging at a higher speed. Even Paula, almost fifteen years old, was getting age lines in her face. The girls had finished school and stayed home. They tried to remain as normal as possible. Paula's friends could visit her and we decided that if Angela went to the mall she could go with her, otherwise she was grounded. Christine and I had arranged with our parents and sisters and brothers to either visit or keep in close contact as time permitted. With school being in its last week the university was empty and only students with exams were present. People wanted to be with their families as the crisis was intensifying. The hospital in Park Falls was asking for volunteers and donations of any kind. They wanted food, clothing, flashlights, batteries, candles, Tupperware, silverware, as well as a list of other essentials that was quite extensive. They were stocking up for the worst-case scenario. The people of Park Falls also began to hoard food and other necessities of life for their survival. These acts of self-preservation were instinctual and it seemed there were many supplies around to be had. I supposed that was another good thing. Most businesses in town began to operate on reduced schedules. The mayor insisted that new hours be posted on the outside of all businesses in large lettering. This was decided by council to keep order in the town.

On television and radio, the news became more grim and desperate. Calibrator readings from most countries were announced daily. The readings were the same of course. The calibrators were running like synchronized clocks. They used the repetition for confirmation and back up of the others and vice versa. The speed in which time passed increased to a faster rate with the dawning of each new day. People around the world prayed to God, asking God for a miracle, for the Pegasus Effect to cease, and for life, as they knew it to return to normal. The global death rate soared as hospitals of the world were overwhelmed. Medical camps were constructed by militaries as doctors tried to alleviate the suffering of the first waves of victims.

Fighting and general mayhem throughout the streets of the world was epidemic. In Park Falls, people were assaulting one another and losing control of their emotions and their anger. People were no longer civil to each other. However, they did not mean to do or say the things they were in most cases. The stress levels of the planet were rising dramatically as they were fuelled by the fact that stress was bringing on more stress and the faster passing of time was firing the brain faster, in effect overloading its capabilities.

Astronomers from around the world were fighting with each other. Their postulations were too many and the scenarios seemed plausible but they could not even agree on a few choice theories. They could not tell how fast the universe was slowing its expansion or if the whole of the universe was slowing. They also questioned their readings from telescopes and other measuring devices as to where the universe really was. The speed of the universe's expansion could no longer be measured. Because of inconsistencies in the passage of time, both perceptions in velocities and/or distance were distorted and not able to be gauged on man's now perceived as, feeble measuring devices. Astronomers began to question whether the whole of the universe was moving or had velocity, or whether space itself had velocity. The one thing they agreed upon was that known space-time and the universe itself could no longer be measured with any precision. As long as the

SOLTES calibrator was showing a shift in time speed, nothing else could be measured accurately in interstellar space or the universe. This was seemingly the only consensus among the scientists and astrophysicists. We could not tell accurately what was happening in the universe with any device of precision that was reliable. Measurements of telling how far away the stars were was no longer possible with any steadfastness. The scientific community wondered how much of the universe was actually out there. Astronomers were looking so far back in time that a lot of the universe was probably gone some hypothesized. They surmised that the universe maybe dying and a lot of it might have already died off. Stars could not be living as far back as astronomers were looking, in the stages of life that the stars were at, in relationship to our present time and place in the universe. This was the basis for them to make their new postulations as to what was happening. The universe was dying and ending. Then again, it was always ending as everything does with the exception of immortal life. Was the whole of the universe slowing, or its contents, or parts of it? Was it slowing from the outside in or the inside out or erratically or what? There was no way for anyone to tell. The astrophysicists were conjecturing. What if the universe slowed down from its outside perimeter to the center? How fast would it die? They wondered if the universe's death was only a stone's throw away. Was it possible that most of the universe was already gone and we may witness the end of the universe firsthand? The scientists were thrown for a loop. They had no real idea of what was happening with any reliability. They also postulated that time speed and time speed changes were a major factor in evolutionary development. Adaptation and transformation were primarily based upon the rate of time speed passage, and secondarily, adaptation was based upon environment and circumstance.

The problem with the science was that it was not helping us. It was not explaining anything to us accurately or with any meaning that might help us get out of this crisis. Medical science was doing the best it could with what it had. Pharmaceuticals were being manufactured in huge quantities for what the world needed most, the simple ones like aspirin, valium, vitamins and others. These were the staples they figured we would need but I didn't think it was going to make a difference.

The date was Saturday, July 11, 2012. The summer breezes were warm and the days were long or so it seemed. The schools were closed and the young people were home with their families. Families were staying home and coming together in this extraordinary yet critical time in humankind's existence. Park Falls was in a state of emergency. In addition, like any other place in the world we wanted to be close to home in our last days. We planned to have our parents over and see them for the last times and maybe they would stay. Huneo and Helen were our friends that visited on a regular basis along with Bernard Wakefield who was spending most of his time with us since the passing of, Stella. Bernie had been alone and needed someone to be with in these awful times. The summer was as beautiful as ever but it was probably the last summer for everyone on earth the way events were unfolding.

We spent most of our time being around our home trying to enjoy ourselves, as things were not good and by no means improving. Huneo and Helen would come to visit that day and we would have a barbeque. The whole family as well as Bernie, Helen, Huneo, and Christopher would have dinner together. Paula and her mother were not talking to one another and we confined Paula to staying at home for the most part. She had been getting many headaches as of late and I had seen her throw up. She was rebellious these days and she swore and cursed all the time. We have scolded her but eventually we gave her the freedom to talk the way she wanted. She had become a delinquent that was hell bent on immoral behavior. We had to watch her constantly. Paula had also become depressed and she complained about nightmares. This had become another phenomenon arising out of the Pegasus Effect. These dreams were widely reported. Medical science was at a loss to explain the increase in dreaming and in particular the nightmares, sometimes quite vivid nightmares. I had also experienced the nightmares and they could be disturbing to the point of waking me up in a cold sweat.

My dreams would come shortly after I would fall asleep and they seemed to last only a few minutes. In the recurring dream I've had, everything seems to start out okay as my family is enjoying themselves in a park or field and the sun is shining. We are doing summer things, walking or tossing a ball or whatever and then the dream starts to become sullen. In my dreams, the sky becomes dark and we become frightened and decide to leave the park. As we leave the park, more people enter the dreams who are also frightened. As my dreams progress, the sky turns black and then the sun turns dark. People in the dreams start to panic and fight as they try to escape. As we run, we pass huge glass houses on the landscape with people inside them, cringing in pain. Trapped in these glass houses, they watch us as we run in fright. The sky fills with debris that looks like pieces of bricks falling from above, as they get closer to the ground, the bricks catch fire and begin to pummel the fleeing hordes. At that point, in the dream, I am only a spectator and I can see Angela and her baby and Paula and Christine trying to run from the fiery bricks. The sky is black and there are fiery bricks falling around the glass houses but they do not hit the glass houses. The people in the glass houses are in pain. They are scratching at the glass trying to get out. It is a scene of carnage as people are bleeding, disheveled, and in various states of undress as the bricks pound them. The dream becomes a surreal stark madness. Blackness then ensues throughout the landscape with a tremendous hail of screaming, shrieking and scraping blasts. I would then bolt upright from the ghastly images. The most unsettling part of the dream is the fact that it is so seemingly real and so vivid that it has a shock effect. After the dreams, I need ten to fifteen minutes to come back to coherence and escape the images. This dream and others similar were affecting about half the population worldwide. There was no commonly shared or consistent explanation for these dreams. Perceived as a prophetic dream that was part of the Pegasus Effect, a divine happening was the way the dream was construed. At least half the world's population believed that this was the hand of God in his wrath and judgment. I believed this also. As for the rest of my family, Christine was also having a hard time. For Christine the problem was fighting off depression and delusional thinking. Christine was easily frightened and had crying fits. She thought that people were in collusion against her and that the people of the world were not what they seemed. She was also starting to hallucinate. Out of the corners of her eyes, she saw shadows of what she perceived were people or things approaching her. She had also developed more gray hair and looked haggard. It was not just her though as we all looked haggard from the stresses of the effect and its ever-increasing pressures. As for Angela, she was fairing out the best so far. I did not know if it was her pregnancy helping her but she was not in as bad of shape as the rest of us. Most people were developing twitches and tremors. This seemed to be the most common manifestation of the effect. I believed everybody was afflicted with these tremors to varying degrees. I had them the worst in our family. We were trying to live our lives as normally as possible as the effects were taking over. When we went into town, we saw people as they were falling apart and succumbing to the effects as well. The people were sad and it was commonplace these days to see people crying or praying in the streets. There were no more smiles. It was rare for happy moments. The Pegasus Effect had set in and like other drawn out tragedies; it brought us despair and hopelessness. At the hospital in Park Falls, there were increasing fatalities. There were more deaths than usual. At night, we gathered around the television and watched the world slide into chaos, like in our dreams. Throughout the world, people were losing control of themselves, as fighting, raping and killing were rampant. Governments were doing their best to keep the peace with their militaries but it was easy to see that this would not be the case in the not so distant future. Around the world, people stopped working and went home to be with their families. People were praying and urging others to pray for help in the world's hours of need. People were praying for divine intervention. We were praying for divine intervention. Our destiny was out of our hands.

Huneo and Helen pulled into our driveway and we went out to greet them. They looked tired and a little downcast but we managed to get a bit of warmness going with a few jokes and hugs. We were together and we would sit around the house and enjoy the day in the warm sun. Angela and Christopher sat cuddled on the porch swing. They had become closer to one another. Paula stayed in the house and watched television and we retired to our garden and patio to sit and rest. Bernie, Helen, Christine, Huneo, Cindy, and I started to make some semblance of a happy day. We planned to sit around and possibly do some light chores. Later in the day, we would have a nice meal on the barbeque. Helen and Christine decided to pot a few flowers for in the house while we guys decided to throw the football around. I turned the radio on to some light music. As we threw the ball, our conversation veered to the situation in town. "You know, Jim, Helen and I just came from town. The people seem to be quite depressed. I saw a few people just standing or sitting with tears in their eyes. I think we're coming to the apex of the effect for humans and other animals." Huneo said, as he threw the ball.

"I think you're right, Huneo. I was in town near the hospital and the people were lined up outside the doors and there was a lot of despair in those eyes." Bernie added.

"I know we're coming to an apex guys but whether it's sooner or later, I think things are going to get a lot worse." I said.

"Have you checked the calibrator readings lately, Jim?" Huneo asked.

"Not since, Wednesday. You guys want to have a look?"

"Yeah, let's all go up and have a look." Bernie suggested.

"Okay, let's do that. Does anyone want a drink first?" I offered.

"I thought you'd never ask, Jim, I'll have a beer." Huneo replied.

"Make that two, Jim." Bernie chirped.

"Okay, three beers it is then." I threw the football one last time. At the moment I threw the ball, the radio chimed in with a live bulletin. As we listened in, a newscaster spoke. "This is CRWW Radio in Winnipeg, John Parker reporting. It has just been reported on the American National News network and the wire services that a major volcanic eruption is currently taking place in Italy. Mt. Vesuvius has erupted. These are preliminary reports and no details have been given," the reporter stated. We looked at each other with indifference. "The only information available at this time is that people are being evacuated. This eruption is reported to have started forty-five minutes ago as information is now just filtering in," the newsman said. He then signed off with a tag to stay tuned for further updates. "Sounds serious." I said. Bernie and Huneo agreed. I went into the house to get the beer and then I returned. Everyone seemed contented today and I was thankful for that. I looked at my family and friends on this warm day and they looked so fragile and precious. They were greatly loved. As I went into the barn, I could hear Bernie and Huneo up in my observatory. They were getting the calibrator warmed up and having a few laughs. I grabbed hold of the ladder with one hand and had the beer in my other. "Hey guys, I got the beer here." I called out.

"Well come on up, Jim, that makes you, VIP." Bernie said.

"Hey listen, after we have a beer, do you guys want to help me run a railing up the side of this ladder to make it easier to go up and down?" I asked.

"Sure, Jim."

"Yeah, we'll help you, Jim but it's going to cost you." Huneo said. He chuckled at me struggling up the ladder.

"Cost me, like what?"

"It'll cost you another beer, Jim and a barbeque dinner,"

"That's a good deal, Jim." Bernie added.

"I'll say." I made it to the top of the ladder. I handed out the beer and then I opened my observation doors. The sun streamed in to take the humidity out of the air. We sat around the calibrator as it did its thing. My telescope was also in the barn. We sat and admired it as we drank our beers.

"That's a nice scope, Jim, I'm anxious to come over and peer through it with you one day."

"Well, Huneo, if you're here at dusk tonight you're more than welcome."

"Oh, okay, that sounds good to me."

"The calibrator is just about to give us a reading." Bernie announced.

"Alright," We gathered around the calibrator. We watched it for a few moments and then it gave us the reading. The reading from the digital incremental/exponential time increase indicator came up.

"Well, the reading is 7.531%, 7.531%!" Huneo stated. He shook his head and sighed.

"My goodness, is the percentage that high? You've got to be kidding!" Bernie exclaimed. He had a shocked look on his face.

"Huneo, what does that convert to in minutes?" I asked.

"Just a minute, Jim, I'll have to calculate that," Huneo took out his calculator and began to punch in the numbers.

"My God, Jim, I can't believe the increase is so high! No wonder we feel so bad and were getting worse so fast." Bernie said. He shook his head as he looked at the SOLTES calibrator.

"Jim that works out to 108.44 minutes difference in time speed as compared to the November 12th, 1995 time speed recording. That's a lot, Jim. We're in big trouble, very big trouble." Huneo said, and he was right. We had no way of knowing what was going to happen next but we knew that we probably did not have much time left on this planet.

"Listen guys, not a word of these time speeds to the girls alright. This'll only upset them. They're going to find out about this on the news anyway so let's give them the day." I wanted to protect them from the bad news we had just discovered. We decided after a short while that we would go down and put on our best party faces and enjoy the day with our loved ones.

We went back to the patio and I offered the guys another beer, which again they heartily accepted. Christine and Helen walked around the corner carrying the flowers they had just pulled up and potted. We then sat in the shade of our big oak tree and began to relax. "Christine?" Bernie spoke. "Why don't you ask, Angela, Christopher and Paula to join us out here for the afternoon?"

"That's a good idea, Bernie! We need someone to operate the barbeque and it's almost that time. I'll go get them."

"Never mind, Christine, I'll get them. I'm going in to get some drinks. Sit and relax, hon."

"I won't argue with you, Jim. I don't have the strength." Christine replied.

As I passed Angela and Christopher, I invited them out to the patio and they eagerly moved out to join us. I then went into the house to get Paula. I found Paula upstairs staring at herself in the mirror in her room with a sad look in her eyes. I began to speak with her. "Paula dear would you like to join us outside on the patio for a while and have a barbeque with us?"

"I'm not in the mood, Dad," she replied, in a sullen tone.

"I know you're not in the mood, Paula but we really want to see you outside and it would make your mother happy."

"Why would I want to make her happy?" she retorted.

"Paula please. Paula listen to me! For me today, would you please try to find it in your heart to be with us, your family? We love you very much, Paula and we want you with us." I pleaded.

"Okay okay, Dad, I'll come out. I'll be out in ten minutes,"

"Thanks Paula, you're going to have a good time sweetie, don't worry." Paula had been a source of great consternation for her mother since their fight a month ago. Christine had tried repeatedly to get Paula to forgive her. However, Paula would not relent. Maybe today I hoped. At any rate, I got the drinks for everyone and I went back to a scene of laughter and humorous stories. Huneo regaled the gang with tales from his university days. Bernie also amused us with his stories of how he helped me get my degree. He had everyone in stitches. We were having a good old time. There were so few of them in the last little while. Paula came out and everybody cheered her. She finally had a smile on her face. I hoped we could have some fun that day and we did. The whole family was together for the first time in a month. It was hard to get everyone together as the family had one reason or another for not gathering. The Pegasus Effect was taking over our lives in what seemed a sneaky and sinister manner. It was only three months previous that we were a happy and balanced family. Three months later we were shells of our former selves using every fiber in our bodies to hang on to what we once took for granted, a normal life. After a fun afternoon, we had a barbeque. We could smell the barbeques of other

Park Fallsers wafting in the breeze. I had a warm feeling as I looked at my loved ones. It was on this afternoon that I began to feel contentment. I felt contentment, as I never had before. I felt that everything that I wanted to know about life, I knew. I felt whatever my fate was or that of my loved ones, was the way it was going to be. I felt that a divine plan was being imparted upon us. I could feel it inside my chest as I felt safe yet I knew I would probably die soon. We were on the patio, Angela, Christopher, Christine, Bernie, Helen, Huneo and even Cindy. They looked happy and at ease for the moment. The only exception was Paula. She sat with a somber, glum look in her eyes. This was the spoiler for me but I tried not to let that get me down. She would come around in the end I surmised. We enjoyed the day with gusto as we ate a healthy feast of chicken and ribs followed by apple pie and ice cream. Even Paula perked up and smiled as we ate our dinner. She laughed and even told a few jokes, which for that moment gave me an impression of the happy young girl I once knew only a few short months previous. It gave me hope. After dinner, we loosened our belts. We cleaned up and the younger ones went their own way as Paula went to her room to listen to music and Christopher and Angela decided to go and visit Christopher's parents.

The rest of us retired to our old rocker swing out alongside the barn to watch the sunset. We had an old swing that Christine and I had refurbished to almost brand new condition. The ball bearings on it were well oiled and it rolled back and forth silently and smoothly. We could sit on the swing in comfort for hours. Huneo, Helen, Bernie, Christine and I hopped aboard. We had some fine wine to sip on as we watched the sun go down in the western sky. It was a beautiful evening. As the sun disappeared, wispy clouds rolled in to fill the sky in a light haze just enough to block out the stars. I decided to light a fire in our outdoor fireplace to add to the ambience. It was a warm evening that only required the lightest of clothing. As I filled the fireplace with logs, the rest of the gang reminisced about better times of summers past. We were laughing when suddenly the sky grew bright in the distance, south of where the sun had set an hour or so earlier. This light garnered our attention. "What's that light do you think, Jim?" Christine inquired, perplexedly.

"Yeah, what's that light, I wonder?" Bernie said.

"Jeez, I don't know what that is. Maybe a large airplane's landing lights?" I replied.

As I spoke, the light grew in intensity and started to spread throughout the sky. Everybody was wondering aloud as to what it was that was glowing. "What's that light?" "What is that?" everyone was commenting. Paula came out of the house and stared up at the sky.

"What's that light, Dad?" she asked.

"I don't know sweetheart. Let's turn on the radio and see if there's anything on the news."

"Whatever it is it's not the usual that's for sure, is it, Jim?" Huneo inquired.

My cell phone rang, it was, Angela. "Hello, Dad, it's me. Do you know what that light is in the sky?" she asked.

"I don't know sweetie, I can't really say. We're baffled here as well my dear. Maybe we'll find out something on the radio." I said.

"Dad, I'm going to come home, I'm frightened." Angela responded.

"C'mon home sweetie if you want, we'll be here for you." I said goodbye and hung up. I noticed lights going on and people coming out of the adjacent homes. I imagined this was happening throughout Park Falls and far beyond. We could not figure out what the light might be.

"I think it could be a reflection off the moon, Huneo. What do you think?" Bernie queried.

"That's possible. That's quite possible, Bernie. I think you might be right." Huneo replied. The light intensified further. The whole sky was bright as the point just south of the sunset was ablaze with intense light. This became a worrisome happening whatever it was. We flipped through the radio stations and then we found some news. The radio announcer said that people were reporting a bright ball of light in the sky in Winnipeg to the east of us but they had no idea what it was either. The clouds were distorting the view of whatever it was that was in the sky. However, it was mesmerizing nonetheless. We watched the brightly glowing object in awe.

The light then leveled off at a high intensity. It was moving off in the distance and seemingly setting on the horizon. After about twenty minutes, it disappeared.

"What was that, Dad?" Paula asked, again.

"I don't know sweetie, I just don't know."

"What do you think, Huneo?"

"I don't know, Jim but maybe it's a reflection off the planet Venus, that's all I can think of. It happens from time to time."

"That could be, Jim. That has happened before around these parts." Bernie added.

"I know, I think that sounds about right." I said.

We were standing around watching the sky and listening to the radio for news. Angela and Christopher pulled in the driveway. They came over to us as they looked up at the sky.

"What was that light, Dad?" Angela asked. She had a strained concern in her voice.

"I can't tell you for sure sweetie but we think it might be the reflection of the sun off one of the planets."

"It scared me, Dad. I thought something bad was happening again,"

"I know, we were wondering that too."

At this point, as I looked at my kids, I felt like one of them. I felt like a kid because I could not give them any of the answers they wanted. I felt vulnerable and fragile to the events and the not knowing. We were calming down as it was dark again. "Wow, I feel light on my feet." Christine said, unexpectedly.

"So do I, I feel like I don't weigh anything." Helen stated.

"Me too, me too!" Angela squawked. The fire in the fireplace burst skyward. I ran to spread the wood and calm the flames but as I moved, my steps became eight or ten feet apart. "My God, what's happening!" I exclaimed. I was at the barbeque in a flash and I felt weightless as if I was about to float. Suddenly, everyone started freaking out.

"What is happening? What's Happening!" the girls yelled.

"I don't know, Christine!" I went to hold her. Huneo ran to Helen. Bernie went to Paula and Angela went to Christopher. We clumped together looking at the sky in frightened bewilderment.

"What's happening? What's happening?" each clamored.

After another minute, which seemed like an hour, our weight seemed to come back. Cindy was barking frantically at the sky. Then, unexpectedly, we felt heavy. We were freaking out. In town in the distance, the lights of every home came on at once, it seemed. Fire sirens, car alarms and police sirens were blaring. The noise was coming from all directions. Our weight returned to normal. We panicked. Next, the old air raid sirens from the hills went off. The girls screamed. "What's happening? What's happening!" they yelled.

"I don't know sweetie, I just don't know!" I responded. I was panicked and frightened. We huddled together in shock and stared at the landscape around us. We were frightened to our inner cores. After approximately ten minutes of this panic, the air raid sirens finally subsided and we breathed a collective sigh of relief. We were frightened witless but we began to calm down somewhat.

"Let's all go in the house and put the television news on to see if we can find out what's going on. C'mon everyone, let's go in the house!" I commanded. We headed towards the door. We filed in and went straight to the living room. I turned on the television and started to flip through the channels to see if we could find out what was happening. We sat in front of the television for almost a half hour before we started to get any news stories. The gang was reliving the event. They were chattering away at a hundred miles per hour. I tuned in to a breaking news story on one of the networks. "Quiet everyone, quiet please the news is coming on!" I ordered. We listened up. The news anchor came on the television. "Good evening everyone this is John Barkley for ACN bringing you a special breaking news bulletin. Tonight at approximately 10:33 pm Eastern Daylight Time, a large ball of light was seen in the skies over the western hemisphere. We now understand that hundreds of thousands and possibly millions of people reported this event to all manner of authorities. Power outages are being reported worldwide and it is now believed that some type of astronomical event has taken place in deep space. Reports from around the world are starting to filter in. The President of the United States has been alerted and is preparing to make a statement at 9:30 am tomorrow morning and we will carry that event for you live," the anchor stated, "As far as we can ascertain, the military is on high alert and experts from all over are trying to decipher what has happened. The light continues to be visible over the Pacific Ocean and it is believed by some reporting observatories that maybe a near earth supernova has occurred, that a near earth star has exploded." the news anchor reported.

"My goodness, that's what it is! I'll bet it's a supernova!" Huneo exclaimed.

"I think you're right, I think that's what it is too." Bernie concurred.

"You're right guys, it has to be. I mean what else could it be." I said.

The reporter continued. "For the moment there is no conformation in any way as to what has happened. We will keep our viewers informed with our next update at 12:00 am. In other news, the eruption of Mt. Vesuvius in Italy has grown in size considerably. It has now claimed the lives of more than ten thousand people. We will keep on top of these stories for you for our upcoming broadcasts and we will have live updates of the Pegasus Effect and the increasing death toll. This is John Barkley reporting," The ACN Network then signed off until later that evening.

"Oh my God, what has happened in Italy? All those people dead." Christine asked.

"There was a volcanic eruption in Italy today, Christine. We heard about it earlier but it slipped our minds. It didn't sound that bad when we heard about it." Bernie said, almost apologetically.

"The whole world is coming to an end, isn't it?" Paula blurted. She stared at the television.

"Please, Paula try to take it easy, it's going to be okay." I said. Christine went over and tried to comfort her. Paula pushed her away. This made Christine start weeping, Paula began to cry and then she left the room. Everybody's day had come to an abrupt and depressing end. Everyone had a sad look in his or her eyes. I became unhappy as well. Everybody excused him or herself. They went to their rooms. Huneo and Helen said their goodbyes and left for their home. Bernie stayed in our guestroom most of the time these days as he went there to retire for the evening. Christine and I sat in the living room. I turned off the television and we sat in the dark. I held her and tried to comfort her best I could. When things went bad it was harder to recover as we were more affected by the time speed changes. We went up to our bedroom eventually as everything seemed to calm down in the town. All was quiet. We were exhausted after this day and went straight to bed. We muttered words of 'good night' to each other. We went to bed indifferent to one another that evening.

As I awakened Sunday morning, I looked at the clock and it was 8:20 am. I looked over at Christine and she was still sleeping. I watched her sleep. She breathed softly. I thought about what she has meant to me over the past twenty-three years. I thought about all the beauty of life that we were fortunate enough to share together. I thought about how much I loved her and how precious she was to me. I realized that life would be difficult to live indeed, if I were to lose her. I thought of what Bernie must have been going through. At that point, I felt two eyes staring at me. "Good morning Christine, I love you." I said.

"Hey you, I love you too." she replied. We cuddled together as a light rain fell outside. Our window was open and we could smell the freshness of the foliage in the air. I felt well rested that morning.

"Did you sleep well, Christine?"

"Yes, I slept very well."

"Do you want to get up?"

"Go ahead, Jim. I'll be ten minutes behind you."

"Okay, but hurry, The President is supposed to be on the TV at 9:30 am don't forget."

"Alright, I'm coming, Jim, I'm right behind you." she said.

I washed up, went downstairs, and started breakfast. Angela was already in the kitchen and was cooking her own food. "Good morning, Angela, how are you today?" I asked.

"Not too bad, Dad, but I have stomach cramps again this morning. I have some diarrhea too. I need something to eat right away,"

"Eat my dear; eat as much as you want. Oh by the way, I love you." I said. She smiled.

"I love you too, Dad," She came over and gave me a hug. I started the toast and eggs for Christine and me.

"So how about your sister, how's she doing this morning, did you see her?" I asked.

"Yes, she was getting up slowly earlier this morning. She's really depressed, Dad. I think she's giving up on herself. I think she's losing hope."

"I know dear, I know, but I am not sure how to deal with her any longer. She's been so silent and not willing to talk with us. She used to be such a boisterous and fun loving young girl, now look at her. Well, look at all of us, I guess." I said, shaking my head, "Are you going to watch the President with us?"

"No, I'm going to go to the, Helgesons and spend more time there. Last night was cut short and I want to make up for it." Angela replied.

"You don't have to explain, Angela, we know you have to spend time with, Christopher and his parents."

"I know, Dad. I want you and Mom to be so much a part of my life so I want to tell you everything, well most everything."

We sat waiting as our food cooked. I began to feed scraps to Cindy who seemed to be oblivious as to what was going on around her. She seemed to be a contented little dog. How I envied her in these troubled days where sometimes I wished I had her inability to understand the natural world around her to the degree that an animal does. Christine and Paula came downstairs. We said good morning and "I love you" to them. We gave them hugs.

"Paula, what's that you've got in your nose?" I asked.

"It's a tissue, Dad. I'm having a nosebleed."

"Do you think you need to see a doctor?"

"I think she's okay for now hon, it's an isolated thing, I think." Christine said.

Bernie came into the kitchen and sat at the table. "Something smells good in here." He commented. He seemed to be in a better mood than usual.

"Good morning, Bernie! Would you like some bacon and eggs this morning?"

"Sure, so how are you guys this morning?" Bernie asked.

"Not bad, Uncle Bernie." Angela replied. The rest of us responded in kind.

"I guess we're all going to watch the President this morning." Bernie commented.

"Yeah, it's almost time. I'll tell you what, let's get our breakfasts and go into the living room and we'll eat in there while we watch him." I suggested. Everyone enthusiastically agreed.

"I hope he's got some good news today, we sure could use it." Bernie stated.

"I hope he does too, Bern." I said. We picked up our breakfasts and headed into the living room.

"I thought you were going to Christopher's this morning, Angela?"

"I'm here now, Dad. I'll go after breakfast."

"Whatever you want, dear."

We took seats in the living room and I turned on the television. "It should be on any minute." I said. The time was 9:27 am. We sat eating and watching the television. There was an array of commercials playing as we ate and then the station-changed networks. A news anchorman appeared on the screen. "Good Morning everyone, this is John Barkley reporting for American Cable News. This morning we will be bringing you a live event. We will be bringing you the live news conference by the President of the United States from the pressroom of the White House. We will be going there in just a minute or two. Wait, hold on, I'm told we will be going there immediately," the news anchor stated. He was receiving instructions through his earpiece. The camera cut away and a scene of the pressroom appeared. It was filled with reporters and photographers as the podium with the Presidential seal was centered in the main camera's view. We were sitting at attention in the living room and watching with anticipation. A spokesperson came down the walkway and up to the podium.

"Good morning ladies and gentleman. The President will be giving a brief statement followed thereafter by a short question and answer session. So, Ladies and Gentleman, if you will, The President of the United States." the representative proclaimed. The President of the United States and an aid appeared and walked up to the podium. The aid then stepped back. The President put some papers down, straightened his jacket and took a sip of water. He began to speak. "Good morning my fellow Americans and a special good morning I wish to you all, and to all listening in other countries, welcome. I will try to be brief and get right to the point for you. I will add as a precursor to this press statement, if I may, I want to ensure you that this statement will be complete with no information being withheld as I have promised the American people. The situation that has become commonly known as the 'Pegasus Effect' will be reported to you without censorship whatsoever." The President stated. He paused to take another sip of water and adjust his suit. He continued, "We're in times of great distress my fellow citizens. Therefore, as of today, I'm declaring that our nation, The United States of America, to be in a state of emergency, and we are on full military alert. I am also encouraging other nations to do so forthwith. I will start with the events of yesterday, Saturday, July 14. As of last night, an event in our skies has occurred that prompted millions to get on their phones and find out what was happening. Today, I can report to you with certainty that a major anomalous astronomical event has taken place. In the skies, we have seen the light from what has now been confirmed to me as being a supernova explosion in our own galaxy of, The Milky Way. A star has exploded. It is believed by astronomers working at our largest telescopes that this supernova is in close proximity to our earth, possibly as close as one thousand light years away. This is the closest known event of its kind ever recorded and because of its brilliance we cannot tell which star or exactly how far away it was that this explosion has taken place." The President explained. He paused again for a sip of water, "So far as we can ascertain, this event will have no effect on us in the immediate future. Last night it was widely reported that people have had lightening effect or floating sensation that went along with our experience. We now know that a gravity wave following the light has passed by the earth and affected our gravity for a minute of two. Astronomers with special gravity wave detectors have had for the first time their detectors impacted by a change in gravity. They tell me that gravity is normal now and will remain that way. This is the first time in history a known gravity wave or gravity change has ever been detected. We are also lucky to have no transportation accidents due to this event. I want assure the American people and the rest of the world that we are in no danger from this event. However, I've been told that when the supernova becomes visible on the eastern seaboard at approximately 2:00 pm, it will be very bright. The Supernova will rival the sun. We warn everyone not to look directly at it without eye protection and we guess that over the next few weeks its brilliance will subside." He said. He paused again and the continued.

"All that is left to say on this supernova event is that it may be one of the most beautiful astronomical events ever and if you can take time to enjoy it, do so. If the situation were different, we may have all enjoyed this event as a world community in peace and harmony. Next, is the time speed effect and where that is taking us. As I have said before and with my words, it is now official, that we are in a declared state of emergency. Our time speed recordings and their incremental increases indicate the death rate will soar shortly. I encourage all nonessential people of the nation to stop working and be with your families. Simply because of the nature of this emergency, I am asking you to be with your families in your homes. I have put the military on high alert to take care of any contingencies and protect the public from all threats otherwise. The military will be more visible to help the nation throughout these times. We have come to some very grave and severe conclusions. I will try my best not to be alarmist. However, our best scientists concur that if the Pegasus Effect does not subside or desist, the general population of humans on this planet will be decimated in a two to six month period. If this effect does not stop, we will have a global extinction event take place with no biological life above the one celled organism left alive on this planet within one year of this date." The President stated. He paused again and the press tried to interject. "Mr. President! Mr. President!" they yelled. A spokesperson came up to the podium and quieted them directly. "Quiet now or this press conference is terminated! Quiet!" he yelled. The reporters stopped their outburst and took to their seats.

"The President will continue with his statement interruption free and questions, like I said, will be answered after!" he exclaimed. He then stepped back. The President stood up to the podium again. "My fellow Americans, we are at a juncture in human history where our global mortality is no longer in our hands and it is up to a divine providence and Almighty God to change this event. I encourage families to stay together and pray for our collective safety and to be safe as individuals. I encourage communities to stick together and do their best in these critical times. On a personal note, I encourage the people of the world to pray for our survival and that we may somehow come through this astronomical event alive and well." The President stated. He paused again. "May God Bless you." he said, "Lastly, I want to give our sympathies to the Italian people and our heartfelt support and aid for the victims of the huge volcanic eruption that has taken place that has claimed so many lives. This has truly been a catastrophe for the people of Italy and I would like others to help in our quest to give aid and comfort to their people. Again, may God Bless you. Alright, I will take questions," he said. The pressroom broke into pandemonium. The press gallery went wild with questions. I decided to turn off the television at this point. I turned around and looked at the girls and Bernie. I could see in their eyes the awfulness they felt inside knowing that we were probably going to die.

No one said a thing. I could feel their sadness. I knew we tried with our lives to live the best we could and now our lives would be taken from us.

"I know this sounds bad." I said, "I know that we're in a situation that will probably take our lives, but we're a family and we must live in these days together the best we can until we can't anymore."

"We're going to die, Dad! We're going to die!" Angela cried out.

"I know Angela, I know! Listen this is not just happening to us, we're not singled out in this. This is happening to everyone and every living creature on earth!"

"But why, Dad, why?" Angela begged, "Why does my baby have to die? Why do I have to die? Why are we all going to die!" she exclaimed. Angela started crying. Christine grabbed her and held her.

"Listen up!" Bernie said, "I want to ask you something. You all believe in, God don't you?" he asked.

"Yes, we do." I said.

"Well, this is a divine happening and that is the only explanation for this event. This happening to humankind is taking place by the movements of the whole universe. God created this universe for us. This is an act of God." Bernie stated. He directed his words toward Paula and Angela.

"But why is God doing this to us?" Angela begged.

"God is not doing this to you or us, Angela. I don't know why God is doing this but he has a reason only known to him. We know he works in mysterious ways and I don't presume to say that he is doing this for one particular reason or another but I do know in my heart that this is in God's providence, that this is a divine event that we are part of. This event shows the power of God in the universe and how fragile we are to the power of God." Bernie explained. Angela listened intently but for some reason I could see that Paula was indifferent. I was starting to worry about Paula. She was becoming withdrawn and isolated from the rest of the family and her friends.

"Listen up everyone!" I said, "I know we're in a serious situation and you girls are old enough to understand the grave nature of this, Pegasus Effect. It has been hard for the whole world to accept but it is now accepted. We have accepted it. There's nothing we can do now except to love each other and pray to God for divine intervention. We must pray for forgiveness for others and ourselves. This is our hour of need and we must pray in our hour of need. Your mother and I love you so very much and you too, Bernie, you're part of our family. We must move on with our lives the best we can and not waste time on dwelling on the negative. We must try our best to put negative thoughts of the, Pegasus Effect to the back of our minds and try to live for whatever time there is that we have left, whatever that is, do you understand?" I beckoned onto them.

"Yes, Dad." Angela responded.

"Paula?"

"Yes, Dad."

"Alright then, I want you girls to try to lighten up. I want you to do something that you enjoy. I know it will be hard but try, please try, do you understand me?"

"Yes, Dad."

"Paula?"

"Yes, Dad." she said, sheepishly.

"Okay, it's a beautiful day outside so let's try to enjoy it. Let's clean up, go outside and enjoy the summer. Remember girls, we'll all get together at around two o'clock and watch the supernova as it rises in the east. It's something that man has never seen before this day, up this close. So we'll watch it together, okay?"

"Alright, Dad." Paula and Angela answered.

"Helen and Huneo will be coming over for a barbeque again around noon so we'll have a late lunch today." Christine said. We were trying to pep up the girl's spirits as well as our own and I think it was working. We sort of broke up our little gathering for the press conference and decided to get on with life for the moment. Trying to stay positive was difficult. We were getting weaker by the day, albeit slowly. We were getting more gray hair as well as lines and age spots. Paula and Angela started to look like they were beyond their years. Our tremors had become more pronounced as other ailments such as stomach upsets, nosebleeds and vomiting became more apparent. For some reason the least affected person was still Angela. She had displayed the least amount of effects and the least severity. Mentally we were becoming shells of our former selves. We became depressed in addition to being sad most of the time. A state of confusion was starting to rein in our thoughts as a bad memory was starting to set in. In any event, we tried to press on, and as the day progressed to lunchtime, we were each doing our own things. Christine was in the garden tending to her vegetables and flowers. Angela was playing with Cindy and reading baby books in the shade of the big oak tree. Angela was waiting for Christopher to come over and join us for lunch. I was in my observatory with Bernie cleaning my telescope and putting a solar lens on it for viewing the supernova when it came up at two o'clock and Paula was in the house listening to her music. I had wished she would come outside but that was what she wanted. I did not want to force her to do anything she didn't want to do at this juncture. It was later when Helen and Huneo pulled in. Christine went to greet them. They had big smiles for her and that was good to see. Bernie and I came down from the loft to greet them and get something to drink. Christine had made two large pitchers of iced tea and lemonade for the afternoon and I figured now was as good a time as any to have a nice cold drink. We sat on the swing again and then about half an hour later Christopher came over with his parents Diane and Bruce. I was not expecting them. I went up to Christine and asked her if she had invited them and she said that she did not know about this either. We went to greet them. They said they were bringing Christopher over and thought they would say "hello" and be on their way. We had not really gotten close to the Helgeson's but they were nice people we thought. We had seen them on a number of occasions and although we would be grandparents-in-law, we did not seem to click. They were virtuous we thought but we seemed not interested in each other. I guessed our interests differed, I supposed. That was what it seemed like. We invited them to stay for hot dogs and iced tea but they declined. A close friend of theirs was in the hospital with a terminal illness. They said because of the Pegasus Effect the end of her life was hastened and they wanted to share some last moments with her. We expressed our regrets and sympathies and invited them to join us on another occasion. They then took their leave as we settled back in and had our barbeque.

It was latter afternoon and we were doing our own thing again. Paula had come outside and sat with Angela and Christopher. Helen and Christine were in the garden together and we were in and around the barn digesting our lunch. We were talking and tossing a Frisbee around when the awesome vision of the supernova started to appear in the east. As the supernova began to ascend on the horizon, I called everybody together. "Hey everyone, come here! Come here! C'mon everyone, come here!" I yelled.

"What is it? What is it! Everyone clamored.

"It's the supernova over there, on the eastern horizon, its coming up!" I told them.

"Wow, look at it!" Christine said.

"Listen everyone look at it but only for a few seconds until I know how bright it is, don't damage your eyes!" I told all. We stood with our eyes transfixed on the sky for the next fifteen minutes.

"Oh wow, Dad, it's amazing, wow! It's all orange!" Angela exclaimed, exuberantly. I looked at her in the glow of the two bright stars in the sky. At that moment, my daughter Angela looked happy and beautiful. She radiated as the starlight beamed upon her. Everyone was smiling and looking at the supernova. Angela was just over seven months pregnant and she looked radiant as she looked to the sky. Christopher was holding her as they basked in the beauty of the event. Christine came over and wrapped her arms around me as we looked at the exploded star.

"Remember now, don't look at it for too long or it might hurt your eyes!" I warned.

"Its okay, Dad, the radio said it's okay to look at it because the UV light isn't strong enough to be damaging." Paula said, to my surprise.

"Are you sure they said that sweetie?" Christine asked.

"Yes, they've been saying that all day on the radio."

"Thanks, Paula." I replied. We stood there and watched the supernova as it rose into the early mid day sky. It was amazing to see this event happening right before our eyes. We were transfixed watching it ascend.

"Every night for the next two weeks it'll probably get a little bigger with each day and night as we see it." I explained.

"Will it hon, really?" Christine asked. She had a look of wonderment in her eyes and a cheek-to-cheek smile. I thought how wonderful it was to see their smiles brought on by an astronomical event of such great magnitude.

"Yes, it will get bigger, it's a star whose explosion is still expanding and will do so for days." I told.

"Wow, Dad, how far away is it?" Paula asked.

"It's so far away, Paula, my dear, that what you're witnessing, actually happened more than a thousand years ago, maybe thousands of years ago. They have not figured that out yet because of the distortion from the explosion, but they figure it's around a thousand light years or beyond." I told them boldly. This was my favorite thing in the entire world, looking at and understanding the heavens. I was in my glory and I felt like I was in synchronization with the entire universe. I was happy even if it would probably not last. This event was more visually stunning than I had ever imagined.

"What do you think of it, Bernie, Huneo?" I asked.

"I'm speechless, Jim! It's astonishing! That's the only way I can describe it. It's more than I ever thought I would ever see in my lifetime from the heavens. It's no doubt the greatest astronomical event in human history!" Bernie said, in a euphoric ambling.

"How about you, Huneo?"

"Ditto, I couldn't say it any better! It's really in class all by itself."

"Helen, what about you?"

"Wow, I never thought I'd ever see anything like this in my life! This is something every human that ever lived should be able to see at least once." Helen said. She had awe in her eyes.

As the supernova rose into the sky that day and eventually occupied the noonday sun position or just past it, I noticed that the sun was moving over to the horizon to set. It was dazzling. Time was passing fast that day, no pun intended. This event was awe-inspiring. I could only imagine there were hundreds of millions of people in the western hemisphere that were outside like us, seeing this with their own eyes, as we were witnessing this together. As the day wore on we had to make dinner and the girls decided to make a hasty barbeque meal to get some food in us and not have many dishes to do. We had an impromptu party going and the best was yet to come. We were sitting around the picnic table, talking and enjoying the warm breeze as the sun was beginning to set. Because of the close proximity of the supernova, there was no need to use any optical devices to get a better view of the event. The girls brought out some wine as we started to get a little tired but we definitely had enough energy to stay up to witness this once in a lifetime event. I went in the house and grabbed a few bags of marshmallows to roast on a fire that Bernie and I decided to light in the fireplace. The sun was close to setting and then only the supernova would be present in the sky. I mentioned to Huneo and Bernie that in all the dismay of the Pegasus Effect we were still sometimes able to live with a relative degree of normalcy. They agreed that the human spirit had the resilience to overcome adversity and to prevail in a positive way. Everybody was looking for a stick to skewer his or her marshmallows to roast on the fire as we enjoyed some easy listening I had put on the CD player. As the sun set beyond the horizon, it was a remarkable sight. It was as if the supernova was chasing the sun across the sky. We had cooked a few marshmallows and we sat and watched the supernova in the night sky by itself. Dusk passed into night and the supernova changed colors in the sky as it astounded us.

"Wow Jim! This is the most amazing thing I've ever seen in my life." Christine whispered. I put my arm around her.

"I can't believe how amazing it is either sweetie. I never thought I would ever see something like this in my life." I said. As the sun went about twenty minutes past the terminator, semi darkness had set upon the night and the great beauty of the supernova showed itself. Everyone was either speechless or gushing over the spectacle as the nova was two colors in the night sky. It was a bright yellow with red around its perimeter. From the perimeter radiating outward were streaks of red, like a starburst from a fireworks display. We were amazed as none of us expected to see a sight like this. It was truly a gift from the heavens. "Look at the shape of it. It seems to have almost a heart shape. I bet they call it 'The Heart Supernova.'" I said.

"Do you think they will, Dad?" Angela asked.

"They might, they have to call it something."

"I think your right, Jim. It has the shape of a heart almost." Bernie observed, "It sure is something though isn't it?"

"It sure is!" We stared into the night sky. We stayed out and stared at the supernova until each one of us could no longer stay awake and had to go to bed. Helen and Huneo went home around 11:00 pm. Christopher's parents had picked him up a little earlier. I was the last to go at 12:30 am when I could no longer stay awake. I went to our bedroom and Christine was already fast asleep. I was so tired that I was asleep before I actually laid down I think. I slept well that night and finally got some rest.

When I awakened the following day, everyone was already up. I got up slowly. I showered, got dressed and went downstairs. Christine was cooking breakfast with Bernie, in the kitchen, and I could see Angela outside with Cindy on the swing.

"Good morning, Christine." I greeted. I gave her a hug and a kiss. "Good morning, Bernie, how are you this morning?"

"Oh, I feel a bit depressed this morning, Jim, I can't help it." he said.

"That's alright, Bernie, you can feel anyway you like. You'll feel better after a coffee and some breakfast." I commented, "Quite a show last night, eh?"

"That was something else, that's for sure, Jim." Bernie replied. "I must say we're getting pretty lucky for weather so far this summer. It's one of the warmest we've had in a long while, don't you think?" Bernie asked.

"Well, I think the weather for the last few years has been a little warmer than usual for us, and you're right, we're lucky in that respect." Christine said. I noticed that her tremors were more pronounced this morning. Then again, my tremors were worse as well, probably more so than anyone else's. The bacon sizzled on the stove as we basked in the morning light. Outside, I could see Angela starting to stir. She was walking around the yard as she was baring the weight of her baby to come. She was in her pajamas and sun hat. She appeared contented this morning not to mention beautiful.

"Look at, Angela, Christine." I said.

"What's that, Jim?"

"Look at, Angela, I say!" She and Bernie looked out the window.

"She's pretty, eh?" Christine expressed.

"She certainly is a lovely young woman, Jim." Bernie commented. Angela must have felt our eyes on her as she turned around and looked directly at us.

"Oh, oh, she caught us." I said. We laughed. We waved at her as she smiled and waved back. She was perplexed.

"I think she could feel us looking at her, eh Jim?"

"You're right. I think she has a sixth sense." I told, Christine.

"Alright here we go, you're first, Bernie." Christine offered. She served the bacon and eggs with hash browns and toast plus juice.

"You're next, hon." She stated. My mouth began to water with the anticipation of squelching my morning hunger. We began to eat heartily. I began to talk about the day ahead. How I wanted to do some chores around the house. I was talking and looking out the window as I ate when I noticed Angela walking in front of the open door of the barn with Cindy in tow. Suddenly, from what I saw, a look of horror appeared on her face. She clasped her cheeks with both hands and began to scream. She ran into the barn and then ran out and fell to the ground screaming.

"Oh my God, something's wrong with, Angela, Christine!" I exclaimed. I started trembling. I knew deep down at that moment that something was terribly wrong.

"What, what are you? Oh, my God what's wrong? Where's Paula?" Christine inquired. We panicked and rushed to Angela's side. Angela was retreating from the barn and Bernie followed us. As we reached Angela, she was frantic and incoherent. The dog was panicked and barking.

"What is it, Angela? What is it!" I beckoned.

"What is it, where's Paula!" Christine yelled. Angela screamed, cried, and pointed into the barn.

"What is it in there!" Christine exclaimed. She looked in and screamed. I ran to look.

"Agh oh no! No Paula, Paula no, aeie nooo!" Jim screamed and yelled as Christine was also screaming. Paula was hanging by the neck from a low beam that was adjacent to the ladder leading to his observatory. Her lifeless body dangled and twisted slowly. I, Bernard Wakefield, had been either friends with or mentor to James and Christine since they were both in their late teens. I would have done anything to change this day as adrenaline filled my bloodstream. I watched Jim, Christine and Angela panicked and screaming and crying as they ran to Paula and tried feverishly to cut her down. I took my cell phone out and tried to dial for help. I was shaking uncontrollably at the horror of seeing my dearest young friends in the worst scenario a man, woman and child could face. I could barely dial 911. As I tried to dial, Jim was scrambling and yelling Paula's name, trying to find a way to get her down. Christine and Angela were jumping, screaming, and crying when Jim found an old pair of scissors-type grass cutters and scrambled up the ladder. He tried to reach out and cut Paula loose as he cried out. I heard a voice on the other end of my cell. "911" The dispatcher answered. I then began to get the words out of what was happening.

"Sir where are you? You are on a cell phone, Sir. We need to know where you are." The operator requested, sternly.

"1121 Mountain view Road!" I blurted out. Jim fell from his grip as he tried to cut Paula down and then scrambled back up as I watched in horror. I saw them as I had never seen my three beloved friends as they tried to save their loved one. I threw my cell phone to the ground and ran to help Jim. I held Jim up by his knees as I pushed his knees against the steps so he would not fall again. Jim feverishly cut away at the rope around Paula's neck and then Paula plunged to the barn floor. Christine jumped on top of her and tried to get the rope off her neck. Paula's pallor blued and she was not breathing. I could hear the siren of the approaching ambulance. Christine and Jim struggled to get the rope off her neck. They finally got it free as the ambulance pulled in and came to the barn, clued in by the frantically barking dog and the yelling. The paramedics raced to Paula, as she lay lifeless on the barn floor. The paramedics had to remove Jim and Christine so they could work on her. They did their job and got her ready for transport. They were giving her CPR when they got her into the ambulance. Christine then collapsed on the ground and Angela and Jim panicked as Christine was overcome by the events. I was feeling sick to my stomach and was not being much help but I did the best I could. I noticed a note on the floor. I picked it up and put it in my pocket. The paramedic yelled for us to go to the hospital. Through the tears and crying, we struggled into Jim and Christine's vehicle and then I drove us to the hospital. Angela and I were sitting in the front. Jim and Christine sat in the back. As we traveled, Christine blamed herself for this tragedy. Jim and Christine lamented painfully as to what Paula's condition might be. Angela sat in the front crying. "Please God, don't take my sister, don't take my little sister!" She repeated. I cried for Paula as well. It was my turn to help Jim and Christine in their hour of need. I raced behind the ambulance as we headed towards the hospital. It seemed like it was taking forever as the adrenaline in my blood began to abate. Finally, we pulled into the emergency entrance of the hospital. The hospital looked so crowded. There were people everywhere, in the parking lots, on the lawns, and even on the lower roofs. I never thought I would see a scene like this. The paramedics rushed Paula into the emergency department. I noticed they were only giving her artificial respiration. I wondered what this meant. We ran in as they took her to an emergency room. They held Christine and Jim back and told them they would have to wait for at least twenty minutes. They protested, as they wanted to be with Paula. I went to Jim, Christine and Angela and tried to calm them. They were in pain and vulnerable and they needed some kind of reassurance that everything was being done. I tried to ease their worries. They could not be calmed for their youngest daughter and sister's life was hanging in the balance. The hospital was a madhouse. I had never seen so many people in Park Falls General Hospital. It was so crowded with so many people in trouble. It was the Pegasus Effect. We were having so much fun for the moments that morning and it all ended in a flash, which was how quickly life could turn on you. However, it was as plain as paper. Time was passing swiftly as Christine and Jim paced in the crowded waiting room. Suddenly a petite female doctor appeared and introduced herself. "Hello my name is Dr. Joan Blanchard. Are you Mr. and Mrs. Reynolds?" she asked.

"Yes, yes I am and this is my wife, Christine. How's our daughter? Is she okay? How's my daughter, Doctor! How is she?" Jim asked, frantically.

"Mr. and Mrs. Reynolds your daughter is breathing on her own and her vital signs are good right now. However, we had to sedate her to prevent brain damage from occurring. This is a precaution performed with this type of injury. We have also given her anti-coagulants and vitamins. Did she try to commit suicide?"

"Oh God, yes. I don't know why!" Christine cried out.

"That's alright, Mrs. Reynolds. We've had over 30 suicides and at least 200 attempts in the last three weeks alone. That's more than the combined total for the hospital for the past eleven years. It's the Pegasus Effect, so don't feel as if you're alone." Dr. Blanchard explained, "Paula is it?" the doctor asked.

"Yes, that's her name." Jim replied.

"We're going to keep her in here for observation and treatment for a short while only, we hope. Our resources are stretched beyond the threshold of safe limits. You're going to have to stay here and help take care of her. When we think she's well enough you'll be asked to leave to make room for other patients. This is all in accordance with the emergency protocol. Do you understand Mr. and Mrs. Reynolds?" the doctor asked.

"Yes we do, we understand and we'll stay here to help take care of her if that's what you're asking?" Jim responded.

"Good, good then. That's exactly what we wanted to hear. There are so many sick and injured. We can't even keep up, in some cases, with dire emergencies."

"Don't worry, Doctor, we aren't going anywhere." Jim said.

"Alright then, you can see her in half an hour and be prepared for any eventualities please. Make sure you fill out the necessary paperwork before you go to her room. A nurse will come and get you, so hang in there, alright?"

"Alright Doctor, we will." Jim answered.

"Okay then, I'll get the papers for you and you can take your seats and be prepared to do some waiting."

"Okay thanks, Doctor." Christine replied.

Jim and Christine sat down to do the paperwork and that seemed to calm them. Angela came over and sat with me. "Uncle Bernie, I'm so scared for myself and everyone." She whispered.

"I know you are, Angela. We all are. You must remember that you're one of the strong ones and you should try to put on a brave face for the ones who aren't in as good of shape as you." I said. I tried to build her confidence. She put her hand in mine and then she leaned on my shoulder and sobbed. The hospital was filled with sad souls that day as it had been for a long time. A television in the waiting room was tuned into the news channel. A sign over the television read: "Do not change the channel please." I think it was for the benefit of everyone that it was on the news channel to keep everyone informed. The hospital staff looked ragged and run down. There were also many volunteers by the looks of things and that's what was holding the hospital together. There were also stockpiles of food, clothing and other essential supplies in every other available space. I could see how this was truly becoming a catastrophe in the making if things continued on the current path. Angela sat next to me. She stirred at the sight of the doctor coming down the hallway as she approached Jim and Christine. We went over to them and listened in.

"Hi again, Mr. and Mrs. Reynolds, I have some good news for you. You can go in and see, Paula now. She's sedated and she'll be in a fog through the next six to ten hours. You'll not be able to communicate with her that she'll understand but go ahead in and talk with her just the same. Paula, I don't think, has suffered any brain damage and you got her down just in time before any major damage or death would've occurred. I think she'll have a full physical recovery and she'll recover fast." Dr. Blanchard said.

"Oh thank God! Thank God!" Christine cried out. She almost collapsed in the moment. Jim reached out to steady her.

"Thank you, Doctor Blanchard, thank you so much." Jim said. He had tears in his eyes. Angela moved over to them as they put their arms around her and they held each other tightly. They hugged one another with the vigor of their love in their powerful dismay.

"Unfortunately, however, I cannot help you with any mental problems she might have and I suggest that you keep a close guard on her. Try not to smother her. Well, I wish I could do more but I'm just swamped here." Dr. Blanchard said. She prepared to move on. "You might try the mental health department for suicide prevention for your daughter but they have their hands full as well, I'm sorry but that's about the best we can do. Things around here are just going from bad to worse and there's no end in sight." Dr. Blanchard added. "Take care of your family Mr. and Mrs. Reynolds. God bless you," the doctor said. She then excused herself.

"Come here, Bernie, come over here, I want to talk to you." Jim said. I walked over to the family and they put their arms around me.

"Thanks for helping us out, Bernie. We wouldn't have made it here without you. Thanks Bernie, join us, you're part of the family and don't you forget it!" Jim said.

"Thanks, Uncle Bernie, it means so much to us." Angela said.

"Yes, thank you, Bernie, we owe you so much. You're the closest person to our family. What am I saying? You are family, Bernie." Christine stated.

"Oh, no, you don't owe me anything, don't say that." Bernie said. It was because of Bernie's calmness that we made it this far without a hitch.

"Alright everyone lets go see, Paula." I said. "Let's buck up and put on a brave face for her."

"Okay let's go." Christine said, and then we walked down the hall to the room in which she convalesced. She was still in the emergency department when we walked nervously into the room. We looked around to see where she was and found her behind a curtain that bared her name. She looked so small. "My God, Jim look at her, she looks so weak and hurt, oh my." Christine said. She put her hand on, Paula.

"Hi Paula, its, Dad, how are you?"

"Hi Paula, it's your sister, Angela, I'm here for you my sister." Angela rubbed her leg. Paula's eyes remained closed and her breathing was labored. We stood there and looked at her for the longest while, as she would stir from time to time. She looked fragile. I wanted to touch her but I thought I would wait until she had awakened. Christine lay partially beside her hugging her and saying how much she loved her and we loved her. She tried to tell her how sorry she was for being so angry with her.

"Paula, we just want you to get better and come home with us. Please forgive me, Paula, I love you so much. Mommy loves you so much." Christine said, ailing over our daughter.

"We all love you, Paula. We just want you to get better and come home with us." Angela beckoned unto her.

"Daddy loves you too, sweetheart. You just do your best to get better." I said.

"We're all pulling for you, Paula. This is your Uncle Bernie. I'm waiting to see you at home, so get better sweetie." We took turns talking with her as she slowly recovered that day. Paula stirred more as the time passed and she occasionally opened her eyes. As we kept our vigil, the hospital was a scene of chaos simply for the fact that it was grossly overcrowded. From time to time, we would each take breaks and get a bite or a drink. I took a time out and decided to give Huneo a call and tell him what was going on. Huneo immediately said he was on his way to the hospital and hung up on me. I did not expect him to be so impulsive. We were just happy that Paula was going to be okay. As I checked my phone for messages, I heard the hospital come alive with chattering. I could see in the main lobby that patients and visitors as well as hospital staff had gathered around the main television. They were displaying concerned looks. I had to see what was happening. I walked over to the television and saw a scene that I did not recognize. One of the attendants turned up the volume. I looked like a volcano but it was different somehow. A newscaster came on to speak. "These are pictures from an ocean freighter forty plus miles away," he said, "This is an extraordinary sight as we look at the far away coast of Greenland as an eruption or explosion of some sort has taken place," he said. Everyone was glued to the screen. It looked like a volcano. However, it seemed larger than anything I had witnessed before. The news channel took a break for announcements and the staff tried another station. They found another news channel and they were showing images from weather satellites. It was showing what was left of Greenland after some kind of massive event had taken place. The people watching collectively gasped as they looked on in awe. This was something I had never seen before and it was scary from the sheer magnitude of whatever had happened. The news channel cut to a reporter who was shuffling papers frantically while he talked with other newspersons. He then faced front and center and began to speak. "Ladies and gentleman because of a massive natural disaster taking place on Greenland it has been reported to us that major seismic activity has taken place. We are therefore instructed to inform our viewers that there is a tsunami or tidal wave warning for the entire Atlantic Basin. We are passing on an advisory from the National Seismic Institute in California. It is advised that people lining the immediate coastlines of the Atlantic Ocean move inland immediately as a precaution," the reporter stated. He spoke in a grim tone. The hospital became tense as everyone was in dread of what was happening. I decided to go back to the room to see my family and by the time I arrived, the news had already spread throughout the hospital. I went to Christine, Angela, and Bernie. They wanted to know what was happening. "Jim, what's going on? Everybody is saying the world is ending. What's happening?" Christine begged.

"I don't know you guys but a large explosion or volcanic eruption has happened on Greenland and it doesn't look good."

"Another volcano?" Bernie asked.

"Well, I don't know, Bern. I seen it on the TV and it looked kind of like a volcano but I think it was something bigger. I've never seen anything like it." I explained. He listened with a growing concern.

"Holy Christ! This world is coming to an end isn't it?" Bernie said, with an anguished tone. Bernie was starting to look pale, and as I noticed this, I saw that Christine was looking flushed as well.

"Are you guys okay? You don't look so good." I asked.

"I don't feel well at all hon, I feel light headed." Christine complained.

"I don't really feel so good myself, Jim. I've been feeling a little worse over the past day and a half. I feel nauseated all the time. Not really nauseated, but nauseated just the same." He said.

"Listen to me, keep an eye out for a doctor and hail one if you find one and tell them how you're feeling, alright? I'll go and try to find a doctor for us right now." I said.

Huneo and Helen came into the hospital at that time with Helen's parents and her brother in tow. I could see that Helen's mother was looking ill and they were more or less carrying her to the admitting. The hospital it seemed was becoming collectively sicker and I was not feeling so good myself.

"Dad, don't panic. You and I are the least affected by this. We have to be there for the others, so buck up!" Angela scolded.

"I know sweetie, I'm just a little overwhelmed by this. Thanks sweetie, you keep telling your dear old, Dad that. Don't let me forget it, we have to push on. Are you okay?"

"I'm not too bad right now, Dad."

"How's, Paula?"

"She's okay."

"Alright, you stay here with everyone and try to comfort them. I'm going to try to find a doctor and go see what's happening with, Huneo and Helen. It looks like, Helen's mother is sick."

"Alright, Dad, hurry back please."

"You bet sweetie, I'll be back as soon as I can." I said. I left to look for a doctor and Huneo. As I walked, I began to pray. "God, please let these events stop. Please, Lord, let these events stop. Please bless us, God. Please bless my family and everyone else." I prayed. I prayed this repeatedly. I was scared and I did not know what else to do. Ever since the Pegasus Effect started to disrupt our lives, I had been praying constantly. I had been asking God to protect us and stop this from happening. I was so scared for all of us. I wondered if my prayers would get answered. I saw Huneo at the admitting desk and I rushed to see him.

"Hey Huneo, what's going on?" I asked. I had panic in my voice.

"Hi, Jim. Helens mother is having heart palpitations so we rushed her in here right away. How's, Paula doing?"

"She's supposed to recover fine according to the doctor. My gang is in the waiting room. Where are, Helen and her parents?"

"They took them upstairs, Jim. They're taking the cardiac patients upstairs where it's quieter for them."

"I hope she's okay."

"I don't know, Jim?"

"Did you hear about, Greenland?"

"Yeah, it's all over the news." Huneo replied.

"Listen, Huneo, I have to find a doctor and get back to, Christine and Bernie. They're feeling sicker and getting pale."

"I'm going to see, Helen, Jim, so go to your family. I'll try to come and see you in half an hour if I can."

"Okay, or I'll come and look for you, if I can," I said, "Huneo, are you as frightened as I am?"

"Oh yeah, Jim, you're not alone."

"Okay, I'll see you shortly then, Huneo."

"Okay, Jim, I'll see you in a bit." he responded. We headed in our prospective directions. I headed back to my girls and Bernie. When I got back, a doctor was with them taking their blood pressure, temperature and pulse. I walked up to Christine and put my arm around her as they tested. Paula started to moan beside us and we went to her side to comfort her. Her eyes opened and I could see that she recognized us but she was still under the influence of the drugs. She was mumbling incoherently as she slipped in and out of consciousness. Eventually, she went back to sleep. The doctor that was there mentioned that she would probably be fully alert in about a half an hour. He said that Christine and Bernie should try to lay down somewhere to get some rest. The doctor said that Christine and Bernie were the most suscep-tible to the Pegasus Effect and they should be getting as much rest as possible to conserve their energy. He said with the way things were going they would need as much of their reserves as possible.

"The only thing I can tell you is that rest is the key to surviving the Pegasus Effect. It's the only thing we know of what to do in this dilemma," the doctor said. Bernie and Christine got into some chairs that were handy in the room and got their feet elevated. Over the public address speakers, there was a code blue call for a cardiac arrest on the second floor. Patients and visitors were congregating around the television for hourly news reports. It was four o'clock in the afternoon. "Christine, I'm going to the lobby to listen to the news, will you be alright?"

"Yes dear, I'll have, Angela with me and, Bernie, so don't worry."

"Okay, hon, I'll be back as soon as possible." I left for the television in the lobby. There were televisions scattered throughout the hospital but some did not work and others had the volume turned down for the comfort and welfare of the patients. I entered the lobby again but I did not see Huneo. I thought I might meet up with him again. I supposed he was with his future mother in law and the rest of Helen's family. People were gathering around the television as the news began. "Good afternoon. This is, Randall Cunningham reporting for, American Cable News Network, bringing you the latest in the fast breaking news stories for today," the anchor announced. He held his earpiece as a coworker dropped a paper on his desk. "Today governments from around the world as well as independents are reporting greatly increased calibrator readings. The Pegasus Effect is to blame for the huge and growing numbers of deaths and sickness' throughout the world's populations. Hospitals the world over are working well beyond capacity and hospital staffs are now becoming victims as well. It is widely reported that all sectors of society are breaking down and are becoming unable to function including food distribution and the military, more on this story is upcoming." The anchor stated. He shuffled his papers and was prompted through his earpiece. He continued. "In another breaking news story from, Greenland, a catastrophe of mammoth proportions is unfolding. It is now suspected that a, Caldera eruption event, has taken place. For those viewers not familiar with the term, Caldera event, this refers to a collapse in the earth's crust causing eruptions that are much larger in scope than volcanic eruptions. We bring you live pictures from the Atlantic Ocean some forty miles away, as well as images from weather satellites," the anchor stated, and then the broadcast cut away to the live feed. "We are officially warning the public on the coastlines of the Atlantic basin that tidal waves and tsunamis will most certainly be forthcoming. We are urging the public at large to move inland for their safety and protection." The reporter beseeched. Live pictures of awesome and incomprehensible destruction were shown on the televisions. The scene was surreal, both on the screens and in the hospital. I was in disbelief. The news continued. "We have reports now of earthquakes in Vancouver, Japan and Russia. These reports are now just coming in. The following are satellite photos from space above Greenland." The anchor said. We saw the photos from space. They were shocking. It looked like about ten percent of the Atlantic Ocean around the area of Greenland was blacked out. A reporter voiced over the images. He described the caldera event once more in detail and explained the size and magnitude possible with these events. He explained that mountains of debris had been blasted up into the jet stream and were headed towards the continents at high speed. It was explained that not since the beginning of modern recorded history up to the Krakatoa volcanic eruption had another event spewed pyroclastic and volcanic debris up into the jet stream, almost a hundred thousand feet above the earth.

The pictures were frightening to say the least. All watching were shocked at what they were seeing. An appalling silence permeated for a few moments and then the sounds of people suffering started to amplify in my ears. The reporter went on but I stopped listening and out of the corner of my eye, I could see Huneo coming towards me. I looked at him to greet him but he had a somber face. He walked up to me and began to speak. "Jim, have you seen what's been going on?" he asked.

"Yes, Huneo, I've been watching this TV out here."

"Jim, Helen's mother just died of a heart attack!" he blurted out.

"Oh my God, Huneo, oh my goodness, are you alright? I'm sorry, Huneo, are you okay?"

"I'll tell you, Jim, I think Hell has come to earth! I mean not that it wasn't here already, but I think we're in the throes of all that is Hell now. I mean how else can you explain this?" Huneo stated. He had a frightened look in his eyes and his voice trembled.

"Easy, Huneo… take a seat with me and we'll take a few deep breaths." I suggested. We sat down in front of the television. The whole of the hospital it seemed would lose composure, then there would be a respite and then the cycle would repeat itself, each time becoming worse. "You've got to hang in there, Huneo. Helen's going to need you."

"I know, Jim. I'm alright, I haven't been affected too badly yet. I'm just having a mini breakdown, I guess."

"That's okay, Huneo, just walk yourself through it."

"Thanks, Jim, I will, I'm feeling better already."

"Remember, we'll try to be here for you and, Helen as much as we can." I said.

"I know, Jim and vice versa."

"I think, Huneo, I'm going to get my family out of this hospital and get them home. This is not the place for us any longer. I know that sounds a little selfish perhaps. Many people here need help and we can't do anything for them. I have to take care of my own."

"I know, Jim; I'm going to get out of here too." Huneo said, with a look of foreboding.

"I think Christine and Bernie are starting to get pretty sick and the best place for everyone is at home. I mean this Pegasus Effect is going to kill us, and if we're going to die, we're going to die at home." I said. I could not believe the words I was saying.

"I know, Jim. It's becoming a hopeless situation."

"Huneo, let's keep in contact by cell phone every couple of hours okay, or try to anyway." I suggested.

"Yes, Jim. I'll call you every couple of hours or so."

"I'm going to have to get back to, Christine and my girls."

"I have to get back to, Helen, Jim."

"Okay then, I'll call you shortly, alright?"

"Alright, Jim or I'll call you."

"Take care, Huneo."

"You too, Jim." We parted and went our separate ways. I walked back to the emergency room. I began to pray again. I asked God to bless us and to forgive us for our sins. I asked God to intervene in our lives and let us live. I prayed more than I had ever prayed. As I walked into the emergency room, I saw Paula half propped up and alert as Christine was on her side holding her and weeping. Angela was holding her sisters' hand and Bernie sat in a chair beside the bed. I walked over and Christine looked at me and spoke. "Jim, Jim we forgot, Paula's birthday!" Christine said. She cried aloud.

"Oh my goodness, I'm sorry, Paula, I'm so sorry sweetie." I said. I got on the bed and held my family as tightly as I could. "Listen to me everyone, we're going home!"

"We're going to go now, Jim?" Christine asked. She looked puzzled."

"Are you sure, Jim?" Bernie asked.

"I'm sure; this is the best thing for us. The doctors can't do much anymore. The Pegasus Effect is going to either kill us or I don't know what but I do know that man has no more control over the events that are taking place. Home is where we need to be in our final days or whatever."

"When do you want to leave?" Christine asked.

"Let's pack up our things and wish these people well and go." I said. As we packed up, I filled the family in on what was happening in the world with the latest news reports. They were shocked to hear that things were getting so grim and agreed that we needed to be at home. We had to contact our loved ones to talk to them and possibly say our final goodbyes. It was a depressing and traumatizing day for us and we needed to get home and rest. Paula was alert and we would talk with her when we got home. She said repeatedly that she was sorry and asked for forgiveness. We reassured her that we were not angry with her. I decided that I would get the girls out of the hospital and on our way before I would tell them about the death of Helen's mother. We went to the car and left for home. All were silent as we traveled along the roads. I thought to myself that we probably did not have that much time left before the Pegasus Effect would become lethal for everyone. I wondered what the day might have been like if time was traveling at the speed it once had. As we traveled I could feel some of my tensions from being at the hospital abate. When I looked in my rear view mirror, I noticed all were asleep, and looked to be at peace for the first time in the past few days. I drove the car gently over the roads so I would not awaken them. Between the clouds, I could see the supernova and the sun. I must say it was a remarkable sight. The air was warm and moist and the haze in the sky made me drowsy. It looked like it was going to rain. As I pulled in the driveway, I looked at my brood again and I thought of how, if we were going to die, we would be together at home. I was tired but I pressed on. I awakened everyone and I gathered up our things to go into the house. "Come on everyone let's go in and eat something." I said. Christine, Angela, Paula and Bernie got out of the car, started gazing up at the supernova, and wondered aloud how beautiful it was in the sky.

"C'mon everyone lets go in and eat and then you can come out and watch the sky." I commanded. They turned to come in the house. We straggled in the door and each found a spot to drop and take the weight off. I took about five minutes to catch my breath and then I got up to start a meal for us. I took out hamburger and macaroni, simple but filling. After a few minutes, Angela got up to help me. Christine, Paula and Bernie slept in their respective chairs in the living room while Angela and I prepared supper. We were the healthiest of the family members and had to take over the primary care and household chores for the others. "Dad?" Angela spoke.

"Yes, Angela?"

"What are we going to do about, Paula?"

"What do you mean dear?"

"What if she tries to do it again?"

"Listen sweetie, the doctor told your Mom that it's unlikely that she would try to make another attempt so soon in the immediate future, but we'll keep our eyes on her regardless." I said, "The doctor also gave your mother some pills for her to take and a prescription for more pills if we think she might need them."

"And that's it, Dad, that's all we do?" Angela questioned.

"No that's not all we do, we also show her love and understanding and be there for her when she needs us or wants us. Your mother and I are going to have some long talks with her and see if we can't help her overcome her feelings of whatever it is that's bothering her. That's also maybe where you can come in and try to help us see things through her eyes. We need to appreciate what's happening inside her to help her, do you understand?"

"Yes, Dad, I do." Angela said, in a downcast tone, "I'm scared, Dad!"

"I know you are, sweetie. I'm scared too. Everyone on earth is scared, sweetie, but we have to try to do our best to push on to the end."

"Dad, that sounds so hopeless the way you say that."

"Sorry dear, I didn't mean for it to sound like that. That's certainly not what I meant." I said. She bore a tiny smile. "There's a little smile there, that's more like it."

"I'll try my best, Dad."

"That's my girl!" I said. The food was almost cooked.

"You can go and wake everyone, Angela and tell them that dinner is ready."

"Alright, Dad."

I thought about how nice it was to be home again but I knew that the good feelings would not last. I knew that after a while the Pegasus Effect would come back to haunt us as it continued its destructive path throughout the world and probably throughout the universe. In these times as we headed toward the great beyond, I would try to make my family as comfortable as possible. I would try to entertain them and I would try to keep them happy, as I knew in the back of my mind that I was starting to hurt bad myself. I saw that Bernie and Christine were becoming the most affected by the Pegasus Effect. They were beginning to look quite ill. The family started to congregate for dinner. We sat down and I served dinner with Angela's help. Christine, Paula and Bernie looked meek as they sat getting ready to eat. They had these sweet appreciative smiles on their faces that deeply touched my heart. I could see how precious and beautiful they were and even more so in these times of distress and impending doom. My thoughts were confusing sometimes but my love for them was certainly intact. Angela for some reason was the healthiest of the bunch. It must have had to do with her pregnancy I was sure.

"Before everyone digs in I want to say grace tonight." I said.

"Okay, Dad."

"Yes hon that would be nice." Christine commented.

"Thanks, Jim." Bernie said.

I sat down and clasped my hands together, then prayed.

"Dear God, I ask you tonight as we sit here to eat, my family and me. I ask you, God to bless them. I ask you, God to bless, Angela and her soon to be newborn baby. I ask you, God to bless, Paula, our daughter, a daughter that we love more than life itself. I ask you, God to bless my dear beloved wife, Christine. I ask you, God to Bless, Bernie and Stella and Huneo and Helen, all our family, and all our friends. I ask you God to bless everyone all over the world. Lastly, God, I ask you to bless me for I sin and I am a sinner. I ask you for your forgiveness. I will try to do the best I can with the life you have given me. Dear God, I ask that we may have love in our lives and that all may survive through this terrible time. Please bless us. Amen." I prayed, "Okay, that's it, let's eat."

"Thanks, Dad." Angela and Paula said.

"That was a nice blessing hon," Christine said.

"Thanks again, Jim." Bernie replied. Everybody began to eat. After a while, when we were pretty well fed, I announced to everyone the passing of Helen's mother. My family was shocked and dismayed by this news. We shed some tears and talked about her. We only knew her from church and shopping but she was a nice woman. Catherine Mary Hamilton had a big heart that was filled with kindness that she shared with everyone. The night moved along rather swiftly and before we knew it, it was time for bed. We were exhausted. We took care to make time and pay some extra attention to Paula and made sure that we would see her to sleep and be up for her in the night and in the morning. We talked to her about taking her pills and she had no objections. We apologized for missing her birthday and we would celebrate it the following day. She was in good spirits and asked us to forgive her for her actions. We told her that she had nothing to ask us for forgiveness. We went to bed. I made a mental note that I would have to call Huneo first thing in the morning. I said goodnight to Christine and gave her a kiss as she was falling asleep as I spoke. In minutes, we were asleep.

LIFE OUT OF BALANCE

I AWAKENED THE FOLLOWING morning at 7:00 am. I felt ill but I got up and washed along with checking on Paula. I peeked in her room and she was still sleeping. That was good. Christine started to stir but said she would stay in bed for another half hour. I told her to do whatever she wished because there was no schedule for her any longer. As I washed, shaved, and got dressed I noticed that it seemed to be dim around the house for that time of day. I thought it was dark outside and maybe there was a storm coming. I went downstairs to read the paper and make breakfast but the dimness felt unnatural. I went outside to see what was happening. I walked out the kitchen door facing the barn and looked up. The sky had filled with a dark pall of colors streaking to the horizons. I had never seen this before. However, I figured it had come from the caldera eruption in Greenland. I took out my cell phone and called Huneo. His phone rang. "Hello, Huneo, how are you? It's, Jim. Have you seen the sky this morning?" I asked. He told me that he had and that the dimness in the sky was from the caldera eruption. He said that he had been up for most of the night with Helen in her grief. Huneo had said the news reported that most of Greenland was, as far as anybody could ascertain, destroyed, and they did not expect to find survivors. He said debris blown up into the jet stream by the caldera eruption would eventually bring down showers of volcanic rock and dust on Canada. The atmosphere filled with debris from the initial blast he explained. "Is everything alright over there, Huneo?" I asked.

"Well, Helen's in a bad way but she'll pull through. We're starting to get sicker from the Pegasus Effect. I wanted to come over there around noon to have a look at the calibrator, Jim, if that's okay?"

"Huneo, you don't even have to ask, just come over whenever you like."

"Thanks, Jim, I'll be seeing you soon, when I get there."

"Alright, bye for now." I said. I hung up the phone. I had noticed that my symptoms were also becoming worse. I had trouble concentrating on almost everything and my tremors were visible to everyone as they had in some instances turned into painful spasms. I could feel a sense of uneasiness in my chest. It was not painful but sickening to my stomach at times. I would get tired easily. I knew that the time speed was picking up and I could feel it, it was palpable.

The phone rang in the house and I ran to answer it before it awakened anyone. It was Christine's father. He sounded awful over the phone. I asked him if anything was wrong and he announced that Christine's mother had fallen to a heart attack and died. "Oh my God, oh my God!" I said. I immediately expressed my sorrow and that I would wake up Christine and bring her to the phone immediately. He told me not to bother and that he could not talk with her right then because of his circumstances, and that I should tell her. He asked me to get Christine to call him back later in the day, perhaps just before dinner, and they could talk then. I expressed my deepest sympathies along with my sadness again and then I said goodbye. I was saddened by this mostly for Christine. I knew this was only the beginning of things to come, if we survived. I went back to the kitchen, sat quietly, and had a bowl of cereal. I began to reflect on our situation. I felt things were hopeless for the first time. I felt this to be a hopeless situation we were in and that God was taking away our mortal lives.

God was passing judgment on all humanity and humankind as he laid waste to the earth. I did not know how or when I would tell Christine that her mother died but I knew it had to be soon.

I heard a stirring upstairs. Everyone was getting up for the day. I fed Cindy and gave her some water. The dog for the most part seemed to be quite contented throughout all of this. There was a lot of moaning coming from upstairs. I knew that everyone was starting to feel worse. Angela was not far from delivering her baby as I wondered if any of us would be around for that event or if that event would even take place. As I sat at the table, I heard the sound of someone vomiting upstairs. I called out. "Is everything okay up there?"

"I'm okay hon, I'll be okay!" Christine called back. She had an exasperated tone.

"Okay dear, I'm downstairs if you need anything." I replied.

"Alright hon."

Bernie came around the corner from the guest room and he did not look so well. "Good morning, Bernie. How are you today?"

"Oh Jim, I don't feel so good. I've had sweats and chills as well as some discomfort in my chest during the night. I threw up twice."

"I'm sorry to hear that, Bernie. Do you want me to make you something to eat?"

"Actually yes, Jim, my stomach is empty and I feel hungry. I better eat now while I'm hungry, to keep my strength up."

"Good idea, Bernie, I'll whip something up right away."

"Goodness, Jim, it looks like hell outside. Are we in for a storm or what? It's dark out there isn't it?"

"Bernie, that's the debris from the caldera eruption, it's probably spreading all over the world."

"My goodness, that's awful."

"That's not the half of it, Bern. Christine's mother died from a heart attack yesterday." I said, just loud enough so that he could hear me.

"Dear God, Jim, I'm sorry."

"Thanks, Bernie. I'm going to have to tell, Christine and the kids as soon as they're all down here together."

"Do you want some privacy, Jim?"

"No, no, Bernie, you're part of the family, you can stay here if you don't mind."

"I'll be here, Jim." At that moment, the girls started coming downstairs. First Angela came down. "Good morning, Angie." I said.

"Oh Dad, good morning." she replied. She displayed a chuckling smile.

"How are you today my dear?"

"Not too bad, Dad but this baby is giving me a sore back something fierce." She said. She tried to massage herself.

"Well sit down. I'll make you something to eat."

"Why is it so dark outside?" Angela asked.

"It's the debris from the caldera eruption in Greenland, Angela. The volcanic plume of debris is spreading over the world through the trade winds in the upper atmosphere."

"I'm going outside to look. Are you coming out to look, Uncle Bernie?"

"Yeah, I'll have a look too. Let's go outside." They went out the patio door and gazed up at the sky. I could see them outside talking. Christine and Paula came down next and Christine had her arm around Paula. This was the first time Paula let her Mom touch her since their big fight. It was heartwarming to see them reconnect but that was going to be shattered in a short while.

"How are you girls this morning?" I asked.

"Oh Jim, I just threw up and I have a headache but I'm hungry." Christine said.

"I feel good, Dad." Paula replied.

"I don't feel too bad." I said. I approached her and gave her a hug. She hugged me back. That made my day. It was also this day that we would celebrate her belated birthday. I told her the previous day we would and I planned to do it big. A surprise indeed was at hand for Paula.

"Why is it so dark outside, Jim? What are, Angela and Bernie doing outside?" Christine asked.

"Yeah Dad, why is it so dark outside?"

"It's debris in the upper atmosphere from the caldera eruption in Greenland. Go out and have a look." I said. They made their way outside to observe the sky. They were outside as I cooked. I could see them looking up at the sky in bewilderment. The sky looked ominous. Cindy was in tow sniffing and licking at their ankles. About ten minutes had passed and I called for them to come back into the kitchen. "Come on in, come and get it!" They came in right away and they were hungry. We sat down and started eating. I waited for a good ten minutes until they had eaten most of their food before I began to speak.

"Okay listen up everyone, I need to have your attention." I said. All ears perked up and I had four sets of eyes trained on me. "Alright, girls, I have some bad news." I stated. I paused and took a deep breath, "This morning, Christine, I got a call from your father." Christine's eyes widened with dread as if she knew the words already. "I'm sorry my dear beloved, but this morning your father called and told me that your mother passed away from a heart attack." I said, softly. My girls burst out crying. There was no other way to describe it. They just burst out crying. I jumped up, kneeled before Christine and put my arms around her. She wailed and cried. Bernie went over to the girls and put his arms around them. We were suffering, as this pain seemed like an unbearable load. We moved into the living room and the girls sat on the couch together and consoled one another. We tried to comfort them the best we could, Bernie and I, and after an hour the situation calmed. I thought this was going to be the norm then as the Pegasus Effect was going to claim life indiscriminately. Christine phoned her father and they consoled each other over the phone. I asked Bernie if he would be able to watch the girls while I made a run into town for some supplies. Bernie confirmed he was up to the task. I told Christine where I was going and then I left for town as fast as I could. I wanted to do my thing and get back as quickly as possible. The weather was warm with a light breeze but it was dim with the dust in the upper atmosphere. I constantly looked up at the sky. I went to downtown Park Falls to see what was open for retail. Most stores were closed but some of the more important stores remained open with the strongest of the people working who could still manage them. Christine's hair salon was open on a rotating basis. Her salon would be open three days a week with the healthiest of the staff doing the best they could. That was how business was operating, on a "best you can" basis. This was the only option for commerce and retail in this global emergency. I was downtown shopping for Paula's birthday gift. I figured near lunchtime we were going to need a pick me up and today of all days, the price or the amount spent was not an issue. I went into the mall to my bank and withdrew one thousand dollars from the ATM. I then grabbed a shopping cart and proceeded to buy gifts and things we might need over the next few days with reckless abandon. I bought Paula a cake, a new CD player, some CD's, a new purse, two new pairs of shoes, some DVD's and a mini-TV for her bedroom. I bought my other girls and Bernie anything and everything I could think of, including books, CD's, movies, magazines and games. I bought some flowers, a cactus, candles, flashlights, and batteries. I went to the supermarket and bought food for a barbeque. I was then finished shopping and I would head home. I did not spend all of my one thousand dollars but I had put a good dent in it. As I got everything loaded into my car, my cell phone rang. It was Huneo. Huneo said that he was going to come over for his visit to read the calibrator. I explained to him that Christine's mother had died and the girls would be sad when he got there. Huneo offered to cancel but I insisted that he come over and we continue with life as normally as possible. I asked him to bring Helen as well if she was up to joining us for a while and he agreed to come as planned. I had also mentioned it was Paula's birthday and he brightened right up. He said he would be over near lunchtime. I hung up and was on my way again but I was feeling a bit woozy from rushing about. I was having lots of twitching and trembling as I made my way around. I told myself that I had to slow down. I took my time on the way home. In retrospect, downtown was functioning but it was on a much-reduced level and the people tried to be as pleasant as they possibly could. There was not much of a crowd at the mall, which was good for the people working there. Downtown was turning into a proverbial ghost town as people stayed home sick or to be close to their families. I looked at the sky and it actually became cloudy under the higher layer of the dusty volcanic upper atmosphere. The day was going to be downright dim. As I looked at the people around the town, I could see the strain in their faces and the despair and sadness in their eyes. I could tell that people were giving up hope. As I drove, I saw that our town of Park Falls had transformed from a sunny town with a happy go lucky disposition to a dark heartrending place, engulfed in a slow and painful demise. When I got into the driveway the house looked quiet. I walked in and all were in the living room. I greeted everyone and each gave me a halfhearted greeting in return. "Is everything alright, Christine?" I asked.

"Yes Jim, hon. I was just talking to my, Dad," she said, somberly, "We agreed I would not go back home for the funeral." She wiped tears from her eyes. I sat by her on the couch and put my arms around her to hold her and comfort her. "Dad said that with the way things are with our families and the Pegasus Effect that it would be unwise and unfair to uproot everyone to attend the funeral or it would be unfair of me to leave you all here and go by myself." she said. Christine looked uncertain and confused.

"It's completely up to you my dear but I just want to say that I think both those thoughts are reasonable. We would not want you to go away in this time of distress for us, Christine. It's up to you sweetheart whatever you want."

"I'm going to stay here with my family and I'm not going to go to my mother's funeral," she said, and then she cried. I held her tightly. Angela and Paula hugged their mother. Christine decided she would stay with us and that she would call her father everyday to keep in touch and grieve. Her father was lucky in the fact that another of Christine's sisters and all of her father's siblings lived in close proximity to his home in Surrey, British Columbia. He would have plenty of support.

The girls decided to go and sit outside. Despite the gloominess, the air was warm and moist. They dressed and went out. Bernie and I decided to watch the news and then go out and join them. I turned on the television. It was on the news channel as a commercial had ended and a newscaster came on, introduced himself, and began the broadcast. He announced that the governments of many countries had declared full states of emergency. He announced that the readings from the SOLTES calibrators were increasing and that death tolls from around the globe were soaring. Large numbers of people were succumbing to the Pegasus Effect. The pictures from the cities of the world painted a grim reality of what life was becoming. The newscast then switched to the Greenland Caldera story where it was reported that no one had been able to get within ten miles of the Greenland coast. The entire population was presumed perished. The eruption continued and the rest of the world would probably suffer some difficult repercussions from the fallout of the blast. They believed the sky over most of the middle earth, the equatorial center, would become dimmed for an unspecified period and the night and day sky would be of limited vision. We would not see the sun, the supernova, or the stars well again until the sky cleared. When that might happen was anybody's guess. As subtle as the Pegasus Effect could be sometimes, its horrors were becoming more pronounced and self-evident. The news ended with reports of death rates and predictions of the time left. The news again displayed pictures of the caldera and the people of the world who were praying for mercy. The pictures were sad to watch as they showed how hopeless our situation was becoming. "I'm having trouble watching this, Jim. The horror of what they're showing is happening to us. I don't know if I want to be reminded." Bernie lamented.

"I agree, Bern. It's awful!" I replied. I turned the television off.

Huneo and Helen pulled in the driveway and got out of their car. Helen and Christine embraced, cried, and attempted to comfort one another. It was at this point that I knew that we were not going to have too many more happy days ahead. I was giving up hope. Huneo, Bernie and I got together and went up to see the readings on the calibrator. We went directly to the loft in the barn and started the calibrator. As it booted up, we talked about how dark it was getting due to the natural weather and the dust from Greenland. After a few minutes, the reading popped onto the digital readout. "What does it read, Huneo?" I asked, intently, "Is it going up?"

"Yes it is, Jim, I'm afraid."

"Afraid of what," I quipped.

"Jim it's reading a 7.778 % increase in time speed as compared to the 1995 time speed recordings. That's the biggest single increase we've witnessed, Jim!" Huneo said, excitedly.

"I know, I know."

"My God, we haven't got much time left, have we?" Bernie commented.

"This gets more depressing by the minute I tell you. Let's get out of the barn." I said. We went out with the girls on the patio. They seemed to be in a better mood and for the time being their grief had eased up on them somewhat. They were talking to Angela about her baby and asking her if she had thought of any names she might be interested in. We sat down with them and began to talk about the losses we had suffered. Angela then went off to make a phone call to Christopher. Paula came over and sat beside me. She offered to get everyone refreshments and we each placed an order with her. She then went into the house to oblige us.

"Hey everyone!" I said, "Listen up! It's Paula's birthday today. Well, it's not her actual birth date but we're going to celebrate a special birthday for her today. Do you guys want to help us out?" I asked, enthusiastically.

"Sure Jim, just try and stop us!" Huneo said. He had a smile to light up everyone's face.

"What did you want to do, hon?" Christine asked.

"Well Christine, when I went into town for the groceries this morning, I went to the bank and went crazy at the mall with some gift buying. My Paula deserves it."

"Oh Jim, you didn't?" Christine said. She had a surprised look on her face.

"Yeah, I bought a birthday cake and a new CD player for her, with CD's, DVD's, flowers, new shoes and a whole bunch of stuff for everyone."

"Oh Jim, that's fantastic. That was the sweetest thing to do. Paula will be so happy."

"That's what I'm hoping for."

"What do you want us to do, Jim?" Bernie asked.

"Well, how about when she comes out with the refreshments, I'll say that we have something to say to her and only one thing. And, when she looks puzzled and maybe a bit surprised, I'll say 'We all have something to tell you sweetie' and that will be our cue when all of us will say 'Happy Birthday Paula!' and then we'll sing 'Happy Birthday' to her. And then, after that, Huneo, you can help me carry the presents from the trunk, alright?"

"Certainly, Jim." Huneo replied. The rest of the gang enthusiastically agreed to participate. We sat there for the next few minutes in anticipation of Paula's return when I saw Angela in the study window and gestured for her to come outside. She smiled and indicated that she would be out in one minute. Angela came outside again and Christine began to explain to her what was happening. At that moment, Paula came out with a tray of drinks and two bowls of potato chips. She began to serve everyone when Christine asked her to sit down and said that everyone could serve him or herself. Paula sat down a little puzzled as Huneo and Helen were talking with Bernie. They then looked over at Paula and I spoke. "Paula, we all have something to tell you!" and right on cue everybody exclaimed "Happy Birthday Paula!" and then we began to sing a chorus of "Happy Birthday". Paula cupped her hands on her cheeks, smiled, and laughed as we regaled her with our version of the ever-popular birthday song. After that, everyone congratulated her individually as she blushed and was humbled by the experience. I nodded to Huneo and we went to the car and retrieved the presents. We came back and I presented everyone with the gifts. Paula was ecstatic when she saw her new gifts. This made us feel good. Paula was a young girl on the verge of finding out who she really was and if only for the moment that we had, it was nice to see her happy. I had not seen her happy in a long while. "Speech! Speech!" Angela beckoned unto her. She looked at us and became shy but managed to get out her words. "Thanks so much, Mom and Dad and everyone. I know I haven't been so good lately but…."

"Oh no, that's okay sweetie, don't say that!" Christine interjected. We listened and watched.

"I'm sorry for the way I behaved. Thank you so much, thanks," she said. Tears ran down her cheeks. I went over and told her she did not have to say that she was sorry to us and that her mother and I loved her very much. Christine came over and said the same thing as we hugged her and gave her kisses. Everyone hugged her and gave her a kiss. It was a happy occasion for us and we enjoyed it immensely, even if it was to be short lived. Paula was happy and that made us happy. She was so excited that she asked to be excused so she could start enjoying her new gifts. We were happy for her because like the rest of us she had been through a lot. It was a happy time for us, as they were getting fewer and farther between. We enjoyed Paula's birthday cake while she cut the slices. The rest of that day was spent being contented for the peaceful moments that we had. Again, Huneo and I agreed to stay in close touch with one another and then after a while longer Huneo and Helen made their departure. I would phone him later that day. Bernie and I then decided to go to his home that afternoon and make sure everything was okay and intact. The girls decided to do their own thing around the house and we would be back by suppertime. We left right away as it was starting to get a bit closer to dinner. As we drove to Bernie's house we noticed how much darker the sky had become. The sky looked ominous as it seemed like an early sunset was about to take place. When we got to Bernie's, everything seemed to be in order. Bernie and I did a few minor housekeeping chores and then we headed back home. Bernie expressed to me that his house held many memories but it really meant nothing to him any longer without Stella. I knew he would change his mind one day if there were to be another day. As we drove back home we talked about how much things have changed for us in the few short months that have passed and how Park Falls had changed. The people we saw on our way home who were outside had become frail as we were becoming frail. It seemed that no one was strong and robust anymore. When we got home, we were tired. When we walked in dinner was ready to be served. Angela had made dinner with her Mom and they were both tired from the simple chore.

Christine was exhausted and she was achy and trembling. She told me that she would not go to work the following day and had phoned her employee Sheila to cover for her. Sheila had accepted saying that she was in good condition. Sheila was younger and more physically fit. We sat down and had dinner as a family. After dinner, I washed the dishes with Paula as Christine, Angela and Bernie watched a movie in the living room. It was then 6:30 pm and as I looked out the window it looked like the sun had set. It was almost dark outside from the dust and the clouds that were moving in. Usually at this time of the year, it did not get dark until past nine o'clock. I called out for everyone to go outside and we would have a look at the surroundings. We congregated in the backyard on the patio and stared up at the sky. It was warm and humid again. We were sweating in the early evening heat. However it was what we were seeing and hearing that was so unnatural for us. We were witnessing something we had never seen before and it was quite eerie indeed. "Dad this is scary!" Angela lamented.

"Oh, I think we're okay, sweetie. Try not to fret over a little early day darkness. It's just the dust in the upper atmosphere." I responded.

"I've never in my days seen anything like this, Jim. This is certainly one for the books I'll say." Bernie commented. Paula and Christine huddled together and looked at the surroundings. In Park Falls, the streetlights had come on as we could see others out in their yards as they looked to see what was going on around them. People had their lights on, in and outside their homes. We decided to spend the evening in the backyard for a while as this odd natural event played out. This was a natural event precipitated through a natural disaster and maybe was the cause in the making for another, which in fact was all probably caused by the Pegasus Effect. Why not be in awe of it while we could, even if we did not know what the outcome might be. Just like life. As we sat and talked, we got comfortable and turned on some music. We could see people in the distance doing similar things around their homes. It was getting harder to see them though as it got darker and we were not even close to sunset. As we sat and talked we got around to discussing the future and what was going to happen.

"What do you think is going to happen to us, Dad? Are we going to live?" Paula asked. She expected me to tell her the truth.

"I honestly don't know, Paula. I know that all over the world people are suffering and dying because of the Pegasus Effect. I don't know what's going to happen to us. I do know, Paula my dear that your mother and I are praying to God that he may deliver us from this terrible situation with you girls and everyone else intact. We hope you girls say your prayers to God and ask him to help you make it through this with us." I told her, in my fatherly way.

"I do, Dad. I want to live, Dad. I don't want to die," she said. That was music to our ears as she displayed a will to live.

"Paula, your father and I love you so very much and would give up our lives in a heartbeat so that you may be healthy and happy and that's all you have to try to be and that would make us happy." She told her. Christine ran her fingers through her curly red hair and smiled.

"I think you girls will do alright in life. I've known you two girls since you were little babies and you're survivors and you will survive." Bernie said, to Angela and Paula. Suddenly, the power went out. It was 8:40 pm. We had a power failure throughout Park Falls. The town went dark and we could barely see anything at a distance. I decided to go into the house and get the radio, the flashlights and one of the gas lanterns. I lit the lantern and we listened to the radio for news on the blackout. A radio station reporter announced that they were investigating the power outage. It was not so serious as we were in the summer season and it was warm enough so we could live without electricity if we had to for an extended period. However, it added to our worries and fears. We worried about our dwindling ability to persevere in these adverse conditions. We sat by the lamp listening and talking until the sun had set. It became dark and it was silent. As matter of fact, it became so dark that I have never experienced this type of darkness unless I was indoors in a lightproof room. I told the girls not wander off in this darkness or they would surely get lost. I turned off the radio so that we could listen to the sounds around us. It was silent in the yard. The silence was unnatural for being outdoors. It was unsettling. We could not see anything past our lamplight. We could not see the stars or lights emanating from anywhere and we could not hear a sound except from ourselves. It was a creepy feeling. A short time later while we were listening to the radio again, an announcer came on for a news update and reported that a lightning strike had knocked down a large transmission line. He went on to say that the power would not be restored until early the following day. We breathed a sigh of relief as it started to rain lightly. I expressed with optimism how this would help cools things off for a while. Paula then spoke out. "Dad, this rain is black!" she exclaimed.

"What?"

"This rain is black, Dad!" she exclaimed, again.

"It is, Dad!" Angela called out. She concurred with her sister. I looked at my arms under the lamp light and there were black raindrops on my skin.

"Must be from Greenland, Jim." Bernie said.

"I think you're right, Bernie. Okay we'll all have to go in the house for now." I said. I heard no arguments. After we went indoors, I lit some candles. I wanted to save the battery flashlights for emergency use only. We would huddle in the living room for a while before going to bed. The rain got heavier and we started to get thunder and lightning. The wind picked up and we began to hear what sounded like hail hitting the house. As I investigated, I saw that it was indeed hail but I also noticed that tiny rocks and pebbles were falling from the sky. I told everyone that we could no longer go outside because it would not be safe. After a short while, the wind gained intensity and the tiny pebbles turned to small rocks and stones. I told everyone that we would have to stay downstairs until the storm passed. The noise of the storm and the rocks hitting the house was frightening for the girls. I was getting scared and commanded everyone to move into my study, which was surrounded by four walls and no windows. It was the safest room in the house downstairs. The storm raged on relentlessly. "Oh no, the cars are going to be destroyed by this." I said.

"Do you want to move them into the barn, Jim?" Bernie offered.

"I don't think so, Bernie, it's too dangerous out there right now." I replied. Right then we heard a big crash and I looked outside but I could not see anything because of the darkness.

"Okay girls, I think we're going to have to move into the basement for safety now." I said.

"Let's go girls!" Christine commanded. We followed them as we heard another big crash. I could tell these were large stones or some sort of volcanic debris that was hitting the house. We stayed downstairs for most of the night. The storm was ongoing throughout the evening as it made for a frightening night indeed. At one point in the evening, there was a direct hit on the house and I was glad we were in the basement. I knew that the debris had landed on the roof as the whole house shuddered when it was struck. It was 2:00 am, when abruptly, as the storm raged, the whole house began to shake. "Earthquake!" the girls screamed.

"Its okay, it's okay girls, we'll be okay!" I shouted. The shaking stopped after about twenty seconds. At approximately 3:00 AM, the storm abated and we began to feel better. The girls and Bernie fell asleep on the spare furniture in the basement so I let them be. I went upstairs to investigate. It was too dark to see anything really and I did not want to go outside just then. I went into the living room to lie down on the couch. I was tired and not feeling well as I proceeded to fall asleep. The following morning when I awakened it was still dim outside in what would have been a bright part of the day had the sun been shinning. It was 8:15 am. I decided to go outside and investigate the damage. It was shocking. I never expected to see what I saw. The whole town was black with the residue from the storm, as the dimmed sunlight did not help the ghastly sight. Everything was wet and there was lots of damage but not as much as I had initially anticipated. When the girls would get up, they were going to freak out when they saw this specter. This was not Park Falls any longer. This was an ugly hell of a town, the way it looked. Our cars sustained the worst damage. However, the damage to everything else looked like it was easily fixable. The days after that night went on as the Pegasus Effect became more entrenched in the human population and the cosmos. The town managed to recover from the storm, and that storm never repeated itself, fortunately for us. Over the next few weeks, Christine was only able to get in to work twice and even at that, she could not work full days. I went to the university and it was a skeleton of its former self. The school was empty except for some maintenance personnel. I decided not to go back to the university again until school started, if it ever started again. We began to stockpile food and staples that we may need over the long run in case we were too sick to leave the house. That day was probably not long off, likely. The people of Park Falls were dying and the ones who were not immediately at peril were getting sicker, more depressed, delusional, paranoid and physically ill. Our family members were no exceptions. It was getting close to Huneo's wedding date and he wanted to have an impromptu rehearsal. It was Saturday August 1, 2012. The skies still filled with the volcanic dust from the Greenland caldera. Hundreds of millions of people had died globally and the world had come to a complete standstill. Everything had come to a complete halt except for food and fuel distribution and the public utilities. They were the only functioning entities at this point for the most part and the governing of these essential services was taken over by the world's militaries. The strategy was collectively agreed upon by the governments of the world near the outset of the crisis. The daylight hours on inhabited earth were at best in dim lighting from the sun due to the caldera eruption. There were predictions that this would be a calamitous event over a long period. There were predictions of a new ice age because of this event. However, we were not likely see the end of this event if it were going to happen for we would have long since perished. The daily news continued to play out the dramas and turmoil's of the world. I do not know how we were able to continue with the shape we were in as well as the shape everyone else was in around the world. The daily news continued to be grimmer and more desperate with each day that passed and passed faster. The Speed of Light Time Existence Speed calibrators from around the world were measuring identical readings. They registered increases in time speed as each day passed to compound the compression of time as it compared to the past.

The news reported the distress and hopelessness of people from all over the planet who watched their days dwindle. They were constantly showing the different countries of the world and their populations praying for a miracle to save them. They prayed for their lives and those of their children and salvation. We prayed. The people of the world were desperate as sickness took over their lives and a dismal fate awaited all who breathed. The pall of the caldera fallout made the cities of the world look hellish and that was the only way to put it, the cities of the world looked hellish and perverted. The collective sanity of the people was starting to give way to madness as our brains as well as our central nervous systems overloaded with increased electrical activity. If time was relative to man, of course, this would not be a problem but that would have been magic. Here in the town of Park Falls we have lost approximately four thousand people, which was almost five percent of our population. The streets were mostly empty as people tried to conserve their energy until the end. An exercise in futility that was pointless. However nonetheless it was a human survival instinct. At home, circumstances were coming to the critical limits of mortality. My dear wife Christine was starting to succumb to the Pegasus Effect along with Bernard Wakefield. Christine had been bed ridden for the past few days as Paula and I tried to take care of her. Angela had started to take care of Bernie more as we tried to take care of our sick. Christine threw up every so often and needed a cane to walk to the bathroom. Her once beautiful hair was brittle and gray and her skin was pale. We were at varying degrees of increased aging. We shook and trembled as well as had muscle spasms and convulsions. Christine and Bernie were more affected than Paula and me. Angela seemed the least afflicted and Cindy up to this point in time did not seem to be bothered at all. Bernie was also bed ridden and he was despondent. It was heartbreaking to see my old friend so sad, frail and depressed. Christine also had bouts of paranoid and delusional thoughts. The other day she was convinced we had put something in her food to poison her and she refused to eat. It became more difficult for us to get through each day. Our closest contacts were still Huneo and Helen. They were also getting sicker. Helen's father Dave and her brother Richard were staying with them in their new home. Helen's Father Dave was getting quite sick and her brother was helping Helen take care of him. Huneo and Helen planned to go ahead with their wedding next weekend. We would try to go to the rehearsal that day at their home but I did not know in all honesty if we were going to make it to the wedding or if the priest would be healthy enough to attend and perform the ceremony that following weekend.

We prayed to God to save us and forgive us in our hours of need. We tried to attend our church as much as possible and help where we could but we were no longer able to do much of anything. We had become depressed. However, we had not yet started to resist one another or be mean to each other.

We tried our best on a daily basis. We knew this was a divine event that was taking place in the heavens, and an event designed by God. We knew a little about the astrophysics of the Pegasus Effect. However, the Pegasus Effect for the most part was of a divine providence. I had always been a spiritual man and I believed in my religion. I interpreted my religion in my own way and I tried to live in that manner. I knew God was with us, all of us and our mortality was always in His Almighty hands. I knew God was with me to the end and I would always pray to him for help and forgiveness. I was watching and witnessing an event like no other and I thought I knew why God was doing this but I was only guessing. His grand plan for us I supposed would always be a mystery in our mortal world.

We readied ourselves for the trek over to Huneo and Helen's home to perform the wedding rehearsal. We were about ready to leave as I helped Christine down the stairs. Paula loaded up the car as Angela and Bernie were climbing into the back seat. Paula had a weird look in her eyes and an ashen pallor. "Paula, are you alright sweetie?" I asked her, concernedly.

"Yes Dad, I'm going to make it, I'll be alright," she replied. She seemed to be gasping for air.

"Are you sure about that sweetie?"

"Yes, Dad." she said, again. We made our way to the car.

"Put your arm around me, Christine. I'll help you to the car my love." She tried to make it on her own but could no longer.

"We'll all be together in heaven, Jim, won't we?" Christine asked. She peered into my eyes for an answer.

"We will absolutely be together in heaven my sweet! We will always be together for eternity." I told her. She managed to smile. She pulled me to her and kissed me full on the lips with an intensity I had not had the pleasure of for a long while. I missed those passionate kisses from my wife. Oh, how I missed the things I once took for granted. We got into the car and Cindy jumped in with us. We would take her with us on this day. Cindy was a well-behaved dog and we could trust her on trips like this one. I started the car and began to drive. "How yuh doin back there, Bernie?" I asked. He looked drowsy.

"I'm doing fine, Jim. I'm hoping this outing will help to pick up my spirits." He responded.

As we drove along, it was a warm day and it was not windy. The sky was bleak with dust. I believed the sun would have been out today had the dust from the caldera not been present in the atmosphere. As far as calderas go, as it was reported on the newscasts, this was a small one and we were lucky. How anybody could call any of this lucky I do not know, maybe lucky to be alive I would agree with. Even with the pall cast in the skies, it was comfortable and not threatening. As we drove by the town, we could see the mortuary filled with cars bringing their dead for cremation without service. Many of the healthiest young people, who had been the least affected, commissioned by their own will, took on the daunting task of incinerating the bodies and other morbid tasks around the town. The police department worked and functioned the same way with only the able bodied and willing to perform the services they provided. They tried to keep a low profile for the austerity of the situation at hand. People were active on this day. There were not many people about but they were moving around doing what I was sure was only the necessary things that needed to be done. As we drove along, the town looked sad and beaten up but somehow it did not bother us so much anymore. We resigned ourselves to this predicament.

"Everybody okay back there?" I asked, again, as we drove along. "You're awfully quiet back there?" I commented.

"I'm alright, Dad. I'm just in a quiet mood." Angela replied.

"I'm okay, Dad." Paula said.

"Bernie, how about you?"

"I'm feeling a little better than this morning, Jim. I think I'm starting to look forward to this now."

"That's the spirit, Bernie!" I said, enthusiastically, to try to raise their morale.

"How about you, Christine?"

"I'm fine hon but my body doesn't want to move anymore."

"That's alright sweetheart, I'll carry you if I have to." I said. She smiled at me and we held hands as I drove.

We arrived at Helen and Huneo's home. I pulled in the driveway and Huneo came around from the backyard to greet us.

"Hi Jim, hi Christine, hi gang, how are y'all?" Huneo greeted us. We responded with positive greetings in return. We got out of the car and then Huneo led us around to the back yard. Cindy jumped out of the car and she started with a few barks. Cindy would become used to the surroundings in a matter of moments and then be off doing her own thing.

We got to the back of the house and the yard was already done up in a wedding motif. There was an archway and a little white altar as well as a podium for the service. Chairs in white picket and two covered picnic tables were set up. Huneo and Helen had refreshments already laid out. It was inviting and homey. "Oh my God, Helen, it's beautiful, it's simply beautiful." Christine commented. She gazed upon all the work they had put into their back yard. Christine and Helen hugged and kissed one another on the cheek.

"Hi Helen, this is beautiful. This is really beautiful, congratulations." Angela said. Paula and Bernie chimed in and then Huneo reintroduced us to Helen's father Dave and her brother Richard.

"Jim this is, Dave, Helen's father, you remember him?" Huneo said, as he introduced me.

"Yes of course, Hi Dave, it's nice to see you again. On behalf of my family and me, Dave, please accept our deepest condolences on the loss of your dear wife Catherine." I said, stoically.

"Thank you, Jim, thank you kindly." Dave said, as we shook hands. Christine then spoke. "Yes Dave, you have our deepest sympathies for your loss, I'm so sorry."

"Thank you very much, Christine, your words are most appreciated by us." Dave responded. At that point, we paid our respects to Helen, Huneo, her father and her brother for the loss of the wife and mother of that lovely family. The Parkas-Hamilton's also paid tribute to Christine's mother and Bernie's Stella in a touching and profound half hour of our afternoon. We hugged and held each other and smiled to show that we cared for one another and that we were there for each other. After some closeness that we shared, we began to take seats to take the loads off our feet. We were a group of dying people and I guessed that in the grand scheme of things, we are always on a path towards death while we are alive. As I looked at everyone, I was amazed at how fragile we had become and how frail we appeared. We were shaking, twitching and lethargic. It would have been funny if it were not so sad.

Huneo invited us to dig into the refreshments and we would start the wedding rehearsal in a short while so that anyone who had to leave for whatever reason could. "Please everybody enjoy the spread we have put out for you all. Don't be shy. A little later I'm going to cook some steaks on the barbeque, if you want to stay!" Huneo expressed, with an unexpected exuberance. Well, I was hungry and so was everyone else. It's funny how when you are a guest in someone else's home how much hungrier you can become. We started in on the appetizers and the beverages. We got together in groups of two or three and talked incessantly. We tried to get in as much as we could. I began to talk to Huneo for a while. "So Huneo, you're in fine spirits today aren't you?" I asked.

"Yeah Jim, I am. I just feel today is a lucky day and it's so good to have my friends and family here. I have a family here. That's something to be happy about isn't it?" Huneo lamented.

"Of course, Huneo, that's fantastic. It's fantastic to have a family in your life and the love that that brings. I couldn't imagine life without mine." I said.

"It's just sad it'll probably be so short lived. Well, I've lived a fairly good life. I didn't get to have children or really settle, but, I'm a fortunate man. I was able to help many people in South America, in Argentina. I've lived a mostly spiritual life and I have a lot to be thankful for."

"That's good, Huneo, a spiritual life is rewarding and fulfilling, I'm happy for you. We've had the pleasures of living that type of life as well. The rewards are plenty and the peace of mind is the best. You know, I've never been as contented in my life as I am now and I really can't put my finger on why. I'm not too worried about the answer to that though as I have a pretty good idea what that is and that's good enough for me. You know, Huneo, over the past few weeks; I've noticed that even though our time has sped up, it seems as if events of the past have happened longer and longer ago, do you know what I mean?" I asked Huneo, perplexedly.

"I think so, Jim. Do you mean to say for example like the symposium? To me it seems like that happened years ago and it's only been a few short months."

"Yeah, exactly, that's exactly what I mean, it's strange. Also, over the past few weeks, I've been having this feeling of a constant déjà vu. It seems like everything I do I've done before even when I know for a fact it's the first time I'm having the experience."

"Yes, Yes Jim, I've been experiencing that too. I know what you mean. This is part of the Pegasus Effect as we slide deeper into the future time faster. They were reporting this on a news show a few nights ago. So, I guess what's supposed to happen is happening. You know they also reported or had a report saying that a lot of astronomers and astrophysicists theorize that the Pegasus Effect maybe a recurring anomaly and that it has occurred before but not in such a pronounced manner." Huneo stated.

"Well, I still kind of subscribe to the theory that this is a universal event and involves a great part of the universe." I said, "You know,

Huneo, I think this is happening on such a grand scale and involves space and time as far back as billions of years ago and that we'll only ever be able to make a best guess as to what's happening. I mean we're only here for a short time on this earth and we're just kidding ourselves if we think we're going to find the answers to how the universe actually works. I mean, could it even be explained in a language and science we could even comprehend?" I stated, "There's just so many theories, Huneo. I mean who's to say really?"

"Have we had this conversation before, Jim?"

"Hah, hah, that's funny, Huneo. Well again, this is a beautiful spread, Huneo. Everybody's really enjoying themselves, I must say."

"Thanks Jim, I was hoping we could make this day a happy one for everyone." The doorbell rang and Huneo excused himself.

I went over and joined Bernie, Angela and Helen as they talked about her upcoming wedding. Helen was talking specifics on how she would like things done. I quickly got bored with that and went over to Paula who was sitting with Christine, Richard and Dave. "How are you making out sweetie? Are you enjoying the food?" I asked her. She actually looked quite pale, but then we all did.

"I feel a little sick, Dad, like I'm going to throw up," she said.

"Sorry sweetie, are you going to be okay or would you like me to take you home?"

"No it's okay, Dad, I'll be alright."

"Are you sure?"

"Yes, Dad."

"If you have to throw up sweetie, go beside the house okay?"

"I will, Dad," she said.

Huneo entered the backyard again through the house as he had Father Alan Mulvey in tow.

"Hello again everyone!" Huneo said, loudly, to garner our attention.

"I have a new guest for the afternoon and I think some of you already know him. This is, Father Alan Mulvey." Huneo said. He introduced the Father to all at the gathering. Everyone greeted the Father and then Huneo and Helen stood at the back door and looked at us as they were going to make what I think was an obvious announcement.

"Well everyone it's been a difficult past couple of weeks and while we were in good spirits mostly, for today, we gambled, Helen and I. We thought if things felt right and they do, we're going to get married today, this afternoon, right now as a matter of fact!" Huneo announced. Well, my girls gasped. They had a look of shock in their eyes. Dave and Richard also looked surprised. A few of Helen and Huneo's neighbors within earshot began to wander over and as the fact set in, Helen spoke.

"Yes, you're all here, the one's we want to celebrate with us. Christine, you're my bridesmaid. Angela and Paula, you're my maids of honor and, Jim, you're the best man." Helen stated. Whoa, I thought to myself, I didn't remember agreeing to be the best man. I would warmly accept this offer however.

"We'll start the ceremony in thirty minutes." Helen announced, "C'mon Christine, will you help me put on my wedding dress?" Christine walked towards her. They disappeared into the house. We were in a bit of shock as Huneo invited the neighbors to come and mingle with us. His neighbors were a little older but seemed receptive to the event. We gathered around the altar and the Father while he went over the basics to a basic wedding. Helen then came to the door and asked Angela and Paula to help her as well. Huneo came over to me and asked me if I was okay with this surprise being sprung on me. I told him that it was an honor and a privilege to be part of the wedding like this.

"I know we didn't have a bachelor party. However I have a few beers left if you guys would like some?" Huneo offered.

"Sure I'll have one. This is a celebration now." I replied. He gave us each a beer and his neighbors as well. Huneo proceeded to get dressed outside with us. Huneo had already been wearing the pants to his suit and continued by putting on the shirt, the coat and the cumber bund as well as a carnation he had in a small box. Huneo then handed me a suit jacket I could wear and we were more or less ready. It was a nice day when I realized and I thanked God for the small things in my life, the small miracles and the small things that happen when you least expect them. I noticed that the sun was starting to burn through the dust and it was beaming its rays down upon us. Everyone noticed the sun as it was truly uplifting to the point of almost bringing tears to our eyes. The thirty minutes had passed and the girls were not back. Father Mulvey said he would step in the door and call out for them. Huneo put some appropriate music on and then we waited. I chatted with Dave and Richard some more as they seemed to be such nice people. Richard the son and his Father were gentleman in every sense of the word. The Hamilton men were excited at the prospect of seeing their daughter and sister getting married. We were excited as well. Finally, we saw some shadows and heard some giggling at the back door. They were about to come out.

"Richard could you come and hold the back door open for us, please?" Christine asked. Richard bounded onto the deck and held the back door open. Christine walked out first and astounded me. She was wearing a beautiful satin, white and green dress with a stunning tiara on her done up hair. She had put on a little make up as well. She looked more beautiful at that exact moment with the smile she was giving me than all the beauty I had known in my life. I began to tear as I smiled back at her in her radiance and her angelic loveliness. Helen walked through the door next and she beamed in her white wedding dress. I looked over at Huneo and he was glowing. He was lit up like there was a light surrounding him. Paula and Angela walked through the doors next as they had tiaras and dress coats on with bouquets of flowers. They had ear-to-ear smiles and looked a little quirky but beautiful nonetheless. Angela looked to be glowing and very pregnant. Paula was smiling but I knew she was hurting on the inside. As the music played, the girls walked toward the altar. Huneo and I rushed up to the altar and I stood at his side as we awaited Helen and Christine. The Father then started the ceremony and excused Christine and me as we went to our seats. We sat down. The families and the neighbors listened as Father Mulvey performed the service. The sun shone down on us that afternoon as we watched a perfect wedding ceremony. In a world that was dying, this was a wonderful event. As the ceremony ended, Bernie jumped to his feet and announced that he had his trusty digital camera out in our car and went running off to retrieve it. The Father then presented the happy couple. We stood up, clapped, and cheered them. At, which point, Cindy started barking at us as she ran around excitedly. We laughed at her wild antics, as our dog could be quite a source of amusement in these days of her youth. She could be precocious and devilish at times. Bernie returned from the car and began snapping pictures of the happy couple. I had not seen Bernie move like that in years and I knew he would probably pay for it later on in that day and the next. That was life however and we do what we like to do. We started to congratulate the happy couple, Mr. and Mrs. Huneo and Helen Parkas. They kissed and held hands as Christine and I kissed and held hands. All the while, we were being admired I think, by our children, and a brother and father. After the ceremony, we went on to celebrate with our steak dinner reception and then the sun faded as if on cue. We grew tired and it was only five o'clock. Our youthful stamina's were gone. We were succumbing. It was unexpected events that day, that brought us joy, and a break from the realities of what awaited us. We were truly grateful we had this time together. After a while longer, the party settled down and we decided to stop for the day. The girls changed and then came back out as I could see Christine was hurting. After all the exertion, it took her to make things look normal, I knew she would pay for this. We would all pay for this. As fast as the party began, it ended. We packed up the car while Angela tried to corral the dog. We said our goodbyes in the driveway and said that we would try to get together again as soon as possible.

When we said goodbye that day I wondered if we were ever going to see one another again. I knew the end was near and it was only a matter of a short time before the whole world would succumb in totality to the Pegasus Effect. Huneo mentioned as we left that he would check with me every day on the calibrator readings and that he would visit on occasion. This was certainly fine with us. Well, it was a beautiful day I said to him and then we said goodbye and thank you to Helen and Huneo. We then left for home.

Hanging by a string

When we arrived home, we were exhausted. We sat around for the remainder of that evening speaking quietly to one another while we each performed some small chores and went about having our little pleasures. Bernie and Christine got sick to their stomachs in the bathroom and I was shaking quite a bit along with having spasms in my legs. Christine and Bernie went to bed to rest at about 7:30 pm and that was it for them for the evening. Angela watched television and Paula played games on our computer in the den. I went into the den to sit and rest for the remainder of that day and maybe catch up on some reading. I noticed that Paula had a strange look in her eyes. "Paula how are you feeling, sweetie, are you okay?" I asked. I was becoming more concerned about her as the hours passed.

"I feel a little strange, Dad," she said, weakly. She looked pale and a little grey.

"Do you think you'd feel better if you lied down and maybe had a glass of water and some aspirin?"

"I think I'll do that, Dad and I'll go listen to my music instead." Paula replied.

"Well go get in your bed then and I'll bring you up some aspirin with a glass of water."

"Alright, Dad."

"I'll be right up in a minute, sweetie." I went off to fetch a glass of water and some aspirin. I passed Angela sitting in the living room watching television. She looked well.

"What are you watching, Angela?" I queried.

"I'm watching the news, Dad."

"Anything I want to hear?"

"You don't want to know, Dad," she said, shaking her head.

"That bad, eh?"

"Oh yeah!" she said. I continued to get the aspirin and water. I went to Paula's room where she was in bed listening to her CD player. I brought her the water and sat on the edge of her bed. She reached out for the aspirin. She proceeded to swallow the aspirin and consume the entire glass of water. "Well you're awfully thirsty!" I said. I looked into her eyes and she seemed to look better than she did previously.

"Thanks, Dad."

"You're welcome, Paula. So did you have a nice time today, at Huneo and Helens?"

"Yeah, it was nice. It was funny to see them get married like that. I mean they did it all of a sudden. It was funny. You looked funny, Dad, when he said you would be the best man." Paula said. She giggled at the thought.

"So you had fun then?"

"Yes, I played with, Cindy a lot and fed her some food off the table."

"Yes, I saw that. She was pretty hungry after all that running around wasn't she?"

"Really hungry!"

"Do you like your new CD player, Paula?"

"I do Dad, thank you so much. Thank you and Mom so much." She then gave me a hug. I hugged her tightly. I did not lately get to hug or be so close to my youngest daughter. It was heartbreak. I realized that I was drifting apart from my daughter without even being aware of it happening. As I gazed at my little red haired beauty, I felt the loss of the time we missed together, and the time that we could have had. I felt that deep inside.

"Well Paula, you know your mother and Angela and me we love you with our entire hearts sweetie, you know that eh?" I stated, with conviction.

"Yes, Dad. I love all of you," she said, and then she hugged me again. I hugged her back with all the love that I had.

"So, are you feeling any better now?"

"Dad! Dad!" Angela's voice rang out, from downstairs.

"Are you okay for now, Paula? I'm going to run to see what your sister wants." I said. I sensed urgency in her tone.

"Yes Dad, go ahead, I'm okay."

"Thanks dear, I'll be back as soon as I can." I said. I headed for the stairs.

"Okay Dad, bye."

I ran down the stairs and into the living room to see what was happening with Angela. "What is it, Angela? Are you okay, hon?" I asked her. I felt winded.

"I think I'm going to deliver my baby, Dad!"

"Why are you saying that, what's going on?"

"My water broke, Dad and I'm having contractions every fifteen minutes or so." Angela said. She had a look of not knowing what was going on in her eyes.

"Oh yes, you're going to deliver, you're going to deliver premature!" I said excitedly, "I'm going to have to take you to the hospital right away. Can you get some things ready quickly?"

"I have a bag already pre-packed right beside my bed, Dad, you know that." Angela replied.

"Oh yeah, that's right." I said. She laughed.

"Easy Dad, we have plenty of time." Angela stated. I did not think so and I was not taking any chances. I had never delivered a baby and I certainly did not want to start with my daughter's baby today.

"Okay, I'm going to have to take you to the hospital by myself, Angela. Your mother, Bernie, and Paula are too sick for this. I'm going to go explain the situation and then we'll head off for the hospital right away, alright?"

"That's fine with me, Dad."

"Okay, stay here and I'll be right back, okay?"

"I'm not going anywhere, Dad," she said, laughing. She thought this was quite amusing. I guess from her standpoint it was. Well, it was her first baby so she may as well have fun if she could. I ran upstairs and entered our room. Christine was asleep. "Christine! Wake up hon, Christine!" I exclaimed. I raised my voice to get her to come to consciousness. I gently shook her and her eyes popped open.

"What is it, Jim?" she said. She awakened.

"Angela is going to deliver her baby!"

"What?"

"Her baby, she's going to deliver her baby! She's gone into labor and I'm taking her to the hospital right now."

"Oh no, what am I…?"

"You're not going anywhere my dear, you're staying right here. You're not up to this trip today, Christine, I'm barely up to this trip. You have to stay here and I'll take care of her for the both of us. You have to be here for, Paula anyway, okay?"

"What about, Bernie?"

"Bernie's too sick for this too. We're on our own and we'll just have to make it by ourselves hon, don't worry about us." I said.

"Don't worry! Are you for real?"

"Christine please! I don't have time to argue this out. We'll be okay. Don't worry, ah, I mean, try not to worry. We'll be alright." I said, trying to reassure her.

"Well, you better bring your cell phone and keep me informed and I mean it!"

"Okay, Christine, I will, you know I will. I have my cell phone right here on my belt. I have to go sweetie so I'll call you as soon as I can."

"Okay Jim, tell, Angela I love her."

"I will, Christine, but I think she already knows that." I said. I headed for the door, "Sorry Christine, I love you. Tell, Paula and Bernie for me will you?"

"I will, Jim. Bye, drive carefully."

"Bye Christine, I will." I went downstairs to leave with Angela. I got back into the living room and she looked ready to go.

"Okay, are you ready, Angela?"

"Dad, you forgot my bag."

"Damn it! I'll be right back." I said. I ran up to her room and grabbed her bag. As I passed Paula's room, she called out.

"Dad! Dad!"

"Yes, sweetie?"

"What's going on?"

"Paula, your sister's going to deliver her baby." I replied.

"Do you want me to go with you?"

"No sweetheart, there isn't time. We have to get going right now and besides that you're not well enough so it's best if you stay in bed, alright dear?" I asked, of her.

"Are you sure, Dad?"

"Yes, I'm sure; I'll phone you as soon as possible with the news of her delivery okay?"

"Okay, Dad."

"Bye sweetie, I love you."

"I love you too, Dad," she said. She looked at me with shades of helplessness in her eyes.

OUR FIG TREE,
A HORRIBLE THING, AND
THE VANISHING US.

I THEN RAN DOWN the stairs with the bag in hand and Angela was at the door, at the ready. We proceeded out to the car. We got in and drove off.

"Are you alright, Angela?"

"I think so, Dad. Dad, I'm starting to have another contraction." She replied.

"Are you in pain?"

"Yes Dad, I am, it hurts!"

"Okay, I'll get you there as fast as I can dear."

"Alright, Dad." She winced in pain and squirmed for the next couple of minutes.

"Okay Dad, I think that contraction has stopped."

"Alright, that's good."

"What time is it, Dad? Let's time the contractions."

"Alright its 9:15 pm, no wait, make that 9:17 pm."

"Okay, I'll tell you when the next one starts."

"Don't forget, it's important." I said, "We'll be there soon, Angela."

"Dad, don't drive so fast, you're scaring me!" she exclaimed.

"Sorry, Angela, sorry dear, I'll slow down. I'll slow down, dear." I slowed the car.

"Thanks Dad, that's better."

"So you're okay right now?"

"Yes, Dad, I'm fine now."

"Okay." We drove the winding roads into town.

"So was there something new reported on the news tonight, Angela?" I asked, to pass the time.

"Oh Dad, it's so awful. They said at the rate the Pegasus Effect is happening that all human life will perish in the next two months."

"Jesus Christ! Are you serious? Are you sure that's what they said?"

"Yes Dad, I'm sure. The news channels are even starting to shut down because of the amount of deaths. They said that maybe nine hundred million have died,"

"Oh my, oh my God! Okay, don't think about that right now, Angela, I'll change the subject, you have to concentrate on delivering this baby! Jeez, I'm sorry I brought that up."

"It's okay, Dad." There was a pause in our conversation. A few minutes passed and then Angela spoke.

"Dad, what time is it?"

"Its 9:32 pm, are you having another contraction?"

"Yes, Dad, it hurts. Ou ou ouuu!" she cried out. She winced in pain.

"Hang on, Angela, we're almost there, five more minutes sweetie and we'll be there."

"Drive faster, Dad, please!"

"Okay sweetie, hang on, it'll be all right!" I increased my speed to as fast as I could go safely and then I went a bit faster.

"Alright, I see the hospital, Angela! Do you hear me?"

"Yes Dad, I do!"

"We'll be there in a minute, sweetie." As we drove the last few blocks, I could see that the hospital was jammed and there were people all over the place. Hundreds, perhaps thousands were in the parking lot and around the hospital grounds. I could not believe my eyes. How were we going to manage here I thought.

"What are we going to do, Dad? It's crazy here!" Angela exclaimed. She looked worried. There were people everywhere, in terrible condition. They looked as if they were at deaths doorstep. Many of them were. People were screaming, crying and praying.

"We're going to have to get out here, Angela and walk the rest of the distance. It's the only way we're going to get into the hospital, if we're lucky." I said. I parked the car. We got out of the car and we began to walk towards the main entrance. As we did, Angela started having another contraction.

"Dad, we better hurry, this baby wants out! Aghh, ou ouch! It hurts, Dad!" Angela cried out. She squirmed in pain.

"Hang on, Angela, we're almost there. Just hold on to me and follow me!" I yelled. We made our way to the front door of the hospital. It was pandemonium inside. There were dead bodies piled up in the corridors and the hospital had a rotting smell. I did not think a hospital could go on like that. Suddenly, a young woman came up to us and explained that she was a student doctor in the field of obstetrics. My God, we got lucky I thought, and we had. She instructed us to follow her. In a matter of a few moments, we managed to get up the stairs and into a delivery room that was no longer of any use. I guessed we were only one of a handful of people in Park Falls that was pregnant. The young student doctor stated her name was, Carol Philips. She only looked to be about twenty-one or twenty-two years of age. I asked her how old she was and to my surprise, she was twenty-six. I told her she looked younger and she took it as a compliment. She asked Angela to lie down on the table and she would be back in a few moments with some help. "We aren't going anywhere." I replied.

Angela lay on the table wincing in pain. I went over to hold her hand and comfort her.

"How long will she be, Dad?" Angela asked, in a panicked tone. She was frightened and nervous. Carol Philips came back into the room and walked up to us with a tray. She took out a syringe and prepared to inject Angela.

"What's that?" I asked.

"This is a mild tranquilizer with a vitamin shot." Ms. Philips answered. "By the way, what are your names?" she asked. We told her our names. She began taking vital signs and asking questions. She explained that the hospital was overwhelmed and that most people got turned away because there was nothing left that could be done for them. She said the Pegasus Effect was killing them and they could no longer help the populace. Carol explained that when she saw us she knew that she could help us and that we were in an emergency and that this was her specialty. She told us that this would be her last medical procedure at the hospital. She said that she was leaving the hospital to be with her family to die with them. She stated that our deaths were inevitable and that there were no more babies in Park Falls ready for birth. I told her that she sounded a little cynical and she shot right back.

"I have a life too and I can have compassion for my family as well. They're dying too and I won't be able to function much longer. I'm finished and that's it!" she yelled. She had a perturbed demeanor about her, "This hospital is closing shortly. The staff here are dying too and we're all in the same boat!" she snapped, getting even more upset. I apologized and she calmed down. Angela was about to deliver, Carol Philips said. She asked if I wanted to watch or go outside. Her helper came in and they started to work on Angela in tandem. I could see that Angela was in capable hands with Dr. Philips. I was no longer worried about her. Dr. Philips asked Angela if she wanted me in the room. Angela asked if I would leave. I was taken aback by this but I understood and I left the room. I was confident in them. They asked me to find them some coffee and to brew it myself if I had to.

I went to find the medics some coffee. That was the least I could do for their help. I saw that the hospital was in a nightmarish predicament. I had never seen anything like the scenario I was witnessing. I had viewed scenes like this on the news but that was the closest I ever got. The misery was incredible and the stench of death was everywhere. I could only imagine that this was what a hospital might be like during a bad war or a terrible earthquake. I looked at the television monitors as the same scene I was in was all over the screens coming from all parts of the world. I realized that this was the end coming. Carol Philips was right. We were in the hours of our deaths. I would call Christine after the baby arrived. I figured at least for my loved ones at home I would have some good news and they would be spared the horrors of this place. People died right in front of me and the doctors could only stand by and watch and record the event. They did not even try to resuscitate the people any longer to the dismay of screaming family members who watched helplessly as it happened. I could see that the Pegasus Effect was the most insidious and odious killer I had ever seen. There was no rhyme or reason for its purpose except that time was not relative to man and if it changed too drastically, we died. As I wandered around the hospital, I finally found a kitchen. There were volunteers trying to help the victims with what food and beverages they had left. The hospital was in a frantic state of desperation. I asked if I could take some coffee and they said it would be okay. I grabbed a tray and two cups of coffee and headed back to the delivery room. When I got there, I saw that Carol Philips had left and the other medic was there with Angela and my new grandson. I offered the medic some coffee but he declined. He said they had sent me for coffee to get rid of me. I approached my daughter and my grandson as Angela was just beaming as the baby was sleeping. I congratulated her. "Look, Dad, you're a grandfather." she said. She laughed and held the baby to her breast.

"Oh my goodness, he's beautiful, what a beautiful little boy! You're a beautiful, beautiful boy."

"He's beautiful, eh Dad?" Angela asked. She had tears in her eyes.

"He certainly is my darling, he certainly is. I can't wait for your mother to see him. You're going to have to call Christopher as soon as possible and tell him that he's a father."

"Oh yeah, I almost forgot about him, Dad. He's a father now. He's going to be in shock, his Mom and Dad too." Angela said. She had a joy in her heart. The medic then came over to talk with me. The medic said that I should take the baby from Angela and let my daughter sleep for a while. After, when we were both strong enough to travel again we should get out of the hospital and go home. He said the hospital would be abandoned soon and not to come back. He also said that everyone must deal with this on their own and then he wished us good luck and left. We were alone again and we started to get some rest. This room was quieter than the rest of the hospital. I remembered I had to phone Christine.

"Angela, I'm going to phone your mother with the good news."

"Okay Dad." I took out my cell phone and placed my call. I noticed that I had left it on silent mode and that there were four messages on it and they were all from home. They were quite anxious I thought. I pushed my number and the phone rang. It rang four times and then I heard Bernie answer the phone. I could hear what sounded like crying in the background. I called out Bernie's name and I became concerned as Angela looked at me. "What's wrong, Dad?" she asked, intently.

"Shh quiet, Angela, please. Bernie, are you there? Hello, Bernie! Bernie are you there!" I called out. I was hearing a definite loud crying. Christine came on the phone and it was her that was crying. "Agh, agh, Jim, is that you?" she answered, in a faint voice.

"Yes Christine, it's me, what is it? What's going on?" I beckoned unto her.

"Why didn't you answer your phone, Jim? She cried out.

"What is it, Dad?" Angela asked, again.

"Quiet sweetie, I don't know. Christine what is it? For God's sake what's wrong over there?" I implored.

"Oh Jim, Paula's dead! She's dead, Jim, Paula is dead! Christine cried out.

"What! Oh no, what Christine?" I said. My heart stopped.

"Agh aww, Jim, Paula's dead! Paula died!"

"Agh, oh no no, Oh my God, no no!" I cried out.

"Dad, what is it? Dad what is it! Dad, Dad please!" Angela begged.

"Sweetheart your sister, Paula has died, Paula's dead!"

"Oh, Dad no, no Dad no, aw no no!" Angela cried out.

"Oh my God, oh my God, my little angel, Paula!" I cried. We cried in sudden grief and shock.

"What happened to her, Christine?"

"She just died in her bed, Jim, she died in her bed!" Christine wailed.

"I'm coming home, Christine right away. I'm coming home now!" I exclaimed. I cried and Angela cried. I held her as our tears fell on the new baby.

"My poor darling, Paula!" I cried.

"Oh Paula, oh Paula, my sister." Angela cried. We held each other.

"Christine, we're coming home now, I'm going to hang up." I said. I hung up the phone. We were overcome with grief.

After ten or fifteen minutes, I released my hold on Angela and I told her that we must leave. We had to get out of this place and feed her new baby. I packed up Angela's belongings and we headed for the car. She took some blankets along to bundle the baby. I did not know if I was going to make it, I was feeling exhausted and I was shaking and trembling uncontrollably. I was feeling sick but I pushed on towards the car with Angela and the baby in tow. I had to get us home where we would be safe and secure. We needed to get into our beds and get some rest. As we got closer to where I left the car, I noticed that the car was not there. I thought our car must have been stolen or something. I did not know what happened. I panicked and I did not know what to do. I couldn't think clearly anymore. "Angela, the car has been stolen!" I squawked.

"What?"

"The car has been stolen! The car has been stolen!" I barked. I felt like I was coming apart at the seams. "My God, Angela, what are we going to do now?"

"I don't know, Dad, we have to get home." Angela replied. She was concerned for her new baby.

"I know, but how? How are we going to get there?" I begged.

"I don't know, Dad. Can you phone, Huneo?" she suggested.

"Oh yes! That's a good idea, Angela, I'll phone Huneo." I dialed Huneo's phone number. I was grief stricken. His phone started ringing. As I looked at my disheveled daughter and my new grandson and the world around me, I thought I was going to die that night. I'm not going to make it, I lamented.

"Hello." Huneo answered.

"Hello Huneo, its Jim!"

"Are you okay, Jim?"

"I need help, Huneo. I'm in a jam and I'm not going to make it without help. I'm in trouble, Huneo! Can you help me out, Huneo, please?" I pleaded.

"What is it, Jim? What's going on?"

"Huneo, my daughter, Paula has died!" I blurted. I burst into tears.

"Oh my God, Jim, Oh my God!" Huneo responded.

"Huneo, I'm at the hospital and someone has stolen my car. I'm with, Angela." I said, fighting my way through the tears, "She's had her baby premature tonight and we're stranded and we're sick and exhausted. We need help or I don't think we're going to make it!"

"I'll be right there, Jim, buddy, I'll be right there, you just wait for me. Where exactly are you?"

"We're on the corner of Bell St. and Glendale Avenue. Can you come and get us, Huneo? Can you come and get us!" I begged.

"Absolutely Jim, you hold on right there, Jim. I'm on my way. Hold on friend, I'll be there in fifteen or twenty minutes, okay Jim! Do you hear me?"

"I'll be here, Huneo, we'll be here. Hurry please!"

"I'll be right there, Jim, bye." Huneo said, and then he hung up the phone. I turned and grabbed Angela and held her.

"Oh, Dad, what's happening to us? Why is this happening to us!" she cried out.

"I don't know sweetie, I don't know. I just don't know." I replied. I sobbed. It began to rain and the temperature dropped. We were in rough shape. I tried to hold Angela as tightly as I could to keep them and myself warm. All around us was misery and death. We were part of that misery and death. I thought of my sweet Paula and my dear wife. I thought of Bernie and our families as we waited. I thought of how we were not going to make it much longer and of how desperate our lives had become.

I could hear the screeching of tires in the distance. I knew that it was Huneo coming to our rescue. I thought of how close Huneo and

I had become and how decent of a man he was. Suddenly, he came screeching around the corner as his head lights found us on the side of the road. He pulled up alongside us and got out to help. I felt an enormous relief that we had been rescued. "Jim! Angela! Are you alright?" Huneo called to us.

"I think so, Huneo. There are three of us here."

"I see, Jim. Congratulations, Angela. C'mon get in out of the rain," he said. Huneo helped us get into his car. Huneo got in and we drove off quickly.

"I see that it's just mayhem down here isn't it. You must have had a terrible time here. My God, Jim, I'm sorry for your loss. Jim, I'm so sorry,"

"Thanks, Huneo." I said. I cried.

We drove along slowly in silence. Huneo did not say a word as he let us grieve and have our thoughts. Angela and I sat in the back seat weeping as we made our way home. It was 1:35 am as I looked at my watch. Our surroundings were blacker than black as it was usually like this in the evenings. The drive home was a blur and then Huneo finally pulled into our driveway. Our home no longer looked inviting. Our home looked cold and empty. Huneo pulled to a stop and we got out of his car. He grabbed our things. We walked up to the door and stopped. I took a deep breath and opened the door and we entered the house. I could hear crying coming from the direction of the living room. "Come in, Angela." I said. We walked toward the living room. I rounded the corner and I saw Christine crying and being consoled by Bernie on the couch.

"I'm home." I said. I dropped the bag I was carrying.

"Oh, oh oh, Jim, Jim!" Christine cried out. She came to me. Her weight fell into my arms as her weakness pulled her down. We cried together. Huneo gestured to Bernie to help him with the baby so Angela would be free to grieve. After ten minutes, the baby began crying and Angela had to care for him. Angela had to feed the baby as Christine got her first bittersweet introduction to her new grandson. I went to the bathroom to get washed and then I returned to the living room. We sat and waited until Christine, Angela, and the baby returned. The house was foreign as I sat in my chair. "Are you okay, Bernie?" I asked.

"I'm feeling quite ill, Jim." Bernie looked like he was about to throw up.

"Try to hang in there, Bern. I'm sure you'll feel better in a while." I tried to reassure him.

"Thanks very much for helping me, Huneo." I said. Huneo stood by ready to help if the need arose.

"You're welcome, Jim."

Angela and Christine came back into the room. Angela gingerly cradled her newborn baby.

"How is he, Angela?" I asked.

"I think he's fine, Dad. He's asleep."

"Come and sit down and rest for awhile."

Christine and Angela came and sat on the couch. Christine used her cane all the time then for support. She was beginning to look more weak and haggard. Christine was losing her energy.

"Christine, where's Paula?" I asked, softly.

"She's in her bed, Jim, where I found her." Christine answered.

"I'm going to see her." I responded. She winced in anguish. "Angela, are you going to come with me?"

"Yes, Dad. Mom can you hold my baby?"

"Of course, dear, you go see your sister," she said. Huneo helped them transfer the baby to Christine.

"Come Angela, let's go upstairs."

"Yes, Dad."

We started our trek up the stairs to say goodbye to my daughter and Angela's sister for one of the last times that we would see her. We approached Paula's room. I pushed the door open. We walked in and I saw her in her bed. She had one of the sheets pulled up over her head. I approached and beckoned Angela to approach. We sat down on either side of the bed.

"Are you ready?"

"Yes, Dad."

I began to pull the sheet down. There laid my deceased daughter as the blanket passed over her face. I began to cry. She was the same as when I left her. She laid there in peace with her CD headphones still on her head. I removed them carefully and slowly.

"Oh Paula, oh Paula!" Angela cried out. Paula was just a she was when I last saw her. Her beautiful soft red hair was in a ponytail as I looked at her. I looked at her face, her soft young face. I looked at her eyes and the soft freckled skin and button nose. I looked at her soft puffy lips that I would not see smile again. "Good bye, my dear sweet daughter, Paula. Go and be with God until we see you again." I said. The tears welled up inside me again.

"Good bye, Paula, I love you so much! I love you so much, Paula," Angela cried out, and then she burst into tears. We cried. I went to the other side of the bed and comforted my eldest daughter as we mourned. Christine, Bernie, Huneo and the baby came upstairs and sat in our room. For the rest of that evening we went in and out of her room saying good-bye and I love you to Paula for the last times. We spent most of the night crying until we could not cry anymore. We finally got so tired that we had to get some sleep.

The next day I got up and went downstairs to see if Huneo was still there. He was sleeping on the couch in the living room. I woke him. "Good morning, Huneo. You'd better get back to your own family, eh? They're going to be worried about you." I said.

"It's okay, Jim. I phoned, Helen in the night and she said to stay here until morning if I had to. So, how are you today?"

"I feel sore all over. Not so good, but I think how else would I feel on a day like this."

"I think nearly everyone on earth feels that way today, Jim, you're not alone."

"Thanks again, Huneo for last night, for helping us. I wouldn't have made it without your help. I mean it, Huneo. I would not have made it without you." I said. I expressed my appreciation.

"It's okay, Jim, you're welcome."

"So what are you going to do now?"

"I've got to get home and tend to things there. Helens' Dad is getting sicker and I want to be with her in our hours of need."

"Goodness, Huneo, by all means don't waste anymore time here, you've done more than enough. Again Huneo thanks."

"You're welcome, Jim." There was a pause and then Huneo spoke again. "Listen Jim, last night while you were asleep, I went into the barn and brought the calibrator down with your winch and brought it into your den."

"What! You're kidding, Huneo!"

"It's in your den."

"Why did you do that?"

"Well, I'll be with, Helen mostly now, Jim and I would like to know that I could still get readings from the calibrator. So would you mind turning it on once a day to take a reading for me?" he asked, with trepidation.

"No no, Huneo, not at all, not at all. Huneo you can phone at anytime of the day and I'll give you a reading."

"Well, I'll call each day at about 1:30 pm and maybe you will have looked at a reading by then for me, if that's okay?"

"Yes Huneo, I'll do that, no problem. I want to know the readings as well."

"Do you know how to do the conversion to minutes compared to November 12th, 1995?"

"Yes, that's a simple one; I can make the conversions too."

"Alright then, I'll be off then, Jim. What are you going to do now?"

"Well Huneo … I'm going to phone the police station to see what I can do with, Paula's body."

"Yes of course. Again Jim, I'm so sorry for your loss."

"Thanks, Huneo." I walked Huneo to the door and we said goodbye to each other. I told Huneo that I would be making a trip to get some food over the next day or two and that I would call him to see if he needed anything. He appreciated that and we made it a point to try to get together over the next few days just to have contact. "By the way, Huneo, when you moved the calibrator did you take a reading?

"Yeah, Jim, I did, it was 8.897% or 128 minutes a day passing faster than on November 12th, 1995."

"We can't take much more of this can we?"

"We're at the end of our ropes, Jim."

"Okay, Huneo, I won't keep you, see you later. I hope."

"Don't worry, Jim, you will, bye for now." I closed the door and he left. I turned and went back into the house to be with my family. The house felt like it was home again. I heard some stirring and then my new grandson began crying. I shook my head. What kind of life was there for us if we only had a few weeks left, I thought. I was raised to stay in there and fight to the end, and not give up hope. I would try my best until my last breath I promised myself. I went to the bottom of the stairs and called up to my daughter. "Is everything alright, Angela?"

"Yes Dad, I'm feeding, Paul James." Angela replied. This took me by surprise. My grandson had a beautiful name that Angela had chosen, I thought in honor of her sister. With that said, I went to my office to call the police station. I bumped my knee on the calibrator as I walked to my phone in the dark. I made a mental note to move things around to accommodate the calibrator. I phoned the police to ask what to do with Paula's body. They explained that they were no longer dealing with dead bodies and that the mortuary and funeral home was not dealing with them either. They told me that I must deal with the body myself. They explained that the situation was just too grim and there were too many deaths for them to manage. They said that the able-bodied personnel and volunteers as well as what military personnel that were left were allocated to food distribution only. They told me that by the looks of things that they would be able to distribute food for five to ten more days and that would be the end. They advised me to bring identification to the supermarket over the next few days and the food for the family would be given in one last one-month supply. They also informed me that in five days approximately the electrical power would be cut off because of safety and failure reasons. They said I should stockpile water if I did not have another source because with the loss of the electricity we would lose our ability to pump water. This news shocked me. I did not expect that things would get so bad and so desperate so quickly. I guessed nobody did and that was the nature of this extinction event. Lastly, they told me that they had to get off the phone to accommodate other callers. They wished me good luck and said goodbye. I decided that I would go for food the following day.

The next task I had to complete while I still had the strength was to dig Paula's grave. I had breakfast with Bernie and Christine and we discussed Paula's burial. Christine and I decided Paula's internment would be by a flower garden adjacent to a great oak tree that was on our property. I asked Bernie if he was up to the task of helping me. He said that he would and that he would try his best. I was sad for us as we were becoming so meek and unable. I would not expect Bernie to do much, even if he could.

As that day passed, we got Paula's grave dug and we managed to have good lunch. As we toiled outside, Angela and Christine sat on the patio with Paul James and admired him lovingly the way mothers do. They spent their time doting on him as they bonded. All the while throughout the day, I noticed that the sky was starting to clear slowly and the pall of dust was starting to fall. I did not know if this was good or bad because I was indifferent to the changes. I had become numb to the disaster unfolding across the globe for it was not on my doorstep any longer. I could do nothing to help or make a difference anymore. It was coming down to each family or group had to take care for themselves. We decided to bury Paula at 4:00 pm that day and have a prayer vigil for her and let our grieving continue. I tried to remember my own words throughout this ritual, the words I spoke to Bernie when he was first grieving. That God wanted us to grieve. God wanted us to show our grief and not be afraid. That grieving was love and we showed our deepest love in our grieving. The day went on and I finally had some time to sit and meet my new grandson. It was in his new life that I could face my death and the death of all of us. This was all I could say for that. We buried Paula and said our final goodbye's to her. The grieving would follow us in time. At the end of the day with the exception of Angela, we were so sick that all of us had vomited during that day. I had painful tremors as well as spasms in my muscles so much so, that I could no longer get up and walk without difficulty. We went to bed early that evening and tried to rest up for the next day hoping it would not be as traumatic as the previous few.

The next day arrived and I was able to get up early enough that I arose at a normal time. As I moved about to get up, my muscles were terribly sore from digging Paula's grave. Moving around was tedious but I managed to make it downstairs for breakfast. Christine would stay in bed for a few more hours for she no longer had the strength to get through the day. The Pegasus Effect left Christine almost fully incapacitated. Bernie was in the same boat. They would not rise up out of their beds until ten or eleven o'clock. Angela was in the kitchen with Paul James, feeding him. I entered the kitchen and greeted her. "Good morning, Angela, how are you and my little grandson doing today?"

"I'm not too good, Dad. I was up all night with Paul James. He needed to be fed once and he cried a few times. Dad, I think I'm starting to get sicker, like you and Mom."

"Goodness, are you having any trouble taking care of, Paul?"

"No, but I'm not used to this either, it so difficult, Dad."

"Babies are sweetheart, but you'll get used to it. What makes you think you're getting sicker?" I asked.

"I'm having spasms in my legs and I threw up last night."

"Are you fatigued?"

"Not really, not yet, Dad." I could see in her eyes that she knew that the end was coming. That she was going to succumb to the Pegasus Effect as well.

"Well Angela, I'm going to have to help you since I'm the healthiest or the least sick of the three of us. Angela when you need a rest or need the baby to be held for a while, don't hesitate to come and ask one of us dear. Your mother could probably take the baby in our bed as well."

"Alright Dad, I will."

I cooked some bacon and eggs for us and we had some coffee. I sat with them at the table in the quiet of the morning and we ate our breakfast. After eating, I asked Angela to give me her hand in prayer.

I prayed aloud for God to forgive us for our sins and that he watch over us and bless us. I asked God to save us so we could live out our lives and love each other. We said Amen. For a while, we talked about Paula and grieved. We talked about the good times we had together and about her life. Angela suggested we get out the photo Album later that day and remember her in pictures. I agreed that would be a good idea. Angela and I moved into the living room to watch the morning news. I turned on the television and of the dozens of television channels we had there were only three remaining on the air. Two of them were news channels and the third one was an entertainment channel for children that seemed to be just playing in a loop. Of the two news channels, one was intermittent. It displayed a screen that informed us of when the next news report would begin by text. The other news channel was pretty much a twenty-four hour broadcast. As we sat and waited for the 9:00 am news to begin, Angela fed Paul James again and after that, I helped change his diaper. This was a laborious chore for the both of us because she was not used to this and I was tired and sore. We finally got the diaper on and sat down for the news. After a few moments, the news began. A newscaster came on and introduced himself. He led off the broadcast by informing us of the death of the President of the United States and the deaths of other world leaders and famous figures. He announced the replacement for the President and showed video of the transition. I could see how bad things were for the government as none of them wore their suits any longer and they looked sick and disheveled. The next topic was the deaths around the world. They announced that due to the huge losses there was no way to count accurately how many people have perished. The news anchor said that an official from the government pegged the best estimates at over a billion perished. Angela and I looked at each other and shook our heads. "God help us!" I said. The newscaster went on with the report showing the calibrator readings that they had. The SOLTES calibrator readings that they reported were different from the ones that Huneo, Bernie and I would see on the calibrator that we used. The calibrators that the rest of the world used based comparisons of time speed increases to the day their calibrators started recording. Their calibrators were just over five months old perhaps. However, they also had the one calibrator with the November 12, 1995 recording on it but only referred to it infrequently. The calibrator numbers that they reported seemed less dramatic but were still indicators of a calamitous extinction event. They showed pictures from around the world of the deaths and of people praying. It was all the world could do for itself. Lastly, they reported that the caldera aftermath was beginning to settle and that the volcanic dust was dropping out of the trade winds. The fine dust was clumping together and falling back to earth. There were predictions of the skies clearing in the days ahead. "Can you please turn that off, Dad, I've seen enough." Angela said. She looked thoroughly dejected. "I guess there's nothing else to do except pray and die."

"Let's try to concentrate on praying, Angela and taking care of, Paul." I said. She did not say a word after that. I decided I would go and get the food at the supermarket. I phoned Huneo and asked him if he wanted to go as well. He asked me to pick him up on the way. I went upstairs to tell Christine where I was going. She was in the process of getting out of bed. I told her I was going to get the last thirty days staples of food. She was indifferent to my announcement but gave me a hug and asked me to hurry back. I told her that I would. I checked on Bernie and he was getting up as well, slowly, but nonetheless he was getting up. I grabbed the car keys and took off for Huneo's place. As I drove, I grieved for Paula. I thought of how much we loved her so. When I got close to Huneo's, I saw that he was in the driveway waiting. He jumped in the car and we headed for town. "How's things going, Huneo?" I asked.

"We're all getting pretty sick now, Jim. Helen's Father is in the worst shape and contrarily I'm in the best shape but I'm hurting pretty bad, Jim. How about you and your gang, Jim, how are you guys holding up?"

"I'm getting pretty run down. Angela's in the best shape and Christine is almost incapacitated. Bernie's in the same condition as Christine. Also I suppose, Paul James is unaffected at this time, so far as we can tell."

"So that's his name, eh? I can tell where he got that moniker. Again Jim, please accept our condolences for your loss."

"Thanks." I replied.

I drove fast until we got to town and then I followed the speed limit. Park Falls was active but on a much reduced level and for survival reasons only. The only people out were people traveling for food and people traveling to graves. They buried the dead in mass graves. Local contractors and the military dug large pits. Only the fittest could move about. Aside from that, the town was a ghost of its former self. We got our food and packed it into the car. The military who was distributing the food told us that we were some of the last ones to pick up and they would close the food depot early so they could go to be with their families. They said that whatever food remained would be kept in the open and the doors would be left unlocked. We decided to take a drive around Park Falls to see it maybe for the last time. We drove by the university and the main street shops and it was ghostly, that was the only way to describe our town. As we drove, we talked. "Huneo?"

"Yes, Jim."

"I remember once, the U.S. State Department came to see you for what you might know. You had told me that you were working on a hypothesis or postulation that related to the Pegasus Effect. You didn't want to tell me then. Would you tell me now?" I prodded.

"I'm sorry I mentioned that actually. I was working on something that was related, Jim. However, it was not something that has any bearing on the current events that are taking place. I haven't told, Helen and I have decided to take it to my grave. Again, however I don't think you have anything to worry about, Jim. You do have a future and that's all I will say on the topic. Does that ease your conscience?"

"Awe come on, Huneo, what is it?"

"Like I say, Jim, I won't say what it is and that's that!"

"I won't press you then, Huneo. Sorry."

"Good, because it would be a waste of time." Huneo stated. We drove around a while longer and then we headed for home. Huneo asked me to read the calibrator when I got home and call him around

1:30 pm. I dropped him off and quickly said Hello to Helen who was out in the yard sitting, waiting for Huneo. We unloaded their food. I said goodbye and drove home. When I got home, Christine, Angela, Paul and Bernie were sitting near the old oak tree near Paula. The day was warm and we needed only light clothing. Angela came and helped me unload the food. We then went out to join the others. We spent the remainder of that day out by the tree, except for my stopping to read the calibrator. The calibrator read 8.937% or approximately 129 minutes faster that the 24-hour day passed compared with the original day captured by the calibrator on November 12, 1995. The conversion of the percentage to minutes was simple. It was the percentage multiplied by 1440 minutes in a day. This percentage was the largest increase yet and it was demoralizing. I fell to my knees when I read this and asked God to please bless us and save us. I asked God to please, please save my grandson, my daughter, and my wife. I asked God to save Bernie. I asked God to save our families and everyone. I asked with all my heart and all that I had in my soul that we be saved. I begged God to help us. I begged. After reflecting for a while, I phoned Huneo and gave him the numbers. We talked for a time and before I hung up, I told him I would call him each day until I died.

After gaining some composure, I went back outside. Angela had brought the photo albums out and we took the opportunity to go through them. As we did, we recalled many fond memories of Paula as well as the great moments of poignancy that were so defining of our lives. At the same time we were mourning the loss of Paula, we were celebrating, although reservedly, the birth and new life of Paul James. As we did so, small waves of fine dust would fall out of the sky throughout the afternoon and early evening and on into the next day. The sky was clearing itself and the sun was starting to peek through the dimness. Our day passed as a melancholic one. Our lives were melancholic. It was depression. We had to accept that. It was our fate and when we saw our lives lasting into the future only days and not years it was a completely different outlook and that was hugely understating the feeling. As the days passed over the next few weeks all we could do was survive. By that, I mean we ate and slept and sat around being sick, trying to nourish ourselves and keep alive until the end. I would phone Huneo over the future days and give him the calibrator readings. August 8th, the calibrator read 9.463%. Two days later on August 10, the reading was 9.993% and then again, two days later on August 12, the calibrator read 10.441%. I phoned Huneo that day to give him this reading and asked him why he even wanted the readings any longer. He responded by saying that he was hoping the readings would change and then he broke down and cried. "It's not fair, Jim!" he screamed, over the phone. "It's not fair. It's just not fair!" he cried. I heard Helen in the background come to comfort him. Both cried. They told me how sick they were and that they expected Helens father to die at any time. I told Huneo I would keep giving him the readings from the calibrator for as long as I could. I promised him. I said goodbye to him that day and asked for God to bless them and for them to take care of themselves and love each other in their final hours. I phoned him on August 14, with the reading of 10.942% and then I phoned him again on the 16th with a reading of 11.553%. It was then 8:30 am, August 17. I knew today would probably be our last day. The end of time as we experienced it and our mortal world had finally come to an end. The sun was shining outside as the dust from the caldera eruption had fallen back to earth and gave way to the light and warmth of the sun. It was on this beautiful warm summer day that we would perish. We would perish without a fight. We would perish and be with God. I read the calibrator today and it read 11.724%. The passage of a twenty four hour day was taking 169 minutes less time than it did in comparison to the day that the Speed of Light Time Existence Speed calibrator first recorded it on November 12th in the year 1995. Angela and her baby were in their beds and were on the verge of being bed ridden and then death would be soon to follow, to be for sure. Christine and Bernie were in their beds, barely breathing. They were turning a pale grey and coughing. They could no longer get out of bed or go to the bathroom. They had been defecating and urinating in their beds, as they would surely not make it through another day. The Pegasus Effect had ravaged their bodies. Cindy our dog was lying on the floor at my feet having convulsions and seizures. I was no longer able to get off the couch for more than five minutes at a time. I would become severely nauseous and would have to lay down wherever I was. I could not carry my body weight any longer and my heart was not pumping in rhythm. I gasped for air at the slightest efforts that I would endeavor to take on. The electricity in the house had gone out a few days previous, maybe even a week ago, I could not remember. Before it went out there was nothing on television any longer except test patterns. The airwaves of the radio had fallen silent. To look outside there was no movement anywhere to be seen, except for the trees and the grass bowing in the wind as the breezes passed gently by the house. It was the only sound left other than the cries and the moaning of our demises. In a few hours, it would be the last time that I would try to contact Huneo. After today that would be it, I would say goodbye forever. Huneo and Helen were in the same boat. They were bed ridden. They were surprised that the father had survived to be with them up until that point. It was futile to bother anymore with calling him. The effort was just too much and besides he knew we loved him and he knew how to let go. I laid on the couch by the calibrator as it merrily hummed away and showed the percentages as well as a few other measurements. It seemed the only use for the calibrator of Huneo Parkas' inventiveness was to tell us how fast we were going to die. As I lay there, I prayed as I went in and out of consciousness. I was sore and depressed beyond what I had ever known before. A fast depression had set in and it brought me to the deepest depths of my morbid thoughts. I could no longer communicate with Christine and Bernie. They seemed mostly unconscious over the past few days as a desperate Angela tried to keep them alive by feeding them in their lucid moments.

"Agh! Dad help me! Help me!" Angela shouted. I tried to get to my feet. I struggled. I crawled up the stairs on my hands and knees.

"I'm coming, Angela, I'm trying. I'm trying." I called back, in helplessness and frustration. "What's happening up there?" I called up to her. I climbed to the top of the stairs.

"Paul James, he's not breathing, Daddy, help me! Help me! Please Dad!" Angela screamed. I pushed on. I had a rush of adrenaline and made it to their bedroom. Angela was trying to breath into the baby's mouth. I yelled to her. "Lay him down on the bed!"

"Okay, Dad. Oh, please no! Don't let this happen, God, don't let this happen!" she pleaded. The baby was turning blue. I grabbed him and started performing CPR for infants. I was dying doing this. I gave the baby good firm slaps on his back, and then I flipped him on his side. I tried to jolt him. It didn't work. I continued CPR for another minute and then I tried the slap on his back again. He burst out crying and wailing. Angela was crying hysterically. We were in the throes of fighting for our last breaths. Paul James color had returned. He was crying and flailing. I told Angela that she must feed him and change him right away and then I fell onto the bed and passed out. When I came to, Angela was over me with a cold compress on my head.

"Dad, please don't leave me, Daddy, Daddy please stay with me! Please! Don't leave me." She implored.

"Agghh, I think I'm okay now sweetheart." I replied. I looked at her as her face and neck as well as her shirt was wet with tears and she was in a state of utter devastation as was I.

I knew that we were passing through the final hours of our lives. I held onto Angela for about half an hour and then I told her that I had to get some rest and phone Huneo for the last time. I held onto the walls as I made my way to the stairs.

"Daddy, please don't leave me!" Angela implored. The tears ran down her face. She sat on her bed crying and cradling Paul James in total despair and hopelessness.

"Angela, I'll make the call and have a small rest and then I'll come right back, alright sweetie?"

"Are you sure, Dad? Are you sure?" I don't want to be alone," she begged.

"Yes Angela, I'm sure, I'll be right back." I then made my way down the stairs on my bum and my hands and feet. I was feeling nauseous as I came into the den. I threw up all over the floor and knew this was bad. I had to keep my stomach contents in for nutrition and hydrations sake. The room started to go black as I aimed myself for the couch and passed out.

I came too and it was still light out. I then heard Angela yelling. "Dad, are you there? Dad, can you hear me? Dad, please, please, please Dad, answer me!" she cried out.

"I'm here, Angela, I'm still here!"

"Oh Dad, Dad, what happened?"

"I fainted dear. I'm okay now!"

"Dad, I've been calling you for fifteen minutes,"

"I'm okay sweetie, I'm okay, I'll be up shortly." I replied.

"Please hurry, Dad."

"I will sweetheart, and will you just give me fifteen minutes more, please."

"Alright Dad, please hurry, Dad!"

I was lying down and still felt nauseous. I looked at the clock on the wall. It was 12:55 pm. I thought I must have passed out for a few hours. The house was quiet. I lay there with great pain in my body and a horrible sick feeling. I looked over at the calibrator and it reminded me to call Huneo for the last time. I reached over and turned it on. It came to life as usual. The calibrator was a well-built instrument. I could give Huneo credit with that fact. It whirred away and beeped as usual, as I waited for the reading. I laid there praying and I was resigned to my fate. The calibrator made its final beep indicating a reading displayed. I looked over at the digital incremental/exponential time speed indicator and it read 11.545%. "What's this?" I said. "My last reading I think was 11.7 something…" I said, "Oh my God, is it going backwards!" I said, aloud. "Oh my God, Oh my God, is it going backwards?" I said, again. I stared intently at the calibrator as it whirred along and then it happened. The calibrator reading dropped to 11.543%.

"Oh my God! I don't believe this. Is this true? Can this be true?" I watched the calibrator for the next fifteen minutes. Angela called down.

"Hold on dear, I'm doing something important!"

"Hurry Dad, please!"

"I'll be there soon, Angela, please hang on." I responded.

I stared at the calibrator and then it happened again. The indicator gauge dropped to 11.541%. "Oh my God, it's a divine miracle! Thank you, God. I praise you, God. I thank you. Thank you, God. Oh thank you, God!" I beseeched. I stood up, fell to my knees, and looked at the calibrator again. It was still the same. I stared at it for another fifteen minutes and it dropped again to 11.537%.

"Agghh thank you, Lord Jesus, and thank you, God!" I shouted.

"Dad, Dad! Are you alright?" Angela called down.

"I'm okay darling. Can you give me a few more minutes' sweetheart?" I asked. I still could not believe it as I sat there and stared at the calibrator. Another fifteen minutes had passed then there was another drop in the reading. The calibrator was registering 11.531%. I knew it was true, I could feel in my heart that we were going to survive. It was a divine miracle. A miracle by God had happened and our prayers were answered. It was a divine miracle. It was a divine happening and we would survive, I hoped. I looked at the phone. I welled up in tears. I decided to make that last call to Huneo. It would turn out not to be my last call. I dialed his number. I trembled. I became happy and nervous suddenly and rejoiced in that feeling. I began to cry as I waited for him to pick up. Finally. "Hello." a ragged and groggy voice answered.

"Huneo, it's me, Jim!" I bellowed.

"Jim are you okay? We're in bad shape," he said. I could hear the sadness in his words.

"Huneo, this was going to be my last time to be phoning you."

"Why, Jim?" he inquired.

"Huneo, I read the calibrator this morning."

"What was the reading, Jim?"

"It was 11.724% Huneo!"

"My God, it's going up fast, Jim. Maybe your right, I think this might be the last time you could've phoned. I'm sorry, Jim, I should have known this. You shouldn't have had to call me every day. I'm sorry for asking you to waste your time with me, Jim, I'm so sorry, Jim." Huneo said, despairingly. He began to cry.

"I'm looking at the digital time speed indicator right now, Huneo."

"What's it reading now, Jim?" he asked.

"Well, it was reading 11.724% this morning, and now, well, its reading 11.521%!"

"What? What Jim, say again!"

"I say to you, Huneo clearly now, the reading this morning at around 8:30 am was 11.724% and it now reads, let's see it's almost 1:35 pm and the reading is, oh! It just dropped again, its 11.519% Huneo!"

"Oh my God, Jim, are you serious! Are you telling me the truth, Jim! Are you serious, Jim?" He asked. I could hear his tone go from hopelessness to hope as he asked the most important question of his life.

"I would never lie to you about a mortal situation, Huneo or anything else for that matter buddy!"

"I can't believe it, Jim! I just can't believe it's true!"

"It's true, Huneo, believe it." I replied. Huneo became elated. He yelled for Helen. At that moment, Angela came downstairs with Paul James and asked me what was going on. She was crying. I told Angela that the calibrator was going in the opposite direction and that time was now slowing down. I could not believe the words I was saying as I was saying them and that time was slowing down. "We're speeding up in the universe again sweetheart. I don't know why but we have a chance that we may live!" I exclaimed. Angela became ecstatic as she looked at the calibrator and I explained it to her. I could hear Huneo on the other end of the line with Helen and they were celebrating. I did not know if this was premature but it was positive. I told Huneo that I had to go back, check on Christine and Bernie, and see if in fact they were still alive as they were still very sick from the Pegasus Effect. Huneo told me to get moving and to see to my loved ones. Huneo begged me to call him back within a couple of hours with the calibrator readings. I promised him that I would call him and then I hung up the phone.

"Come on, Angela, let's go up and see your mother and, Bernie, and see if their still with us." I said.

"Dad, I can't believe this. I hope, God has saved us,"

We made our way to the top of the stairs. I crawled up and Angela made her way in better shape. We went to my bedroom first to check on Christine. I opened the door and the smell from the feces and urine was overpowering. We made our way over to the bed and I checked for her vital signs. She was still breathing. I told Angela to give me the baby and try to get some water into her as I thought she could recover. She was unconscious. After getting her aroused and forcing a bit of water into her, we went to check on Bernie. We made the trek downstairs to Bernie's room. He was in a similar condition as Christine so we did the same. The three of us then lay down on the carpet in Bernie's room to rest. I cuddled up to my daughter and my grandson and felt myself at peace for the first time in a long while. We fell asleep for approximately a half an hour.

After I had awakened, I could see that Angela was up feeding Paul James. "How's he doing?" I asked.

"He seems to be doing okay, Dad. He's hungry and thirsty."

"I think that's a good sign, Angela dear. How's, Bernie doing?"

"He's still breathing, Dad and he's moaning a bit from time to time."

"Okay, that sounds good. I'm going to check on your mother again. You can go into the kitchen or living room and I will be back as soon as I can, okay sweetie?"

"Alright, Dad."

I went back to the stairs and crawled back up to our room. I walked slowly to the door and made my way into the room. The room smelled putrid as Christine still lied on the soiled sheets. I sat down beside her to see how she was doing. Her eyes opened as she felt my presence on the bed. "It's me, Christine, Jim, can you hear me?" I said, firmly.

"Yes." she answered, in a rough gravelly voice. Her eyes were glazed over as she sweated from her brow.

"I think we might be alright, Christine. I think our luck might have changed, hon," I said. She was coughing and moaning in response. I could not make out what she was trying to communicate. I asked her to speak louder. "I'm hungry." she grunted. I laughed and said that I would fix her something to eat and drink. I told her that we would get her cleaned up. I told her to wait just a bit longer and she would start to feel better. I went directly to the SOLTES calibrator to take another reading. I wanted to make sure I was not dreaming this turn of events, this miracle. I went into the den and looked at the calibrator. It was not working. I panicked and did not know what was happening. I then remembered that it was running on battery power and must have lost its charge. I phoned Huneo to tell him my predicament. Huneo said that a car battery could be used in place of the wall outlet on the auxiliary power input. He said I could cut the leads off a voltmeter, wire them to the battery, and use them as the plug-ins to the input. I told him that I did not have any voltmeters or anything like that. Huneo said that he had the proper connections and would be over directly to do it himself. I did not argue with him and then we hung up. As far as I was concerned at this point, I was going to go on the assumption that the Pegasus Effect had reversed itself. My main goal was to get my family back to health. I would start by checking on Angela again and then I would take care of Christine. My main goal would be to get Christine back to health. I would of course nurse Bernie back to health as well. I started to feel vigor inside me and worked with that momentum to get Christine cleaned up and fed. Next, Angela and I got Bernie cleaned and fed. We maneuvered them off their beds to flip their mattresses. We threw the soiled sheets out the windows along with their soiled clothing. We washed them the best we could as they started to come around. It was 6:00 pm. Huneo pulled into the driveway. He got out of his car slowly with a tired look in his movements. He grabbed a shopping bag that was on his seat along with a bottle of water. He made his way to the house. I opened the front door for him. He gave me a hug as he walked through the door. "I never thought I'd see you again, Jim. I never thought I would." Huneo said.

"I didn't think I'd see you either, my friend!" We hugged with what strength we had left in us. Huneo and I then talked for a few minutes about our ordeals as well as our survivors. It looked like we all made it, those of us who were alive past Paula, Stella and Helen's mother Catherine. The rest of us, so far, were intact. We went straight to the calibrator and began to wire it up to my battery, which I went out to retrieve from the station wagon. It was finally ready to go. "Okay, Huneo, it's your baby, turn it on." I said. I looked at him and crossed my fingers. At that point, Angela walked into the room with Paul James. Angela was trembling at the prospect of the next reading. "Oh God, please let it be, please let it be good!" she implored. Huneo pushed the power button and the computer came to life. It whirred and beeped as it always had before and we waited for the verdict of our fate. We stared at the calibrator in anticipation. Then, finally, the number popped up onto the digital incremental/exponential time speed indicator and it read 11.477%. "Yahoo! Alright!" I yelled. Huneo shouted out with happiness too. Angela smiled and laughed as tears rolled down her cheeks. We were in a state of utter joy. A great weight had been lifted from our shoulders. The weight of the world had lifted from us. As soon as Huneo got some strength, he said, he would run into town and spread the word that the Pegasus Effect had reversed itself. Over the next few hours and days we started to feel better as the time speed began to slow down. Cindy our dog began to recover. Over the next few weeks, life became exciting as everyone on earth recovered. The power came back on and things were slowly starting to assemble themselves again. The infrastructures and the networks as well as all the necessary social systems recuperated. As those weeks went on, people would recover and become their old selves, or should I say we became new people. In those days, we felt a great happiness in the reversal of the Pegasus Effect and our lives were renewed in the sense that we knew that an Almighty power was watching over us. On television, we got back the stations and we could see people through-out the world in every country rejoicing vociferously, very vociferously. Tears of joy abounded all over the planet. A river of tears flowed for the joy of our good fortune. People the world over prayed together in rejoicing that an Almighty God had mercy on us. The world was a changed place. Although everything we owned and all material pos-sessions of the earth's countries and peoples were intact, we knew it would be a long time before the people of the world would recover emotionally, physically and spiritually. This turn of events transformed us. Most of all in the immediate weeks following the reversal of the

Pegasus Effect my dear wife looked like she was going to have a full recovery. Angela and Paul James were doing fine as well and Bernie had a smile painted on his face for weeks as he recovered with blinding speed. I think Bernie may have had the quickest recovery. I, well, I was in a state of perpetual elation just for the very fact that we were going to live. Moreover, that was exactly what we would do, live. As for Huneo and Helen, they experienced the same recovery processes we went through. Helens dear father had also made it through this event, this disaster. This was Mother Nature's worst natural disaster. The Pegasus Effect was a natural disaster of biblical proportions that showed the power of the Almighty's swift sword. It showed us the divine power of God and the universe. As life went on, the world was a more peaceful place. The town of Park Falls got its personality back and then some. There was joy in the streets. Astrophysicists and astronomers measured the Pegasus Effect with great accuracy. After five months, the Pegasus Effect slowed incrementally and then finally it leveled off. The Pegasus Effect stopped at a time speed that Huneo and I figured out mathematically to be slightly slower than the November 12, 1995 time speed recording. Astrophysicists were at a loss to explain the event. There was speculation but it was inconclusive. The universe and space-time were beyond our capabilities as humans to know and figure out in certain aspects and maybe that was for the best. For the universe was gigantic and time was different everywhere and could be different by colossal amounts. We could not comprehend it for that reason. In the end, Huneo became one of my best friends and Helen became best friend to Christine. After a year had passed, we were having a picnic one day in late August at the Park Falls Lookout. Over five thousand Park Falls residents came out that day to be on the lookout hill as we spent the day reflecting back on our lives. As the world counted its dead, it had tallied almost a billion and a half perished. A great aberration of the Pegasus Effect was the fact that almost every family on earth lost at least one family member. The phenomenon was an anomaly that the people had not taken lightly. We looked out over our town, prayed together, and loved together. We sat that day and remembered our loved ones. We remembered deeply and fondly our sweet Paula Lynn Reynolds who at tender sweet age of fifteen was taken from us. We remembered Bernie's wife Stella Bernice Wakefield, sixty-one years, who was too young to pass on and we remembered Helens mother Catherine Mary Hamilton, forty-eight years, who was dearly beloved. We loved, laughed, and cried that day. I had my dear wife back to her normal self, and with a bit more zest, I do believe. We had our grandson whom was now the apple of our eyes and the extended family that that had brought us. We had our daughter Angela, whom we loved and cherished more than life itself. We looked out over Park Falls that day as a warm breeze wafted through the trees and we counted our blessings. I also tried one more time that day to get Huneo to divulge his secret to me, but again to no avail. I would try again another day. We had dinner on the hill that day with our fellow Park Fallsers. We gathered on the lookout to remember our loved ones and look out over our beautiful town. We remained after dinner to bask in that glow as we watched the early evening arrival of what became known as The Heart of an Angel Supernova Remnant. It was a dazzling display of beauty and color in the heavens as the stars shone brightly in the clear sky. I went back to teaching that fall and Huneo became part of the faculty as well. Life was sweet again. Life was sweet again indeed. If I have but one thing only left to say of our experience, it is that love is where life is, and God is where you find it. Amen.

The End.

Lightning Source UK Ltd.
Milton Keynes UK
10 June 2010

155409UK00001B/190/P